mc
it

'G
abou
tenc

'Good
roman whimsy that will charm even the most sceptical amongst
us. If you're hoping to find a book that escapes beyond
its pages to fill up your heart as well as your imagination,
look no further'

HANNAH BONAM-YOUNG

'*Good Spirits* is the most wonderful read of the year. The twists, the turns, the candy canes – it's a magical book by every definition of the word . . . Fresh, fun and original, B.K. Borison can do no wrong'

LINDSEY KELK

'Heartwarming, hopeful, and inspiring, this book will have your heart aching in the best way'

A.T. QURESHI

'This story is tender in all the right ways. It's magical in the quiet moments, and unexpectedly funny when you need it most. All the softest parts of me lit up, then split wide open. Shiny. Glittery. Golden. I could read it a dozen times'

KI STEPHENS

'*Good Spirits* is holiday romance perfection, with B.K. Borison's trademark mix of witty banter, a cosy setting that feels like being wrapped up in the warmest blanket, and a love story that makes you want to scream into a pillow . . . Borison is a gift to romance readers, and fully in a league of her own'

JESSICA JOYCE

'*Good Spirits* brings us a clever, funny, and enchanting world that perfectly captures the wholesome spirit of the holidays. This love story is for the true romantics at heart'

JULIE OLIVIA

B. K. Borison is the author of cosy, contemporary romances featuring emotionally vulnerable characters and swoon-worthy settings. When she's not daydreaming about fictional characters doing fictional things, she's at home with her family, more than likely buying books she doesn't have room for.

Also by B. K. Borison

The Lovelight Series
Lovelight Farms
In the Weeds
Mixed Signals
Business Casual

The Heartstrings Series
First-Time Caller

B.K. BORISON

GOOD SPIRITS

ONE PLACE. MANY STORIES

HQ
An imprint of HarperCollins*Publishers* Ltd
1 London Bridge Street
London SE1 9GF

www.harpercollins.co.uk

HarperCollins*Publishers*
Macken House, 39/40 Mayor Street Upper,
Dublin 1, D01 C9W8, Ireland

This edition 2025

1

First published in Great Britain by HQ,
an imprint of HarperCollins*Publishers* Ltd 2025

PB ISBN: 9780008760434
Export PB ISBN: 9780008804190

Designed by Diahann Sturge-Campbell
Holiday illustrations © Shajamal/Stock.Adobe.com

Printed and bound in the UK using 100% Renewable
Electricity by CPI Group (UK) Ltd

FSC™
www.fsc.org

MIX
Paper | Supporting
responsible forestry
FSC™ C007454

This book contains FSC™ certified paper and other controlled sources to ensure responsible forest management.

For more information visit: www.harpercollins.co.uk/green

For the lost and forgotten ones.
And the believers who hold on tight.

GOOD
SPIRITS

Chapter One

Harriet

*O*n the first day of December, the universe gave to me—

A busted knee, a twisted string of garland, and a cat with an attitude problem.

I don't need any of these things, but I have all three, warring for my attention as I roll to a stop at the bottom of my porch steps after tripping over a rogue cat. She meows and scampers after me, offering a sandpaper lick on the back of my hand—like she's not the reason I'm stretched out across the sidewalk in front of my little house like a *CSI: Annapolis* cold open, sparkly garland twisted around my ankle.

Oliver lets out a plaintive meow as I haul myself into a seated position, inspecting my knee. My tights are ripped and I'll have a hell of a bruise, but it's not bleeding . . . much. I suppose it could be worse.

Then I see that the feline responsible for my early-morning acrobatics is holding a piece of heavyweight cardstock with gold foil between her tiny, pointed teeth and my positivity plummets.

"It could have waited until later, Oliver," I grumble, giving her a pet while she deposits the invitation in my lap.

Frankly, it could have waited until *never*.

She meows again, butting her forehead into my arm before bounding off. A silent *Buck up, buttercup*. She disappears around the corner with a swish of her orange tail, off to do whatever it is she does during the day.

I look at the envelope in my lap. Twenty-five years and my mom hasn't changed the design once. When I was a little girl, I would hide in the entryway of her office and watch her slowly write each name. I used to think her care and attention to detail meant she wanted it to be special. Now I know she just likes the performance.

I trace over my name: *Harriet York.*

Not a lick of personalization or a single indication that the woman who addressed this card is the same woman who raised me. It's the same invitation my father's accountant gets, as well as the rest of the guest list for the annual York Family Christmas Gala. The envelope arrives every year on December 1 like clockwork, my mother's commitment to tradition and etiquette unmatched.

I place it in my bag, taking care not to bend the cardstock. As much as I wish it didn't, it matters to me that I received an invitation. It means I'm still considered part of the family, despite how strained our relationship has become.

I haul myself off the sidewalk, untwist the wayward garland from my leg, and collect the bags that landed in the bush next to my railing. I always have my decorations up by the time my mother's invitation arrives. My own little tradition for my favorite time of the year. I spent the weekend digging everything out of my attic and arranging it in appropriate piles, not that it matters now. The garland artfully looped around my banister is hanging limp. The giant poinsettia I spent twenty-six minutes adjusting *just so* is missing a petal.

I fix the edge of the oversize flower so the brand new bare spot is hidden.

"There," I say. "Good as new."

My aunt Matilda used to tell me there are few things that can't be solved with a shift in perspective and some shiny new trinkets. I've applied that to my own life by buying obnoxiously oversize Christmas decorations. I try to find the silver lining and when all else fails, there's always a blueberry Danish from the tiny bakery down the street to chase the bad mood away.

I don't like focusing on the bad. I never have.

So, I don't.

"Okay there, Harry?" A shadow falls over the short wooden fence that circles my property. Darryl, the postman assigned to our block, is doing his best to peer over the top of the boxes stacked in his arms.

"All good, Darryl." I limp over and meet him at the fence, taking the top package off his massive stack. He grins in relief, his thick mustache hiding most of his mouth, but not the deep smile lines by his eyes.

"How'd you know that was about to fall?"

"Probably because you can't see around it." The tower in his hands wobbles precariously, the bag over his shoulder bulging. I frown at it. "Holiday rush? So soon?"

"Nah. I'm just correcting some misdirected mail." He turns to look over his shoulder. "I don't know how I keep getting mixed up."

He's been getting *mixed up* for the duration of his career, delivering the wrong packages to the wrong people for well over twenty years. I don't know why a man with no sense of direction decided to become a postman. I spare a quick look at the package in my hands, then turn him toward the green sign on the corner. "You're on the wrong street. This label says it needs to get to Morris Street. You're on Murray."

He squints at the letters on the paper, an astonished *huh* caught in the back of his throat. "Can't believe I didn't notice that."

Neither can I, considering he made the same mistake last week. Most of us spend our Sundays sorting out who got what and where it's supposed to be. Last week there were so many mismatched packages, we decided to have a potluck, too.

"How about"—I wedge the wayward package under my arm—"I take this and drop it off on my way into work. That way you can finish up this street without backtracking."

His face brightens. "You'd do that for me?"

I've done more complicated things for less appreciation. I smile at him. "I love playing Santa," I tell him with a pat on the shoulder. "See you later?"

He gives me a quick wink over his shoulder, already moving down the sidewalk. "Not if I can help it."

On the first day of December, the universe gave to me—

Two more misdelivered packages to be corrected, a side trip to get Band-Aids, and no blueberry Danish in sight.

"I'm so sorry, baby, but we're all out." Paula frowns at me from the other side of the counter, the lines on either side of her mouth deepening in concern. I've been coming to Paula's bakery since I was six years old, my face pressed up against the display with blueberries staining my cheeks. "You want a cranberry apple one instead?"

No. I want a blueberry Danish. The promise of that sweet, sugary delight is the only thing that's gotten me through this hellscape of a morning. I've dangled it in front of my nose like a carrot on a stick. But it's not Paula's fault she ran out, so I force a smile and nod, willing to accept literal crumbs from this woman. "Cranberry sounds great, thank you."

She reaches into the long glass case while I inspect my knee. The hole in my tights has expanded, a slash across my upper thigh. I look like some sort of holiday grunge-rock princess with my tweed skirt and knee-high boots. The unicorn Band-Aid adds a little color, at least. That's nice.

"Uh-oh."

I look up. Paula is bent in half, searching her pastry display.

"What's *uh-oh*?" I ask. I hate *uh-oh*. I don't know how many more *uh-oh*s I can handle today.

"I think we're out of Danish."

"All of the Danish? Even the cranberry? It's gone?"

Her face softens at the utter devastation that seeps into my voice. I *always* get a Danish on December first. *Always.*

"You're here much later than usual," she says, casting a critical eye over the counter. She nods at my busted knee. "Did you get in an alley fight? What happened to you?"

"Life happened to me," I mutter. I'm here later than usual because I was trying to do a good thing, but I guess no good deed goes unpunished.

Mindful of the line starting to form at my back, I scan the selection. All she has left are some butter croissants and a couple of powdered doughnuts.

"I'll take a doughnut." I glance over my shoulder. "Sorry to keep everyone waiting."

"Don't worry about that." She scoops up a doughnut with her metal tongs and places it in a to-go bag. "Why don't you grab a coffee on your way out? We've got that peppermint mocha you like. Tell Imani at the register I said it's on the house."

I force a smile. "Thanks, Paula."

I eat my pity doughnut while sipping at my pity coffee on the way to the Crow's Nest, the antiques shop I inherited from my aunt Matilda a handful of years ago. Powdered sugar decorates the front of my sweater as I turn down one of the many crooked avenues that twist around downtown Annapolis, following the cobblestone path along the harbor that leads to the Crow's Nest. Nestled at the very end of the street, it waits for me—my home away from home—framed on either side by glittering water.

Cedar shingles. Green trim. A sign in arching gold letters above the door. When I get closer I'll be able to see the faded pencil marks on the inside of the doorframe from where my sister and I used to measure ourselves every summer.

While my parents kept our physical reports in a tidy manila envelope in their shared office, my aunt Matilda carved our childhood into her walls. I've always been able to find a home among the forgotten things that clutter and crowd the shelves. They've given me hope. Kept me company. More than once, I've picked up a lost little bobble and seen the beauty in its imperfections. I've wondered if I worked hard enough at my bruised and broken bits, if I could be shiny again, too. I've wondered if anyone might ever see me as something precious.

I step over the sidewalk and onto the small wooden bridge just in front of the entrance, the heels of my boots nearly clicking. *Walking the plank*, Aunt Matilda used to say with a wink. I do a little hop skip over the last board and greet the two massive Douglas firs waiting patiently by the door, a delivery from a Christmas tree farm a couple of towns over. I plan to decorate the shop while Bing Crosby croons on the ancient record player in the back and shovel enough peppermint bark into my face to make this morning nothing more than a bad memory.

But my carefully laid plans stay tucked beneath the trees. I never even get to put them in their stands. As soon as I flip the CLOSED sign to OPEN, we're inundated with a steady stream of customers. I should be grateful for the foot traffic, but they're the sort of customers who ask a lot of questions and buy exactly nothing, testing the positivity I'm holding on to by sheer force of will. Usually I don't mind the conversation, but one woman spends fifteen minutes on her speaker phone, another tries to sell me on some sort of hair mask she's been using religiously for ten years, and a middle-aged man in New Balances huffs and puffs his way around the furniture section.

"You don't have any unassembled nightstands?" he calls, hands on his hips and one off-white sneaker kicked to the side.

This isn't an IKEA, I want to snap. But I bury it down in the same place I keep my grief for the blueberry Danish and fix a smile on my face.

Silver living, I tell myself. *Silver lining, silver lining, silver lining.*

"No, we don't sell unassembled antiques." I'm proud of myself when my tone stays even. "But we do have some really lovely pieces."

By the time the sun is melting through the back windows, I'm tired, my knee hurts, and not a single decoration is up in the shop besides a half-hearted sprig of mistletoe over the back storage closet. I flip the sign on the door and pat one of the trees, dragging my fingers along the prickly branches.

"Don't worry, pal. Tomorrow is a new day."

Hopefully a better one. Hopefully one where I can string lights on my trees.

Wind whistles off the water as I lock the door to the shop behind me, the ornate brass key heavy in the palm of my hand. Another one of Aunt Matilda's whimsies that I haven't had the heart to update. I press the key into my pocket and turn up the street, the lanterns that line each side of the road slowly flickering to life in the settling dusk.

There are no wayward cats on my walk home. No misdelivered packages or oversize Christmas decorations crumpled in a heap against the porch. It's just my quiet craftsman house on a side street of Annapolis and a door I need to kick on the bottom right corner to open.

The glow of my tree welcomes me as I drop my things in a heap by the door, shimmying out of my tights. I tug on my favorite pajamas—a matching red and white flannel set with dancing reindeer—and toss my curls into a ponytail. Tonight, I'll soothe the day's disappointments with *White Christmas* and peppermint tea. Tomorrow I'll try again.

Christmas has always been my favorite time of year. It's the only time of year when it feels like magic might be real, hovering somewhere close to the surface. Like you can reach out and touch it. Cup it between frostbitten fingertips like sugarplum kisses and popcorn strung on ribbon. Crackling fires beneath the hearth and gingerbread cookies fresh from the oven. Christmas has always felt right. Christmas has always felt true.

I sink into the comfort of my couch and watch my movie, unwrapping a candy cane while Betty and Judy sing about sisters. Something thick and heavy settles at the back of my throat. *Sisters*.

Growing up, my sister and I used to lie on the floor with our heads tucked together and watch this scene over and over. We'd promise each other that we'd be the same way, laughing and smiling and dancing—*together*, always. We watched our mother and our aunt tear into each other until their relationship was a pile of ash. We knew we wanted something different. Something better.

But the last time I talked to my sister, cherry blossoms were on the trees and tears were on her cheeks. Somehow, despite our best intentions, we managed to become exactly like them.

I took one path. Samantha took another.

I force the thought away. Today is December 1. It's not a day for painful memories. It's a day for Danny Kaye and peppermint candies and my coziest socks.

Tradition. Hope. Kindness.

I'm so busy trying to suck down tea and convince myself that I'm fine that I don't notice the important things. Namely, the strange man in my living room. It's the scuff of his boots against the floor that finally catches my attention, his shadow large and looming in the glow of my Christmas tree. He clears his throat, my head snaps in his direction, and I—

I scream. I scream at the top of my lungs and hurl the closest projectile I have. The TV remote sails over his shoulder, landing next to an ornament of a lighthouse.

He doesn't so much as flinch, gazing at me steadily from the shadows.

"Hello, Harriet," he says easily.

His voice is rough. A faint accent I can't pinpoint or recognize. I don't *recognize* a single thing about him, most of him hidden in the shadows. All I can make out is a strong jaw and broad body, his hands held loose at his sides.

I press myself farther into my couch. My breath goes shallow. Every murder mystery podcast I have ever listened to has started exactly like this.

The stranger raises his hands, palms facing out. "Don't be alarmed."

Don't be alarmed. Okay. Says the man who is standing—uninvited—in the middle of my living room. He moves closer and light dances over his angular face. His jaw is brushed with scruff, heavier over his top lip. An implication of a mustache, if he were to grow it out fully. He drags one of his hands through his messy, windswept hair.

I grip my candy cane. It's not sharp enough to stab him with, but I've got enough adrenaline coursing through my system to probably cause a little damage.

"What do you want?" I breathe.

"I want to help you." He moves closer. "It's not too late, Harriet. You can mend your ways."

I blink. "Is this, like, a door-to-door thing? I'm not interested in joining your cult, thank you." His face remains blank. My eyes dart to the door and back again. "How did you get into my house?"

"I—"

"More importantly, when can you leave?"

"I don't—"

"I don't have anything valuable." I drag my teeth over my bottom lip. "Actually, that's a lie. That gingerbread house by your feet is hand-painted. You could probably get something for it on the black market."

He studies the gingerbread house in question, eyebrows raised. "Black market," he repeats slowly.

"You can have it," I whisper. "Please leave now."

He shakes his head, dragging his attention back to me on the couch. His eyes linger a beat too long on the patterned material of my pajama bottoms. He drags his hand over his jaw. "I have no interest in your gingerbread house."

"What do you have interest in, then? Murder?"

Good job, Harriet, my brain chirps. *Very subtle.*

"I have no interest in murder either." The light shifts over his face. He is all angles and sharp, knowing eyes. His jaw firms and he tilts his chin up. "I'm interested in your soul," he says ominously, and my stomach lurches up to my throat.

I pause, waiting for him to continue. He doesn't. "See, that sounds a little bit like murder."

"It's not murder."

"It *really*, really sounds like murder."

"It's not," he insists. "I'm not—"

"It's just, if you're not a murderer, you should really work on your presentation because—"

"I'm here for your reckoning." He cuts me off quickly, raising his voice. He sounds frustrated, like none of this is going to plan. Good. That makes two of us. His lips flatten into a line and he gives me a look, something flickering behind his eyes. A flame. Or a candle, almost. "I'm a Ghost of Christmas Past, Harriet. Your reclamation awaits."

My jaw hinges open. My candy cane falls to the floor.

On the first day of December, the universe gave to me—

A string of bad luck and a . . . ghost, apparently.

Chapter Two

Nolan

She watches me in silent, frozen astonishment from her place on the couch, her brown eyes blown wide, her blanket clutched tight to her chest. After a passionate initial response, it seems she's decided to pretend she's invisible.

That's perfectly fine. I'm a patient man.

I'm still recovering from the shock of the television remote nearly clipping my ear. While violent reactions to my appearance are not out of the ordinary, I can't say I was expecting it from this tiny woman in ridiculous pajamas.

I turn halfway and reach into the tree behind me, extracting the slim device while she processes. I set it neatly on her coffee table.

She makes a garbled, sputtering sound.

Lovely.

"You don't—" She swallows, sucks in a sharp breath, then exhales again. "You don't look like a ghost," she finally says.

"Well . . ." The word falls out of my mouth and hovers there, uncertain. I'm not used to people doubting my existence as I stand in front of them.

"Well?" she repeats, staring at me in bewilderment. There's a mug in the shape of a Christmas tree at her elbow and enough candy canes hanging from various light fixtures to probably be a fire hazard. Clutter occupies every inch of available space. This house is a disaster, but . . . festive, I suppose. A festive disaster.

I try to summon all my ghostly bravado. "I am one."

"A ghost?"

"Yes." I nod. "I am a ghost. Or a spirit. Whichever you prefer."

She gives me one slow blink in response. Her hair is a mess of wild, blond curls, tied back in a haphazard ponytail on the very top of her head. Two strands break free, brushing along her high cheekbones. She digs her fist into her eye, seemingly trying to clear her vision, then drops it again, blinking blearily at me.

"Of course. That makes sense." A slightly hysterical laugh bubbles out of her, her eyes rolling to the ceiling. "You're a ghost," she says under her breath. "He's a ghost."

I nod. "Yes. I am a ghost."

The smile drops from her face in increments. "You're a ghost," she repeats, sarcasm fading into disbelief.

"A Ghost of Christmas Past, yes."

"Sent to haunt me?" She digs a finger into the middle of her chest. "Me?"

I hum in the affirmative.

"I'm being haunted? Right now?" She squints, her nose wrinkling. "This is—I'm having trouble believing it."

"That's a fairly common reaction."

"You're haunting *me*? Me. I'm a good person. I pay my taxes. I feed my neighbor's cat." She squints. "Are you sure you're not just breaking and entering?"

I shake my head, gesturing at the room. "I didn't break or enter. I appear where I am summoned. It's an unintended consequence of the general haunting."

She shifts beneath the blanket, mouth twisted in thought. This happens, too. The slow bleed from shock to confusion to denial. The way people try to make sense of my sudden, unexpected appearance. I *know* I don't look like a ghost. I look like an ordinary man. Brown boots. A pair of dark jeans. A warm flannel. I've never bought into the flash-and-bang routine the way some of my colleagues do. There's no point in a costume, really, when my appearance out of thin air usually does the trick. I'm not about to start wearing a long white cloak for the drama of it all.

Though perhaps I should. It might speed things along.

A note for next time.

Her eyes slowly crawl back to mine and something about her expression scratches the back of my mind. I tip my head to the side and study her. She feels . . . familiar. Like the edge of a memory I can't quite grasp. Or an . . . impression, almost. A song I've heard before.

"Have we met?" I ask.

"I don't know," she says, voice faint. She shifts on the couch and the light hits her from a different angle. The feeling drifts away. "You tell me. Are you a stalker in addition to a vandal?"

I roll my eyes to the ceiling. "I did not break into your home, Harriet. I used my magic."

"Magic," she repeats, skeptical. "You do realize that the method of breaking and entering doesn't invalidate the actual breaking and entering, right?"

I pinch the bridge of my nose. "Can we please move on from the breaking and entering bit?"

"You'd like that, wouldn't you?"

I would. Desperately. I've barely started this assignment, and I'm irritated. Typically, this feeling settles in around the second or third memory. Spending my holiday season haunting the very worst of humanity hasn't exactly softened my edges in the afterlife.

Some of my magic escapes my careful control, the lights in the room flaring and then dimming. Her eyes grow wide.

"Do that again," she breathes.

"No."

"Why not?"

Because it wasn't intended, but she doesn't need to know that. "Because you're not in charge."

That seems to ignite a fuse of rebellion within her. She sits up straighter on the couch, the blanket she has wrapped around her shoulders slipping a bit.

"I want proof," she demands.

"Of what?"

"Of your . . . ghostliness. Do you have some sort of documentation?" A slender hand emerges from beneath the blanket, holding a candy cane. The end of it is sharpened to a point. "A . . . badge, perhaps?"

"A ghost badge?"

"I don't know how these things work."

"We don't carry badges. Or any sort of documentation."

Her eyes narrow. "That seems convenient."

I shrug. "Something for me to bring up at our next staff meeting, then."

"Staff meeting? There are more of you?"

I nod. There are hundreds of us. Surely, she doesn't think there's just one Ghost of Christmas Past, haunting the world's worst offenders. It would be an impossible task.

"Okay, fine. That's fine. This is fine," she whispers to herself. Her eyes flutter up and then away. Back and away again. The third time, her attention sticks.

"Do something ghostly," she demands.

Good lord. This woman. "No."

"Prove that you're a ghost," she insists. "Do something only a ghost would do. The light thing again."

I cross my arms over my chest. "It's not a *party trick*."

She grows smug. "That's something a not-ghost would say."

"I just appeared in your living room. I believe that should be sufficient."

"You emerged from behind the tree," she clarifies. "It's possible you came in through the front door."

I turn my head and stare pointedly at the deadlock on her door. The chain is still notched. "I didn't."

"The window, then."

"The window is also locked."

Her eyebrows inch up her forehead, her mind searching for an explanation.

"Maybe I'm having a very elaborate dream," she says, her voice going faint. She pinches the inside of her wrist.

I smirk. "You're not."

She huffs out an irritated breath. "You're a little young to be a ghost."

"Says who?" I shrug. "I died young."

"And your voice. What's going on with that?"

I arch an eyebrow. "My accent?"

She nods.

"I died Irish."

Her brows pinch together. "You're not Irish anymore?"

"No, I'm still Irish."

"Why aren't you haunting a nice gal in Ireland, then?"

"I don't know. This is the location I've been assigned." I scratch at my jaw. "Probably because you Americans need more haunting than most."

She gasps, affronted. "Rude."

I shrug. "'S true. You lot are a narcissistic bunch."

She goes quiet, thinking it over. The only sound is the hum of her television at my back and the crunch of her candy cane when she bites off the end of it. She's wearing flannel pajamas with little reindeer all over them, her feet in thick red socks. The outfit is oddly endearing, if not wholly absurd.

"I'm being haunted by a ghost," Harriet states. "I've done something terrible, apparently, and now I'm being haunted. By a ghost."

"That's the general gist of it, yes."

"And you're *sure it's me you're supposed to be haunting*?"

I snap my fingers and a piece of paper appears in my palm. I unroll it and squint at the messy handwriting. Isabella, my supervisor at the Department of Hauntings and Spirits, prefers old-school methods. Our assignments are always hand-written and hand-delivered.

"You're Harriet York, yes? Twenty-seven years old? Owner of the Crow's Nest?"

She blinks at me, staring hard at where the paper materialized.

"You have a piece of paper with my name on it?" she whispers.

"I was given one, yes."

"You're really not doing much to dispel the stalker theory, buddy."

I sigh. "This isn't stalking. This is haunting."

"Sure."

"This is how things are done."

Every Ghost of Christmas Past, Present, and Future receives a missive from Isabella on the final day of November and—off we go. We have the month of December to change the ways of our recalcitrant subjects or they're doomed to a life of misery and sadness. I am to pass off Harriet to her next ghost before Christmas Eve or she'll forever be doomed.

Or something. I've never cared enough to investigate the details of what happens when my work is done. "Should we start from the beginning?" I ask. "Will that help you come to terms with what's happening here?"

She tucks her legs beneath her on the couch. Another curl makes a mad dash for freedom. "We might as well try."

"I am a Ghost of Christmas Past. I've been sent to help you mend your ways. We're going to look through your past, so you can learn from your mistakes."

"Okay," she says slowly, drawing out the word until it sounds more like a question than a statement.

"Yes? Good? Ready to go?"

"Not quite." She wedges her candy cane firmly in her cheek. "I have some questions."

My shoulders slump. "Of course you do."

"These mistakes—" Her voice softens. A flash of regret in her brown eyes. She blinks and it's gone. "What are they?"

"All will be revealed when we visit your past."

"That's it?"

"More or less."

She doesn't look convinced. "And you're sure I've made these mistakes? To have earned this haunting?"

I almost reach for the paper still crumpled in the back pocket of my jeans and thrust it under her nose. *The paper has your name on it*, I want to yell at her. *Why are you questioning the magic of a Holiday Spirit?* I drag one hand through my hair in frustration and anchor my palm at the back of my neck. "The magic decides. You've been deemed salvageable, if only you mend your ways. You must make amends."

These mortals are always the same. They fight it at the start—say they're *good*, they don't deserve it—but they can't outrun the truth. The memories don't lie.

And I can't move on until I fulfill my ghostly duties. I have no interest in lingering any longer than I need to in this infernal place. I've spent a hundred years *lingering*. I'm tired of standing still.

I hold out my hand, impatient. "Let us begin."

"I mean, we could. I guess," she says. "Or we could wait."

I barely resist a groan. "*Why* do we need to wait?"

"Because I'm not convinced this isn't a medical event and I don't feel up to a haunting tonight, thank you very much. You can proceed back to whatever corner of my mind you emerged from, and I can go to sleep and chalk up this entire evening to a weird batch of peppermint tea." She frowns and presses two fingers to her temple. "Or a concussion."

"While I'm delighted to hear that I align with whatever dreams you might be having, that's not how this works. I can't just disappear. I am bound to you for the holiday season until you recognize the errors of your past and I can hand you off to a Ghost of Christmas Present."

She laughs, borderline maniacal. "Oh good. More rules."

I nod. "Yes. There's a transition process."

She mouths the words *transition process*. "This is all very organized."

"Yes," I concede. "It's not how I expected it to be either."

I didn't have a choice when I died, but if I did, I wouldn't have chosen this. This utterly mundane existence, watching other people go about their lives while I stay exactly where I am. Haunting terrible humans. Watching their dismal, sad memories.

After more than a hundred years haunting the worst humanity has to offer, I can hardly remember my human life. It comes and goes in flashes of color and sound. Robin's-egg blue. Sea-glass green. Pale, pale pink. Waves lapping at the side of a ship and a church bell, somewhere in the distance. A lighthouse on the shore.

Flashes, instead of moments. I've lost everything I used to be. Now I'm this instead. A shell of a man forced to endure the worst of others.

I hold out my hand again, frustrated. "Time to begin."

She doesn't move. "No thanks."

I drop my hand. "Harriet."

She picks up her mug. "Ghost man."

"You can't avoid your fate."

She arches an eyebrow. "Oh, that's a very good line."

I shift on my feet, uncomfortable. I heard another Ghost of Christmas Past say it once. It always seemed very powerful.

Apparently not.

"How can I get you to take my hand?"

Her eyes trail along my shoulder and down the length of my arm, considering. Being a ghost means I'm rarely seen—almost never studied. It's an unusual feeling. Her slow perusal sends awareness tingling down the length of my spine.

My fingers twitch.

She snaps her gaze back to mine. "I'd like to talk to your supervisor, Ghost of Christmas Past."

"Oh, please. Don't be that person."

She laughs. A bright burst that slams out of her body. She laughs like she's made to do exactly that, and it's enough to have me teetering on the edge of indecision.

"Then *you* talk to your supervisor," she says, still grinning. "That's how you can convince me to examine my past, or whatever it is you claim you do." She tugs her discarded blanket back into place, wrapping herself like some sort of burrowing creature. Her cheeks are pink and her lips are candy-apple red. She matches the lights on her tree, all colorful and bright. A little frazzled at the edges. "If you show up again tomorrow, maybe I'll believe this wasn't some weird fever dream."

"That's all you need? For me to return?"

She nods, looking past me to where the movie is still playing on her TV. I remember the year *White Christmas* came out. I sat in the very back of the movie theater with all the mortals, a box of Hot

Tamales in my lap and my heart in my throat. I watched Danny Kaye spin Vera-Ellen around and around in a pale pink dress and felt an ache in the palms of my hands. Homesick, or something like it. A tug beneath my breastbone for something I couldn't reach. Something I couldn't even *name*.

That wisp of familiarity grips me again.

The creak of a boat beneath my feet. Sea salt air and my hands on burnished metal.

Pale, pale pink.

"Tomorrow," I repeat slowly, trying to grasp the feeling but failing, dallying in the middle of her living room. This has never happened before. I've never had someone refuse to take my hand and . . . ask to speak to a manager. Short of tackling her to the couch and forcing her to agree, I can't make her relive her past. She needs to choose it.

Another one of our little rules.

"Yes. Tomorrow." She uncovers a popcorn bowl from out of no-where. Her own sort of magic. "If you use the window when you leave, please remember to shut it all the way. It gets drafty."

I blow out a breath, amused despite myself. "I won't be using the window, Harriet. I'm a ghost."

"So you say."

I take a hesitant step back toward the tree. "I'll see you tomorrow," I tell her firmly. Perhaps by then, I'll gather my own resolve.

She shoots me a distracted thumbs-up. I roll my eyes and tug at my magic. It sweeps up and over me before she can offer any more excuses.

Or lob anything else in my direction.

Chapter Three
Nolan

*H*alfway down the cobblestone street that leads from the Annapolis State House to the harbor is an empty storefront. Unassuming, it's tucked right between an ice cream parlor and a maritime shop. The windows are lined with faded brown paper and the awning hangs at an angle, the green material torn like someone reached up and attempted to rip it down.

People pass by without a second glance, ignoring the dusty windows for the promise of candy farther up the street. This time of year, everything smells like butterscotch and cocoa. Hot fudge. Crushed velvet and fresh pine.

I go just as unnoticed as the empty window I'm bound for, tucking my chin into the collar of my coat as crowds of holiday shoppers drift around me. I step off the sidewalk and a woman barrels into me, her shoulder slamming into mine, a bright red bag with gold trim almost taking me out at my knees. I grip her arms to hold her steady and she gives me an embarrassed, unfocused smile before chirping an apology and rushing off to join her friends.

She won't remember me. She won't ever think about me again.

With the exception of my assignments and the handful of ghosts that occupy this town, no one has looked directly at me in more than a century. People keep a natural distance, moving past me like a river runs around a rock. There's a sixth sense buried somewhere in their head that tells them I'm something else, to keep away. I'm not from here or there, but another place entirely. Another time. I wait and I listen and I watch as the world grows and shifts around me, never moving anywhere myself.

If I were a morose man, I'd call it a half-life.

As it stands, it's just my afterlife.

The door at the abandoned store creaks as I open it, a bell on a tidy red ribbon announcing my arrival. For a long time, someone thought it would be a good idea to have the office access point in the towel section of a Bed Bath & Beyond. The *Beyond* a reference to the *Great Beyond*, I guess. But there was an incident with a Poltergeist and a beanbag chair in the shape of a cheeseburger and the mortals started asking questions. Now a more subtle approach is taken.

The room is bright with sunlight despite the shabby, deteriorating facade, a wide skylight stretching across the length of the ceiling. A massive yew tree splits through the tile floor in the middle of the room, its gnarled and knobby branches reaching up. Two comfortable chairs sit at its trunk and a large mahogany desk fills the space behind it, situated intentionally in front of a single door.

"Nolan!" A small woman with sleek blond hair waves to me from behind the reception desk, bracelets dancing up and down her wrist. She has jam on the front of her shirt and a half-eaten pastry on the corner of her desk. "What a surprise!"

The man standing patiently in front of her desk turns halfway, a worn cowboy hat tucked under his arm. He gives me a nod and I lift a hand in greeting. I don't recognize him, but that's not unusual. I sometimes think there might be more spiritual beings in this town than people.

Betty, the receptionist for as long as I can remember and probably a time longer than that, too, gestures toward one of the chairs. "Let me help this gentleman and I'll be right with you."

"Take your time. It's not a bother." I drop down in one of the seats and stretch out my legs beneath the tree. "I'm comfortable waiting."

I busy myself with watching the clouds through the skylight while she finishes up her low conversation with the wayward cowboy. Sitting in this room always makes me feel like I'm wedged at the bottom of a kaleidoscope. Muted, blurry colors and hushed sounds.

Harriet's house made me feel that way, too, but with more enthusiasm. A Christmas kaleidoscope.

The candy canes. Her wild, almost-sentient hair. Those reindeer pajamas. I've never seen pajamas so ridiculous in my life, and that includes the time I haunted a man who thought it was appropriate to wear a spandex one-piece to sleep.

Were they a gift from someone? A joke? Did she buy them for herself?

What a strange, whimsical woman. A right pain in my ass, too.

The door behind the desk opens and shuts, and my attention darts to Betty.

"Nolan." She beckons me forward, a jelly tart held primly in one hand. "I'm ready for you now."

She takes a gargantuan bite, crumbs raining down the front of her blouse. Her eyes close in rapture.

I stare at her. "Are you sure? If you need a moment alone, I could come back—"

"No, no." She finishes the rest of the tart, cheeks bulging. "A little mess with the inn on Church Circle," she explains, words muffled by pastry and jam. She swallows and presses her fist to her mouth. "Reed is having a bit of trouble with his assignment. There's a new owner and she insists on burning sage in the upper rooms. It displaces him every time, and he has nowhere else to go." She gives me a tight smile. "But enough about that. What can I help you with? I don't usually see you so early in the holiday season. How's your assignment going?"

My assignment is a disaster. She believes nothing I say and insists on maintaining her innocence. Oh, and she demanded I come here and speak to my manager.

I scratch at my jaw. "I've run into a bit of a hiccup," I hedge. "I was hoping to discuss it with Isabella."

Betty's face twists in sympathy. "Did your assignment try to sage you?"

"No. There was no sage involved."

"Those cheap candles from the psychic over in Waldorf?"

"Not those either." A good thing, too. I heard the headaches from those candles last a decade. "Just hoping for a moment of Isabella's time, if it's not too much trouble."

Betty gives me a knowing look. "Well," she says, brushing the remainder of the crumbs from her skirt. "You know Isabella."

I do know Isabella. I've known Isabella since the day I dropped into her tidy office, bewildered and still soaking wet from the ocean I drowned in. She took one look at me, arched her eyebrow, and said, *Why are you looking at me like that?*

Like I chose to fall overboard in the middle of a winter storm.

Delicacy is not a quality she possesses.

"I'd like to see her all the same."

Betty picks up the phone on the edge of her desk and taps out three numbers. Another pastry magically appears right next to it, like the universe or fates or whatever it is that governs this world knows she needs the fortitude.

"It's your funeral," she tells me.

I give her a small smile. "Wouldn't be my first."

She snorts a laugh. "Make sure you hold on to that sense of humor when you see Isabella."

I hear the lazy buzz of a dial tone, a sharp voice, and then a pause as Betty explains the situation. The pause goes on for several uncomfortable seconds. Even the tree behind me rustles its leaves in agitation.

Betty returns the phone to its cradle with a wince. "She'll see you now."

I don't move. "Is she mad?"

Betty knits her fingers together on the desk. She opens her mouth, closes it, then tries again. "I'm not at liberty to say."

I sigh. "That's a yes."

"Best just to wait and see," she offers. She gestures behind her at the closed door. "You know the way."

The nondescript door behind Betty's desk leads to an equally uninspiring hallway, the natural light swapped for the glow of fluorescents. Neatly labeled doors line either side, each office perfectly spaced at even intervals. I make note of them as I pass.

Phantoms, Ghouls, Malevolent Spirits on the left. *Guardian Angels, Cupids, Conscious* on the right.

Harriet's voice drifts back to me. *This is all very organized.*

If she only knew.

I wasn't joking about the staff meetings. There are quarterly reports, too. A benefits center I haven't quite figured out how to utilize and a summer picnic we're always expected to attend.

The door to *Possessions* rattles ominously as I pass it. A water cooler drips in front of *Grim Reapers*. I pass *Poltergeists* and a heated argument drifts through the door, the thick drawl of an accent rising in volume and drifting away again. I wonder if that's where the cowboy from the lobby disappeared to.

Holiday Spirits is at the very end of the hall, marked with a dark wood door and a shiny gold handle. There used to be a jolly sprig of mistletoe over the door. I never could figure out why Isabella ripped it down.

I knock twice to the vague tune of "Jingle Bells," hoping to curry a little favor.

It doesn't do the trick.

"Enter," echoes a voice from within.

I poke my head through the door first, cautious of entering fully. Isabella is already frowning, the severity of her expression somehow heightened by the blinking reindeer headband she's wearing. Leave it to Isabella to make novelty Christmas headwear intimidating. Her dark hair is tucked neatly behind her ears, her tan skin smooth and unblemished. Sharp cheekbones. Dark, knowing eyes.

Rumor has it she died just before her twentieth birthday and was too angry over her early death to properly move on. She started in the Department of Déjà Vu, but transferred to Hauntings and Spirits sometime in the late fifteenth century. She's been head of Holiday Spirits ever since.

Her office is just as sparse as the rest of the department, except for her desk and the bookshelf behind it. Every inch of available space is covered with snow globes of various sizes and shapes. Some are mid-flurry and others are completely still. She's holding one with an obscure city skyline in her hands, small white snowflakes drifting lazily across the glass.

She places it to the side as I pull the door shut behind me.

"Nolan," she greets me evenly.

"Isabella." I dip my chin. "Always a pleasure."

She hums, dragging one blood-red nail across the edge of a different snow globe. "You've either set a remarkable record or you're here to irritate me." She pauses. "Which is it?"

I clasp my hands behind my back. "I have not set a remarkable record."

Her lips purse. The reindeer headband alternates between red and green.

Red. Green. Red. Green.

"What's with the headband?" I ask. I've never seen her in so much as jaunty earrings.

Her face darkens. "The executive team thought I needed to show a little more holiday spirit. For team morale. Did you come here to ask me about my headband?"

"No, I—"

"The holiday potluck, perhaps?"

"Not that either. I was wondering if—"

"I presume you were *wondering about something* if you're here. In my office. At the start of the holiday season." She leans back in her chair. "Spit it out, Nolan."

I clench my jaw and then release it. Safe to say the headband isn't lifting any spirits today. "Am I currently involved in a training exercise?"

Her frown is a slash across her face. "What?"

"Is there a training exercise happening that I'm not aware of?"

Isabella stares at me for so long, I contemplate disappearing back through the door. I eye her warily.

"What's today's date, Nolan?"

I inspect the bookshelf behind her. In the middle of all the snow globes is a small, square calendar. DECEMBER 2 practically glares at me from over her shoulder.

"It's the second day of December."

"Correct." She lightly touches her headband and the flipping colors switch to a steady red. It casts her face in sharp angles and shadows, the deep crimson of her lips looking a little too much like blood for my liking. She really could work in Malevolent Spirits if she wanted. I have no idea why she's never transferred.

"And do you think," she continues, "that on the second day of December—the very start of our busiest season—I'd orchestrate a training exercise?"

I shove my hands in my pockets, properly chastised. "No."

"Are you in need of training, Nolan?"

"No?"

"That sounded like a question."

"No," I say again, making sure I clip the edge of my answer. "No, I am not in need of training."

"You've been a ghost for over a hundred years. I should think not." She taps her headband again and the blinking resumes. "Why are you here asking me about training exercises? Don't you have work to do?"

"That's why I'm here. There's something wrong."

Isabella stares at me.

"With my assignment," I clarify.

"What do you mean?"

"She's . . ." *Chaotic. Messy. Honest.* "Young."

"Age doesn't define character, Nolan," she says, dismissal in her tone and in her face. "You've had younger hauntings than her."

"I know. But something feels off about this one."

Like a book out of place on a shelf. A single note out of tune. A rope frayed in the middle. There's something different about Harriet York, and I can't put my finger on what it is.

"She's nice," I tack on awkwardly, trying and failing to articulate the bizarre conversation I had with Harriet last night. "My assignments . . . they're not usually nice."

A bit obsessed with candy canes and an irrational choice of bedwear, to be sure, but there was something about her that seemed genuine. Authentic. She told me she's a good person and I—

I think I believed her.

That hasn't happened before.

Isabella looks bored. "And you came to this astounding assessment of her character from one conversation?"

I scowl, some of my restraint fading in favor of frustration. "Haven't you told me repeatedly to trust my gut?"

"You don't have a gut," she says, dry as a bone. "You're dead."

"There's something about her that feels different." Familiar, almost. Out of place, maybe. "I don't think she's meant to be haunted. I'd appreciate it if you could check if there's been a mistake."

Isabella's lips flatten. She picks up another snow globe—a harbor this time, with a lighthouse in the middle. She shakes it with a graceful twist of her wrist and white obscures the glass. When the snowflakes settle, the lighthouse is wrapped in twinkling lights. A faint glow from the lantern within flares and then dims.

"I've been here for thousands of years, Nolan. I've seen every past, present, and future you could possibly imagine. I've seen things you couldn't even begin to understand." She looks up from her snow globe, her dark eyes serious. Tired. It's the most human I've ever seen her.

"Mistakes aren't made," she says. "Not here. Not with this. You have your assignment for a reason. It's up to you to figure out why."

The heartbeat I don't need begins to pound out an uneven staccato in my chest. There's a threat in there somewhere. Or, at the very least, a warning.

"And if I don't?"

Isabella twists the snow globe again and the light abruptly goes out. "Then you'll face the consequences of your failure."

Chapter Four

Harriet

 There's a crack on the bottom. See? It's right there."

I bite the inside of my cheek and feign interest as I examine the minuscule crack at the bottom edge of the music box I sold last week. This piece is one of my favorites. A gilded cage with a songbird in the middle, wrapped in flowering vines. I had been happy to sell it to someone who wanted to give it as a gift. I spent extra time on the packaging.

I used the good wrapping paper. I curled the ribbon.

Now there's no ribbon. Or delicate gold paper. I imagine my hard work discarded in a trash bin somewhere and frustration licks at the inside of my chest. I let it have its moment, then take a deep breath and push the irritation somewhere else.

It's just paper. Just ribbon. Easily replaceable.

The woman in lululemon leggings turns the music box on its side and jabs her finger repeatedly at a crack the size of a thumbtack.

"I can't give my sister a broken music box for Christmas," she says. "I can't believe you even sell broken music boxes."

"It's not broken," I explain. I turn the box carefully in my hand

and twist the hinge at the bottom. The bird begins to spin and a lovely, tinkling melody spills out. "See? It plays music."

The woman ignores the song, tipping it back on its side. It makes a dull *thunk* against the countertop and I clench my jaw so tight my teeth snap. She's not being careful.

"But there's a crack," she says again.

"Yes, but—"

"There's a crack," she repeats, slowing down her words and enunciating each syllable like I didn't hear her the first forty-seven times she said it. The frustration in my chest spreads to my cheeks, my face burning hot. The urge to apologize bubbles in the back of my throat, but I ignore it. She narrows her eyes. "A crack means it's broken."

A crack doesn't mean it's broken. A crack means it's done exactly what it's supposed to do for generations. A crack means hundreds of hands have held it . . . have listened to that little bird sing. A crack means it's one of a kind. Different from anything else.

A crack means it's special.

One tiny imperfection and this woman is ready to abandon it.

I pull the music box closer and push down on the parts of myself that want to argue. I'm tired today, and no amount of fancy coffee from the café across the street is reviving me. I had strange dreams last night. A handsome man in an old, faded flannel. A frown on his face and his hand outstretched toward mine.

That's what I get for falling asleep in the glow of my Christmas tree after drinking half a box of expired peppermint tea. I woke up on the couch with my hair in my mouth, *White Christmas* somehow still playing on my television, no sign of the man who claimed to be a ghost.

I checked the locks on my windows just to be sure.

"What would you like me to do about the crack?" I ask. I know what I'd like to do. I'd like to press pause on this entire day and go back to bed. I feel like I'm two steps behind every conversation and annoyed because of it.

"Well, I'd like another music box," she says, still talking to me like I'm stupid. "Without the crack."

I frown. "I don't have another music box. This is an antiques shop. Everything is unique."

Unique and original and handpicked by me from online auctions and estate sales and Goodwill bargain hunts across the state, just like my aunt Matilda used to do. I spent my childhood running up and down the crowded aisles while my parents attended to business at the statehouse. It seemed magical back then. Necklaces and rings the size of my palm with shiny, colorful gems. Music boxes and plates with painted horses. Handwoven baskets and crystal glasses casting rainbows across the ceiling. Aunt Matilda used to say walking through the front door of the Crow's Nest was like stepping into a treasure chest.

It still has that magic, but I'm having trouble feeling it this morning. I don't like when people come in here and treat everything like it's an amusing little novelty.

And I still haven't had a chance to put my trees up.

The woman's frown deepens. "You're telling me you don't have another music box like this? Not even one?"

That's exactly what I'm saying. That's exactly what I've *been* saying. "We have music boxes. Different music boxes," I say, settling on brevity. "Not one exactly like this, but something just as special. Would you like to look at the rest of our selection? I'm sure we have something—"

"I want this one." She taps the top of the gilded cage. "The bird one. My sister is an avid bird watcher. She loves sparrows."

I stare at her. The bird in the cage is not a sparrow. It's a dove. "Would you . . . would you like me to rewrap it for you?"

"No, I'd like the same one *without* the damage to the base. I can't believe how many times I've had to explain this to you."

Around and around we go. I wonder if this woman is related to the man who wanted the unassembled nightstands.

"How about I give you a refund instead?" It's always been easier for me to take the hit than fight the fight, and this fight is hardly worth it. I lift the music box. I'd rather keep it with me anyway. "And then I can direct you to a shop two blocks over that you might have better luck with."

It only takes me a few moments to issue the refund and then the woman is sweeping back through the front door, oversize glasses perched on the end of her upturned nose. I twist the knob on the bottom of the music box and listen to the first few warbly notes as the door shuts behind her.

"You're not broken, are you? Just a little bruised." I trace the tiny crack along the bottom. "That's okay. It's her loss."

I set the music box down and close my eyes, digging my knuckles into the middle of my chest. There's an ache there I can't quite chase away, no matter how much I try.

Maybe that weird dream last night was some sort of prophecy. A mirror held up to my consciousness. Maybe I have made bad choices. Maybe I *am* a bad person.

"Well, she sucked." Sasha, my store manager, emerges from the shelves like a wisp of smoke. I jump slightly and she gives me a narrow-eyed look. "What's got you so twitchy?"

"You mean, besides your lurking?"

Sasha shrugs.

"Nothing." I push my hair away from my face. "Weird dreams. Expired tea." *A man who says he's a ghost sent to haunt me as retribution for being a terrible person.*

She gives me a considering look as she shuffles behind the counter to her rightful place. The place I left her twenty-five minutes ago so I could finally put up my trees. The place she certainly wasn't at when lululemon came through the door.

"We can add her to the banned list," Sasha says.

"We don't have a banned list," I tell her, watching as she taps away at the ancient cash register. Her nails are topped with chipped black polish, a number of mismatched rings decorating her fingers. Her strawberry blond hair glows pink against the black of her sweater, the muted light from the stained glass lamp above us making her sparkle. For someone who looks like she belongs on the top of a cupcake, she's never had any trouble holding her boundaries.

I want to be her when I grow up.

"We also have a no return policy," she says, singsonging the words. "But that's never stopped you from giving in."

I ignore her. The state of the return policy is not something we agree on, nor is the banned list. Sasha and I have sort of a good cop/ bad cop routine. I give in to every customer demand and Sasha stares blankly without responding whenever she's annoyed.

"Where did you go?" I ask. "I thought I left you behind the counter."

She pushes her glasses up her nose. "I could smell the Victoria's Secret Love Spell when she opened the door. I was needed in inventory."

"Who needed you in inventory?" We're the only two people in the store.

"I needed me in inventory."

I snort. "You mean you needed to sit on the beanbag in the back corner of the inventory room that you think I don't know about and catch up on your reading while I handled the difficult customer."

A small, pleased smile curls the edges of her mouth. "Poh-tay-to, Poh-tah-to."

She jabs another button and a receipt slowly starts chugging out from the top of the register. We really need an upgrade, but every time I hear the squeaky bell that accompanies the change drawer being ejected, I swear I can hear Aunt Matilda cursing under her breath. Missing her still feels like a heavy stone in the middle of my chest. I'm too sentimental to part with anything that makes me think of her.

The register lets out another beleaguered groan. I wince. "Can you fulfill the order for the staging company today?"

Sasha nods, her dark eyes already scanning the report. "Yep. I'm loading pallets in the back. Everything should be ready to go for the truck this evening."

"Excellent. Thank you." I might let customers walk all over me, but that same positive energy has helped me secure a number of contracts with local partners that have scraped us out of a decade of debt. For the first time in a long time, the Crow's Nest is operating with a profit.

Sasha rips off the receipt that's dangling limply above the floor and folds it into three neat squares. "The girlies love an aesthetic moment."

"And we love them for it." I bump my hip into hers. "Don't act like you haven't been hoarding the bronze candlestick holders."

Sasha snickers. "Guilty." She reaches under the counter for a clipboard and a small bag of trail mix she must have hidden at some point last week. "All right. I'm going to be in the back. Shout if you need me."

I watch her weave through the shelves. "Will you come if I do?"

"Debatable," she responds, breaking the word into multiple syllables so she can sing it. She slows to a stop near an ornate, evergreen wardrobe. I can see only the very top of her berry-pink hair.

"Remember to stand your ground!" she shouts. "Stop giving people refunds and stop letting them steamroll you!"

I pick up the music box again.

"I'll do my best."

I don't intend to follow through. People have always pointed to my subdued nature as a weakness. Every time I had to participate in a debate at law school, I'd get the same feedback. *Too timid. Gives in to external pressure. Hesitation lessens the impact of argument.* Everyone expected more from the youngest York, a sentiment that has more or less followed me for the duration of my life. I've always been better on paper.

But there's strength in picking your battles. I'm good at reading a room and setting my expectations accordingly. It's a skill I perfected while growing up in a cold house with cold parents. Sometimes it's best to make yourself as small as possible so you can go unnoticed.

Even if going unnoticed breaks your heart.

"I can't imagine she was talking about you," a familiar voice drawls from the other side of the countertop. "Stand your ground?" He clicks his tongue. "I didn't think that was something you had trouble with."

My head shoots up so fast my neck cricks in protest. It's the so-called ghost man from my peppermint-drunk-concussion-addled dreams. He's standing on the other side of my register, a cup of coffee in each hand.

Last night, I couldn't make out his features, but I can see the details now.

Midnight blue eyes. Thick eyelashes. A nose that's slightly crooked, like it's been broken a time or two. Full lips that tug up slightly on one side. A thin white scar above his left eyebrow.

If he's a ghost, he's a handsome one.

"You," I whisper.

"Me," he says. Amusement makes the lines by his eyes deepen. Two dimples wink to life in the scruff of his beard.

Fuck, my brain whispers.

He drops a coffee cup in front of me and braces one arm against the countertop. "Hello again, Harriet."

The thermal he's wearing is dark green and well-loved. There's a small tear at the base of his neck. I study it instead of meeting his eyes. His throat strains with a swallow.

"I thought you were a figment of my imagination," I whisper.

He grins in response and the dimples deepen, two divots in his cheeks.

Or the subject of a particularly indecent dream. He looks like the type of man from those old-school romance covers. The ones my aunt

Matilda used to keep in a haphazard stack on her nightstand. He's strong. Rough around the edges.

The dimples are an unfair—and frankly unnecessary—addition.

"Nope." He pops the end of the word, then nudges the coffee cup closer to me. "Here. I brought you this."

"Did I fall down the steps again? Did I drink NyQuil?" Once I accidentally had too much cold medicine and thought there were dancing gophers on my windowsill. I tried to call an exterminator. I'm sure that voicemail lives on in infamy. They probably play it during their new employee orientation. "Am I in a coma?" I ask in a whisper.

"No. You're not in a coma." He glances at the beautiful stained glass lantern hanging between us. Aunt Matilda got it at an estate sale in Baltimore and then went on a bender, picking up about sixteen more. They hang throughout the store at various, haphazard heights. "Though these lights are pretty low. It's entirely possible you smacked your head on one."

"Am I asleep?" I pinch the inside of my wrist again. "Did I take a hallucinogenic?"

"You're conscious and unharmed." He frowns at the red mark left on the inside of my wrist, then plucks the cup from the counter and dangles it in front of my face. "Drink your coffee."

I frown at the cardboard cup, suspicious.

"It's peppermint mocha, not arsenic." He wiggles it back and forth. "Drink it."

"I'm not sure I should take strange drinks from strange men."

He drops the cup back to the counter. He swaps it with his. "Take mine then."

"You drink coffee?"

He brings the peppermint mocha to his lips and takes a sip. His shoulders push up to his ears as he swallows with obvious difficulty. "I'd hardly categorize this as coffee."

"But you said . . . you're a ghost?"

Blue eyes slant to mine. "I am. Nice to see you do indeed remember our conversation."

"Ghosts drink coffee?"

One of his dark eyebrows jumps up. "That's what you're choosing to fixate on?"

I nod. It's either that or reevaluate everything I've ever known. I'm not sure I have the mental capacity to wrestle with the universe right now.

He scrubs his hand against the back of his head, then drags his palm down the line of his jaw. I can hear the way his scruff scrapes against his skin. It's a middle-of-the-night sound, paired best with rustling sheets and bedroom whispers. Wind at the windows and hands tracing over sleep-warm skin.

I pinch the inside of my wrist so hard I suck in air through my teeth.

This is what happens when I don't get proper sleep. My brain starts wandering down alleyways it has no business traveling. I start thinking inappropriately about *ghosts*.

"I drink coffee. I eat food," my ghost says slowly, oblivious to my mental deterioration. "I sleep in a bed and I have a rather torrid love affair with Hot Tamales. I don't need to do any of those things to exist as a spirit, but old habits are hard to break."

"Habits from . . . when you were a human?"

"Yes."

"Because you're a ghost."

"Yes," he says again, more than a little exasperated. "Because I'm a ghost."

"Hmm."

His eyes narrow. "You told me you'd believe me if I came back."

"Yes, well, I also thought you were an imaginary person. Dream bargains don't count."

"It wasn't a dream."

"Apparently not." After a moment of hesitation, I reach for the coffee cup he's not holding and take a sip. It's a dark roast from Paula's without any of the fun stuff. It tastes awful.

"Would you like your peppermint mocha back?" he asks, voice laced with more smug amusement than any man—living or dead—should possess.

"Ugh, yes please." I practically throw his cup at him, reaching for the other with two hands. I guzzle at it like a greedy little goblin. It's the perfect balance of sweet and rich, chocolate and peppermint exploding on my tongue.

He props himself up on his elbows, leaning up against my counter. He's one long curve, his sleeves pushed up over his forearms. His hands are covered with scars. Thin white ones that overlap his knuckles.

"Better?" he asks.

"This coffee is much better, thank you." My life, on the other hand, continues to spiral.

"Excellent. Shall we discuss the rest of this now?"

"Bold of you to assume I have any idea what *this* is," I say under my breath. Summoning my courage and suppressing the ten thousand questions ping-ponging around in my head, I shake my hair behind my shoulders, a stubborn strand or two caught in the collar of my sweater. I try to corral it with my hands, struggling to contain the entirety of it.

It's particularly out of control today, the dry, winter air infusing it with static. Some days I try to shove it under a beanie or subdue it with a braid, but I was too tired after a restless night to do much of anything with it. Now it's letting its displeasure be known, probably rising above my head like a sea creature. I bet I look like Medusa.

I drop it with a sigh. There are bigger things to deal with than the state of my hair. Like the self-proclaimed ghost standing in front of me and his so-called soul-reckoning. I study him. There's nothing out of the ordinary about him.

"Sasha is here," I tell him abruptly.

He drags his eyes with obvious reluctance from my hair to my face. "Who?"

"My store manager. She's here. If she comes out, she's going to see me talking to no one and probably check me into one of those special spa clinics."

He hides his smile behind the lid of his motor oil disguised as coffee. "People can see me, Harriet."

"They can?"

He nods. "They see, but they don't remember. Ghosts skirt around the edges of your consciousness."

"Yeah, right." I snort. It bursts right out of me without permission or thought.

His blue eyes turn sharp, curiosity burning cobalt. "What is that supposed to mean?"

I gesture at his overall person while my cheeks burn hot. The scruff. The jaw. The hair. The . . . forearms. The almost-mustache. Didn't think that would do it for me, yet here we are. "You're telling me people don't notice you?"

A smile hooks the corner of his mouth. It's almost as devastating as the dimples. "Flirting won't win you any favors, Harriet."

"I'm not flirting," I tell the top of my coffee cup.

His eyes crinkle at the corners.

"I'm not."

"Aye, all right." He laughs. He takes another long sip from his coffee, then scratches at his jaw. His gaze turns thoughtful. "Have you ever gotten goose bumps for no reason? Been in a room and felt like there was someone there with you?"

My breath catches. Sometimes when I'm here by myself, I swear I can hear a low voice in the back corner humming the chorus of "I'll Be Home for Christmas." The floorboards creak with the pattern of footsteps I know by heart and I expect Aunt Matilda to emerge from an aisle with a wind chime or a ring plate, proudly showing off her latest treasure.

"Sometimes," I croak.

He takes another pull from his coffee. "Probably a ghost nearby. You feel it, even if you don't understand it. Children can usually tell better than adults." He pauses and tilts his head to the side, thinking. It's a painfully human gesture. Entirely earnest. "Cats, too," he adds with a small smile.

"Cats?"

He nods. "Cats can always tell when there's a ghost."

"Is there—can you tell if there's another ghost here? Right now?"

He frowns. "In your shop?"

I nod, scarcely daring to breathe. He looks around quickly, eyes darting over the back corner without bothering to linger. My hope sputters and extinguishes.

"No," he says slowly. His eyes crawl back to mine. "No, there's no one else here."

"That's okay," I say quickly, even though he doesn't offer an apology. He's looking at me like he's waiting for an explanation, but I don't want to unpack that particular hurt. "I have another question."

He huffs, lips quirking up at the corners. "Of course you do."

"Do you have a name, or do you prefer your . . . title?"

His forehead creases in confusion.

"Your name," I say slowly. "Surely you have one."

Or maybe he doesn't. What do I know? My brain is still fourteen miles behind, eyeing this entire situation with thinly veiled skepticism.

A Ghost of Christmas Past. Haunting *me*.

A straight line appears between his eyebrows. "I haven't mentioned it?"

I shake my head.

"My apologies." He stands to his full height, only a handful of inches taller than me but somehow managing to seem more. I tip my chin up to look at him, watching as a shadow passes behind his eyes. He holds his hand out between us, almost painfully old-fashioned. But then, I suppose he would be, wouldn't he?

"My name is Nolan. It's a pleasure to meet you."

I stare at his hand suspiciously. Last night he offered me his hand for an entirely different reason. "If I grab your hand, you're not going to suddenly whisk me off to a ghost realm, are you?"

His chest shakes in silent laughter. "No. I'm not going to whisk you off to a ghost realm. I'm going to shake your hand with mine. This is an introduction, yes?"

Fair enough.

I slowly extend my hand toward his and he clasps my fingers gently, his big palm dwarfing mine. His hand is slightly cold, calluses at the base of his palm. I expect a jolt or a shower of sparks, but nothing out of the ordinary happens when we touch. I'm not jerked to an alternate reality. No swirling portal of doom opens at our feet. We stand there, shaking hands, at the front of my cozy little antiques shop.

"It's nice to meet you, Nolan."

His chin dips. "Likewise, Harriet."

We continue shaking hands, staring at each other. His grip tightens against mine and the amusement slowly fades from his face. Instead he studies me like he's looking for something, a furrow between his brows. I keep my face open, letting him look. I have nothing to hide.

Somewhere in the depths of the shop, a chair screeches across the floor.

I tug my hand away and cradle it against my chest. Nolan clears his throat.

"I talked to my supervisor, like you asked," he offers in the resulting silence. He picks his coffee back up and takes a long sip. I try not to notice how he places his mouth right over the faint red lipstick mark I left behind.

"Oh, wow. I sort of forgot I demanded that last night." Peppermint Harriet is a firecracker.

Amusement reappears in the lines of his face, softening his harsh angles. "I truly find it hard to believe that anyone thinks you need to stand your ground."

"Yes, well. Like I said, I thought that was a dream." I busy myself with wiping away the condensation ring left on the counter with the sleeve of my sweater. "What did your supervisor have to say?"

I imagine some ghostly apparition sitting on a throne, a long and billowing robe on her regal frame. Nolan kneeling at her feet in supplication. An ancient tome open on her lap, my name underlined twice.

HARRIET YORK, she probably boomed. *DESERVES TO PAY PENANCE. MAKE HER SUFFER.*

"She said mistakes aren't made. If I'm haunting you, there's a reason."

I frown at the wet spot on my pale green sweater. I think of a cold night in the middle of December, my hands clenched into fists against my skirt. My mother's face, anguished before she became angry.

"What are the reasons?" I ask.

Nolan raises an eyebrow.

"Like, what reasons do you usually have for haunting someone? Give me an example, so I know what I might be guilty of."

He huffs a breath, turning his eyes up to the tin ceiling in thought. "There was a man once who kept raising the rent on one of his tenants until she could no longer afford her home, purely because she rejected his advances. Another who fired everyone who worked beneath him the day before Christmas."

I flinch. "Oof."

"There was a woman who kept calling the cops on the kids in her neighborhood who liked to play basketball. Another who consistently sent scam emails to her friends and family. Oh, and of course the father who never remembered his kid's Christmas concerts. Instead, he was at the casino, bankrolled by the family savings account."

I frown. "I haven't done anything like that."

"I guess we'll see," he says easily, but there's a wariness there. A low hum of warning that tells me he won't be pushed. Not on this.

I can tell he doesn't believe me—that he thinks I'm hiding some big secret—but the joke's on him. My biggest secret is I sometimes leave my clothes in the dryer for over a week, continuously restarting the machine to ease the wrinkles that never seem to fully come out. I'm hardly the monster he thinks I am.

Except for one night. One mistake.

And I've already paid the price for that misstep.

"And how do you plan on judging me?" I ask slowly. I try to remember what happened in *A Christmas Carol*, but it's a blur. A ghost with a turkey leg, maybe? A door knocker that came alive? I definitely remember a ghost with chains around his wrists and ankles, shuffling about.

I peer over the edge of the counter and look at Nolan's legs.

Two brown boots, slightly scuffed.

No chains.

"I'll be your guide and together we'll observe your memories. We'll land in the ones that need examining and when you have your epiphany moment, you'll be handed off to the next ghost. It's a fairly simple process."

"Simple." A laugh bubbles out of me. "None of this is simple, Nolan."

Nolan nods, the shadow of a smile appearing on his face. But it's gone as quick as it arrives, a solemn look etched across the lines of his face. Either he's had remarkably easy assignments before me, or he's been doing this for so long he doesn't realize what an absolute trip all of this is.

"It can be if you let it. What else are you doing right now?"

"Right now?" I glance around the shop. "Right now I'm working."

His mouth pulls into a flat line as his eyes scan the empty shop. "Yes, I can see you're very busy."

Indignation straightens my spine. "I have hardware I need to organize. Some paperwork to catch up on. My trees—" I gesture in the direction of the two Douglas firs still standing at attention in the windows, their branches bare. "I need to tend to my trees."

"Your trees will be fine."

"You don't know that."

"When I arrived, you were staring mournfully at a tiny bird. You've got the time." He taps his cup against the counter twice. "Let's go."

"Wait, wait, wait. Right now?"

He finishes the rest of his coffee, tossing the empty cup in the bin behind the register. "Yes, right now." He gives me a stern look. "You're resisting quite a bit for someone who is supposedly a *good person*. Do you have something to hide, Harriet?"

"No," I say, defensive. Crap. That definitely sounds like I have something to hide. Which I don't. "What if Sasha needs me? I can't just disappear."

"We'll come back to this exact moment, down to the second. It'll be like no time has passed at all." He holds out his hand between us again, palm up. I take two steps back and hold mine against my chest.

Nolan sighs, fingers flexing. "Harriet."

"I'm just—I'm nervous." I exhale sharply. "What does it feel like?"

"What does *what* feel like?"

I can hear more of his accent when he's frustrated. A rough start and stop that rolls along the edges of his words. I wonder how it sounds when he's angry or tired. If the same thing happens when he's happy.

He doesn't seem like he's very happy.

I twist my fingers together. "Visiting the . . . ghostly portal, or whatever. Will it hurt?" I ask.

"No, it won't hurt," he says, his face finally softening in understanding. "It feels—it feels like stepping into a dream." He reaches for me and the tips of his fingers brush against the back of my hand, silently urging me to let go. To trust him. To believe this extraordinary fairy tale my life has somehow become. "Like falling asleep when you're on a long and winding road and waking up somewhere else."

"Oh." I blink at him, the tension abruptly leaving my shoulders. The way he described it, it sounds like something I *want* to do. "Have you considered a career in sales?"

"Not remotely," he answers. He swallows, eyes searching mine. "You'll be safe with me. You have my word."

I worry my bottom lip with my teeth and release the tight grip I have on myself. My hands tremble. "You won't let go?"

He shakes his head. "I won't let go."

"Promise me." If I'm going to indulge this exercise, I want confirmation that I won't end up in the eighth circle of hell. Or on the island from *Lost*. I'd die in 0.2 seconds if I saw a polar bear in the jungle.

Nolan steps closer. "I promise you, Harriet. I won't let go."

I could argue some more, find some reason to drag my feet. I'm still not sure how I ended up here, but I suppose seeing is believing. Nolan held up his end of the bargain. It's time to hold up mine.

I suppose I always have believed in Christmas magic.

I extend my hand, press my palm to his, and together we disappear.

Chapter Five

Nolan

*H*er hand is warm. Soft. Small in my tight grip.

It's all I can think about as time starts to spin around us. I told her traveling to the past was like falling into a dream, but it's more like being tossed into a storm. A tide that comes in far too quickly. It whips at your hair and pulls at you like it's trying to figure out where, exactly, you belong. I've done this more than a hundred times, and I'm still not used to it.

But *it feels fucking terrible* isn't exactly a ringing endorsement, so I bent the truth. I don't know what happens if I don't pass Harriet on to her next ghost, and I don't intend to find out. I've spent enough time waiting. I need to finish this assignment. I need to move on.

Harriet's hand tightens around mine on a particularly rough tug and I squeeze, holding her steady. Not much longer now.

The pressure lessens, flashes of colors settling as we skid to a stop in the middle of what looks like a fancy lobby. Time deposits us with the same lack of grace it gathered us up in, Harriet stumbling into my side. I grip her elbow as she finds her footing.

"Oh my god," she breathes. "Oh my *god*. You weren't kidding."

"About what?"

"About *what*? About time travel. About—about the *magic*." She makes a complicated, fluttery gesture with her hands. "You used *magic*, Nolan."

"I'm aware." My hand slips from her elbow to her forearm. I resist the urge to shout *I told you so* like a petulant child. "And technically it's not time travel."

"Whatever." Harriet shakes off my grip and bends at the waist, her hands on her knees. "What the hell did you mean, *it's like stepping into a dream*? What sort of dreams do you *have*?"

"I haven't had a dream in over a hundred years," I answer, distracted. This place feels cold, and it's not just the marble. There are massive, ornate columns anchored on either side of the room, a wreath the size of a small aircraft hanging between them. An elevator bank is on one side, a desk with no one behind it on the other. "I needed you to agree," I add.

"Yeah, well, now my stomach feels like it's trying to climb out of my eyeballs, so thanks for that." Harriet squints at me. Her hair, if possible, is even more wild than it was at her little antiques shop. Blond corkscrew curls fly every which way, half of them in her face. She pushes them back with her palm, straightening slowly. "You don't have dreams?"

"Another ghostly side effect, I'm afraid," I offer. I sleep, but I don't dream. I eat, but I don't taste. Everything comes in vague imprints. Like breathing against cold glass, tracing a picture, then watching it fade away.

"That's sad," she says with a frown.

I shrug. "No harm, no foul."

It used to bother me, back in the beginning. Existing without living. Going through the motions without the satisfaction. Spending my time watching the very worst of humanity with no redemption whatsoever.

But I've had time to adjust. I know what to expect now.

Harriet looks like she wants to say more, but her face pales and she doubles over. She makes a sound like a foghorn.

"Oh my *god*," she whispers, her voice thick. "I think I'm going to throw up."

I pat her back awkwardly while she deep breathes through the worst of it. Her back heaves and I spread my fingers wide, slowing my touch. She releases a shuddering breath. "I can't believe you used magic," she whispers to herself.

I finally give in to the urge. "I told you."

"Yeah, but—" She dry heaves. "I didn't believe you."

I rub another path across her back.

"You'll be grand. Just give it a moment, yeah?"

She's wearing a thick green sweater that's just as soft as it looks. My hand continues its circuit without my explicit consent. Up and down. Across and back. Between her shoulder blades and down to the small of her back. On the third pass, my thumb brushes the top of her spine at the delicate, hidden spot beneath all that hair. I linger there, tracing over soft, warm skin.

I haven't touched anyone in reassurance for decades. No one has touched me for even longer. I've had only sharp edges and curt words. I've forgotten what softness feels like.

Her breath hitches and I pull my hand away, embarrassed.

I shouldn't be touching Harriet. I shouldn't be comforting her.

I should be paying attention to my surroundings. I should be trying to uncover her secrets. Harriet could be an especially earnest con woman, for all I know. I need to crack her open, reveal the skeletons in her closet, and send her on her way.

I need to keep to the plan. I need to *move on*.

I shove both of my hands in my pockets, looking around the room. The memories I typically land in aren't usually so . . . empty.

"I'm never listening to you again," Harriet grinds out, slowly reclaiming her upright position.

"We'll see. Bound to you, remember?" I tip my head back to study the ornate ceiling. There's gold filigree up there. A giant glass dome that's shaded and dark. *Rich people.*

"Do you recognize this place?" I ask.

"Vaguely," she answers, her attention catching on the train garden set up around the base of the large reception desk. A sleek black engine chugs around, pulling six or so colorful cars behind it. Harriet steps closer.

"That train," she says. "There's something about that train that I recognize." She pauses. "I think."

Good. If she recognizes the place, then she'll be able to recognize whatever it is that brought us here. Maybe this will be a short assignment after all, despite my initial misgivings.

I wander through the possibilities while Harriet studies the train. Perhaps this is the start of an elaborate bank heist. Perhaps she has taken a lover and we'll watch as she's discovered by his wife. I've seen all sorts of transgressions. The very worst of people. I doubt much can surprise me.

Harriet takes another shuffling step closer to the empty desk, her face set in concentration. "I remember the sound," she says. "The whistle."

On cue, the train lets out a high-pitched whistle, picking up speed on the turn. From the other side of the lobby, a bell chimes at the elevator bank. Anticipation pinches between my shoulders.

But the shiny gold doors don't reveal a spurned lover, or a disguise, or anything remotely interesting. Two small children spill out from the elevator, laughter bouncing between them.

"Be careful, girls!" a woman's voice drifts from behind. Small shoes clap against the marble, and two figures dash around us. "Mind the floors!

"Harriet!" the woman calls again. "Don't run!"

A little girl with tight, blond curls giggles madly, reaching for the girl struggling to keep up with her. They're wobbly reflections of each other. A stone thrown into still waters, their similarities rippling until they become differences instead.

Next to me, Harriet makes a soft sound.

"My sister," she says, her voice hushed. Like we're in a church or a museum. Someplace worthy of reverence. "That's my—that's my sister. We're children."

Her eyes find mine, shiny and wide. "I think I believe you now."

"Finally," I say, but she pays me no mind. Her attention is elsewhere, watching the little girls bound their way across the lobby.

"C'mon, Sammy," the miniature version of Harriet calls, a slight lisp in her voice. "Let's look!"

"I'm coming." The other girl laughs. "But slow down, okay? I'm not as fast as you."

"Not true! You're faster and stronger and smarter and way, way prettier." Next to me Harriet huffs a watery laugh. The little girl with the curls spins on her heel, arms splayed wide. "You're the best big sister in the whole world!"

They collapse to their knees at the edge of the train set, their hands clasped tight between them. Two adults follow slowly behind, heads bent close in conversation. The woman's face pinches. Whatever they're discussing, they're not happy about it.

"It was Matilda, of course," the woman says with a sneer. "She always has something to say."

"Just jealousy," the man replies, looking bored. Looking like he'd rather be anywhere else, actually. "Simple as that. Ignore her."

"It's not as simple as that," she snaps back. "You wouldn't understand."

They continue arguing, drifting across the lobby after the girls.

"Your parents?" I ask.

Harriet nods, her eyes flicking up to her mother briefly before drifting back to the two little girls whispering in front of the train. The engine zips around again, and little Harriet claps her small hands together in delight.

Their mother approaches. I can see the similarities in the hair coloring, a dark blond that looks more like spun gold in the artificial light. But that's where the similarities end, their mother's expression carved into something severe and unforgiving, even as she watches her girls delight in the trains. She presses her palms over the skirt of her red velvet dress. It's a match to the outfits the girls are dressed in, yet she somehow manages to make it look austere rather than festive. A crystal glass swan, set on the highest shelf.

I've observed enough questionable people with loose morals to recognize a bad apple when I see one.

"Harriet," she snaps again, and I don't miss the way adult Harriet straightens her spine next to me. I watch her carefully, cataloging the details of her response. There will be clues in her reaction, perhaps something for me to use later. My job is to be observant and convincing, and I do both things well.

"You're too old to be playing with trains," she says. "It's not appropriate."

"I'm just looking, Mother," the little girl says, glancing sheepishly over her shoulder. Her cheeks are pink, her hands buried in the tulle of her skirt. "It's so pretty, and they move so fast, and look! They added a harbor this year with little boats—"

Her mother turns away. The little girl chatters on, pointing out various objects, oblivious to her mother's disinterest. Next to me, Harriet steps closer, nodding along like the child-version of her can feel her enthusiasm.

But the little girl eventually notices the absence of her mother and grows quiet, her small voice trailing off.

"Why are we here?" Harriet asks, her attention fixed on the children. The younger Harriet has her head against her sister's shoulder as the train goes around and around, their arms looped together. Somewhere behind us, her parents are arguing about familial responsibilities, the name Matilda cropping up again and again. Harriet knits her fingers together, pressing them under her chin. "Why did you choose this memory?"

"I don't choose the memories. My magic guides us. We see what we need to see," I answer solemnly. I don't control this part. I'm just a chaperone. I accompany my assignments to their past and guide them through the worst of their decisions. I hold up a mirror to their actions and let them see the damage their poor choices wrought.

But none of this seems like a poor choice. She's just a little girl, watching a train.

"Harriet! Samantha!" It's their father this time, bellowing at the insistence of the woman next to him. She's tapping one heeled foot against the marble, staring out the front windows, exasperation and impatience rolling off her in waves.

Samantha dutifully begins to retreat from the train set but Harriet stays close, examining the tiny village and the fleet of wooden boats beneath a bridge constructed out of Popsicle sticks. She touches one of the boats lightly, delighted when it bobs up and down in a sea made of bubble wrap.

"C'mon, Harry," the other little girl implores, shooting nervous glances between her parents and her sister. She tugs lightly on the back of her dress.

Harriet twists away. "I just want to watch the train one more time."

Samantha inches closer. "But they're getting mad."

Harriet reaches her hand across the set again, small fingers stretching for the tops of the trees. "They're already mad," she says in a voice that sounds far too old for such a young girl.

"They're getting more mad, though," Samatha whispers, urgent. Behind her, her mother is striding across the floor, heels clicking with purpose. Next to me, Harriet releases a breath that sounds like a laugh.

I turn halfway. She's watching her mother stomp her way across the lobby, a wry smile twisting her lips.

"I remember this part," she says.

Her mother pulls at little Harriet's arm, guiding her up and away from the train set with insistence. The little girl tries to turn back, but two perfectly manicured hands hold on to her shoulders, twisting her in the direction of the exit.

"Why must you make things so difficult for me?" her mother snaps.

"I don't mean to," little Harriet says, in stereo with the older version at my side. Harriet offers me a tight smile and I get that twisting feeling again. That scratch of recognition, at the very back of my mind.

"You embarrassed me at the party," her mother continues, marching little Harriet across the lobby. She stumbles, and her mother sighs like that's an inconvenience, too. "Is it truly so hard for you to behave for one evening? Look at your sister."

Harriet turns in her mother's grasp and gazes at her sister. Samantha angles her face away, pretending to be interested in her shoes instead.

"Samantha," her mom says, "*always* makes the right decision."

Harriet wilts. "I'm sorry," she says, subdued. "I'll make good decisions. Just like Samantha, I promise."

Her mother arches an eyebrow. "I sincerely doubt that."

I do, too. Because as soon as Harriet's mother moves around her to the door, I see a small wooden boat clutched in Harriet's hand. She tucks it quickly in the large bow at her back and fixes her face in a demure, apologetic frown.

I laugh. A tiny little con artist in a velvet dress.

"In my defense," Harriet says, "I probably wouldn't have stolen it if she just let me look."

I snort. "A right little beastie, you were."

The family disappears through the front door. Next to me, Harriet collects all of her wild hair, twisting it back in a loose knot. "I don't even remember that boat." She stares at the train garden. "I feel bad. Someone worked hard on that display."

I hum and rock back on my heels. Harriet shoots me a dark look. "What? You think I wanted to destroy the Christmas display?"

"I said nothing."

"Your face says enough. The boat didn't even go to a good cause. My mother probably found it and destroyed it."

"She didn't let you keep your treasures?"

"What do you think?"

No, I don't think Harriet's mother let her hold on to much of anything at all. Maybe that's why she has her antiques shop now, the shelves crowded with so many trinkets you can hardly find your way through. Maybe that's why her house is an explosion of color. A dragon hoarding her gold.

"What?" she asks. "What's that look about?"

"Nothing." I school my features back into a neutral mask and hold my hand out, palm up. "Ready to go?"

"That's it?" Harriet frowns, glancing around. "I expected something more . . . substantial."

I don't know how to tell her that I did, too. That a little girl stealing a boat doesn't exactly fall in line with the transgressions I usually bear witness to. But I don't know how much of what she's showing me is an act and how much is true. The past will eventually reveal her secrets, even if it takes the long way around.

I can be patient.

"Is that why you're here?" she asks. "Because I stole a toy boat?"

"I'm here for a reason," I reply evenly. "Perhaps this is the precursor to a lifetime of larceny."

"Larceny?" She laughs.

"It's possible. You're a stranger to me, Harriet. You could be hiding all sorts of secrets."

Her smile fractures and her eyes drop from mine. I frown. There's something out of place, but I can't figure out what it is.

"Maybe you're right," she says. She gazes out the doors where her family disappeared. "Maybe I messed it all up."

I hesitate. My job isn't to make her feel better, but I don't like the look on her face or the way she's holding herself. Hands at her elbows, shoulders hunched forward. She looks smaller here, in the past. Diminished.

"For the record," I admit slowly, "I don't believe stealing boats from train garden displays makes you a bad person."

Her eyes slant toward mine, suspicious. "You don't?"

I shake my head. "No."

A timid smile breaks across her face and the itchy feeling rattling around my rib cage is replaced with a firm pressure. Something heavy and uncomfortable, like I've been pushed.

If I'm a ghost, maybe she's a witch. Stranger things have happened.

"See?" She flicks my chest. "Was that so hard?"

"What?"

"Being *nice*. You catch more flies with honey, you know."

I roll my eyes. "Are you the fly in this scenario, or the honey?"

"Well, that lasted all of thirty seconds." The smile wilts off her face. "You're sort of a jerk, do you know that?"

"And your true colors will reveal themselves shortly. They always do." I thrust my hand between us. "Time to go."

I couldn't get her to grab on in the present, and now she's waffling in the past, too. I'm starting to think Harriet York's true purpose is to be a giant pain in my ass.

Maybe this is *my* karmic reckoning. Not hers.

She ignores my hand between us and rolls out her shoulders instead. She stretches one arm across her chest and then the other.

"What are you doing?"

"I'm preparing myself for the tornado of time, or whatever the hell that magic swirly thing is. And you're being bossy." She lowers her voice. *"Let's go, Harriet. You can't avoid your fate, Harriet. What are you—"*

"I'm trying to do my job," I defend sullenly.

She raises her voice, talking over me. *"What are you hiding, Harriet? What's your secret, Harriet?"*

"What *are* you hiding, Harriet?"

"I'm just saying," she continues, ignoring my question, "it wouldn't kill you to be a little nicer."

It wouldn't kill me. "You do realize I'm already dead, right? It wouldn't kill me because I'm— Harriet. I'm dead."

A small grin quirks at the corners of her mouth. "Then you can afford to be kind."

I huff. Her fledgling smile broadens to a grin. Done with her warm-up routine, she taps one foot against the marble floor, pretending to glance at an imaginary watch. I wish I didn't find it as charming as I do.

"Harriet," I try, softening my voice. I place my hand palm up between us. I'm always reaching for this woman. "Would you please grab my hand so we can leave this place and return to the present?" I add a sarcastic half bow. "If you don't mind terribly."

"It needs work," she says. "But it'll do for now."

She takes one last look around the lobby, her gaze lingering on the train. It's still chugging merrily around the reception desk, the bridge rocking slightly as it powers over it.

"Harriet."

"Yes," she says, dragging her eyes away. "We can go."

"Wonderful."

She snickers. Her hand reaches for mine.

"Hold on," I tell her.

The last thing I see is her smile, subdued but still shining through, like the last slice of sunshine before it melts into the horizon. A flash of light and then—

And then nothing.

Chapter Six

Harriet

I stare out the window behind my couch with my chin resting on my folded arms, watching as heavy clouds gather over the harbor. I've been trying to occupy myself with my favorite things—a fresh (see: nonexpired) box of peppermint tea, a coordinating pair of cotton pajamas, a blanket warm from the dryer, and a bowl of popcorn the size of my head—but my brain keeps drifting back to a train garden with two little girls at the edge of the tracks.

I don't remember the last time I thought about the gaudy lobby of my parents' law firm. Not because of some long-buried trauma. It just never felt like a place I should remember. For all its grandeur and commitment to Greek-inspired architecture, it never awed me as a child. It felt like walking into a showroom. Someplace cold and devoid of life, where everyone talked in hushed whispers.

But that's the memory Nolan decided to take me to. Or follow me to, I guess, since he says he doesn't control where we go. It all seems a little convenient to me, but I've never been haunted before. I don't know the rules.

I frown at my wavy reflection in the window. Experiencing that memory as an outsider had been disorienting. I thought I'd drifted away from the little girl in the red dress with the wild hair, but I think I'm the same as I've always been. Impulsive. Fanciful. Messy.

A disappointment.

Watching from the sidelines, I could almost feel the scratch of that horrible velvet between my shoulder blades. My mother always made us wear matching dresses for the annual holiday gala. She still dictates what I wear for it, unable to release her iron grip on control. I'm sure there's a tiny piece of premium cardstock in the envelope I haven't bothered to open yet with my orders detailed in crisp handwriting.

Floor length. Navy blue. Pearl earrings.

My mom does enjoy her pretty pictures.

I turn the memory over from every angle, examining it. What was significant about it? Why did we visit that time? That place? Did I need to see my mother's disapproval? That was hardly something novel as a child, and it only got worse as I grew into adulthood. Did I need a front-row seat to my father's ambivalence? Same story.

I heard my mother mention Aunt Matilda. Their relationship was always fraught with tension, but it deteriorated as I got older. By the time I was a teenager, they weren't on speaking terms. And by the time Aunt Matilda died suddenly of a heart attack, they hadn't seen each other in years.

I trace my fingers along the edge of the window, feeling the press of cold air from the other side. Somewhere in the harbor, a boat drifts by, Christmas lights wrapped around the mast.

Maybe it was Samantha. Samantha, who I haven't seen in six months. How did we go from little girls holding hands to sisters who barely acknowledge each other? It feels like the second act of my mother and Aunt Matilda, but with less ferocity. We've traded the heated arguments for stony silence. In a lot of ways, that feels worse.

We argued when I took over the Crow's Nest, though anyone

who had been observing us probably wouldn't have noticed. We were calm. We never raised our voices. But that didn't make the barbs we lobbed at each other any less painful. She thought I was being childish and I thought she was being cold-hearted. I wanted to hold on to my aunt's legacy with two hands and she was ready to throw it away. I remember the way her face fell when my frustration got the best of me, angry, spiteful words spilling out of my mouth. *Why can't you care about this? Why can't you care about me?* Clipped questions, delivered beneath stained glass lights.

A lifetime of letting people down and not being the *right* thing cracked me right open, and all my hurt spilled out.

Why didn't we go back to *that* memory? The one where I said things I didn't mean and made my sister cry? If I'm the villain Nolan thinks I am, maybe we should start there.

I pick up my phone from beneath my nest of blankets and scroll to Samantha's number. I hesitate, then grit my teeth and tap out a quick message.

Thinking about you, I finally settle on. *I hope you're doing well.*

It sounds like something my mom would write and I wince as I hit send. I debate for another minute, then rapidly tap out another message.

Miss you, Sammy.

There. That's a step toward reconciliation or . . . something. Nolan should be proud of himself. One little haunting and I'm already making behavioral changes.

Not that he's been particularly helpful since we got back. As soon as we stopped rolling through the ghost version of a spin cycle, we were exactly where we'd started, just as he'd said. Sasha called a question from the back, I yelled an answer, and when I turned around, Nolan was gone. The only trace of him was his discarded coffee cup in the bin beneath the counter and the goose bumps on my arms.

You feel it, even if you don't understand it.

Well, he was right about that. I understand exactly nothing. Magic and memories and stoic men without a sense of humor.

"Stupid ghosts," I mutter, flopping back on the couch and staring at my ceiling. "Coming and going as they please. Not explaining a single thing. Being infuriatingly vague and mysterious."

"I'm hardly mysterious."

I shriek and roll to the side, landing in a heap on my living room floor. My dryer-warm blanket tightens like a noose around my legs. Nolan watches calmly as I struggle to free myself, two mugs of steaming tea in his hands.

He lifts them in silent explanation.

"You left tea on the counter," he says, watching me battle my quilt. "I made us a cuppa. Hope you don't mind."

If I were feeling calmer, I'd be delighted by the way he says *cuppa*. As it is, I'm trying to convince myself I'm not about to be murdered. Again.

"I do mind." I wheeze. "I mind very much."

He frowns at me. "You don't want tea?"

"No, I want the tea. I just don't want an *intruder* to make it for me."

"Intruder," he says, heaving a weary sigh. "This again."

"Yes, Nolan. This again."

"If you didn't want the tea, you shouldn't have left the mug out," he says. He peers over his shoulder at my kitchen. "Though you do seem to take issue with putting things away properly."

"Nolan." *God.* How long has he silently been lurking in my home? Poking through my things?

"What?" His face twists in agitation, his eyebrows a heavy slash over his dark eyes. "You're that upset about the tea?"

"I don't have a problem with the tea. I have a problem with you materializing out of thin air. Again!"

"I didn't *materialize*," he says, offended. "I called hello. I started the kettle. You didn't hear me? I made enough noise to wake the dead."

I narrow my eyes. I can't tell if that's a joke or not. "Are you trying to be funny?"

"Funny is not something I'm often accused of, Harriet."

I believe it. "Listen. I'd like for you to knock at the door like a reasonable—" I almost say *human being*. "Like a reasonable ghost," I finish. I finally manage to untangle my legs from my blanket nest, kicking it away. "How long have you been in my house?"

"Ten minutes or so," he answers, his gaze fixed on my bare legs. His eyes narrow, the line between his brows deepening. He gestures at my legs with one of the mugs. "What the hell are those?"

"What?" I quickly look down, expecting to see an angry horde of fire ants marching over my kneecaps by the severity of his expression. Instead, I just see my pale skin and my oversize socks, one slightly higher than the other thanks to my cartwheel off the couch.

"Those." He nods toward my midsection.

I pinch my camisole. It has tiny candy canes printed all over it. I love it. "These? My pajamas?"

He scoffs. "Those aren't pajamas." His eyes don't move from the fabric around my middle.

"I got them in the pajamas section," I defend. They're buttery soft and deliciously comfortable. Matching pajama sets have always been a guilty pleasure of mine. Something about the silky smooth materials and the utter departure from practicality. It feels indulgent when I wear them. Something just for me.

I climb up from the floor, adjusting the matching shorts that hit mid-thigh. Nolan makes a choking sound.

"I got them on sale at Nordstrom," I offer.

"What the hell is a Nordstrom?" he asks, sounding dazed. His gaze drifts back to my legs. His jaw clenches tight, the faintest brush of pink appearing at the top of his scruff. I didn't realize someone could hate coordinating sets so much.

"It's a store." I shuffle my socked feet and debate wrapping myself in my blanket, then immediately discard the thought. It's his problem, not mine. I don't need to be ashamed of my festivity.

I prop my hands on my hips and try to find the often-elusive assertive part of myself. "If you had knocked at the door as requested, maybe I would have had time to put on something more reasonable."

He drags his attention back to my face with reluctance. His expression is thunderous. "What?"

"The door," I repeat. "I want you to use it when you visit. You've scared me twice now. You can use the door."

"You're serious?"

I nod, resisting the urge to take it back. To tell him it's okay. To make it easy and comfortable and fine. I've always been good at accommodating the needs of others, but I guess something about yesterday's memory sparked a long-buried desire for rebellion. I've been inspired by a tiny wooden boat, clenched in the fist of my six-year-old self.

I wish I were still as brave as that little girl. As hopeful, too.

I lift my chin. "I don't think it's too much to ask for."

His gaze holds mine, his mouth tilted down at the corners. A lock of dark hair flops over his forehead, shadowing his eyes.

"Please," I add.

He rolls his eyes to the ceiling, turns on his heel, and stomps back to my kitchen with the tea. I hear the clang of the mugs in the sink, a muffled oath whispered under his breath, and then—nothing.

Not a single thing.

I take a hesitant step toward the kitchen, regret sinking like a stone in my stomach. I pushed too hard. I was needlessly rude. He's a *ghost*. He's been dead forever. He's seen only the *worst* of humanity. Of course he's a bit of an overbearing asshole. It's the only thing he's known for over a hundred years.

"Nolan?"

An impatient knock rattles my door at the same moment my phone pings with a notification. The pressure in my chest pops like a balloon, replaced with something light and fuzzy.

He didn't leave. I didn't chase him away. I stood my ground and followed through and nothing bad happened.

There's another knock, shorter this time, and I swipe at the alert from my Ring camera while grinning like a maniac. I laugh out loud when I see Nolan's grumpy face appear on the screen, glaring at my door.

I tap the speaker button. "So you *do* use your magic."

How else could he have gotten from my kitchen to my front porch? I doubt he wedged his big body through the tiny window above my sink.

He startles at the sound of my voice. "Of course I use my magic. Was the trip through time not indication enough?"

"For other stuff besides that, I mean. I still want a demonstration."

"That *was* the demonstration."

"Still," I insist, getting a buzz from teasing him through the door. Is this what it feels like to hold your ground? I'm drunk with power.

He makes a rude gesture at my camera and another peal of laughter bubbles out of me. He must have magical powers. It's the only explanation as to how he looks so damn good on this camera. No one looks good with this camera. Sometimes I get alerts when I'm rolling the trash bins out to the curb and I have three seconds of pure, unadulterated fear. Then I remember that the harpy on the screen is actually just me before I've brushed my hair.

Nolan, meanwhile, looks like someone plucked him from a Patagonia centerfold and dropped him on my front porch. He pushes his hair out of his eyes as he studies the door, searching for where my voice materialized from.

It's adorable how irritated he looks.

"You almost got it," I singsong. "Keep looking."

He finally bends at the waist to inspect my doorbell, his nose comically large in the fish lens. I'm delighted I'll get to go back and watch these twenty seconds whenever I want.

"Apparently I'm not the only one with magic," his voice says over the speaker, sounding watered down and far away.

I stride across the room and open the door. Nolan straightens, his eyes taking only a brief detour of my outfit before centering back on me.

"You've really never seen one of those before?" I ask.

"Are you referring to your undergarments masquerading as pajamas or the tiny, malevolent spirit residing in your doorbell?"

I laugh. "It's called a Ring."

"It's insufferable." He drags his hand along his jaw and fixes me with a beseeching look. "May I come inside now, or do you have more hoops you wish for me to jump through?"

I tap my fingers over my lips and pretend to consider the question. I'm cold with the door open like this, but it's worth the discomfort to watch him squirm. Something about Nolan makes me braver than usual. He makes me want to push. To see how much I can get away with. "No more questions, but I do have a request."

He crosses his arms over his chest and leans his shoulder against the doorframe. "I should have known. Proceed."

"I want to see you use your magic," I blurt out excitedly. I've felt it. I've existed within it. But I haven't *seen* it. If I'm going to be haunted, I'd like to reap the benefits. I'd like a little show with my eternal damnation.

What else can he do? Is it holiday related? Can he make sugar-plums dance?

Nolan's eyebrows crash together, all traces of playfulness leaving his features. My gold-medal feeling plummets to the very bottom of my stomach.

"No," he says.

"What? Why not?"

He pushes off the door, his hands hanging loose by his sides. His fingers squeeze into a fist, then relax again. "I told you," he says, his voice sharp. His accent is stronger now. Rougher. "It's not a party trick."

"I know it's not, I'm just—"

"Can I come inside now? Have I sufficiently fulfilled your need for mindless chatter?"

I snap my mouth shut, properly chastised. I debate shutting the door in his face, but knowing Nolan, he'd probably just appear in my fireplace. I step back from the door and he slips past me, his arm brushing against mine.

"I'm going to make us some tea," he says, like he means to argue about it, heading straight for my kitchen. "Again," he adds, somehow managing to infuse that single word with enough venom to have my shoulders inching up toward my ears.

I close the door behind him, shivering in the icy wind that slips through the cracks. My hair lifts and then settles across my shoulders, a wild tangle. Right now, it's the physical embodiment of how I feel inside.

"Help yourself," I call. "Again."

He waves a hand over his head and disappears behind a floral-wallpapered wall. A second later, I hear the clang of ceramic mugs and the kettle on the stove. I settle back into my place on the couch, collecting my blanket and draping it over my lap, while he bumbles around my kitchen.

I wait.

And then wait. And wait some more.

Guilt pricks at me the longer I sit, plucking at the loose threads from a small tear in the blanket. In my attempt to be playful, I think I pressed on an old hurt. I have no idea the circumstances under which Nolan became a ghost. I have no idea the things he's seen, or what he's had to do. I might not have asked to be haunted for the holiday season, but I don't think Nolan asked to do the haunting. He's made it very clear he wants to do his job and move on. I've been making that difficult for him.

Maybe something hangs in the balance for him here. I shouldn't take that lightly.

By the time he returns with two new steaming mugs of peppermint tea, I've sufficiently worked myself into an anxiety spiral. The hole in my blanket looks like a gaping wound.

Nolan sets my mug on the coffee table in front of me and then claims the cozy armchair closest to the tree. He stretches his long body out, his ankle over his knee, his spoon clanking noisily around the rim of his mug. He pauses his methodical stirring when he sees the hole I've transformed into a cavity roughly the size of my fist, loose threads draping over the back of my hand like survivors of a yarn disaster.

He rearranges the spoon and traps it with his finger, lifting the mug to his mouth. "What did the blanket do to you?" he asks.

I clench the material in my fist, hiding the massive hole. I'll fix it later.

"Nothing," I say, feeling clumsy and out of my depth. I hate feeling like this. Like I've done something wrong. Like I need to fill in the empty space between me and someone else until the wobbly feeling in my chest disappears. "I'm— I shouldn't have— I'm sorry."

Nolan's eyebrows rise behind his mug.

"I shouldn't have pressed you about the—" I swallow. "About the thing I wanted you to show me," I finish awkwardly. I couldn't sound more suspicious if I tried.

Nolan lowers his mug slowly. His tongue appears briefly at the corner of his mouth. "The thing you wanted me to show you," he repeats.

Maybe it's because of the slow way he says the words or maybe it's the way he's sitting—his knees spread wide, taking up every inch of that chair like he *owns* it. My embarrassment flares into something else. Something liquid hot that sinks in my belly.

"Don't say it like that," I whisper.

"Like what?"

"You know. Like it's—like I've propositioned you."

"Are you propositioning me, Harriet?"

I groan and tug my blanket up, attempting to hide behind it. Through the gap in the material, I see the self-satisfied smile transform Nolan's face.

"Not so fun to be teased, is it?" He settles farther in the chair.

"No, I guess not."

He laughs. My throat feels too tight. My mouth, too dry. Maybe *this* is his magic. Rendering me speechless.

"That came out wrong." I wet my lips. Nolan takes another sip of his tea, amused. "I wanted to see your magic, but I recognize now that it's not something you want to discuss. I won't ask again."

"You're right," he says slowly. "It's not something I like to discuss, but—" His mouth twists as he tries to untangle his own thoughts, his eyes drifting over my shoulder to the window behind me. "That's not something you need to apologize for."

I reach for my tea and take a sip of it, just for something to do with my hands. Nolan must have put honey in it. It's exactly the way I like it. "You're allowed to feel how you feel," I say quietly.

"And you're allowed to ask me things," Nolan says back, his voice uncharacteristically gentle. He heaves a deep breath, a sigh rattling out of him. "I don't— I don't often talk with people outside of my haunting commitments. You'll have to forgive me if I'm abrupt. I'm out of practice."

"Forgiven," I say easily, meaning it. His forehead creases in confusion. I laugh. "Look at us. We just survived our first argument."

One eyebrow pops up. "First?"

"Okay. Maybe second. Or third," I amend. I wiggle in my seat, beaming at him. "It's almost like we're friends."

He grunts.

"Can I ask another question?"

He closes his eyes before giving me a short nod.

"You really haven't talked to anyone? For a while?"

"I'm a ghost, Harriet." He opens his eyes and a small, sad smile shadows his mouth. "I can't talk to people who don't see me. And the only people who see me are my assignments."

I frown. "That sounds lonely."

"I'm not one for conversation." He takes a long pull from his tea. "Obviously."

"Not just that part," I say. I try to imagine it. Living in this town but not talking to a single person. Seen, but not remembered. Standing at the very edge of things. For decades. "Nolan," I breathe. "I'm so sorry."

He picks at the knee of his jeans, one of his long legs kicked straight out. "I was always a solitary man, and books make good company. I don't remember much of my mortal life, but I do—I remember that. Being alone." The easy look on his face falters and I see the crack beneath. A flash of sharp, intense pain. "I've found ways to occupy myself in the afterlife."

"How?" I ask.

A smile hooks one corner of his mouth. "I've become very good at caring for stray cats over the years. For some reason, they seem particularly enamored with the library I've amassed at my home. They're good company."

"Did you think it would be like this?" I ask, curiosity burning a hole through me. "Your afterlife?"

He shakes his head slowly. "I thought there would be something more. Something that isn't—"

"Hanging out in a stranger's living room and making her tea while trying to uncover her life's greatest transgressions?"

"Aye," he says, his accent stronger in that single word than anything else he's said. A sound dragged up from the very back of his throat. "Something like that."

I didn't realize we're both struggling to find our footing. The thought is oddly reassuring, a delicate thread stitching us together.

I give him a small smile and he returns it. Some of the heaviness disappears, twisting into comfortable silence. He's given me a crumb, and I want to know more.

"What is it?" he asks, tipping his head back against the chair, getting comfortable. "You're buzzing over there."

He did say I could ask him things.

"What did you do? Before? What was your job?"

"I was a fisherman." His head dips to the side, resting almost against his shoulder. One eye squints. "Why do you ask?"

I take in the subtle strength of his body. The sleeves of his shirt pushed up over his forearms and his large hand wrapped around his mug. The scar I can just barely make out above his eyebrow and the scruff along his jaw. He looks indecent, sitting there like that with the top two buttons of his shirt undone, exposing the strong line of his neck. I can see exactly what he must have looked like on the deck of some vessel. Sun on his skin. Wind in his hair.

"You look like you'd be a fisherman."

Something about that statement amuses him. "How so?"

"You look . . . capable," I decide, staring at his hands again. "Rugged."

"Is that a good thing?"

I blow across the top of my mug, watching the steam dance over the edge. "Not for me," I mutter.

Nolan chuckles—a low, rough, rumbling thing—and goose bumps erupt along my arms.

"Ah," he says. "That's right. You thought I was a fantasy that first night." His eyes flash with something cocky and knowing. "I'm your dream man."

I snort. "Let's not get carried away."

He laughs again and I tuck my answering smile into the lip of my mug. I bring my knees to my chest, my blanket in my lap.

"So," I say, eager to chase this easy, warm feeling between us. "What now?"

I love figuring out what people need from me. Sasha would have something to say about my desire for external validation, I'm sure, but it makes me feel good to dig to the bottom of something and slot the pieces together until they make a complete picture. To understand the people around me. To have them understand me.

"What do you mean?" he asks.

"I know you didn't appear in my house to make me tea. What are you doing here? Tonight?"

"Ah. Harriet. Best you get used to seeing me. I'll be occupying all your nights."

I swallow hard.

"I'm bound to you for the holiday season," he continues. "I am to study your past, then hand you to your present." Nolan arches an insolent eyebrow. He really does look like my mind cooked him right up and dropped him beneath my tree. He lifts his mug in a silent toast. "We have work to do, Harriet York."

Chapter Seven
Nolan

Twenty minutes later, Harriet and I are standing in the middle of a tree field with snow up to our knees. When I said we had work to do, I didn't expect it to be quite so . . . rural.

"I'm glad you told me to change. I would have been freezing in my pajamas."

I grunt in response, my hands shoved deep in the pockets of my jacket. I didn't tell her to change because I was worried she'd be cold. I told her to change because if I had to watch the tiny strap of her camisole drift over her shoulder one more time, I was going to put my fist through a wall.

Pajamas. Those flimsy shorts with the slit in the side were not *pajamas*. She was wearing a garment constructed by the devil, designed specifically to bring men to their knees.

"I guess I didn't notice in the last memory, but the past feels different," Harriet continues, oblivious to my distraction. She wiggles in the snow, testing it, then holds out her hand and catches a snowflake in the middle of her palm. It holds its minuscule, crystalline shape half a second longer than it's supposed to, then melts into her skin.

"The cold is only sort of cold. It's like being in a bubble," she muses. "Or a space suit."

"We're observers," I explain. "Not participants."

While current Harriet ponders the logistics of the memory we've landed in, past Harriet is doing her damnedest to cut down a tree. All I can see is her jeans-clad legs from beneath a tangle of branches. She's been trying to cut it down since we arrived. I have no idea what she's doing under there.

And I have no idea what we're doing here, in *this* memory. It's another perfectly innocuous peek at Harriet's past. Completely ordinary. We're in a serene snow-covered field full of rich Fraser firs. Christmas music drifts from the big red barn in the distance. Laughter comes in fits and bursts as kids run by with their parents, and beneath her tree, Harriet persists with what I assume is a horribly inefficient saw.

Maybe she'll somehow set the tree on fire and reduce the whole farm to ashes? Perhaps the tree she is attempting to destroy is a precious heirloom? Maybe she's cutting down the tree to spite someone else with . . . holiday spirit?

What is she *hiding*?

"It's like I'm here, but I'm not," Harriet continues, spinning on her heel while I brood silently next to her. She bends at the waist and scoops some snow into her hands, dumping it out again. "The snow feels like marshmallows."

"It's because we're in the past," I say again, tilting my head in concern as the tree begins to wobble. I take in the empty field. What if it falls? She's out here by herself and there's no one here to help her with the damned tree.

Does anyone know where she is? Is she even using a saw, or is she gnawing through the trunk with her teeth? My hands flex at my sides.

"Stop scooping the snow," I snap, annoyed. Annoyed that I'm *annoyed*. "You'll make your hands cold."

"I don't feel it, though."

"You will when we get back," I explain, watching the tree sway back and forth. "These things tend to linger."

"Really?"

I nod. If she's not careful, she'll feel the chill of the snow for days. I've never cared very much about it, but I seem to care with Harriet.

I am annoyed.

She looks at her hands, flexing her fingers. "How strange."

I fumble around in my pockets, searching. "Do you want my mittens?"

"You have mittens?"

"It's winter. Of course I have mittens."

I pull them out of my pocket, dangling them in front of her. She grabs them and tugs them over her hands. They're comically large. More like oven mitts than mittens.

She claps them together, delighted. "Did you knit these yourself?"

"No." *Yes.* I have an obscene amount of time on my hands and very few hobbies. I knit. I read. I take care of the cats that inexplicably show up at my window every few months. I occasionally steal one of the small fishing vessels docked in the harbor and take it out for a joyride. "I picked them up at that mercantile store by the dock in 1976."

Her thick eyelashes are a fan across the tops of her cheeks and the tip of her nose is pink from the cold. Her coat is pink, too. She looks like cotton candy over there.

But, fuck, she's pretty.

"Nineteen seventy-six?" she asks.

"Mm-hmm," I lie, turning back to the other Harriet and the precariously leaning tree. "They were having a sale."

"A sale on mittens."

"Correct."

"In 1976."

"Yes."

"Okay." I watch her out of the corner of my eye as she digs one mittened hand into the pocket of her coat. "You're lying, but that's fine."

She continues to struggle, her arm fully caught in the confines of her pocket, her elbow winging out like a chicken in distress. She wiggles to the left, then the right.

"All right?" I ask, peering down at the top of her head.

"'M fine."

"You sure?"

She nods, going still. A moment later, she tries to wedge her hand free again. I leave her to it, content to watch her struggle.

Finally, she turns and stares mournfully up at me. Her arm is still pinned to her side.

"I need your help," she says.

I bite the inside of my cheek against my grin. "With what?"

"My hand is stuck." She wiggles her arm around for emphasis. "And I can't get my candy cane out."

"Where's the candy cane?"

"In my pocket. I always keep candy canes in my pocket."

Of course she does. That makes sense, given the sheer amount of them she has in her house at any given moment.

I raise my eyebrows. "And how would you like me to help?"

"Untangle me?" She twists and offers me her elbow. "One good tug should do it."

"A tug?"

"Yes, a tug. I found this coat at Goodwill and the pockets are too small. This happens a lot." I imagine it does, with all the candies she's apparently shoving inside it. Harriet seems like she's a catastrophic mess, 80 percent of the time.

She shimmies closer, pressing her arm against my chest. She nods at it. "Go on."

I hesitate. "You're sure?"

"Yes, please. I'd like to use my arm again today. And I could use a candy cane." She nods at her past self, still sawing away at the tree. There's a muffled thud and a groaning sound. "If I remember correctly, we're going to be here for a while."

"You know this memory?"

She nods, a secret smile flirting with the corners of her mouth. My attention fixes there, holding until she knocks her arm against my chest. I grab it, fingers gripping tight. The coat she's wearing is just as soft as the sweater she had on the other day, but thicker.

"Nolan." Harriet laughs. "C'mon. Help me out."

I adjust our stance and pull gently on her arm.

"What's that? What are you doing?" she asks, sounding like she's on the verge of laughter. I can't see her face like this, her body wedged against mine, her hair obscuring her features. "That's not going to do anything."

"I shouldn't have given you my mittens," I grumble. "You don't have an appreciative bone in your body."

"My hands are nice and cozy, thank you very much. Now try again. Put some muscle into it."

I put more than a little muscle into it. I pour all of my frustration and a little bit of my resentment, too. I have no idea how I keep finding myself in these ridiculous situations with Harriet, but I'd like very much to do my job and call it a day for the holiday season. I shouldn't be offering my assignment the mittens that took me close to a month to make. I certainly shouldn't care whether her hands are cold.

But I did and I do and despite my best efforts to the contrary, I don't regret any of it.

I pull too hard and she squeaks, her hand coming loose in a single, rough movement. She loses her balance in the snow, arms flailing, a rogue candy cane and an obscure box dropping in the bank to our left. I wrap my arm around her waist before she can go toppling over after it, her mittened hands clutching the front of my coat.

I hold her there until I'm sure she has her footing, then hold her for a second longer. She's warm and solid and real and it's been so damn long since I've felt the press of someone else's body against mine.

I flex my fingers against her back. Her hands find my shoulders. She exhales and her warm breath brushes against my throat.

I spread my fingers wide and tug her half an inch closer. She bends slightly, her head tipping back. It does something dangerous to my control. My magic rolls in my chest, a low hum.

"Okay?" I ask.

She nods, silent, her eyes blown wide. I straighten and set her back on her feet. When she's standing without any additional slippery mishaps, I let her go and bend at the waist, plucking her items from the snow.

I hold them out to her.

"Thank you," she murmurs. I'm so busy watching her blush work its way over her skin that I miss her trying to shove the box at my chest.

I grab her wrist. "What are you doing?"

"These are for you." She shakes the box, something rattling around inside. "Candies. You said you like cinnamon right? I got you a box."

I blink at her. "A gift?"

"I suppose it is, sure." She shrugs, her cheeks still a ferocious pink. "It's not a big deal. I saw them and thought you might like a treat."

I don't. The denial sits heavily on the tip of my tongue. It won't be worth it. Whenever I eat anything, I get only a vague impression of the taste. The reason I like Hot Tamales so much is because the cinnamon bites through the numbness. It's the closest I've come to enjoying a flavor in decades.

If visiting the past is like being underwater, then existing in the present is like being frozen solid. Nothing gets through.

Harriet goes to dig in her troublesome pocket again. "I also have lemon drops, if you'd rather—"

I grip her wrist again. "Hands out of the pockets, trouble."

She stills. "Yeah. Good point."

"How much candy do you have stocked on your person?"

She smiles at me. "You wouldn't believe me if I told you."

A laugh punches out of me. She's probably right. I slip one finger in her left coat pocket.

"Lemon drops are in this pocket?" I tug on it, twisting her slightly. I don't know why, but messing with Harriet is like cracking open a rusty door to a part of myself that hasn't seen light in a hundred-something years. I'm stepping down a very dangerous path.

She nods. "Yeah. They're in there."

"All right," I agree. "But I'll get them."

I slip my hand inside her impossibly small pocket without looking away from her face. Her lips part as my fingers come in contact with roughly ten thousand pieces of candy. I can barely fit my hand in among all the sweets.

"You have a problem."

"Never know when you might get a craving," she says faintly.

Her tongue appears at the corner of her mouth and everything in me pulls tight. A snowflake drifts lazily from the sky and lands against her bottom lip, a tiny crystal miracle before it melts into her skin.

I pull in a deep breath through my nose, then release it. I tug the candy out of her pocket and hold it in the palm of my hand.

"Thank you," I manage, my voice sounding like it's been dragged over rocks.

Harriet smiles up at me, shifting her attention back to the wobbling tree. "You're welcome."

I stare at her profile while I unwrap the lemon drop and try to rationalize the knot tightening in the middle of my chest. Harriet is the first assignment I've had in a decade that's been close to my mortal age. I don't usually engage in casual conversation. I can't remember the last time someone touched me that wasn't by accident or a part of my job. She's achingly beautiful with a wicked sense of humor and a desire for kindness that I'm starting to think might not be an act.

Her proximity is affecting me. That's all this feeling is.

I shove the candy in my mouth. For a single, hopeful heartbeat, I think I can taste it. Smooth, creamy lemon and the bite of something sharp. But then the flavor dulls and fades away, my senses muted once again.

I release a sigh. "What exactly are you doing to that tree under there?"

Harriet snickers. "I'm brutalizing the poor thing. I was twenty-one and painfully uneducated on forestry tools. I couldn't figure out how to use the saw." The tree shivers, a victorious screech coming from beneath the branches. "Hold on a second. This is the best part."

"I don't understand why you came out here by yourself." I keep waiting for someone else to materialize. A family member or maybe a boyfriend. Someone to help her with the tree roughly five times her size. "Or why you picked that tree."

Harriet rolls her shoulders back, her candy cane between her teeth like a cigar. "Because I'm a strong, independent woman." A thoughtful look wrinkles her nose. "Although . . ."

A sense of foreboding grips me by the back of my neck. "Although, what?"

There's a loud snap as the trunk finally gives. I watch as the tree begins to fall—forward instead of back. Toward Harriet's outstretched legs.

"I was sawing the wrong way," Harriet supplies next to me, a laugh bubbling up. "Physics never was my strong suit."

The tree lands with a muffled thud in the snow, right on top of Harriet. In front of us, we watch as she struggles beneath the weight of the tree. I've never interfered with the past before, but right now I want to. I want to grab the tree and drag it off her. I want to help her stand up and brush away the needles that are undoubtedly stuck in her hair.

I want to make sure she's okay.

I don't think she has anyone to make sure she's okay.

"You shouldn't be out here alone," I say instead, clenching my hands into fists at my side. I bite down on the lemon drop and aggressively chew until I don't feel so out of control.

Harriet waves her hand, dismissing me. "Everything turns out fine. Look."

The tree tips to the side and Harriet emerges, red-faced and victorious. She does have pine needles in her hair. A pinecone, too. The beanie she was wearing is now tangled in the branches of the tree, an unintentional ornament.

But it's the look on her face that has my breath backing up in my chest. She's beaming down at the tree like she's just conquered something.

"I didn't have anyone to come with me," Harriet explains. "I'm sure you noticed with our last trip to the past, but my family isn't exactly the 'walk through a field and perform manual labor' type. My mom didn't want—" She huffs a deep breath through her nose, then exhales it slowly, letting the rest of that sentence go. "They had other plans and I wanted a tree for my very first grown-up apartment. My aunt Matilda offered to come with me once she heard I was on my own, but I think I wanted to prove that it was okay to do things by myself. That I could want something and deserve to have it. That even if it ended up being hard, it would be worth it."

We watch as past Harriet bends and grabs the base of her spruce. She lifts it with a grunt and begins dragging it backward through the snow.

"Was it worth it?" I ask.

Her smile is wistful as she watches herself. "What do you think?"

The pinecone falls out of her hair when she gives the tree a par-ticularly rough tug, bouncing down the front of her puffy jacket and landing right next to her hat. Harriet stops yanking and stares at it, reaching up with one hand to pat at her head. Realization lights up her face, a laugh following right after. It echoes out across the field, twisting around the trees like tinsel. There's joy in that sound. Relief, too.

She found what she was looking for.

"Yeah," I tell her. "Yeah, it was worth it."

We don't linger in the past much longer.

As soon as past Harriet disappears down the hill with her tree, I hold out my hand and current Harriet takes it without a word, the wind that's been twisting around the trees centering on us instead, wrapping around our ankles and coiling up until her hair is in my face and my stomach is in my throat. I'm aware of all the places we're touching as we tumble through time. Hands, hips, shoulders. Her steady breath on my neck and her palm pressed to mine.

When we slow to a stop, we're back in her living room, our mugs of tea exactly where we left them. I center myself with the things I can see. Her blanket discarded over the arm of the couch. The ce-ramic gingerbread men on the mantel above the fireplace. The tree in the corner.

"Did you cut that one down by yourself, too?" I ask.

"I did," she answers. "I started a new tradition that year, though I like to think I'm better with a saw now. And . . . gravity, I guess. It's much less action-packed these days." Her lips purse in thought. "I order the ones for the store, though. Cutting down three trees in one season feels like pressing my luck."

A self-deprecating smile blooms across her face. I drag my thumb over her knuckles, our hands still locked together between us. I wish she weren't wearing my mittens. I want to feel her skin.

I guess I know a thing or two about pressing my luck.

I drop her hand, pressing my palm to the back of my neck instead. I need to recalibrate. We've taken two trips to the past now and neither has been particularly revealing. I'm looking at a puzzle with half the pieces missing.

"Felling trees and stealing boats," I say, frustrated. "Whatever could be next?"

"I suppose I've burned a gingerbread cookie or two over the years. Maybe when we visit my past again, we'll have to watch me massacre an entire town of licorice." Her smile becomes something forced, her eyes searching mine. I've disappointed her somehow. I've said the wrong thing. "You still think I'm hiding something, don't you?"

I think there's something holding me here. Something I haven't seen yet. Maybe she doesn't mean to be deceptive, but the fact remains that there's something I need to find. To see. And it's not a train garden or trees in a field.

Mistakes aren't made. Not here. Not with this.

"It's my job," I tell her, feeling a prick of guilt for reasons I can't begin to name. "I need to get you to your next ghost."

"My next ghost," she repeats.

"As much as I'm enjoying myself," I say, reaching for sarcasm, "I have other things to tend to. People I answer to." Frustration burns hot at the back of my neck. "You really think you're the exception to the rules that have governed this realm and the next for millennia?"

Harriet's face collapses. She pulls the mittens off her hands.

"Of course," she rasps. "I've made plenty of mistakes. I've hurt people. I'm sure—" She takes a shuddering breath. "I'm sure I probably deserve this."

Guilt pricks at me again. A dull pressure that builds the longer she stares at her feet. "Harriet—"

"I mean, I haven't called the cops on children, or been responsible for someone losing their home, but—" She shrugs listlessly. "Maybe what I did is just as bad."

I narrow my eyes. "What did you do?"

She plucks at a loose thread on the mittens, turning them over and over in her hands. "We'll find out, won't we? I can't hide from my past, as you are so fond of saying." She gives me a tight smile. "But I get it. No hard feelings. I don't want to hold you up or keep you from moving on."

She offers me my mittens back.

That's the thing. I won't move on. I'll stay exactly where I am, shackled to this place until I fulfill whatever requirements it has of me. How many decades have I spent trying to figure out how to move on? How many decades more will it take?

"Keep the mittens," I tell her, suddenly exhausted. "I have other pairs."

I can knit more. It'll give me something to do.

"Oh, okay." She tucks them close to her chest, her fingers gripping them tight. "Are you sure? You got them on sale."

"They're twenty years old. It'll be fine."

Her mouth tilts in confusion. "I thought you said you bought them in 1976."

Shit.

"Time is a fleeting concept for me," I deflect. "There's a lot I don't remember."

"If you're sure," she finally says, her words slow. She reaches behind her and places them on the arm of the couch. "Did you want— did you want to stay for a little bit?" She gestures at the half-empty mug on the small, round table by the tree. Her eyes grow hopeful.

"You could finish your tea. If you wanted. We could talk about . . . whatever you want to talk about. You don't have to be lonely."

I shake my head. The last thing I need to do is spend more time in this house that smells like peppermint and pine. These concessions to Harriet's comfort need to stop. I'm not meant to be her friend. I'm meant to be her reckoning. "I should be on my way."

"Okay," she says softly and that makes me feel worse. Her easy agreement. She doesn't look like the Harriet from the tree farm at all. This Harriet looks tired and broken down. Crumbling at the edges.

She tugs her arms free of her coat and drapes it over the back of the couch. She stretches her arms above her head and I get a glimpse of the smooth, pale skin of her stomach. The rise of her hip and the dip of her belly button.

I swallow hard and avert my eyes to the tree.

"Do you think—"

She stops abruptly. I wait for her to continue, but she doesn't.

"What is it?"

She peers up at me through her lashes. "Do you think—do you think I'll be able to fix it? Whatever it is I've done wrong?"

I don't answer, at a loss. I've never had an assignment ask if they could *fix it*. I've never been with anyone who's even wanted to try. It usually takes until they're faced with their third ghost and their unfortunate and/or untimely demise before they're even willing to consider it.

She rushes to fill the silence, her face earnest. "Do you think I can be a good person again?"

I stare down at her, glowing in the light of the tree. I can't think of a single thing to say. "I guess we'll find out," I finally say, repeating her earlier statement.

Her shoulders fall and she turns her face toward the floor. I'm struck with the irrational desire to cup her face in my palms. Tilt her chin up.

"I should be going," I say instead, stepping backward. My leg hits the coffee table and our teacups rattle. "I'll be in touch."

She nods. "Where will you go?"

"When?"

She tips her face toward mine. Melancholy lingers in the smile she tries to force. "When you're not here. Where do you go? Do you have a part-time haunting gig at the cemetery?" Her smile becomes less forced, delighted by her own joke. "Do you float around the abandoned lighthouse at the inlet, moaning and groaning?"

"I have a home," I answer. Though the lighthouse idea has merit. Maybe if I get bored, I can go down there with my bag of recycling and clang around a little bit.

"I'm glad," she says. At my questioning look, she elaborates. "I'm glad you have a home."

It's fine. It's a small row home on the other side of town with a view of the water that was condemned in the 1800s, I believe. The city of Annapolis believes it to be a hovel, but the department has cleaned it up nicely. I spend my days drinking coffee on the back porch and reading from one of the endless stacks of books that line my shelves. I owned a television briefly in the early nineties. Then I accidentally watched two episodes of *The Jerry Springer Show*, thought I somehow transferred myself to hell, and abandoned it on the front steps of the fire station.

My existence is quiet, small, and easily contained. Nothing like the home Harriet has made, filled with a tree she cut herself and ten thousand candy canes.

It feels good being here. It's like—it's like I'm absorbing some of her light.

Which is exactly why I should go.

But it's hard to leave her when she still looks so defeated, standing alone in the middle of her living room with her arms wrapped around herself.

I could extend an olive branch.

If I wanted.

"Why are you looking at me like that?" Harriet whispers.

The magic in my chest jumps at the sound of her voice, skittering through my bloodstream and settling in the palms of my hands. It's an odd feeling. Not entirely unwelcome, but odd. My magic isn't usually so fickle.

"I'm thinking about something."

"What are you thinking about?" she whispers.

"Peace offerings."

"Oh," she says. Her eyes squint. "I don't understand."

"Just—be quiet for a second."

"Okay," she whispers.

I study her face as I try to find that place in my chest where the magic comes from. That deep tug somewhere near my lungs. A smile flirts with the edges of her mouth and my magic jumps in my chest, a hot flare of *something*. I grab a hold of the gold, glittering thread and tug, the ground rushing out from beneath my feet.

The last thing I hear before I use my magic to jump from her home to mine is her delighted laugh, almost as bright as the magic roaring through my bloodstream.

Chapter Eight
Harriet

"What do you think of ghosts?"

Sasha frowns thoughtfully as she twists her rag around the handle of a large serving fork. She found a stunning silver set at an estate sale in Baltimore and we've spent the first hour of the morning trying to shine it back to its former glory. It's completely intact except for two spoons. I like to think those two spoons are off in a drawer somewhere, nestled together and happy.

"What sort of ghosts?" she asks.

"I don't know. Just ghosts."

She considers the question. "My parents took me to see *Casper* at the Bengies Drive-In Theatre when I was a kid. I thought it was cool." Sasha lifts her fork into the light, squinting at it. "Not as cool as this fork, though. Doesn't it sort of look like a trident?" She thrusts it into the air. "Maybe we should put it in the medieval weapons section."

"We don't have a medieval weapons section."

"We could have. If you bought that mace from that creepy guy."

I grab the fork before she can stab me or herself.

"Would you listen to yourself? I was never going to buy a mace from a creepy guy. I had no way of authenticating it, for one. And two, he had a goatee. Never trust a man with a goatee." I set the fork back in its designated place in the wooden case. "And tridents have three spokes, not two. Tri means three. Polish the knives next."

Sasha grumbles something under her breath that sounds like *wish we had a mace* as I let my mind drift. I haven't seen Nolan in five days. I've been waiting for him to pop up from behind one of the crowded shelves in the antiques store, or maybe knock on my door again, but it's been complete and total silence since he disappeared with a wave of his magic in the middle of my living room.

Where did he go? What's he doing? He said there was a deadline on this whole haunting business. Shouldn't I be seeing him more regularly if there's a deadline? Will he say goodbye, or will the Ghost of Christmas Present suddenly appear in my bathroom? I have no idea.

Maybe I have seen him, and I don't remember. He did say ghosts skirt the edges of consciousness. Maybe he's been in here every day, and I've forgotten him every time.

I stop twisting my polish rag.

"Why are you asking me about ghosts?" Sasha asks, picking up a dainty-looking butter knife. She flips it up in her grip, catching it at the handle. "Did you experience something?"

I think of Nolan's hand around mine. The way he squeezes my fingers every time we visit the past. I think of the way I stumbled in the snow when my hand got stuck in my pocket. How he held me steady with my body tucked against his, my heart thundering in my chest.

He smelled like warm skin and salty air. Something darker. Cloves, maybe.

I've experienced something, all right.

I shrug and reach for another spoon. "Just curious. We work in an antiques shop and we've never talked about it before." I look over the aisles thoughtfully. "I bet some of this stuff is haunted."

"Probably," Sasha agrees. "I bet some of the people who owned this stuff met a grisly end."

"Sasha."

"What? That's just, like, basic math," she quips. "Should I get out a Ouija board? We can try to reach another dimension."

"Do those things work?"

Maybe I can use one to get in touch with Nolan. *Where did you disappear to? Is it because I asked you to show me your magic? Is it because you* showed *me your magic?*

Did you knit those mittens yourself?

He'd probably take a lot of joy in slowly spelling out B-I-T-E M-E.

"I don't know." Sasha laughs. "My knowledge of the undead is contained to what I learned at preteen sleepovers. And marathon viewings of *Unsolved Mysteries* on Lifetime. I guess we could go in the bathroom, turn off the lights, and chant 'Bloody Mary' three times in a row. See what happens."

I shiver. "No, thank you." Now that I know Nolan exists, I imagine there are plenty of other spirits milling about. I don't want to invite anyone named Bloody Mary over for tea, thank you very much. "Why would someone become a ghost, you think?"

Sasha sets one knife down and picks up another. "As opposed to . . ."

"I don't know. Being at peace?" I wasn't raised in a religious home. My parents were the church-on-Easter-and-Christmas type of people, and only because it provided good networking opportunities. My opinions on the afterlife are purely philosophical, at best. "Why would someone choose to hang out here?"

"Entertainment," she answers. "Society is doing a fine job of being a shit show lately. Did you see that new reality show? About the people who are in relationships with inanimate objects? I might pass on the afterlife for that."

"I'm serious, Sasha."

She sets her polishing rag down and gives me her full attention, blinking at me through her thick glasses. Her nails are bright, sparkly purple today, glittering at me as she adjusts her frames. "Yeah, I can see that." She frowns and turns back to her knife, expression thoughtful. "Maybe it's not a choice? I can't imagine anyone choosing this over, I don't know, a golden field with a never-ending sunset." She rubs her lips together, thinking. "All-you-can-eat churros. Nachos that don't get soggy with salsa. Oh! Bottomless brunches you don't need reservations for."

Choice. My brain sticks on that word while Sasha continues to verbally list the amenities in her version of the afterlife, most of them food related. Didn't Nolan say he thought there would be something else? Something better?

Maybe he didn't have a choice. He said he's bound to me for the holiday season, but maybe he's bound to this place, too. Stuck until he does whatever it is he needs to do.

Until I atone for my supposed sins.

I frown down at the silverware set.

"My mom thought there was a ghost in our kitchen pantry," Sasha continues. "She said he had unfinished business with a bread recipe he couldn't perfect, and that's why he kept spilling flour all over the floor." She gives me a sly look. "But she didn't know the flour was from my sister. Elena had a fixation with the lollipops on the top shelf and the flour bag was the best makeshift step stool."

I laugh. "I'd expect nothing less of Elena. Or your mom."

Where my parents are straight-laced and uptight, Sasha's moms are free-spirited and welcoming. They come in every few weeks with fresh-baked organic cookies, delighting over the store's newest finds. Sasha is always horrifically embarrassed, but I'm deeply envious. I'd love to be loved that loud.

"My mom went through a heavy sixth sense phase. She was convinced every disturbance was someone with unfinished business."

She finishes the knife and sets it down. Picks up another. "Maybe that's your answer. Unfinished business."

"Hmm. Maybe."

Nolan doesn't fit in line with my ghostly stereotypes. He doesn't seem driven by anger or malice. He's not particularly enthusiastic or impassioned about his role. Or his magic. Or . . . anything, really. He seems like he's just existing. Drifting along.

The front door of the shop creaks open. My attention snaps toward the door, but no one appears. A second later, a blur of orange streaks by.

My shoulders relax. I haven't seen Oliver since the letter incident on my front porch. I was starting to worry.

Sasha snorts. "That cat is a menace."

"Hush. She's cute."

"She's playing you for your treat stash. And you're nice enough to give in. Every time." She reaches for the polish can and frowns at it. "We're out of polish. I'll go grab some more from the back."

"Nuh-uh. I'll grab it," I tell her. I don't need Sasha disappearing for half the day again. The last time I checked, she'd added string lights to her reading nook. It's a miracle she ever comes out of there. "I'll be right back."

I grab the empty can and head toward the storage closet.

Unfinished business. Could that be why Nolan is here? He said he died young, that he never anticipated becoming a ghost, so maybe—

Maybe there's something he needs to help him move forward. An object, maybe? Something in my shop. Maybe my poor decision making is only *part* of the reason he's here. Maybe I can make up for my past transgressions by helping *him*. I could help him solve his unfinished business—whatever that looks like.

Maybe that's my path forward.

Oliver weaves between my ankles as I wander to the back of the shop, arching her back and nuzzling her head against the top of my boot while I slap blindly at the light switch in the supply closet. She meows into the sudden burst of light, her small face turned up toward mine.

"Sorry, sweetheart. No treats today." I bend at the waist to scratch at her head, but my fingers are covered with a sheen of polish. Oliver hisses and darts off when it pulls at her soft fur, knocking over a small mermaid figurine in her hasty departure. I sigh and try to wipe the cat hair/polish combination off on my skirt.

The light bulb in the center of the storage closet flickers and then blows out with a soft *pop*, cloaking the room in darkness.

"Of course," I mutter, fumbling for the shelf with the polish. "Maybe I'll get lucky and Bloody Mary will decide she's bound to me for the holiday season, too."

"I doubt it," comes a voice close to my ear. Sea salt and spice. Coffee and cloves. "Mary isn't exactly social, and she hates the holiday season."

My hand shoots out and the box of silver polish goes tumbling to the ground. The cans hit the hardwood like raindrops on a window while my heart does its best to beat out of my chest.

Nolan stands behind me, his hands shoved in his pockets. In the dark, he's mostly silhouette, but I'd recognize that low laugh anywhere.

"Hello, Harriet."

I smack his shoulder. I don't care about getting polish or cat hair on him. He deserves both. "I thought we talked about you scaring me!"

He shrugs and angles himself away, bending down to collect the cans that are still rolling around the floor. "Couldn't help myself," he says. "And you were thinking so loud, I doubt you would have heard me anyway."

"Well, try next time," I grumble. He reaches around my leg for a wayward container and his forearm brushes against my calf. Goose bumps pebble my skin. "Where have you been?"

Nolan stands to his full height, my box against his chest. He scans the shelf briefly then slides it back to its proper spot, keeping his hand propped up against the post afterward like he needs the support. The inside of his biceps is half an inch from my face.

"I've been around," he says evasively.

"Around."

"Yep." His mouth pops around the edge of the word.

"It's been five days." I pause, embarrassment lighting me up like a solar flare. "Not that I've been—not that I've been keeping track."

Nolan, thankfully, doesn't seem to notice my misstep. He reaches for his scruff with his free hand, dragging his palm along his jaw. "Apologies. I had a bit of a . . . situation."

The way he says the word *situation* sounds like *I disposed of a body in an alleyway and then feasted on its soul to sustain my life force*. I lean back against the shelves and try to read his face in the dark.

"What sort of a situation?" I ask.

He sighs, his warm breath brushing across the top of my forehead. "Nothing nearly as dramatic as what you're thinking, I'm sure."

"Did you kidnap someone?" I whisper.

"No," he says slowly. "I did not kidnap anyone."

"Eat any souls?"

"What? No. Harriet, I—" He shakes his head. "That mind of yours," he says, with fond exasperation.

"What were you up to, then?"

He grumbles again, something deep and nonsensical. I can almost feel the vibration of it against my chest. What would he do, I wonder, if I leaned into him. Would he curl around me like he did in the tree field? Would he spread his fingers wide, like he's trying to touch as much of me as possible? Or would he push me away? Cut me down with another sharp remark?

"My cat hurt her paw," he finally says.

I blink into the darkness. "What?"

"My cat," he says again, slower this time. "Builín. She hurt her paw."

"You have a cat?"

"Yes." He nods. "I told you I take care of the strays."

"*Taking care of the strays* is different from *I have a cat*."

"Not to me." He pauses. "They're the only company I can keep. I want to make sure they're doing well."

Well, that's . . . cute.

"Was it bad? Five days is a long time."

The metal shelf creaks ominously behind me. I try to picture Nolan nursing a kitten back to health. His big hands. Tiny pink toe beans. A hurt little paw. A fuzzy body cradled close to his bare chest.

In this mental pathway, Nolan is apparently shirtless.

I banish the thought.

"She's fine now," he says. "But she was being dramatic about it. I didn't feel right leaving her."

"That's sweet."

I keep getting flashes of softness from Nolan. Glimpses of the man he might have been before, maybe. It makes me greedy for more.

I shift and brush against the front of him. He's standing so close, practically caging me up against the metal shelf.

After not seeing him for a few of days, his sudden presence in this tiny space is jarring.

I'm a tactile person by nature. I like hugs. Holding hands. Cuddling on the couch. Samantha used to fill that need for me when we were younger—my aunt Matilda, too—but I've been horribly bereft as an adult. I wonder what Nolan would do if I just wrapped my arms around him and squeezed. He looks like he could use a good hug.

"I'm glad she's okay now. Your cat." I pause, sawing my teeth across my bottom lip. "Her name is Builín?"

"Aye," he says. "It means loaf of bread. She looks a bit like one."

I wait for him to say something else—to explain why he's here, to give me the usual speech about my soul hanging in the balance—but he doesn't. He just . . . stands there, the two of us tucked together in the darkness.

I imagine the two missing spoons from the display case in the front.

"I wasn't sure if you'd be back," I try, testing the waters. His face tilts toward mine, though I can't make out any of his features. Warm air puffs against my forehead. Coffee, again.

"We haven't figured out what you've done yet," he replies. "I'm—"

"Bound to me." I sigh. "Yes, I know."

Something in my chest squeezes. I hate the way he says it, equal parts derision and resignation. I can't tell if he doesn't like being a ghost, or if he doesn't like being paired with me. Neither option sits particularly well, but I firm myself up with an internal pep talk. I've dealt with more difficult things than a surly ghost who plays fast and loose with his haunting commitments.

"I was about to buy a Ouija board," I say lightly.

His laugh rumbles between us. The thrill of turning his mood around surges like electricity through my veins. He pushes off the shelf at my side, the metal rattling behind me. "So *that's* why my ears were burning."

My eyes widen to saucers. "Wait. Really?"

He shakes his head. "No, Harriet." I can hear his smile in the dark, the way it works around the edges of my name. I bet his dimples are doing something obscene right now. "Those don't work."

"How should I get in contact with you, then? If I need you?"

His boots scuff against the floor and in the dark, I feel something lightly touch my wrist.

"Been needing me?"

"You said you're on a deadline," I tell him, trying to sound like I'm not affected by the way he's brushing his fingertips along the inside of my wrist. He's trying to rattle me on purpose. I'm sure of it. "I'm just trying to be helpful."

"Helpful." He hums. "Helpful Harriet."

"Yes," I agree, wary. There's something about the way he says it, like it's not something I should be proud of. Like I should try harder to be something different, when *helpful* is all I've wanted to be. Helpful, easy, accommodating. I've given all of myself to the people around me, broken myself down into minuscule pieces to try to be exactly what everyone else has needed. I've tried to shape myself to other people's expectations, but it's only ever left me broken in the end.

And for what? The universe decided it's not enough, anyway. I've been deemed a bad person. Right up there with men who catcall women on the street, apparently.

I swallow around the balloon in my throat. "I try to be helpful. I try to be good."

"I know," Nolan says softly. A rare concession. His hand catches the cuff of my sweater.

Soft, I think I hear him mutter, except I don't think I was supposed to hear it at all. He lets go and I rub at my wrist.

"There won't be any more interruptions," he says. "I intend to see the rest of this haunting through. I'll be around if you need me. Just . . . think happy thoughts, and I'll appear."

I roll my eyes. "Okay, Tinker Bell."

He's silent for the stretch of three heartbeats. "Who is Tinker Bell?" he finally asks.

"Never mind." I hold my hand out to him, palm up, wiggling my fingers. "I'm ready to go now. Let's go watch me ruin the third-grade musical performance of 'Rudolph the Red-Nosed Reindeer' by tripping into one of the elves and tearing down the entire backdrop."

He sighs, wistful. "I've never wished more for the ability to select a memory."

"Think happy thoughts, and maybe it'll happen." I nudge his chest. "C'mon. Let's seize the day."

I'm emboldened by my new theory, energized by the idea that maybe I can be the one to help him. It's a balm to the sharp burn of my *bad person* designation. An alternative solution to this whole, ridiculous situation. He hasn't been assigned to me because I'm *bad*. Maybe he's been assigned to me because I'm *good*.

Because I'm the only one who can help.

"Easy." He grips my wrist, holding my palm away from his. "I'm not grabbing your hand while it looks like that."

"What's wrong with my hand?"

"It's covered in grime." He pauses. "Also, you could use some lotion."

I gasp, offended. "Excuse you, I use very expensive hand lotion." I buy it at the same sale I get all my fancy, matching pajamas. "I think you just hate Nordstrom."

"I still don't know who this Nord Storm is and why he peddles in ridiculous scraps of clothing."

"Nordstrom," I say. "Nord-strom. It's a— You know, what? Never mind." I reach for the polish rag I tossed in blind fear when he made his sudden appearance, tap-tapping my way blindly across the shelf with my palm. "I apply twice a day," I tell him. "After my shower and before I go to bed at night. Maybe your feeble ghost hands are—oh. What are you doing?"

Nolan has my hand in his, his grip gentle around my wrist. He carefully turns my palm up, cradling it with his.

"Feeble hands," Nolan says, reaching somewhere over my shoulder for the rag I couldn't find. His chest brushes against mine as he leans forward. "That's not what you said the other night," he whispers close to my ear.

My breath hiccups at the innuendo. A flash of heat starts at my temples and spreads down until I feel like I could melt into the floor. Like maybe I could be poured into one of those polish containers.

"What did I say the other night?" I breathe.

"You called me rugged, I think." He pulls my hand closer. He starts with my pinky, wrapping it in the rag and working the polish off with firm strokes. I've never had such an innocent touch feel so illicit before. I feel like my clothes could disintegrate right off my body.

"I was high on expired peppermint tea," I explain, surprised to find myself breathless.

"You can't keep using that excuse."

He moves to my ring finger and I shiver. I want him to stop. I want him to *never* stop.

"Okay?" he asks.

I make a garbled, gibberish sound in response and Nolan chuckles. He bends his head between us as he moves to my middle finger, watching his work. I examine his face in the light that filters through the crack in the door.

The thin scar above his eyebrow. The sharp line of his jaw. The dark, messy hair that falls over his forehead and the set line of his mouth as he concentrates.

By the time he gets to my thumb, my breath is a rattle in my chest, my body weight resting fully against the shelf at my back. If Nolan notices my semi-liquid state, he has the decency not to say anything about it.

"There," he says, bringing my hand closer to his face to inspect his handiwork. My belly decides to jump toward my throat. I never knew I had so many sensory receptors in my palm, but I swear I can feel the stroke of his touch everywhere. "All tidied up."

I don't move out of his grip. "Thank you."

"You're welcome." His fingers flex around mine. "Ready to take my feeble hand and be on our way?"

"I haven't let go of your feeble hand."

"Right." He adjusts his grip until we're palm to palm. The butterflies in my belly turn into an avalanche. I blame the world that's starting to fall away beneath my feet, and the sharp tug of magic at the base of my spine. I close my eyes and brace myself, relieved when Nolan holds my hand tighter.

"Away we go, then," he says, his voice barely more than a whisper in the growing roar around us. "Hold on tight, Harriet."

Chapter Nine

Nolan

*W*e land back in the closet with flailing limbs, a muffled curse, and a small explosion of fig jam.

"I don't understand why you felt the need to grab the entire jar." My sticky hand catches in her sticky hair while our sticky sweaters smash together against the now sticky shelves. "There's a reason you don't bring things back from the past."

The trip was a waste of our time—*again*. Not a single nefarious thing was revealed about Harriet, except perhaps an extreme sweet tooth. We watched her make holiday jam with a woman in a catering uniform, wrapping each mason jar with a single gingham bow. She didn't even try to lick the spoon.

An absolute *waste*.

"Maybe that's something you should have mentioned when I *grabbed it*."

"I said *stop*."

"That could have been in regard to, like, a million things, Nolan. You weren't specific!"

I clench my jaw so hard my teeth snap together. This *woman*.

"I've been trying to find that recipe for ages," Harriet continues, her voice muffled in the front of my sweater as we continue to try to extricate ourselves. She shakes her wrist, a clump of jam landing with a wet sound on the floor. "I didn't realize the jar would explode on impact."

"The jar did not explode on impact. The jar exploded somewhere in our travels, as evident by the current state of things. We're lucky you didn't embed shards of glass into my skull."

"You're a *ghost*," she hisses. "As far as I'm aware, you can't die again. And if glass ended up anywhere, you probably would have deserved it."

The jam must have multiplied as we were rolling our way through time. I have no other explanation as to how it's . . . everywhere. It's on my neck. It's dripping down my chest beneath my shirt. It's on my hands and in my hair.

And Harriet is clinging to me with the same tenacity as the jam, her arms wrapped tight around my waist. She plastered herself to me as soon as I tugged us out of the memory, afraid I'd leave her there. I can feel all of the places her body is a perfect fit for mine. The curve of her hips and the soft press of her breasts. Every time she wiggles, I lose a little bit more of my sanity.

This. *This* is why I made up the excuse about the cat and stayed away. I hoped the time away would give me some clarity. I hoped the time away would allow me to straighten myself out.

I'm afraid it only made everything worse. I didn't stop thinking about Harriet once.

"Harriet." I grip her hips tight and squeeze my eyes shut. "Stop moving."

"You're the one who squished me up against the shelf." She twists some more, arching her back. My hips nestle between her thighs, her hair in my face. She smells like honey and sugar. Like one of the sweets she's never without.

"It was accidental," I grind out. She didn't mean to cause an explosion mid-travel. I didn't mean to press her bodily against the wall. Yet, here we are. Two stubborn fools. "My foot must have slipped in your damned jam."

"Well, you're not slipping now," she replies. She finds her footing with one hand braced on the metal shelf, her body finally—*thankfully*—going still against mine. Our chests heave against each other as we try to regulate our breathing. My body feels heavy, my pulse pounding at the base of my throat and in the palms of my hands.

It would be so easy to drag my hand from her hip to her thigh, flex my fingers around her delicious curves, fill my palm with her gorgeous ass, and lift. I could have all of her wrapped around me in a heartbeat, her mouth half an inch from mine. Would she taste like the jam she decided to confiscate from the past? Or would she taste like something darker? Richer?

I don't move. Neither does she. It's the two of us pressed together in the dark. I'm standing at the edge of a choice, temptation tugging at me.

"Good?" I ask.

Her laugh is a whisper against my neck. My skin prickles in awareness.

"Yeah, I'm good," she says. "I just watched my childhood self make Christmas jam with a woman my mother hired because she couldn't be bothered. I'm covered in a jam that I've been trying to re-create for twenty years. I tried to grab one thing for myself and now it's—now it's everywhere but where I want it to be."

"Where do you want it to be?"

"On toast, preferably." She looks at the jam smeared across her sweater sleeve and sighs. "I didn't even get to taste it," she adds mournfully.

I blame the look on her face and the loopy, hazy feeling that's still snug tight around the base of my skull from ricocheting through time. The ferocious, yawning ache in the middle of my chest. There's no other explanation as to why I reach for her, cupping her face in my hand so I can gather the heavy streak of sugared fig just under her chin.

Her skin is warm and the jam is warm, too. Sticky. A complete and total mess.

I lift my finger to my mouth and suck it off.

The taste is muted, but there. Sweet and tart. A sharp burst that sparks, then fades. It's the closest I've come to experiencing a flavor in decades.

I immediately want more.

"Tastes good," I tell her.

"I thought you said—" She swallows, her eyes heavy on my mouth. "I thought you said you can't taste things," she finishes.

"Sometimes I get a hint," I tell her, my voice sounding like it's coming from somewhere very far away. I'm wandering down a path I have no business being on, but Harriet's lips are parted and she has more jam on the long line of her neck and it's been *so long* since I've let myself feel anything other than self-induced apathy.

"Oh," she says.

Harriet hesitates, then reaches for my hand with hers. She traces her fingertips along the base of my palm, lingering over a scar I don't remember how I got before scooping some wayward jelly. She keeps her head down as she brings her pointer finger to her mouth, cheeks hollowing as she sucks it off. My hand twitches in hers. I have to clench my teeth to keep myself from doing something reckless.

She makes a surprised sound.

"What do you think?"

"Tastes good," she repeats, a laugh caught somewhere in the back of her throat, her eyes shining bright in the tiny, dark room as she gazes up at me. They look like whiskey in the dark. A glass half-filled, a single cube of ice at the bottom. "Almost worth all this mess."

I shift and feel the jam on my chest again, sticking to my shirt. "Almost," I agree. "Can I get rid of it, or do you want another taste?"

"I'm good," she says, something husky still in her voice, her hands twisting in front of her. I don't know if she's uncomfortable because of the situation, my inability to hold my restraint in check, or the jam currently making a home in her hair, but I don't want her twisted up because of me. I reach for the place inside myself that holds my magic and I yank on it.

The stickiness on my chest and arms and neck disappears. Harriet blows out a relieved breath.

"Another riveting trip to my past, huh?" She smooths her palms down the front of her sweater, checking for any spots I might have missed.

"Aye." I reach forward and pretend to wipe some jam from one of her curls. Her hair is so soft, it feels like silk. I tuck it behind her ear and let my hand drop. "You continue to be a paragon of good behavior."

She snorts. "Try not to sound so surprised."

"I'm not surprised, I'm—" Confused. Irritated. I'm doing everything exactly the way I'm supposed to be doing it and nothing is changing. She's not the person she's supposed to be. We're trapped in a limbo where I can't move on and neither can she. I'm so tired of being stuck. "I'm trying to figure out how this ends for the both of us."

She hesitates. "I've been thinking about that."

I narrow my eyes. "About what?"

She twists the hem of her sweater over her fists, spreading her fingers wide then closing them again. "Maybe you're not here for me," she says slowly. Her eyes peek up at me to check my reaction. "Maybe you're here for you."

I rub my hand over my mouth. "What does that mean?"

She pushes off the shelf. "Maybe—maybe there's something you need to do. To move on, you know? You said you've been here for a while . . . maybe I'm supposed to help you." She presses her lips together, thinking. "I own an antiques shop. I don't think you were paired with me by accident." Excitement lights behind her eyes, her features brightening in enthusiasm. "Maybe there's something here that belongs to you. Like a talisman or something. Maybe it's holding you in place, or—I don't know. Maybe there's something you're supposed to see with me. We could work together to find it."

A rough sound rolls out of me, too sharp to be a laugh. The idea of moving on after a hundred years spent in one single place is . . . comical, at best. Devastating, at worst. There is nothing to move on *to*. There is just this. An aimless, driftless existence where I don't get to hold on to *anything*. Where I lose all the things that once made me human, slowly and painfully.

And for Harriet—a woman I barely know—for her to somehow be the key to moving on, it's—

It's too much.

It's a joke. It must be.

Except the hopeful look on her face doesn't flicker or waiver.

"Did I say something funny?" she asks.

"You're serious."

"Of course, I'm serious," she says. "What gave you the impression that I'm joking?"

I drag my hand through my hair, then anchor my hand against the back of my neck. I squeeze, hoping the pressure will distract me from the buzzing in my chest. "Your complete unfamiliarity with my existence, for one." I sigh, trying to shake off some of the venom lacing my tone. But I can't. I can't because she has no idea how much it hurts to have the thing I want most dangled like a treat in front of my nose, knowing I can't ever have it. "You didn't know ghosts even existed a couple of weeks ago. These things don't work like that."

"I know there's a lot I don't know, but think about it. We've visited my memories and you haven't discovered anything horrible about me. We've gone to my past several times, and every time it's something completely mundane."

"Harriet—" I try.

"I don't think I'm a bad person," she says, raising her voice and cutting me off. "At least not the type of bad person you typically deal with. I'm just a person trying my best, occasionally making mistakes." She tilts her head to the side. "Tell me the truth. Have you seen anything that warrants a haunting?"

"I haven't, but—"

"Then I think this is the answer!" Her face lights up, her eyes wide and bright, shining like copper. She stops twisting her hands and waves them between us. "You said you've been stuck, that you thought there'd be something different. You said there aren't any mistakes. Maybe we've just been looking at it from the wrong angle."

"The wrong angle," I repeat, a creeping numbness in my chest.

She nods. "Maybe this is something that can help *you*. Not me."

I consider it. When I first became a ghost, this was the sort of thing I hoped for. I spent hours, days, weeks, agonizing over it. And then weeks became months and months became years. I combed over the details of my life, looking for the part where I earned this fathomless existence. I painstakingly picked everything over until the details became muddled. Until I could barely remember the person I was. The things I did.

I kept waiting for a choice—a chance.

But when one never materialized, I realized I was a fool.

There is no happily ever after for me. There is no . . . light at the end of the tunnel. There is only this.

After a decade, I let go of my hope. After a century, I released my expectations, too.

And now Harriet has decided she can fix it. That she can fix *me*.

"How long have you been thinking about this?" I manage to ask.

Her smile wavers. "Well, I was just talking with Sasha this morning and—"

"This morning," I repeat, frustration welling up in my chest. It spills over until I'm coated in it, just like the jam she insisted on bringing back from the past. She has no *right*. No right to give me hope when I've been without it for as long as I can remember. "You've been contemplating something you know next to nothing about for an *hour*, and I am to believe you suddenly have an answer?"

Her shoulders inch up toward her ears. "Nolan—"

"Thank you, Harriet," I say, the frustration twisting into something darker. Rougher. Wilder. My magic licks at the inside of my chest in warning, hot and punishing. I ignore it. "I'm so relieved you've found the solution to this absolute hell I've been living."

"Nolan," she says again, her voice a whisper. There's not an ounce of enthusiasm left in her face. I've pulled out all of her light and crushed it in my fists, but I can't help myself. It feels like the ultimate cruelty, what she's just done.

"A woman who has existed for a mere blink of my lifetime is somehow the key to my salvation. I don't know how I didn't see it before," I continue, my sarcasm like a blade between us. "Thank you, Harriet. You are *oh so* helpful. I can see why you have so many people willing to be around you."

The hit lands the way I intended. She flinches and sucks in a sharp breath.

"There's nothing wrong with wanting to help. That's not the reason I'm alone." She pauses. Swallows. Her eyes turn glassy and wet. "You don't have to be cruel," she finishes with a whisper.

"I don't want your help. I never asked for it. You have no idea what you're talking about," I explain. Ten minutes ago, I was desperately trying not to kiss her. Now I can barely stand to be in the same space as her. She's the one being cruel, and she doesn't even know it. She's offering me things she can't follow through with.

"You can't—" I try to calm down. "I don't want you to bring that up again. Not ever."

Her laugh is stripped of any amusement. Sad and hollow. Her arms hug herself. "You don't have to worry about that."

My magic roars in my chest. I can't catch my breath. I need to not be here. I need to be away from her.

"Good," I snap.

She nods, teeth sawing over her bottom lip. She gives me her back while she collects her cans of polish and the rag I flung on the top shelf, her face hidden by her hair. She sniffles once and my stomach freefalls all the way to my toes. The first bite of regret plucks at the consciousness that should have been abandoned as soon as I became a ghost.

I'm grateful for her turned back so I don't have to see the look on her face. Maybe with enough determination and blind optimism, I'll be able to forget I hurt her on purpose.

But pride keeps me from apologizing. My own hurt.

"I'm going to go," she says, once she's collected all her supplies. When she turns, she barely makes eye contact. I'm so used to her expressive face watching my every move, that the sudden absence of her attention feels like a tether that's been cut. A light that's been snuffed out. She forces a tight smile, her gaze stuck somewhere around my neck. "I'm sure I'll see you in a day or two."

She doesn't wait for a response. She shuffles past me to the entrance of the closet, then pauses for a moment, her head turned halfway.

"I'm glad your cat is okay," she whispers.

She leaves without another word, keeping the door to the storage closet open. I stay behind in the dark, staring hard at the place she just was. Even when I've lashed out and done my best to hurt her the way I've been hurting, she rises above it to be the better person.

Muffled voices drift from the front of the shop. Low conversation and then a burst of laughter. I yank on my magic as soon as I hear Harriet's low, raspy chuckle spinning its way through the shelves to the tiny closet at the back.

I don't want to hear it.

I'm not sure I deserve to.

Chapter Ten
Nolan

Three hours later, and I'm still thinking about Harriet.

The curve of her shoulders. The slight inhale through her nose. Her hair curtained in front of her face, so she could hide from me.

Flat on my back in a bed that's not all that comfortable, I stare up at the ceiling in my bedroom and watch the way the light moves across my ceiling. I see Harriet's face in every beam that spills across the shadows, specifically the way her eyes turned glassy when I mocked her for trying to be helpful.

I've seen enough of her past to know that she feels like she's a burden on those around her. Her parents didn't offer an ounce of affection, and she's struggled to find her place. I know there's a bruise there, but I pressed on it anyway.

She's right. I was being cruel.

"Fuck," I rumble, digging the palms of my hands into my eyes until I see spots. How much of me has been twisted by the people I've been haunting? How much of myself have I lost?

She didn't know what she was saying when she spoke of my moving on, but that doesn't mean she deserved to be the outlet of my frustration. She didn't deserve to be hurt.

I drop my hands to the bed. Tomorrow, I'll go back to the antiques shop. I'll make it up to her. Explain the situation. I'll . . . try to articulate my own feelings, though I should probably untangle what those are.

Regardless, I'll do better.

The floorboards creak in the hallway. I sit up on my elbows, sheets pooling around my hips.

"Builín?" I call.

For years, cats have been attracted to my little house on the water. Sometimes they appear on the porch. Other times, they sneak in through the window that never quite closes all the way. I've had countless ambiguous pets over the years, coming and going as they please.

But Builín has been the only one for the last decade or so. I imagine she's returned for her nightly burrow in my sheets. Or her apparent need to terrorize the stacks of books in my living room.

"Nolan?" a voice calls back.

Harriet appears, framed by the light that seeps in from the windows. She's wearing her minuscule pajamas again—the ones with the candy canes printed all over them—and my mouth goes dry at the sight of her.

Pale skin. Round hips. The smallest sliver of her stomach beneath the hem of her shirt. Bare shoulders and golden hair turned silver in the moonlight.

"Harriet?" My hands fist in the sheets at my sides. "What are you doing here?"

"Couldn't sleep," she slurs, digging a fist against her eye. "Not with how we left things. I don't—" She drops her hand. "I don't do well with conflict. As you've probably noticed."

She shuffles closer to the bed, her feet bare. Her knees hit the mattress, and she climbs up without hesitation, crawling over my body still trapped beneath the sheets. It's too much contact, too fast. I've only allowed myself to touch Harriet in increments, and now she's laying out a feast. I grip her hips as she drapes her arms over my shoulders, her bare thighs hugging my sides. The thin strip of fabric on her shoulder drops to her elbow, the curve of her breast a tease through the material.

"I didn't mean to make you mad," she whispers, her nose digging into my bare shoulder. I am painfully aware of the little fabric that exists between us. "I really did want to help."

"I'm not mad," I tell her, still bewildered by her sudden appearance, but not enough to question it. I press my hand to the small of her back and hold her to me, tracing the line of her spine until I can knot my fingers in her hair. My magic hums in quiet approval, my skin buzzing everywhere we touch.

In the quiet of my bedroom, Harriet shifts in my arms. There's only the rasp of my sheets and the even pattern of her breathing. I don't know how she found me, but I'm glad she's here. I hold her tighter and her chin finds my shoulder.

"I shouldn't have reacted the way I did." I scoop all of her hair up in my hands and let it fall through my fingers. "Are you mad?" I ask.

"No. I'm not mad."

"You should be."

"Yeah, probably." She settles deeper in my lap and I grunt, my hands tightening against her. She feels so good, her weight pressing me down into the mattress. She feels solid. *Real.* I fall backward into my pillows so I can see her, sliding my hands to her hips.

She stays sitting, perched on my lap like some sort of moon goddess. "Maybe I'll be mad tomorrow. Tonight—" She traces her palms over my shoulders, across my bare chest, and down to where the sheets ride low around my hips. My back arches and my eyes fall shut. No one has touched me like this in years. It feels . . . indescribable.

She slips her fingers beneath the twisted material of my flannel sheets and tugs them lower. Cool night air kisses my sleep-warm skin.

"Tonight," she continues, her breath at the hollow of my throat. The ends of her hair tickle my bare arms. "Tonight, I want something different from you."

Her mouth hovers over mine. I want it *so badly*.

Kiss. Devour. *Take.*

I wake with a jolt, my heart thundering in my chest. My bed is empty, my sheets twisted around my middle. I can still feel the weight of Harriet in my lap, taste her peppermint on my mouth. My cock is heavy between my legs, my magic singing in my blood.

I collapse back against my bed and throw my arm over my eyes, exhaling a groan. Heat is pulsing through my veins, centering low between my hips. Harriet, in those pajamas. Harriet, with her mouth on my skin.

Harriet, Harriet, Harriet.

I hesitate, then dip my hand beneath my blanket and wrap my fingers around myself. I squeeze, and my hips arch.

A dream. It was a dream.

For the first time in over a century, I had a dream.

And I dreamed of Harriet.

"Fuck," I mutter.

Chapter Eleven

Harriet

*N*olan appears on my front porch three days later with a cup of coffee in his hand and an apologetic look on his face.

I'm not particularly inspired by either, and I ignore the doorbell when he presses it. I watch him through the camera instead as I continue to wash the figs I impulse bought at the market earlier in the morning.

I've decided I'm going to make my own damn jam. I should get something positive out of this whole ghost arrangement. The jam seems like the most likely candidate.

The jam wouldn't yell at me in a closet.

The jam also wouldn't ignore me for three days, even though he said he'd show. I'm starting to think that cat story was a load of baloney.

In addition to every person who has ever been even moderately important to me, I'm being ghosted by a literal ghost. My life is a joke.

My phone pings with another alert, Nolan bracing himself with his hand against my doorframe. Not that I care, but he looks frustrated in the tiny, grainy picture. His hair is sticking up every which way and the collar of his flannel is twisted. He looks like he hit a tornado on the way over here. Maybe a trash truck.

Good. He was an ass the last time I saw him. He should look worse, frankly. That curl of hair over his forehead is an insult. The shadow of his dimples is an atrocity.

He presses the doorbell again.

I ignore him some more.

"I could just appear in your kitchen, you know," he says conversationally, his voice tinny through the speaker on my phone. He squints at me through the camera. "I'm trying to be nice."

"You weren't trying to be nice in my storage closet," I say to myself, scrubbing one of my figs too hard and sending it bouncing around the inside of my sink. I'm holding on to my frustration with a white-knuckled grip. I'm so tired of people treating me like I'm dispensable, like my feelings don't matter. That if the reality of me doesn't line up with their expectations, I'm not worth their time or effort. All I did was suggest an idea. I didn't . . . hold him hostage in the closet and demand he succumb to my whims. The entirety of my life, I've had to listen to people vocalize their disappointment at how I haven't measured up.

I don't need it from the undead, too.

"Harriet," he tries again. His body is one long line in the middle of my front porch. He drops his head in defeat, like he can't bear to hold himself up any longer. When he looks up again, his face is earnest.

I scoff. I bet he practiced that move in the mirror. I bet he spent twenty-two years doing nothing but that.

"Harriet," he says again. "Open your door."

I tap one soapy knuckle against my phone screen. "Give me one good reason I should let you in," I say through the speaker.

"Well, I'm bo—"

"If you say you're bound to me for the holiday season, I will—I will—" I'll explode into tiny pieces of rage confetti in my kitchen. I'll hurl one of these figs through my historically preserved windows. "I'll do something unkind," I finish.

I watch through the camera as an infuriating smirk tugs at the left side of his mouth. He should be shaking in his boots, not smiling. "And what does that entail, Harriet?"

"I won't share any of the jam I'm making."

His eyebrow jumps up in interest. "You're making jam?"

"I am. And I won't share it unless I get a sincere apology out of you." Some of the wind leaves my sails and I deflate. I'm not very good at demanding things from people, even worse at holding my ground. I'm usually the first to apologize, even if I don't need to. The only thing I hate more than constantly being underestimated and undervalued is making waves. It scratches at the walls of my heart until I'm bending over backward to make sure everyone is okay.

"I understand I might have inadvertently touched on a sore spot with you, but you didn't need to be rude," I continue, still holding my finger to my phone. *You didn't need to hurt my feelings*, I almost say. *Not when I thought we might be friends.*

"Can I come in? I want to see your face when I talk to you." He straightens, holding a to-go cup in front of his face. "I brought you a peppermint drink."

I drop the figs in the colander and shuffle my way to my front door, wiping my hands on my pajama pants as I go. They're cherry-red flannel today, a matching, oversize set I put on as soon as I got home from the farmers' market.

Nolan's eyes light up when he sees me, his gaze quickly traveling down to my bare feet and back up again.

I can't decipher the look on his face. I don't particularly want to.

"You can't buy my forgiveness with overpriced holiday drinks."

That's a lie. My forgiveness can absolutely be bought with over-priced holiday drinks, especially if he remembered to get whipped

cream on top. But I want to try something new where I don't immediately fold for the comfort of someone else.

Nolan holds out the cup. "I know."

I grab it. "And I don't want to hear a single word about my wardrobe choice," I warn. I'm afraid if he says anything else belittling to
me, I'll crack right down the middle.

"I think you look nice." His gaze drops to somewhere around my
hips and he takes a long pause. His throat bobs with a heavy swallow.
"These are—ah. Very cute."

I roll my eyes and take a sip of the coffee. It's still hot. I wonder if
he used the magic he seems to hate so much to keep it warm, or if he
just power walked from wherever it is he calls home.

I wouldn't know because Nolan doesn't talk to me. I'm just a job.
An item to be crossed off his checklist.

"Would you like to compliment my hair next?" I gesture at the
chaos on the top of my head. "Maybe my stunning organizational
skills?" I sweep my arm across my living room. The cluttered, overcrowded bookshelves and the mantel over the fireplace, loaded down
with enough empty frames and knickknacks, it's a wonder it's still
level. "What else?"

Nolan frowns. "You don't think I'm being sincere?"

"I think you're saying nice things because you were a jerk the other
day." I take another long sip of my drink, buying time and building
courage. "But I don't want you to give me compliments because you
feel bad."

"That's not what I'm doing."

"Isn't it?" I know well enough when someone is being genuine,
and when someone needs me for something. Nolan wants to move
forward. He hasn't let me forget it. I'm merely a means to an end for
him. Our conversation in the closet cemented that fact.

"Listen." It's too difficult to keep looking at his face, so I look at
my bare feet instead. I painted my toes bright red last night because

it made me feel good. Because I've always been able to make my own happiness when the people around me decide I'm not worth the trouble. "We can just go about our business. We don't have to do this part anymore."

"This part?"

"The part where you pretend you're my friend."

Nolan edges closer, his boots on either side of my bare feet. His fingers lightly brush beneath my chin until I'm looking at his face. His eyes are storm clouds, a heavy line between his brows. His expression looks like it's been chiseled out of stone, all of his features sharp. For probably the first time, I actually believe he's something . . . other. He looks imposing. Like he took on some of the sea when he died, and now it roils around inside of him.

"I'm not pretending anything," he says. "When I say you look lovely, I mean it." He traces the curve of my chin. For a fleeting moment, I think I can feel him tremble. But then he drops his hand and I tell myself to stop imagining things that aren't there. "Sometimes I think I'm too honest with you."

I scoff. "You haven't given me anything honest."

"I've been more honest with you than anyone else, Harriet." He rubs his hand against his jaw. He's still standing so close. "I owe you an apology."

"Yes," I agree. "You do."

His eyes search mine, his mouth set in a firm line. "Harriet, I—"

My phone rings from the kitchen, interrupting him. My stomach twists. That ringtone only sounds when a very specific person is calling. It's my very own tornado siren.

When it rains, it pours, I guess.

I start my slow, defeated walk toward the kitchen. Nolan follows closely behind.

"What is that sound?" he asks. "An emergency?"

I don't know why he thinks I'd categorize an emergency call on my phone with "Misery Business," but I suppose there's a technology gap in his knowledge. Probably a pop culture one, too.

"Do you know Paramore?" I ask.

He stumbles behind me, his knee hitting my gingerbread house. Something rattles. He barely notices.

"You have a lover?" he asks.

I swipe my phone off the counter. "What? No. I—" I've already let this phone call ring for too long. God help me if it goes to voicemail. Donna York does not leave *messages*. "I need to answer this call from my mother and then we can finish our conversation."

Nolan leans back against the counter at my side, making himself comfortable. "All right."

"You can wait in the living room."

He shrugs, interest blazing in his eyes. "Here is fine, too."

I roll my eyes, hitting the answer button before the call trips over into voicemail and I rain hellfire down upon my existence.

"Hi, Mom." I try to force my voice into something chipper and enthusiastic, not the bone-deep dread that settles every time I see her name flash on my screen. I'm out of practice, though. "How are you?"

There's a brief pause and I hear the clink of a china cup in the background. She must be having her scheduled 11 a.m. tea. Earl Grey. One sugar. Served in the same Hermès china cup she's had since I was a child.

"Harriet," she says in greeting. "What took you so long to answer?"

My eyes slant to the man responsible for the delay, leaning against my sink and observing me with quiet, watchful eyes. I feel like a wombat in an enclosure at the zoo. Maybe a particularly distressing art exhibit at the Baltimore Museum of Art. One of the high schools had a performance of *Sweeney Todd* a couple of years ago, and everyone in the audience had the same look on their face as Nolan does now.

Trepidation. Concern. A slight hint of entertainment.

I push some of my hair away from my face. "Misplaced my phone," I lie smoothly. "But I'm here now. What can I do for you?"

"You and that cottage of yours. It's so cramped. That's the trouble with surrounding yourself with mess, Harriet. You never can find what you're looking for."

My house isn't a cottage. It's a historical restoration. And it's not a *mess*. It's cozy and comfortable, with all the things that make me happy. But my mother is nothing if not predictable, and she has perfected the art of roundabout insults.

It doesn't matter how many times my mother proves she's disinterested in the life I've made for myself, I always hold on to a kernel of hope that this visit, this phone call, this conversation, might be different.

But it's not. It never is. And if my hopeful heart could learn that lesson, I'd be better for it.

"That's a good point," I tell her, and Nolan shifts in my periphery. His legs are crossed at the ankle, a frown on his face. I have no idea if enhanced hearing is part of his ghostly superpowers, or if he's just being a Nosey Nelly. I give him my back and pace over to the fridge. "I assume you're calling about the gala."

"So she does remember she has family commitments."

"I was going to call this afternoon," I lie again. "Time got away from me." My *time* went all the way back to when I was six and she was still rocking shoulder pads. I roll my lips together. "You really need me to RSVP to the gala I attend every year?"

"It's the polite thing to do," my mother responds evenly.

"Right. Consider me RSVP'd then. I apologize for the delay."

There's a pause. "You'll respond in writing, too, of course."

I stare hard at the envelope attached to my fridge with a dancing strawberry magnet. I never bothered to open it. "Of course," I answer.

"Wonderful," my mother says, the word sounding foreign from her mouth. I can't remember the last time my mother truly thought anything was wonderful. "Thank you. If you could save me another phone call by responding within the appropriate window, that would be helpful. My schedule is very full."

Suddenly I'm a little kid again, in an uncomfortable red dress and shiny shoes that pinch at my toes. *Why must you make things so difficult for me?* Sixteen and standing outside a banquet hall, trying not to cry. *Don't make a scene, Harriet.* Twenty-five and sitting at a fancy table, staring down at my plate. *How could you do this to us? How could you be so selfish?*

I swallow around the sudden thickness in my throat. I've always worn my guilt like an itchy sweater. "I understand," I manage.

"Good. I'll see you on the eighteenth." She hangs up without another word, but I keep the phone to my ear, listening to the dial tone. I'm overly aware of Nolan behind me, still leaning against the sink.

"Bye, Mom," I say into the silence, hoping I sound convincing. "See you soon."

I drop the phone from my ear and slowly pack away all my prickly, turbulent feelings until I'm calm waters again.

Calmish. Calmish waters.

"So," Nolan says. "Your mother sounds like a treat."

I look at him over my shoulder. "How much of that did you hear?"

His face is unreadable. "Enough."

I turn away again, busying myself with the magnets on my fridge. I arrange them in a smiley face, hoping that maybe if I try hard enough, I might feel it, too.

"You shouldn't have listened," I chide.

"I've visited your past, Harriet. Me listening to a phone call should be the least of your privacy concerns." I turn and he gives me a look. "Why are you upset about it?"

"Because it's embarrassing," I whisper, my voice wobbling at the edges.

"Why?"

Because my mom treats me like I'm an inconvenience. Because the universe or the fates or whoever it is that Nolan answers to isn't the only one who thinks I'm a bad person.

Because not even the people who are *supposed* to love me can find a way to do it.

Because I'm so fucking tired of trying, only to come up short. All the time.

"I don't know," I answer, unwilling to share those pieces with Nolan after what happened at the shop. "It just is."

Nolan stares at me for a long time, eyes flicking back and forth.

"You're not the one who should be embarrassed," he finally says.

He cuts his eyes away, glancing at the colander full of figs in the sink. He plucks one up and takes a bite, like that simple sentence isn't a balm to over two decades of heartache. "She wanted to confirm your attendance at a party?"

I nod. "My family has a winter gala every holiday season. I usually RSVP by now, but I forgot about it with . . . everything else going on."

He takes another bite of his fig. Some juice from the fruit runs over his knuckles. "That sounds formal."

"It is." It's my mother's yearly opportunity to show off for her friends in the name of altruism. To spend far too much money on a grand display of her success. My presence isn't demanded out of a desire to see me. It's my role to play. The ornamental daughter that completes the family portrait.

I'm surprised they still want me there, all things considered.

"You don't seem happy about it," Nolan says, finishing his snack and reaching for a towel.

"I'm fine," I answer automatically. Or I will be. The gala is far enough away for me to still have time to stitch my armor together.

I'll pull it together in time. I always do. "Let me get changed and you can whisk me away."

"And where am I whisking you today?"

"I'm sure we'll find out. I wouldn't want to delay the haunting agenda."

I'm still angry and he knows it. Nolan watches me carefully, angled up against my kitchen sink. His stormy eyes crinkle at the corners. "You didn't let me finish earlier. I've changed my mind."

"About what?"

He tosses my kitchen towel on the countertop, folded just the way I like it. "We won't be visiting your past today."

"We won't?"

"I still owe you an apology." His face melts into something solemn. Honest. *Shy.* An offering, if I'm brave enough to take it. "I thought today we could take a look at your present."

Chapter Twelve
Nolan

When I told Harriet we could do whatever she wanted, I didn't expect her to pick ice skating.

I thought we'd watch one of her movies. Maybe make the jam she seemed so intent on when I arrived at her home. I thought—worst-case scenario—she might potentially take me to one of those tree farms she seems so fond of.

I didn't anticipate gliding along a frozen slab of water with razor blades strapped to my feet while the overhead speakers scream at me about the twelve days of Christmas.

Harriet whizzes past me for the sixth time in as many minutes, her blonde hair flying around her. She does a graceful spin in front of me then winds her way back, circling my slow shuffle across the ice.

"If your hope was to kill me," I say while gripping the side of the rink, "let me remind you that I'm already dead."

She beams at me, her earlier melancholy melted away. "For a Holiday Spirit, you're awfully grumpy about holiday things." The song changes to the one where Mommy kisses Santa Claus. I groan.

Harriet rolls her eyes with another fond smile and zips off. Despite the music and my inability to skate, I'm glad we're here instead of somewhere in her past. I have no desire to watch Harriet fold herself into an even smaller shape, broken down by disappointment after disappointment. Especially after the call from her mother.

I hate that I added to that feeling. I hate that I was another person who diminished her.

"Come on," she calls from the other side of the empty rink. She does something complicated with her feet and executes another jump-spin that leaves me an odd combination of aroused and terrified. "I thought you were supposed to have sea legs, Mr. Fisherman."

"This isn't the sea," I yell back. "This is a frozen death trap."

Harriet's laugh echoes off the backboards and I feel a reluctant smile pull across my mouth. It's just us in the large rink, golden globe lights strung around the perimeter, a large white canopy overhead. According to Harriet, this space is used for a family holiday skate in the evenings, but the owner lets her come whenever she wants. She struck some sort of deal involving a discount on costume jewelry at the Crow's Nest in exchange for free skate time.

The woman who unlocked the door for us had a crooked smile and massive, blue gemstone earrings. She handed Harriet a small package, complained about a man named Darryl delivering the wrong things to the wrong places, then proceeded to talk about online auctions for seven minutes.

Harriet manages another five laps while I complete one, slowing her pace to meet my stride on her final loop. I'm getting better, steadier on my feet, but I'm no match for Harriet.

Harriet with her hair tied back in a high ponytail, curls just brushing her shoulder blades, her hands swinging loose at her sides. I feel like I can barely look at her.

I haven't slept since I dreamed of her. I won't let myself. I'm afraid of what my subconscious might come up with if given the opportunity, and my body doesn't need the rest anyway. I'm embarrassed I jerked myself off to the thought of her. Frustrated I gave in to that drumbeat of desire. I'm not a man easily swayed by whims, but with Harriet, I've completely lost control of the situation.

"Thank you for bringing me," she says. She's wearing her pink coat and the mittens I gave her. "It's been too long since I've skated."

"Then I'm glad we could come," I tell her. "I meant it when I said I was sorry, yeah? You didn't deserve that from me." She makes a soft sound of acknowledgment, but doesn't say anything else as she turns to skate at my side. We move together silently for another lap, nothing but the scratch of our skates against the ice. Our hands brush between us, bumping together and then away again.

I want to hold her hand so bad my bones ache with it. Would she let me hold her hand?

My magic zips up my spine, settling between my shoulder blades. *Wait*, it says. *Not yet*.

Her anger has melted into something softer, more malleable. While it's what I wanted, I'm not sure it makes me feel better. I think Harriet waters her feelings down to make them easier for others to deal with.

If she's mad, I want her to be mad. If she's sad, I want her to be sad.

"When I became a ghost—" I hesitate, my skates tripping beneath my feet. Harriet sets me to rights with a gentle hand at my elbow and I try again. "When I died, it all happened so fast. I was on my boat, and then I—" Dark, heavy skies. The deck lurching beneath my feet. Salt water in my nose and something gold, just out of reach. It's been reduced to sensations after all these years. A creeping numbness and a hand gripping the back of my coat, tugging me away.

"One moment I was on my boat, and the next I wasn't," I finish. "I was dead and there wasn't time for me to come to terms with it. There was a job to do, and expectations, and it all felt like a—like a nightmare. There was an orientation, of course—"

An astonished laugh chokes out of Harriet. "Of course."

"—but I felt trapped. I didn't even get to choose this place. I didn't get to choose *anything*. I was here and I was alone and it was—" *Jarring. Horrible. Terrifying. Lonely.* "Those first few decades, I kept waiting for the next step. I tried to do my job well and I hoped—well, I think I hoped that if I fulfilled the requirements, I'd move on to something else."

Harriet considers that. "You thought you'd have an afterlife. Rest, instead of work."

"Aye." We turn another lap around the rink, Harriet quiet next to me. "But there's never been anything else. Nothing has changed. I've had to let go of my expectations. It's easier for me than the alternative."

"The alternative?"

"That perhaps, for me, there is nothing else."

Harriet frowns. "You really believe that?"

"I don't want to hope anymore. If I don't bother with hope, then I can let go of the impossibility of change. Everything is more tolerable because of it. I don't dislike being a ghost. Not when I forget about what was before and ignore what might come after." I give her a tight smile. "Denial suits me well."

She gives me a matching smile. "I'm familiar with the concept," she says softly.

"Your mother?"

"Yes. It's different for me, though. With her, I can't seem to help myself from hoping."

"Why is she so—"

"Cold?" Harriet offers.

"Horrible," I correct.

Harriet ducks her head, hiding. I want to touch her chin and guide her face back to mine. I meant it in her kitchen when I told her she had nothing to be embarrassed about.

"My grandfather was a difficult man," Harriet says slowly. "My mother was the eldest, and I think she bore the brunt of his expectations. He spared his softness for my aunt Matilda, and I think my mother resented it."

She tips her head back, staring up at the canopy above us, the golden lights twisted and swaying in the cold air. "He died young and it drove a wedge between them. They had a falling out over his will and didn't speak for years. Then when my mother got pregnant—first with Samantha, then with me—they attempted a reconciliation. But the damage was done. Almost like scar tissue, you know? They always seemed stuck in an argument the rest of us didn't know anything about. And neither ever wanted to talk about it."

"But I gravitated toward my aunt." Harriet smiles. Soft. Unfocused. *Sad.* "She gave me the affection I so desperately craved and I think it hurt my mom. That I chose Matilda. I pressed on a bruise I didn't even know was there, time and time again. So, it's not exactly her fault."

"She punished a child for wanting to be loved. Who else could possibly be at fault?" I ask. Harriet gives me an exasperated look. "It's the truth," I defend. "Between the two of us, I think I'm the expert on bad behavior."

"It's not as simple as that," Harriet explains. "She just wants me to fulfill my full potential."

I barely resist the urge to roll my eyes. Harriet is very good at making excuses for the shortcomings of others.

Even me.

"I owe you an apology," I say, rounding back to the reason we're here. "It seems you're not the only one who can press on bruises."

Harriet's expression flickers. "I cornered you," she says quietly. "You were right. I didn't think it through."

I shake my head, frustrated. "And I overreacted. I should not have lashed out the way I did. It was poor form, Harriet. It won't happen again."

Harriet exhales a slow breath. We skate in silence for one lap, then another. I give her the space to consider my apology without pressing for more.

"Do you promise?" she finally asks.

"I do."

"Good." She nods once. "Then you're forgiven."

I feel my eyebrows rise. "Just like that?"

A smile curls one side of her mouth. "I'm not in the habit of holding grudges, especially with beings that have existed before I roamed the planet."

I laugh. "Fair enough."

She gives me a sly look, her ponytail swinging over her shoulder. "Would you rather I make you work for it?"

A slow smile tugs at one corner of my mouth. "I wouldn't mind working for it," I say lightly.

She holds eye contact. We're wading into different territory now. The place where I was in that dream, with her hands in my hair and my face in her neck. Her little candy cane top around her waist, her bare breasts against my chest.

"That's, um, th-that's good to know," she stutters, color appearing across her cheeks. Harriet wears everything she's feeling on her sleeve, right where anyone can see it. I can't tell if it's a good thing or not, but I do know I've never met anyone like her before.

We take another lap in silence and the string pulled tight around my chest lessens with every rhythmic push of our skates. It's the closest I've come to feeling settled in a while.

"C'mon," she finally says, slowing to a stop as the music changes to something light and whimsical. "I'm hungry."

I follow her dutifully off the ice and back to the lobby of the rink, an open area with long wooden benches. There's a stone fireplace on one side with a fire roaring in the hearth, a string of fresh garland looped across the mantel. Harriet dropped our boots in front of it before we put our skates on and I bend to collect them on our slow hobble across the room.

My fingertips brush against the leather and I immediately drop them.

My boots are hot.

I could *feel* them.

Harriet turns toward me. "Everything okay?"

I nod, still frowning at my boots. "Aye," I answer slowly, rubbing my fingers together. They're red. Irritated. "I'm fine."

I'm dreaming, and now I'm feeling, but everything is *fine*.

Denial, as always. My faithful friend.

I drop down onto the bench next to Harriet, my hip pressed to hers, still staring at my fingers. She grunts next to me, almost slicing my calf with her skate.

"And what about you? Everything all right?"

Her mittens lay abandoned at her side, her ponytail over one shoulder. She tugs at her skate some more with a frustrated grunt. "The knot is stubborn. I can do it."

"Give me your foot."

"What? No. Why do you need my foot?"

"So I can help." I bend down and grab her ankle, lifting her leg onto my thigh. I pick at the frayed laces. "Are you always so stubborn when people want to help?"

I untangle the knot, working the strings free from the front of her skate. I grab the blade at the back and wedge it off her foot, then grab her boot. It's still warm from the fire and she watches as I tug it over her reindeer socks. I pat her ankle and set her foot on the ground, reaching for the other.

She lifts it dutifully onto my lap.

"People don't usually offer help," she says as I work, her voice low. I look at her face, but she's watching my hands work at the laces. These are far less tangled, but I still take my time. My hand not working against the knots grips her ankle, my fingers fanned wide.

"I'm offering."

I shouldn't. I know I shouldn't. She's my assignment. I'm on a ticking clock. I've been sent here to reveal her worst bits.

But I can't seem to help myself.

Fingertips brush over the back of my hand. "Maybe we could help each other?" she asks, a thin thread of apprehension in her voice. My magic pricks at the back of my neck, admonishing. I put that anxiety there. I made her wary of asking me for things.

I want to fix it.

I finish unlacing her skate and drop it with the other. I reach for her boot. "I'd like that."

"Yeah?"

"Yes," I tell her, my useless heart hammering in my chest.

I don't believe in her theory. There's nothing she can do to move me forward. But if it makes her happy to try—if it chases some of the sadness off her pretty face—if I can be one person that doesn't disappoint her or let her down—

Then I can endure it.

I'll finish the job. Harriet will move on with her life and I'll—I'll be here. She won't ever know that her work was for naught. She'll forget I ever existed and that hopeful heart of hers will find another lost cause to indulge in.

We can help each other. Just not in the way she thinks.

"Ready to go?" I ask.

She nods and holds out her hand. "Yup."

I stare at it. "I meant back to your shop or your home or . . . whatever you have planned for the rest of your day."

"You're on a deadline. Let's see what my past reveals today." She nudges her hand against mine. "I promise not to grab any jam."

"We don't have to," I offer. "We can wait another day."

We shouldn't. The other ghosts will likely be getting antsy. I'm shortening their timelines, making it more difficult to turn around a successful case. But I can't be bothered. If they have issues with the way I'm operating, they can file a formal complaint with Isabella.

"Let's go now," Harriet says, insistent. "I'm feeling good about this one."

"Are your secrets about to be revealed, Harriet?"

She grins. "I guess we'll see."

She wiggles her fingers, bouncing on the balls of her feet.

I grip both of her hands, squeezing once. Her skin is so much softer than mine. Pale. No scars over her knuckles or calluses against her palms.

My magic sparks and rolls in response, a warm wind coiling around my ankles, spinning up and out until it catches in her ponytail, the end of it brushing at her cheeks. Her smile widens until she's laughing, her hands held tight in my own, color and sound swirling around her as we're tugged away to somewhere else. The ice rink fades away and is replaced by flashes of other places as my magic decides where to drop us.

A candlelit dinner. A brick-lined alleyway. An overcrowded aisle and a hospital corridor. Everything passes too fast for me to hold on to while Harriet and I face each other in the storm.

Like this, she looks like she's at the center of all of it.

Maybe she is.

When we finally slow to a stop, there's not a soul in sight. It's just the two of us and an open stretch of beach, waves lapping at the shore. Gray sand beneath our boots, stretching all the way to where the coast abruptly tumbles into lush, green hills, rising above us on a gentle slope. There are homes in the distance. A single lighthouse painted in thick black and white stripes.

"I don't recognize this place," Harriet says next to me, shielding her eyes as she looks out over the water. Her hair twists around her face as she turns back to me. "I'm not sure I know this memory."

My stomach is in knots. A tremble starts in my hands and crawls along my spine until I feel like I'm vibrating.

"That's because it's not your past," I hear myself say. It's a wonder I can manage any words at all. "It's mine."

Chapter Thirteen
Harriet

Nolan looks like he's going to be sick.

The ocean breeze ruffles his hair, his cheeks a startling shade of white as he stands unmoving on the beach.

I've never seen him look more like a ghost.

"Nolan," I try. He's looking at the row of buildings behind the beach with wide, unseeing eyes. His hands release from fists at his sides, but it's the only part of him that moves. "What do you mean? How did we get to your past?"

"I don't know," he whispers. He cups his hand over his mouth. "I don't know. I don't—"

A loud laugh bursts from the other side of the beach and a little boy appears over the crest of the hill. Nolan turns to watch as the boy charges down the slope, his little legs barely keeping up with the rest of his body. His pants are too big, hiked up high and secured with a belt that's holding on for dear life. Behind him, an older man gives chase, a wide smile on his bearded face.

"Nolan!" the man shouts. "Come back here, you wee scoundrel!"

The little boy screeches in delight, tumbling onto the beach. He tries to roll in the sand to avoid the man behind him, but he's not fast enough. The older man picks him up and tosses him over his shoulder, swinging him around and around. The little boy laughs, a joy so pure I want to bottle it up and keep it.

"That's my da." Nolan swallows heavily. "That's me and—that's my da."

He takes two steps backward, his feet in the surf. But I don't think he feels it, too busy watching the two figures on the other side of the beach with disbelieving eyes. I don't understand what's happening, but I do understand the look on Nolan's face.

Longing. *Heartbreak.*

"I don't—" Nolan pulls in one deep breath and then another, his body struggling to keep up with his panic. "I don't remember this day." His wide eyes look around, frantic. "I barely remember this place. This beach. And I don't—I can't remember this day."

"You're all right." I grab him right above his elbows and hold on. He keeps moving backward and I follow, the water lapping at our knees. "Nolan. Look at me."

His wild eyes connect with mine. His chest rises and falls with every choppy inhale and exhale. I smooth my hands up his arms to his shoulders and back again, hoping my touch might ground him.

"You're okay," I tell him. "I'm here with you. You're not alone." I reach for something to say. Something to erase the desperation etched into his face. I try to find the thing he needs, but I don't know where to start. He looks like he wants to sink under the water and disappear. I grip him tighter. "It's just a memory."

He nods, hands reaching for my jacket. He knots his fingers in the thick, soft fabric, gripping tight. Behind us, the little boy on the beach is gathering sticks, his father watching with a fond smile.

Nolan doesn't look in their direction. He keeps staring at me.

"I need to leave," he says.

"Are you sure?" I glance over my shoulder at the little boy throwing sticks in the surf. They're closer now, the man ruffling the little boy's hair. What if this is Nolan's only chance to see these things? To remember? To get this piece of himself back?

What if this is part of moving him on?

Nolan shakes his head, his jaw clenched. His pupils are so dilated, his eyes look almost black. "I can't be here. I can't—I don't remember and I can't—" His bottom lip trembles before he sets his mouth in a firm line. "I need to leave. Please. It's too much."

"Okay," I answer. I'm a little worried about him using his magic when he's so wound up, but I trust him to keep me safe. With one last look at the lighthouse on the hill, he reaches for my hand, tangling our fingers together. Palm to palm, the ground starts to fall away beneath my feet. The last thing I hear is the crashing surf, the call of a sea bird, and the laugh of a little boy. Nolan grips me tighter and a second later, we're standing in front of the fireplace at the ice-skating rink.

He immediately drops my hand and turns away, both of his arms raised, his fingers clenched tight in his hair. I stare at his back as he paces toward the fireplace, then leans heavily against the mantel. Each breath is more labored than the last. My hand hovers over his spine.

"It's all right," I whisper, wishing I knew what to say. The part of my heart that craves making other people feel good aches at the sight of him. He's barely holding himself together. I trace a path up and down his back and feel his lungs expand beneath my palm.

"We're not there anymore. We're back at the ice rink and there's—there's Mariah Carey playing on the speakers. The rink is closed and it's just us right now. Us and Denise, who is probably in her office looking up jewelry auctions online. I've told her a million times to stop buying things from Facebook Marketplace, but I think she's addicted to the fight or flight of it all. Last year around Easter, she went to someone's house for these earrings that looked like oranges. She's lucky she's not a ghost now. A ghost of bad online purchases."

I'm babbling, talking nonsense, but with every word that falls out of my mouth, Nolan seems to collect himself. I press my hand harder against his back, slowing my strokes to firm presses. I spread my fingers wide, seeing how much of his back I can cover. He tilts slightly until his head is pressed to my shoulder instead of resting against the curve of his biceps, and my heart almost breaks clean in half.

"I don't know if you noticed, but I have reindeer socks on today. They're wet right now, from the—from the ocean, I think, but—" He shudders, and I abandon that particular thought. "You seemed to like my reindeer pajamas," I say.

It's an invitation to react. I know how much he hates my reindeer pajamas. He looked at them like he'd never seen anything so offensive in his life. But he lets the comment sail by, his head still against my shoulder, his trembling hands hanging limply at his sides. "Okay, no comment on the reindeer." I sneak a look around the open space. There's a snack bar in the back corner, tucked next to the skate rental. It's abandoned right now, but I know they have hot chocolate in the back.

"C'mon. I have an idea." I grab his hand as he reluctantly unfolds his body, but he doesn't give in to my persistent tugging. He is an immovable object in front of the fireplace, his hand clamped around mine.

"This way." I nod toward the snack bar. "Hot chocolate will help."

"In a second," he tells me, his mouth barely moving. He's not as pale as he was on the beach, but he still looks vacant. A little bit lost. "I need a second," he says again.

"Can I—" I watch him carefully. "Nolan. Do you need a hug?"

I still don't know where Nolan and I fall on the scale of appropriate physical touch, but I know hugs always make me feel better. He doesn't say anything and I'm just about to backtrack—make an excuse, give him some space—when his arms band around my torso.

He wraps himself around me like a vine, gathering my body

against his until his face is in my neck and my arms are draped over his shoulders. His hands are so big, cupped on either side of my rib cage, his arms crossed over one another. My feet dangle off the ground as he lifts me up closer against his chest, the toes of my boots skimming the tops of his.

I blink at the wall in astonishment, then wrap my arms around him and squeeze.

A deep sound rattles out of him.

"Okay?" I ask.

He nods, then shakes his head. I drag one hand through his messy hair and he holds me tighter. I scratch my nails against the back of his neck and he shivers.

I hold him in the lobby of the ice-skating rink with my body wrapped around his, my feet dangling at his shins and his arms snug around my waist. I hug him until my arms go numb.

"Another moment," he begs, after I've combed all his hair off his face and traced the curve of his ears enough times to know that he has a scar shaped like a crescent moon on one, the delicate skin slightly raised beneath my touch. Nolan presses his face farther into my neck, nose nudging. "I just need one more moment and I'll be grand."

"Take as much time as you need," I say quietly, starting another meandering path against his scalp. His hair is so soft. I drift my touch over his ears again, lower to the warm skin of his neck. I trace his shoulders, then circle one hand back up to cup the side of his face.

"Feels nice," he slurs.

I retrace my path along his jaw. "What does?"

His arms tighten around me. "Holding you," he says, and I can feel his mouth move against my skin. "'S been a while since I've had a hug," he adds, quieter.

I blink against the sudden pressure behind my eyes and across the bridge of my nose. How lonely he must have been, all of these years. Waiting for something that never arrived. Wanting for something to change. No wonder he lashed out when I offered him the hope of something different.

He releases another deep breath and his arms loosen.

No, I want to protest. *Not yet.*

But he sets me back on my feet with an embarrassed wince, lines from my jacket on the side of his cheek. I reach up and rub at them.

"Better?" I ask.

He nods, distracted, a downward twist to his mouth. "Aye. Thank you." He reaches for my hand with his, pulling it away from his face. "I need to go."

My stomach twists. "Right now?" I look over my shoulder at the abandoned booth. "But the hot chocolate. It'll help. I promise." I pause. "We don't have to talk about anything, if you don't want to. But I don't think you should be alone."

You could stay, I almost tell him. *I could try to make it better for you.*

His hand squeezes mine, his eyes fixed on the door. "If we visited my past, there's something wrong. That's not supposed to happen." He swallows, flinching again. He looks so *tired*. Rattled. "I need to talk to Isabella."

"Isabella?" My heart gives one uncomfortable thump, right in the middle of my chest.

His expression softens, his hand rising to brush at my elbow in reassurance. "My supervisor," he explains. "I need to get this sorted. I'll be back tomorrow. The next day, at the latest."

Where will you be? I want to ask. *How will I get in touch with you? Are you all right? Do you need another hug?*

He still looks like he's clinging to his composure through sheer force of will. His eyes are bloodshot and his hands are trembling. I want to reach out and grab him. Sink my hands back into his hair and hold on. Wrap him in a blanket and stick him on my couch. Hug him until he remembers what it feels like.

I don't know why, but it feels like when he disappears this time, I won't ever see him again.

"Do you promise?" I ask.

He hesitates, then nods. "Tomorrow," he says. His hand drops from my elbow. "I'll find you."

I look at my feet instead of his face, nodding absently. "All right," I agree. "Be safe—"

But when I look up, he's already gone.

"—and I'll see you soon," I finish. I blow out a breath. At least I didn't have to watch him leave.

I stare at the door of the ice-skating rink for another minute, then head toward the snack booth in the corner. I ignore the knot in my gut and try to decide if I want marshmallows or not.

This is familiar territory. I know how to hold myself up against disappointment. I've been left behind by every person who has ever mattered.

A forgotten thing, just like the treasures I keep stocked on my shelves.

Chapter Fourteen
Nolan

"She's not here?"

Betty straightens the phone on her desk, then picks up a monstrous cupcake. She plucks the fondant snowflake off the top and takes a dainty bite. "Unfortunately, Isabella is out of the office with a departmental emergency." She gives me a sunny smile. "You're welcome to leave a message."

I exhale a harsh breath. I don't want to wait. I don't want to leave a message. I *want* to talk to Isabella and figure out why I'm suddenly visiting my past instead of Harriet's.

"It's urgent," I try again.

"So you've mentioned," Betty says, patient as always. Behind me, the massive yew tree stretches, branches rustling in a nonexistent breeze. A warning to behave myself.

I've been vibrating since I landed on that beach with Harriet, her hand in mine and my—my father on the sand in front of us.

I don't remember that day. I barely remember that beach. The only memories I have of my father are faded at best, worn down like a river stone.

My parents loved me with everything they had, and I couldn't even honor them by *remembering*.

What other things have I forgotten? What else has time taken from me?

And why in the hell am I visiting these memories now?

"Please, Betty. If she has any availability today, I need you to slot me in."

She sets down her cupcake.

"As I've said, Isabella isn't here today," Betty offers, her face apologetic. I guess I've displayed enough desperation to warrant concern from the afterlife receptionist. "She won't have any availability for the remainder of the week. There's been an incident with a Reaper. It's all hands on deck."

I frown. Reapers are notoriously solitary spirits with powerful magic. They're ruthless and unpredictable. Calculated and cold. Coincidentally, they also demolish the competition at the annual departmental bocce ball tournament.

"What's happened?" Death magic is ancient magic, older than the Earth itself. It was here before we came and will remain long after we've gone.

It's eternal. Unmoving.

Unforgiving.

The day I died, a man in a black robe with a scythe across his back grabbed me by the collar of my sweater and pulled me from the water with a low *for fuck's sake*. Then he flicked his wrist and his magic was coiling around us. It felt like tar on my skin, heavy and thick, sliding up my arms before I found myself in Isabella's office, dripping on her carpet. The Reaper deposited me in a chair, complained about water in his Italian loafers, then promptly disappeared.

I haven't talked to a Reaper since.

Betty peeks over her shoulder at the door behind her, then leans forward, dropping her voice to a whisper. "Rumor has it that one of the Reapers failed to report for her shift. She's gone missing."

"Missing?"

Betty nods. "No one can find her. And as I'm sure you're aware, we can't have that sort of magic out in the world without the proper precautions in place. Isabella and the rest of the department heads are trying to locate her."

I scratch at my jaw, agitated. That's all well and good, but I have a problem, too. A problem that needs sorting sooner rather than later. Reapers don't have holiday countdowns to contend with.

"I suppose I'll leave a message then," I say, frustrated.

"Wonderful!" A pen instantly appears in Betty's hand, hot pink with a sparkly poof ball on top. "Ready when you are."

"Let her know there are additional complications with my assignment and I wish to discuss it with her in person." There. That's reasonable. And better than *What in the hell is going on?*

Betty scribbles against her sparkly notepad, head bent in concentration. "What sort of complications?"

"Harriet's memories haven't revealed anything." I swallow. "They're mundane, at best. And our last trip to the past was . . . complicated."

"How so?"

"Well. It wasn't her past."

Betty's pen stops scratching. "Whose past was it?"

"It was mine."

The pen snaps in two. Ink explodes from the top of it. Betty lifts her head and stares at me with her mouth open, blue ink splattered across her cheek.

"What did you just say?"

"We went to my past instead of hers. It was—it was one of my memories."

Betty stares at me, flabbergasted. Her brows furrow. "Are you sure?"

I nod. My father. *Me.* The beach in our small fishing village. The lighthouse on the hill.

All of it aches like a newly set bone. The most important person in my life, and I'd forgotten him.

"I've never heard of such a thing," Betty says. I don't know if that makes me feel better or worse. She taps the pieces of her pen against her mouth. "Maybe we should have you talk to someone. Get you reassigned. Another ghost can take on Harriet while we figure this out."

"No." My response is visceral, without conscious thought, coming from somewhere deep in my chest. The tree at my back shudders, a low groan as the branches sway back and forth.

"No," I say again, softer. "Isabella said she's my assignment for a reason. I can—I can figure this out. I had merely hoped for a little guidance."

"But if you're visiting your past, Nolan—" Betty sets her broken pen to the side. "That's a serious wrinkle. It's not something that happens."

It's a good thing I didn't mention my dream, then, or how I was able to taste the fig jam Harriet brought with her from the past. Or that since my last trip to this office, I've been able to *feel* things. Heat from the fireplace at the skating rink and the scratch of ice against the palms of my hands.

Standing in this office, my socks are still wet from standing in the surf of my memory. I've *never* brought the past back with me before.

Betty would probably toss me in the back and throw away the key if she knew. Harriet would be alone, and I—

I'd be alone, too. Even more so than I already am.

"It's possible I'm exaggerating things," I try to backtrack. This was a mistake. I shouldn't have come here. I panicked and acted rashly. "I'm sure it was just a blip."

"A blip," Betty repeats, her mouth settling in a firm line. "Visiting your past is more than a *blip*, Nolan."

"I wasn't completely in control of my magic during the last trip. I was distracted." Only half of that statement is true. I was distracted, but not enough to end up somewhere completely different, in a time I shouldn't have access to.

But I don't want to be taken away from Harriet.

I back toward the door. The branches above my head rustle again, like the ancient tree can sense my dishonesty. Some of the thin, delicate leaves break free, fluttering to the ground at my feet. "I'm sure Isabella will have an explanation when she returns. No rush. I'll just be—I'll be with Harriet until then." I force a smile. "In fact, I bet this assignment will be wrapped with a bow by the time Isabella returns. No need to worry."

Betty tilts her head to the side and picks up her cupcake. She peels off some of the wrapper and flicks the crumbs toward a small wastebasket at the side of her desk.

"This can sometimes happen to ghosts under stress. Anomalies. Ending up in places you shouldn't be. Did I ever tell you about the time a Poltergeist ended up with the Guardian Angels?" She laughs. "Can you imagine? It was pandemonium for weeks."

She takes a massive bite, thinking while she chews. "When's the last time you had a rest? I can give you the contact information for the Malevolent Spirits' book club. I think you could really benefit from some interaction with—"

Betty continues rambling on about book clubs and potlucks and socializing with my coworkers while I tune her out.

Rest. I don't need rest. My job requires one month of the year, and other than that, I sit at my condemned home on the water and knit half-assed mittens and adopt wayward cats that break into my kitchen and steal my pot holders.

All I do is rest.

I rest and I wait.

I *wait*.

I wait for something to change and from the very moment I

stepped out from behind her Christmas tree and spotted Harriet on her couch, things have been changing. It's like I've been shoved awake, feeling returning to my limbs after lying too long in one position.

I drag my hand over my mouth, awareness lighting me up like a firecracker. Perhaps Harriet is right. Maybe she is the key to moving me forward. It could be possible that she has something in her possession that once belonged to me, but perhaps—

Perhaps she's the hopeful, optimistic antithesis to the dark cloud I've become, meant to hold up a mirror to *my life* and *my actions*.

"Hell," I whisper, dragging a hand through my hair. She could be the key to everything, and I let my emotions get the best of me.

I've gotten this all wrong.

Betty stops short in the middle of her impassioned speech about the importance of sun exposure.

"You're leaving?" she asks. "So soon?" She stares at her desk and the cupcake she's somehow managed to already demolish. She snaps her fingers and another appears. "Want a cupcake?"

"No, thank you." I clear my throat. "I should get back to Harriet. Close out the assignment." I shove both hands in my jacket pockets. "Time is ticking and . . . all that."

"It's true you are under a tight deadline. It's already December tenth. Can you believe how time flies?" She laughs while I try not to scream, wiping a bit of frosting from the corner of her mouth. "I don't know if it's ever taken you this long to hand off an assignment."

I usually have my assignments wrapped in a week before I return to my otherwise tedious existence at the water's edge. But Harriet has set us on a different path and I only have fourteen days left before my hard deadline of Christmas Eve. Fourteen days left to figure out why.

And if Harriet is indeed the key to moving me forward . . . if she's meant to help me discover my unfinished business . . .

I plan to run that time down to the wire.

Chapter Fifteen

Harriet

I rush down the stairs while a mad man pounds at my door, my toothbrush wedged in my cheek. I wasn't expecting company, and I certainly wasn't expecting Nolan. Not so soon after he left.

I fumble with the deadlock while his shadow paces on the other side of my curtains, his hands on his hips and his head tilted down.

"You were right," he says, breathless, as soon as I get the door open. He spent the entire four minutes it took me to answer alternatively poking at my doorbell and grumbling at it, knocking with the side of his fist when neither of those seemed to work. His hair is all over the place, his jacket is inside out, and his eyes are bright.

He looks like he just consumed an entire vat of espresso. That, or he's found a new hobby in between time traveling and past exploring and haunting. Like snorting Pixy Stix, maybe. Or base jumping.

I eyeball him, concerned, my toothbrush still hanging out of my mouth. When he left me at the rink, he was barely holding himself together. Now he's practically crackling with energy.

"*Yewgood?*" I ask.

He stares at me. "Was that English?"

I take my toothbrush out of my mouth. "Are you all right?" I say slowly, trying to enunciate around a mouthful of toothpaste.

He props one hand against the doorframe, squinting at me. "You want to fight?"

I roll my eyes and turn, heading to the small half bathroom at the front of the house. I leave my front door open behind me in silent invitation, confused by the abrupt change in his attitude.

There was a student in one of my law school classes that lost it in the middle of a lecture once. He started laughing uncontrollably while tearing pages out of a book. He put his socks over his ears and said he was an elephant. He had to be escorted out by campus police.

I wonder if Nolan will have his socks over his ears when I join him in the living room.

I spit out my toothpaste and grab the hand towel, burying my face in the soft material. When I look up again, Nolan is standing right behind me.

"Jesus," I gasp. "You need a bell."

"A bell?"

I turn, the small of my back pressed against the sink. There's not enough room in this space for two adults. There's barely enough room in this bathroom for one adult. His chest brushes against mine every time I breathe.

"Why are you in my bathroom?"

Nolan frowns and studies the toilet. He looks a combination of confused and surprised, like he didn't expect me to have indoor plumbing. "Is that what this is? I thought it was a closet."

"You thought I was spitting my toothpaste out in the closet?"

"Mortal customs elude me." He waves his hand over his head. "I need to talk to you."

"In my bathroom?"

"Location doesn't matter."

"All right." That's . . . fine. Doesn't explain why he's standing so damn close, looking at me with an intensity that borders on manic. Dark eyes. A clench in his jaw that stretches and pops as he studies me. I turn halfway and drop my toothbrush into one of the spare cups, then bury a yawn against the back of my hand.

"Did your boss have an explanation for you?" I ask, fighting with the tail end of my exhaustion. I suppose I should make peace with never having any idea as to what is going on. I blink away the tired tears collecting in the corners of my eyes. "Did she have any advice?"

"No," he says, still staring at me. He reaches up and fingers a lock of my hair, tucking it behind my ear. His knuckles graze my cheek. "Your hair." He sighs. "There's so much of it."

"I'm aware." I gather it in one hand and push it behind my shoulder. "What's going on with you? You're being weird."

"I'm not being weird."

"You are absolutely being weird."

"It's a matter of perspective. I'd prefer the term *energized*."

"Okay," I say slowly. "What's got you *energized*?"

He drops one shoulder against the wall. "I didn't get a chance to talk to my boss."

"No?"

He shakes his head. "There was an emergency with a Reaper."

"A Reaper?"

"A Grim Reaper," he explains, like mentioning the embodiment of death will suffice and not immediately ignite about seventy thousand additional questions.

"Those exist?" I whisper.

"That's not the point of this conversation."

"I wish I knew the point of this conversation."

I don't want to be in here with him. I want to be in my bed, halfway to unconsciousness, trying desperately not to think about the way it feels when Nolan gives me his full and undivided attention.

I've dreamed of him every night this week, mostly new interpretations of real-life memories. A left turn instead of right. Others are complete fabrications. Fantasies. Nolan at my kitchen table stringing cranberries onto ribbon. Nolan reclined on my couch in just a pair of red reindeer pajama pants. Me in the matching shirt, straddling his lap. My mouth on his neck and his hands in my hair.

Nolan in the antiques shop, reading in the back corner with his ankle crossed over his knee, his face lighting up when he sees me.

It's becoming a problem. I think I'm developing feelings.

I'm developing feelings for a ghost who will disappear before the end of the month.

But I can't help it. Nolan doesn't feel transient when we're together. He feels like a man. A man with a reluctant smile and a sharp mind and a devastatingly soft heart beneath all that flannel padding. Someone that's just as lonely as me.

"I couldn't wait," he says, resting one hand at the sink by my hip. "That's the point of this conversation."

His pinky reaches out, tracing the soft material of my pajamas. I chose a green pair with dancing nutcrackers for tonight's hibernation.

"I didn't want to wait," he adds softly, dragging his gaze up from my pajama bottoms to my face.

My stomach performs an Olympic-worthy somersault.

"Our conversation the other day," he says, still studying me. "When we discussed my unfinished business. I think you were right."

I flinch, frowning. *Discussion* is a polite term for what that was.

"I'm not sure we should talk about this again," I say.

I'm not sure my heart can take another battering. Not after the ice-skating rink, when it felt like we might be creeping closer to something that feels like friendship. Not after he clung to me in front of the fireplace, his face buried in my neck and his body trembling. Not after I've acknowledged that I'm starting to like Nolan very, very much. Too much.

"Why not?" he whispers.

"Because you seem a little worked up." I push past him to the living room and head straight for the cookie jar shaped like a snowman on the mantel. I keep a stash of candy canes in there for emotional support emergencies. This feels like an appropriate time.

Unfortunately for me, there's a distinct lack of candy canes in the jar. I guess I've needed my fair share of emotional support over the last month and a half.

I abandon the empty cookie jar for the gingerbread house under the tree, lifting the lid and peering inside.

Nolan trails dutifully after me, from the gingerbread house to the couch to the bread box in the kitchen.

Every hiding spot is empty.

"Do I really consume this much sugar?"

Nolan leans against the frame of the door, his arms crossed over his chest. "Yes," he states. "You do."

I blow out a breath through my nose and stare up at the ceiling. I'm frustrated, but more than that I'm irritated.

In my periphery, I see Nolan move closer.

"Why are you following me?" I snap.

"I go where you go, Harriet," he replies.

I barely resist rolling my eyes. I never asked for any of this. I certainly never asked for a pity ghost, sticking around because he has to. The constant reminder is a sprinkle of salt in barely healed wounds.

No one has ever stuck around. No one has ever chosen me. I don't need him to constantly remind me that he's here only because he has to be.

"Because you're haunting me," I say to the ceiling, sharper than I mean to.

Fingertips gently touch my cheek. Nolan holds a candy cane in front of my nose.

I hesitate, then take it.

"Why are you upset?" he asks as I aggressively chew on the end of the peppermint stick. It's the brand I prefer, with the thin red stripes instead of the thick ones. "I thought you'd be excited."

"You changed your mind fairly quickly. Pardon me if I'm less than enthused."

"Not as quick as you think, and it's not just the past that's changed my mind."

"What does that mean?"

"There are other things, too. Things that have . . . persuaded me that perhaps you can help me. Just as you said."

I switch my candy cane to the other side of my mouth. "And what are those things?"

A blush colors his cheeks right above the scruff of his beard. It's blood in the water for my curiosity.

"Must I share them?"

I nod. There is absolutely no way I'm letting him out of this room without an explanation. After everything, it's the least he can do.

He sighs and turns his face to the ceiling, his neck and jaw in sharp relief. He really does look like he's from another world, another time. Like a faded photograph at the very bottom of a chest, warped at the corners, the edges peeling up. Dark in some spots, light in others.

Something left behind. Something forgotten.

"Things are changing. I can *feel* them changing. It's like—it's like the sky, yeah? Right before it snows. When the night is holding its breath and everything feels heavy. When it's not truly dark, but— something else. A lantern behind the clouds. That's what I feel like. Like a lantern has been lit. I don't know how else to describe it." His eyes search mine, dipping briefly to trace the contours of my face. I wonder what he's looking for there, and if he'll be able to find it. His mouth pulls up on one side, the shadow of his dimples appearing in both cheeks. "You're the first thing in a hundred years to make me feel anything at all, Harriet York, and I don't think that's an accident."

I blow out a slow breath. It's hard for me to hear those words and not become attached to the idea of it. I've never been special to anyone. I've never been of use to *anyone*. The only feelings I've ever managed to inspire in others is vague frustration and opaque disappointment.

Or worse, nothing at all.

It's tempting to be something different for Nolan.

Still. I need more.

"What's changed?" I ask.

His half smile sharpens. He reaches for one of my curls, twisting it around his pointer finger and tugging once. "You mean besides ending up in one of my childhood memories?"

I nod.

He blows out a deep breath, the rest of his hand sifting under my hair. He settles it around the back of my neck, his palm flush against the top of my spine. Steadying himself, maybe, or perhaps steadying me.

"I'm afraid," he confesses.

I soften. "Of what?"

His eyes flick back and forth between mine. "I'm afraid if I say it aloud, it'll no longer be true."

"You can tell me."

His fingers flex on the back of my neck. "My coffee was burnt this morning." He swallows. "It tasted like absolute shite."

"Um . . . okay?"

"I could taste it, Harriet. I could taste my coffee this morning and the lemon drop you gave me in the tree field. I burnt my hand in front of the fireplace at the ice-skating rink and I was cold this morning when I left my house. I'm feeling again." His eyes search mine. "I'm feeling quite a bit."

An ache pinches in the middle of my chest. "Anything else?"

"Is that not enough?"

"There's something you haven't told me about yet. I can tell."

His mouth pulls into a grim smile, his jaw flexing and releasing. "I had a dream." He pauses. "About you."

"Me?"

"Aye," he says. "You."

"I thought you said you didn't have dreams."

"I don't," he agrees, his voice tripping into something lower.

"Oh."

I think of the dreams I've had about him. The warm, buzzy feeling under my skin. The way I sometimes wake up with my hand low on my belly. Heat floods my cheeks. "Was it—was it a good dream, at least?"

His gaze takes a meandering path across my face. Lower, to the v in my pajama shirt and where I most definitely am not wearing a bra. His tongue appears at the corner of his mouth, and his hand tightens against the back of my neck. A sigh rattles out of me.

"It was a very good dream," he rasps.

My stomach bottoms out. I wet my lips and Nolan's attention shifts there. He traces another slow circuit across the knob at the top of my spine and I shiver in my matching pajamas.

I bet my pulse feels like a jackhammer right now. Like some sort of heavy machinery, picking up speed the longer I stand here like this, with him.

But I'm not embarrassed. I'm aware of my body and of his. Of the moment that is stretching between us until everything feels languid and slow. Lights from the tree and a horn across the harbor. Wind at the windows and a sticky peppermint stick wedged in my mouth.

"I think you're bringing me back to life, Harriet."

"That's a ridiculous statement."

He shrugs his shoulders. Barely half an inch. "Not if it's true."

I release a slow breath, studying him. He keeps his face open and honest, letting me look.

"I guess that's a good reason, then," I whisper, filling the space between us, trying to cut through the tension that's gripped us both. I want to approach this academically, slot another clue into its proper place, but I also want to lean forward and bury my face in his chest.

"That's—um. That makes sense. If you're, uh, experiencing things. I get it now. I get why you'd have a change of heart."

Some of the tension eases from the lines by his eyes, his face so earnest I could cry. "You'll help me then?" He tries to crack a smile. "You'll end decades of blind desperation and send me off into the afterlife of my dreams?"

I try to see through the bluster. "Is that what you want, Nolan? Truly?"

The teasing smile slips from his face.

"I need this, Harriet," he says. "I need to move on. I need something different."

I try not to let those words sting, but it's a bucket of cold water over the heat simmering between us. I tug out of his grip.

Of course he wants something different. He's been here for decades with no hope to hold on to. He's hated this existence.

I can't be selfish with this. After all, what future could I possible have with a ghost? I've lost myself to a fantasy, and it needs to stop.

I need to bundle it all up and let it go.

"Of course," I tell him, forcing a smile and ignoring the rubber band of disappointment slowly squeezing at the middle of my chest. I can do this. I can help him without falling further into whatever this is. I'll help him move on, he'll disappear, and I'll return to my ghost-free life. I'll have fond memories of this . . . absolutely ridiculous series of events. Like the brass bobbles that hang on my tree in the window. I'll box them up carefully at the end of the season and store them in the attic. I'll take them out every now and again to marvel over how pretty and special and unique they are, then I'll tuck them away.

It will be fine.

I will be fine.

I always am.

I fix my face into a smile. "I'll do whatever I can to help."

I've always been good at being exactly what people need.

Chapter Sixteen

Nolan

I stare at the unmarked door in front of me.

While I don't have the best awareness of passing time, I do know that I've been sitting in this heinous, gold-patterned chair long enough for one of my legs to go numb, an uncomfortable tingling up the back of my calf every time I so much as think about shifting. It's another novel development in my ever-changing existence.

I lift my leg and drop it, a shock of itchy discomfort exploding beneath my skin. One of the sales associates wanders by with a faintly amused look on her face, a bundle of silk and wool in her arms. Harriet has been locked in the changing area for close to twenty-five minutes trying on dresses for her parent's gala, while I remain marooned on this torture device masquerading as a chair.

She agreed to help me, but she's been distant ever since. She was tight-lipped about her plans for the day when I met her on the sidewalk in front of her home, only caving when I bribed her with a blueberry Danish I picked up on a whim. She had stared at it for an uncomfortably long time. I thought I had made a mistake, but then she gave me a half-hearted smile and inhaled it in three bites, reluctantly inviting me to join her for her morning errands.

But she's not making eye contact. Her smiles are harder to earn. I've made a misstep, and I don't know how to fix it. I don't even know where to start.

I thought she'd be pleased. Smug doesn't suit Harriet, but I thought she'd at least be cheery about being right.

There's a ruckus behind the closed door and another navy blue dress flies over the back of it, draped haphazardly with the others. A carnage of heavy, starchy material. I drag my hand over the back of my head and sigh.

"This was your idea." Harriett's voice snaps beneath the door. "No one said you had to come dress shopping with me."

I *thought* I'd have a front-row seat for Harriet in evening wear, but all I've seen is the flecked white paint of the changing room door, Harriet fighting with various materials on the other side.

I dreamed about her again last night. She was wearing one of her matching pajama sets, one I've never seen before. An oversize flannel shirt that hit mid-thigh, the creamy expanse of her legs bare beneath. I was wearing the matching pants as she crawled onto my lap, setting her elbows on my shoulders and her knees at my hips. I slid my hands up the back of her shirt and traced her warm skin with my palms, just looking at her.

When I woke up, I could have sworn I smelled peppermint.

"Could you get me this one in another size?" Harriet's arm emerges from behind the door, holding a dress. She wiggles it back and forth while I try to clear the cobwebs of my fantasy.

I stand with a grunt and grab the garment, wedging my boot between the door when she immediately tries to close it again. One wide brown eye peers back at me, a haphazard collection of curls over half of her face.

"You haven't let me see a single dress," I say.

"No one said you'd get to see the dresses."

"It was implied."

"By who?"

By me, I think wistfully, *and this ache in my chest. This . . . longing I can't seem to get rid of.*

I haven't wanted anything in decades, but I think I want you.

I study one of the discarded dresses with a frown. "Why are you wearing this color?"

"Because that's the dress code for this event." A wrinkle appears between her eyebrows. I gently poke at it. She swats my hand away. "And I don't deviate from instructions."

I know she doesn't. It's probably the most endearing and frustrating thing about her. Harriet does exactly what she says she will, no matter the cost to herself. No matter how she's treated in return.

"I think you should wear red," I tell her. She belongs in something vibrant. Something that makes her glow.

"And I think you should get me a different size," she singsongs back, nudging me away from the door. I roll my eyes to the ceiling and gather the smooth material of her dress, retreating to the aisle she pulled it from.

I hook the dress on the right rack, flicking through the options. I can't make sense of the tiny tags, so I abandon them, meandering to a completely different section instead. A garment catches my eye and I smirk as I grab it, wandering back to Harriet's fortress of solitude and knocking twice.

The door opens. Her hand reaches out. I give her the new dress.

"Nolan," she says immediately. "This isn't what I asked for."

"You're right. It's better." I reclaim the chair and stretch out my legs. The numbness has receded, replaced by giddy anticipation instead. "Go on. Try it."

She pokes her head out of the changing room. Her shoulders are bare, her hair pulled to one side. I grip the back of the awful chair until the wood creaks in protest.

"I can't wear this."

I stop trying to count the freckles across the slope of her shoulder. "Says who?"

Her nose wrinkles. "My mother. And the previously mentioned dress code."

"Do you always do as she says?"

"Yes," Harriet replies simply. "I do as everyone says. It's a defining character trait."

"You don't do as I say." I gesture to the dress at her side. "Case in point."

"Well, you're you."

I grin. I like being the exception to Harriet's rules, even if it results in my frustration. "I seem to remember a little girl who delighted in stealing a boat."

An answering smile flirts with the corners of her mouth. "That was a long time ago. I've learned a lesson or two since then." The smile fades away, replaced by a thoughtful frown. "It's easier this way."

"For you or for everyone else?"

She doesn't respond, but the downcast look on her face says enough.

I bite my tongue against a sigh. Harriet hides so much of the person she wants to be behind the person she thinks she needs to be. It's clear her mother has played a heavy role in making her think she's not allowed to be anything outside perfect and reasonable, but it's also evident that Harriet feels the need to make up for something. I wish I knew what that was.

"Perhaps you need a nudge in the right direction." I nod at the plum-colored silk in her hand. "Humor me."

She gives me a long look, then disappears back into the dressing room without another word. I sit there and stare at the door and let myself imagine it.

The smooth glide of the dress over her body. The thin straps against her shoulders. Her hair, flirting with the tops of her breasts. The press of her nipples against the delicate fabric. The tiny zipper at the back and how the bite of the metal would feel between my fingers. My mouth at her neck and my nose in her hair. I wonder how far down her blush would go. If I could gather the silky, smooth material of her skirt in my fists and press her up against the mirror. If she would watch me drop to my knees behind her in the reflection, or if she'd turn around. Sink her fingers into my hair while I pressed my face between her thighs and—

"After I finish up here, we can get on the road," she calls through the door. I'm jolted so forcefully from my daydream that I drive my knee into the tiny, ineffectual marble table next to the chair. The sales clerk drifts past with a smug snort, a knowing look shot in my direction.

I stretch out my knee with a scowl. "On the road?"

"Traveling," she says slowly, with all the subtlety of a fog horn. "You know. To places we've visited in the *past*."

Amusement settles in the middle of my chest. "Yes, I follow." I pause, still busy trying to tug my brain back from flashes of bare skin and smooth silk. I click my tongue. "We can get on the road, or we could grab some lunch first. Whatever you prefer."

"Lunch?"

"I'm told that's a thing people do."

She's quiet for the stretch of three heartbeats. "It's a thing *people* do," she finally says.

I laugh into my fist. "I'd like to be a person with you, Harriet."

Harriet hums on the other side of the door. The hum quickly turns into a grunt. There's a sharp exhale of breath and then a thud. It sounds like she's wrestling a badger in there.

"All right?" I ask.

"I think I'm stuck."

"In the dress?"

"Yes, in the dress." She mutters something under her breath that I don't quite catch. "The zipper is twisted or . . . something. I'm not sure you got me the right size."

I'm almost certain I didn't. I only gave the tag a quick look, choosing instead to eyeball the stretch of the material and imagine it over the curve of Harriet's ass. It was not a logical decision.

I'm at the door in two quick strides, both arms braced against the frame.

"Open up."

The sound she makes is offended. "Absolutely not."

"Harriet." I drop my forehead to the door and tap it there twice. This woman. "Don't be proud."

"It's not a matter of pride." She pauses for a long minute. "It's a matter of decency."

Something tight and aching catches me by the throat. I clear it once, then clear it again. I'm imagining plum silk and alabaster skin. The pink of her blush and the honey blond of her hair. "I'll close my eyes," I tell her, my voice like gravel.

"No, thank you. I'll figure it out." I wait, patient, listening to the sounds of her struggle. "Okay. I think I need to be cut out of this dress. Can you get that sales lady?"

I peek over my shoulder. The sales associate is nowhere to be found.

"Sure," I lie. I don't move an inch.

"I can see your feet beneath the door, Nolan."

Damn it. "I don't know where she's gone off to. If you let me in, I'll make quick work of it." I wince. I couldn't sound more like an eager, green boy if I tried. "I just meant—"

The door unlatches. Her face looks like—she looks the same as she did when we spun through her past, that first time. Pink-cheeked and a little thrown off. Frazzled, but brave.

Beautiful.

"I know what you meant," she says, defeated. She reaches through the crack in the door, her hand fisting in the front of my shirt. She tugs me into the minuscule room and then swiftly shuts the door behind me. She turns, offering me her back, her shoulder shrugged up to her ears.

One of the straps is twisted. Caught in the zipper that's halfway down her back.

Her bare back, without an undergarment in sight.

I stare at the collection of freckles at the base of her neck and release a breath from the depths of my soul.

She shimmies her shoulders. "Help, please."

I think I'm the one that requires help. I'm struck speechless by the bare expanse of her back. The gentle curve of it and the two dimples at the base of her spine teasing me from in between folds of rich fabric.

I want to grab both sides of the dress and pull. I want to drop to my knees and see what those indentations taste like.

"Nolan," Harriet snaps. "Fix the zipper."

The zipper. The zipper. I don't see a zipper.

"I'm—what are you—that is to say—" My jaw pops and I snap my mouth shut. I need to collect myself, but I don't know where to start. "I cannot locate the zipper," I grind out.

She peers at me over her shoulder. I drowned in the ocean once and I think I could just as easily drown in Harriet. Sink down into her and lose myself for days.

Perhaps coming into this tiny room with a half-clothed Harriet after a series of illicit dreams about her was not the best of ideas.

I underestimated the dress.

I underestimated *Harriet*.

"You said you'd help," Harriet whisper-yells, her shoulders inching up higher. One of the straps falls down the curve of her arm and I unthinkingly guide it back up.

"I'm trying to help."

"By doing . . . what, exactly? Standing there? Grunting occasionally?"

I answer with another deep sound from somewhere in the middle of my chest. "I'm strategizing."

"Strategizing," she repeats, her voice dry.

"Yes. I'm trying to figure out where to begin."

"*Begin* with the zipper," she snaps. "And go from there."

I hesitate. "Are you sure?"

"Nolan, I swear to—"

"All right, all right." I find the zipper at the very small of her back, twisted in the fabric. She shivers when I grasp it, my knuckles brushing against her skin as I carefully tug at the caught material. I ease one finger in between the dress and her spine to get a better grip and grit my teeth when my touch drifts over the curve of her ass.

"Another moment," I urge, my hand at her hip, fingers fanned wide to hold her steady. All this warm skin. The way her body bends to meet mine. I feel like I'm having a heart attack. "Almost got it."

I free the zipper with another gentle tug and it glides up smoothly, the sides of the dress coming together.

It's a perfect fit, once the material is no longer twisted.

"There," I say, letting my hands drop. I look over her shoulder at our reflection in the mirror. "Fixed."

"Thank you." She sighs, relieved.

"Not a problem," I say, distracted, letting my gaze drop to the dress and the way the deep purple material clings to her curves. The bodice is tight, the soft swells of her breasts pushed up. The skirt spills over her hips like water, gathered at one hip. She shifts on her feet and one pale thigh appears through the high slit on the side.

Christ. She looks like something carved out of marble. Like something that deserves to be worshipped.

"You're staring," she whispers.

"Can't help it," I whisper back.

Her hands flutter in front of her before she fists them in the material of the skirt.

"Is it—does it look bad?"

"Bad?" I snap my eyes back to hers. "Harriet. You're lovely."

Her hands smooth over the skirt again. "It's quite the dress," she says.

"I'm not talking about the dress."

Her head drops to the side and it takes every inch of my willpower not to gather up all her hair and expose that delicate bone at the top of her spine. The place my fingers always itch to touch. Tension leaves her body with a gentle sigh, a pleased smile replacing the distance she's been holding on to all morning.

"You didn't even see the other dresses," she says.

"I don't have to."

She ducks her head to hide the way her smile blooms, but I still see it.

"I'll have to ask if they have it in blue."

"You should stop indulging your mother."

She twists back and forth slightly as she studies her reflection, watching the skirt swish around her ankles. "I've tried that before. It didn't work out for me."

"What happened?"

Harriet's body goes still, her eyes clouding over. "It broke her heart," she says faintly. "The least I can do now is wear whatever color she picks out for me."

"Did stealing boats eventually lead to light vandalism? Perhaps a flirtation with pyromania?"

"No. Nothing as dramatic as that."

I give in to temptation and let my fingers dance through the ends of her hair. "I find it hard to believe you've ever intentionally broken anyone's heart. How'd you manage that?"

Her shoulders rise and fall, listless. Her eyes find mine in the reflection. "I followed mine."

I reclaim the horrific gold chair while Harriet changes back into the tiny tweed skirt and knee-high boots she was wearing earlier, emerging with her hair twisted back in a hastily drawn braid. She avoids my eyes as she hands over the dresses she tried on, plum-colored silk on top.

"These didn't work," she says to the sales associate who has finally deigned to reappear, her fingers trailing over the material like she's reluctant to let it go. "But thank you."

We walk out the glass double doors at the front of the shop into the bright winter afternoon sunlight, Harriet's hand shielding her eyes as she fumbles with her bag. She's only managed to get one arm of her jacket situated, the other half of her body flailing as she attempts to slip the rest of it on. I watch her struggle for a moment, amused. She looks a bit like a dog chasing her tail.

"Need help?"

"No." She spins again, trying to catch the sleeve of her jacket. "I've got it handled, thank you."

I gently grab her collar on her next rotation, guiding it around her shoulders. I reach through the sleeve and loop my fingers around her wrist, tugging until her hand pops free. Then I bend down and collect her dropped bag, and I wedge it under my arm.

She scowls at me. "I can carry that."

"I know you can. So can I." I fix her with a look. "Why are you fighting me today?"

"I'm not fighting you."

"She says, as she's fighting me."

"I'm not. I'm—" She flutters her free hand in front of her in a vague explanation, still digging around her pockets with the other. "I think I'm just tired. I've been having these weird dreams and I can't—"

She cuts herself off, fighting with her pockets now, instead of me.

"What are you looking for?" I ask. She's digging around in her coat like she'll find salvation in there. It's a good thing she's not wearing the mittens today.

"A candy cane," she whines. "I thought I put one in here earlier, but it's not—oh. Where did that come from?"

I unwrap the end of a candy cane and pop it between her lips. "I figured you'd need a fix."

She pushes it to the side of her mouth with her tongue. "Have you been carrying this around in your pocket the whole morning?"

I have six in my pocket, actually, which is ridiculous because I can summon them at will with my magic.

"Got it for free from that man dressed like Santa on the corner," I lie. "Been holding on to it."

Harriet beams at me, the end of her braid swinging over her shoulder. "Thank you."

"Don't be worrying yourself," I answer, still studying the lamp-post so I don't have to watch the way her cheeks hollow as she enjoys her candy. I'm slowly deteriorating into the worst version of myself. Perhaps this is hell, and my punishment is wanting a woman I cannot possibly have.

"We should look for clues today," I say, reluctant, "when we *travel*. Anything that sticks out or seems unusual."

"You mean, apart from all the jam." She smiles at me, her bad mood temporarily soothed by sugar. She considers me. "You think there are clues in the memories?"

I shrug. "I don't know why else we'd be watching you cut down a tree unless it was a metaphor or a hint at something bigger."

I hold out my elbow for Harriet to take. She does so without hesitation, her fingers twisting in the material of my jacket. We wander down the crooked street, red bows on the streetlights, heavy strands of garland strung between.

"There was the fancy lobby at my parent's firm, the jam making—" She holds up a finger for each of the memories we've visited.

"Your tree massacre," I add.

She laughs. "Yeah, my tree massacre. Then we somehow went to your past." She sneaks a look at me from the corner of her eye. "The day at the beach," she says carefully, like she's afraid of my reaction.

I pull in a deep breath and let it out again slowly. Now that the shock of it has worn off, it's easier to think about. Easier to bear. If I treat it like a clue instead of a crucial piece of my heart I've forgotten, it's manageable.

"I don't see a connection off the top of my head. Not besides the obvious."

"The obvious?" Harriet asks.

I nudge her shoulder with mine, turning on the street that leads to the Crow's Nest. It sits at the bottom of the cobblestone like a beacon—like one of the gingerbread houses Harriet loves so much—the windows glowing gold against the sun dipping in the sky.

"You stole a boat when we were in that fancy lobby," I tell her. "I was once a fisherman."

A laugh bursts out of Harriet. "*That's* the connection you've come up with?"

"I don't see you connecting any dots."

She shifts her candy cane to the other side of her mouth, thoughtful. "I don't think it has anything to do with my memories at all. I think—I think it might have something to do with me, and the shop, and the collection of odds and ends we have there. The memories are just your magic doing what your magic does."

She mentioned this before. "You believe there's something in your possession at the shop that's holding me here."

"More or less. I think it's possible there are clues in the past, but—" She rolls her lips together, thinking. "But I'm a collector of very old things. And you're—"

"A very old thing." I laugh, finishing her thought. "Clever."

She squeezes my arm through my jacket. "That's not what I was going to say."

I pat her hand and continue guiding her down the street. "And yet, it's true."

"It's just—who knows what's in my shop? We keep an inventory, sure, but I'm always finding nooks and crannies where my aunt Matilda shoved things. There could be something hidden in there that's connected to you. It's like an interdimensional scavenger hunt."

I consider it. "Is *interdimensional* the correct word?"

"Transtemporal?"

"Possibly."

It seems like too obvious an answer, but I suppose it's worth investigating. A hope to cling to, when I've had so few.

"I don't think I owned anything that I was passionate about. Certainly nothing that would keep me floating in a state of purgatory, waiting for its eventual return."

"Your boat?" she asks.

I arch an eyebrow. "Do you have a boat at the shop?"

She smiles. "No. Though it's an idea to consider." We continue walking down the street, bells ringing from the Santa on the corner with the fake white beard. It's hanging crooked today, the end of it discolored by what must have been a rogue jelly doughnut.

"Maybe you don't remember what it is. You've forgotten things before," Harriet offers as I toss a coin in his shiny red bucket.

"Aye. I have."

She eases closer. "Maybe something will jog your memory, then. Maybe these trips to the past are exactly that. We just have to keep our eyes and ears open."

Easier said than done, when my eyes and ears seem to be fixed solely on Harriet. "An adventure."

Harriet smiles at me. "I like the sound of that." We slow to a stop at the entrance of the Crow's Nest, light from the trees in the window bathing everything in a warm glow. The sun melts into the water over the harbor, the sky cotton-candy pink.

These are the nights I loved best when I was out on the water. When the whole world seems to hush, waiting for that last bit of sunlight.

Harriet reaches for the door handle. An ornate, gold thing, shaped like a lion's paw.

"And for the record," she says, her smile edging into something sly. "I happen to like very old things."

Chapter Seventeen

Harriet

"Are you looking for something in particular?" I call from behind the counter, twisting back and forth on my stool.

Nolan ignores me, sorting through a tray of buttons in the middle of the store like he's diffusing a bomb, nearly bent in half as he examines each one individually.

"You picked buttons." I rest my chin in my hand, watching him. "You really think the key to your salvation is in a button?"

He could have started with the books along the back wall. Maybe some of the mismatched artwork hanging by the windows, but no. He insisted on studying a borderline useless collection of old buttons.

Nolan frowns down at the tray, sifting through the contents. "I wore a lot of jackets in my time."

"A lot of jackets," I repeat.

"Perhaps I lost a button from one."

I wait for him to crack a smile, but he just keeps sifting through the buttons. He picks up an amber one, squints at it as he holds it to the light, then places it back with the others.

"Nolan." I straighten against the counter, settling my hands flat against it. "Do you think it's possible you're afraid of visiting the past?"

The scratch of the buttons against the bottom of the tray abruptly stops. "Pardon?"

I push my hair back, toying with the top of the birdcage music box I still haven't moved from the counter. I trace over one of the intricate vines, feeling the wear in the metal. There's comfort in holding these well-loved things. In knowing someone else has, too. It always makes me feel less alone. More connected.

I choose my words carefully. "Our last trip to the past ended . . . poorly for you. Are you afraid to visit the past again, because you think we might end up in yours?"

I've been waiting for Nolan to use his magic all day. But every time I say I'm ready to go, he comes up with another excuse. First, he insisted on joining dress shopping. Then, he suggested carry-out from Paula's for lunch. Now he's looking at buttons.

He snorts, dismissive. "I'm not afraid."

"Okay."

"I'm not," he says again, looking up from his little treasure chest. His eyes burn midnight blue in the low light of the stained glass lamps. Night presses in on the other side of the windows. The whole day has gotten away from us.

"All right," I say easily. "Forget I said anything."

The muscle in his jaw pops. "Are you calling me a coward, Harriet York?"

For some reason, the way he says my full name makes my entire body flush hot. I press the insides of my wrists together. "No. I'm not, Nolan—"

I hesitate. I don't know his last name.

"Callahan," he says roughly, his accent licking along the edges.

"I am not calling you a coward, Nolan Callahan."

His eyes flash and he abandons the tray, slinking closer to the counter. I feel like a mouse caught under the paw of a cat. A particularly stupid tropical bird, watching the approach of an apex predator. I smooth out my sweater as he sidles up to the counter, both of his hands curling over the edge.

"I like that," he grinds out.

"What?" I ask. "The button tray? If you really want to go wild, I can show you the door knobs."

"No, not the button tray." His eyes are fixed somewhere around my mouth. "I liked the way you said my name. I haven't heard my full name in—" He exhales. "A very long time."

Goose bumps prickle my arms. "I like saying it," I manage, voice faint. The stool squeaks beneath me.

"Good." A dimple flashes in his cheek. "Now, back to the original point. When you called me a coward."

I roll my eyes. "I never called you a coward."

"Are you sure?" he asks. "Because that's what I heard."

"Then you need your ears checked, old man." He drops down to one elbow against the counter and my breath backs up into my lungs. I can smell the salt on his skin from our walk along the harbor. The coffee he's been nursing for most of the afternoon. Flannel and cloves. Warm skin and whispered thoughts and hands on my hips in a dark closet. He smells *delicious*. "I thought we had a plan and you're looking at buttons. It seems like you're deliberately delaying the inevitable."

His eyes flash. "The buttons are important."

I roll my lips against my smile. "Sure."

"Even small things can be important."

I don't even know what we're talking about anymore. "Okay."

The counter is the only thing between us. His arms are planted on either side of my own, his body loose and lazy. The air around us feels like it's vibrating. His magic, maybe. Or maybe just him.

This morning when I woke up, I resolved to pack all these feelings away. But now, faced with him, after spending an entire afternoon together—

It's impossible. I like how he makes me feel. I like the hazy mix of affection and anticipation. I like the way he looks at me and I like the way he touches me.

I can't pack anything away. I don't want to.

Nolan's eyes search my face, calculating.

"Give me your hand," he finally says.

"What?"

"Your hand," he says again, the eyebrow with the scar through it jumping up his forehead. "Give it to me."

With everyone else on the planet, I always do exactly what is asked of me. I take great pleasure in fulfilling expectations. In exceeding them.

But something about Nolan makes me want to push.

"Say please," I breathe.

A delighted grin tugs at the edges of his mouth. His hair falls over his forehead and his tongue drags along the inside of his cheek. He takes his time tracing the lines of my face, his gaze turning hungry, lingering on my mouth.

Do something, I think. *Touch me. Kiss me. Damn the consequences. Stop holding back. Give in.*

"Please, Harriet," he says, his voice low and rough. I feel it like his knuckles against the base of my spine in that dressing room. His nose against my throat at the ice-skating rink. I shiver as he holds out his hand between us, palm up. "Take my hand and let me prove a point."

I tuck my hand into his and the world spins away.

Chapter Eighteen

Harriet

The pull is instantaneous, his magic flaring hot around us. The music box on the counter tips over as we're torn away, twisting and tumbling through time. The hand not holding mine settles on my hip as I clench my eyes against the force of it, his fingers spread wide, edging up beneath the hem of my sweater to the bare skin beneath. I make a shaky sound that's swallowed up by a dull roar as he traces a slow path against my hip bone. Magic and motion and his bare skin against mine. It lights up my body from the inside, a shower of golden sparks cascading over my shoulders like fireflies.

We slow to a stop. I keep my eyes shut tight. Nolan shifts in front of me, his arm around my shoulders, scooping me closer. He holds me there, tucked within the shelter of his body.

"Harriet," he says.

I'm still trying to get my bearings, my nose buried against the front of his shirt.

"Harriet," he says again, urgency in his voice.

I open my eyes. We're behind the counter at the Crow's Nest.

I look around, frowning. "Did we travel . . . ten minutes into my past?"

Nolan looks back toward his button tray. "I'm not certain."

"I think we just hopped the counter."

He gives me a look.

"What?" I ask. "That's the only thing different."

"My magic wouldn't have felt like that if I merely jumped the counter, Harriet."

That's a fair point. I open my mouth for another useless explanation when two voices near the back of the shop catch my attention. One a rough scratch, like she's been crying. The other light and comforting. It's a voice that reminds me of hot sticky buns, fresh from the oven. The windows open over the water and humid, salty air. Cool hands against my cheeks.

I back away from the counter, my hip bumping against a Christmas ornament display. The ornaments don't move at all despite the force, staying eerily silent on the shelf. We moved this display a year ago—farther into the shop—but my aunt Matilda always kept it front and center. She said she liked the way the light played with the brass.

Nolan moves with me. "What is it?"

The light coming in through the windows. The red velvet bows tied around the lamps. The garland I replaced last winter because it was threadbare in the middle, pine needles littering the floor every time I even *thought* about moving it.

"We did travel," I explain, trying to peer over the shelves toward the back. "We went back to my past. When my—" I swallow around the jagged edges that still slice me open. "When my aunt Matilda was alive."

Nolan's hand cups my elbow. "Are you all right?"

I nod jerkily. "Yes," I whisper. "She just—she meant a lot to me. I wasn't ready to say goodbye to her."

"We can leave," Nolan says. The voices from the back of the shop grow closer. My aunt Matilda laughs and tears immediately burn at the backs of my eyes. Across the bridge of my nose. It's been *so long* since I heard that sound and my memory of it is watered down at best. Like looking through a frosted window or trying to see to the bottom of a lake. I have the impression of it, but the reality, the sound of her, *here*, in this place, it's—

It's a gift. It's a gift I thought I'd lost.

"We can leave right now," Nolan says again. I shake my head, moving closer to the quiet voices in a daze.

"No," I answer, my voice hushed. It feels sacred being in this place, at this time. Magical. "I want to see."

I edge around the evergreen wardrobe with the mismatched hardware and down the aisle with the tea cozies and the hand-knit scarves. I turn left at the artwork, drifting closer. I can feel Nolan close behind me, his presence like a warm, comforting shadow. But everything disappears—the oversize painting of a sailboat on open waters, the sound of Nolan's deep, easy breathing, the sunlight drifting through colored glass, and the dust motes twirling up toward the ceiling—it all disappears when I see *them* at the end of the aisle.

Us.

My aunt Matilda with a crate in her arms and me—ten years earlier in my school uniform, tear tracks on my cheeks.

"Your parents are going to be worried sick," I hear my aunt Matilda admonish, reaching up to wipe at my face. I watch as I lean into her touch, running a shaky hand beneath my nose.

"Are you kidding?" I ask, my voice warbling around a watery laugh. "They won't even notice."

Aunt Matilda's mouth fixes into a firm line, her curls pulled back in a ponytail at the base of her neck. It was rare for her to do anything at all with them, the same chaotic sweep of hair as me. But when she was working with a new shipment, she'd always tie it back.

I used to love that we had the same hair. It felt like something special, just for the two of us. Especially since my mom seemed to hate mine so much. It was always *too difficult, too messy*.

My eyes greedily eat up every detail of her standing at the end of the aisle. The festive red sweater with the wide sleeves. Her kelly green clogs and thick, gray socks. The hole in the knee of her jeans and her colorful nail polish, chipped on her ring finger, likely from digging through boxes.

It hurts, but it's the good sort of hurt. There's so much I've forgotten.

Nolan shifts next to me, worried. "Harriet—"

I hastily wipe my hand across my cheek. "'M okay. I promise." I reach behind me and find his hand, squeezing. "Trust me."

He grumbles something but he also listens, twisting his hand so our fingers are slotted together. I watch the two people at the end of the aisle, almost afraid to blink. Aunt Matilda is somewhere in her forties in this memory, gray just starting to appear at her temples. My mom ruthlessly bleached the gray out of her hair, but my aunt Matilda never bothered.

I wish she lived long enough to get more of them.

"I couldn't stay there," I hear myself say, voice thick, one sleeved fist wiping under my nose. "It was horrible."

Aunt Matilda's hands flex around the edge of the crate, ANNAPOLIS CANNING CO. printed in bright red paint on the side. I bet she found it on the side of the road somewhere and decided to bring it home. She was always collecting broken and abandoned things.

"All men are stupid, darling, but teenage boys take the cake." She rearranges the box in her arms. "Tell me what happened."

I remember this day. I took a city bus from my school in the middle of the afternoon to the Crow's Nest, silently crying in the back seat. I remember the ache in my chest. How my cheeks burned from embarrassment.

The young girl at the end of the aisle sniffles some more, shuffling her feet. Next to me, Nolan's hand tightens around mine.

"They put up mistletoe in the cafeteria. I didn't see it at first, but they made me stop, and then I did see it and—"

I press both of my sleeve-covered hands over my eyes. "I thought Tommy Hildenbrand wanted to kiss me, but he didn't. He laughed in my face and said—he said I would never be anyone's choice," I finish with a rough sob. My aunt Matilda sets the crate by her feet and wraps me in a hug. My chest aches for that young, awkward, gangly girl in her odd-fitting sweater who just wanted so badly to be loved. Who wanted to be kissed under the mistletoe by the school's most popular boy, but was embarrassed instead.

Aunt Matilda presses a kiss to the side of my head and I swear I almost feel it.

"I know it doesn't feel like it right now, but this ache will fade away," Aunt Matilda whispers. Her hands soothe up and down my back, a gentle circuit I sometimes imagine when I can't sleep. When I miss her so much it feels like I can't breathe. "You don't want your first kiss to be from some preppy douchebag, now do you?"

"No," I answer. I cling to the back of her sweater. "I guess not."

"No, you don't," she replies, rocking me back and forth. "Especially from a boy named Tommy Hildenbrand." She sways to the beat of an old Christmas song from the record player in the back. "I bet he's not even very good at it. I bet he has chapped lips."

"He probably has chapped lips," I hear myself agree with a snort.

"See? No big loss." Aunt Matilda urges me back and wipes at my cheeks. "Now. Here's what we're going to do."

I nod, my hands on her elbows, staring at her like she's the center of my universe. In a lot of ways, she was. She was the only adult in my life who showed me any affection. Who never tried to shape me into anything other than exactly myself. She saw me. She *loved* me.

It felt like the two of us against the world and when I lost her, it was just me, standing alone.

A tear slips down my cheek and I brush at it roughly with the back of my hand. Nolan shifts closer.

"I'm gonna close up early for the day and we'll go back to my place. I'll make you the potpie you like and we'll use whatever vegetables are left to throw at Tommy Hildenbrand's house." Nolan and I snort in unison. I dart my eyes to his, catching the half smile on his face. His face softens.

"Okay?" he asks.

I nod, then shift my attention back to my aunt. She's still listing out potential vandalism ideas.

"And when we're done wrapping his mailbox in toilet paper, we'll stop for ice cream. Then I'll take you home to your parents."

I watch as I frown in dismay. Aunt Matilda strokes her hands up and down my arms.

"I know," she says quietly. "I know their love for you looks different than the sort of love you want, but it doesn't mean it's not there."

"I'm not sure it's there. Not for me, anyway."

"It is, honey. I promise." She pauses, lips pressed together. "I know your mom and I have our differences, but please don't carry that with you. We made our choices. It's our fight, not yours."

I shake my head, insistent. "I don't fit."

Matilda frowns. "What do you mean?"

The younger version of myself shrugs. It's so easy, watching like this, to pretend that she's another person. But that girl is still a part of me. Her hurts are my hurts, buried deep beneath the bandages I've made for myself.

I still feel like I don't fit, but I've stopped trying to force myself into the spaces that aren't made for me. I pretend, as much as I can, that it doesn't bother me. I do my best to meet my parents' expectations with a smile on my face. But knowing I still fall woefully short, it's—it's hard for me.

"They want something different," I hear my voice whisper. "I've tried to figure out what that is, to be more like Samantha, but it's not—they don't want—"

I dissolve into more tears and Matilda tucks my face against her shoulder. She whispers something in my ear that I can't hear, but I remember the feeling. How she tried to patch all my holes with her affection. She always knew exactly what to say to make me feel strong.

I miss her *so much*.

Nolan tugs on my hand until I look at him again, frowning at what I'm sure is an impressive display of nonwaterproof mascara on my cheeks. He reaches up and wipes at my face gently, just like my aunt Matilda did.

I manage a wobbly smile. His frown deepens.

"Time to go," he says. "We don't need anything else from this memory."

But we haven't gotten anything we've come for either. If there are clues hidden here, I haven't seen them. I haven't even bothered to look. I've been too distracted.

I pull my hand from his. "A little longer," I almost beg. "Please. I just want to—"

He nods, understanding tightening his eyes. "Aye, we can stay a few minutes more. But come here," he grunts, tugging me closer. "You're too far away."

I let him pull me into his body, his arm over my shoulder and his hand spread over my collarbone. Possessive. I'm greedy for it—for the affection, the reassurance, the steady pound of his heart against my back. He rests his chin on the top of my head and I let out a grateful sigh. I feel more grounded like this, wrapped in his arms. Protected, like maybe the ground won't fall out from beneath my feet as soon as we leave this place. Like maybe I can hold on to this memory just like I'm holding on to him.

We watch my aunt and the teenage version of myself cling to each other in the melting daylight and I let myself feel every inch of the grief I so rarely indulge in. But for the first time in a long time, there's a light shimmering just beneath it. A reminder that I can remember without it hurting so bad. That I carry pieces of Aunt Matilda around with me everywhere I go. That I stand in the same place she did, every day, and I can still see her in the fingerprints she left on me.

She doesn't have to be gone. Not if I don't want to let her go.

The two women wander off, leaving Nolan and me alone in the middle of the shop. I cling to his forearm and take one shaky breath. Then another.

"Okay. I think I'm ready."

His arm tightens around me and we're spinning, spiraling, spooling away, his magic threading around my legs and anchoring around my waist. I clench my eyes shut tight, not wanting to watch as we're yanked away from this memory.

I keep my eyes closed when we land. I feel the stillness, feel the press of Nolan's fingers against my shoulder. I listen to our breathing and the quiet way he says my name, his stubble catching in my hair.

"Thank you," I whisper, my voice a rough scratch.

His grip tightens on me. "For making you cry?"

"You didn't make me cry. These are happy tears," I try to explain. "That was—you gave a piece of her back to me. You made it easier to remember." I tilt back to look at him, his arm still anchored across my chest. "Thank you," I whisper.

Nolan's eyes search mine, his face intent. He's quiet for so long, I think I've said something wrong. But then I feel it. Bright and bursting, like soap bubbles popping against my skin. Nolan's magic licks at me and dances away again, playful.

"Nolan, what—"

His hand shifts to cup the back of my head, gently guiding me until we're facing each other. He drops his forehead to mine and I grip his wrists, holding on. My heart is thundering, stomping out a beat I can't catch up with. His magic spins out around us, faster and faster. Coiling up and over. A rising tide.

I catch a flash of green out of the corner of my eye. When I turn to look, I gasp.

Tucked between the stained glass lanterns, mistletoe starts to blossom against the tin ceiling of my antiques shop. Like a living forest, hundreds of sprigs of green leaves slowly burst to life, growing larger by the second. Heavy bundles with glossy red berries push their way in between the panels. Smaller ones with shiny leaves dance down the lamps. The whole ceiling vibrates with mistletoe of all shapes and sizes while a small zipping thread of golden sparks dances between them, bouncing from leaf to leaf.

Nolan's magic, I realize.

I tear my eyes away from the ceiling and fix them on him instead, his mouth inches from mine.

"You used your magic," I whisper, delighted.

He nods, his nose brushing against mine. "I did."

"Why?"

"Because I wanted an excuse."

I barely dare to breathe. "For what?"

"For this," he says.

And then he ducks his head and kisses me.

Chapter Nineteen

Nolan

She tastes like peppermint.

Like peppermint and the first bite of a fresh orange, juice sliding over my chin. I work my mouth against hers, too hungry for the taste of her to take my time.

She keeps taking me by surprise. Even when life has been nothing but cruel to her, she keeps her chin up. She smiles through the worst of it and I can't—I can't keep myself away anymore.

I suck at her bottom lip, drag my teeth across the corner of her mouth, and kiss her like I'm trying to breathe her in. I'm out of practice and out of control, my hands trembling as I try not to take too much, too fast. But I've been lying to myself every time I see Harriet, thinking this feeling would fade if only I dedicated enough time to it. If only I were strong enough.

But I'm not strong at all, and she tastes like peppermint.

I kiss her again, my nose digging into her cheek, my hand at the small of her back, dragging her closer into me. She makes the smallest of sounds—a short exhale of surprise—and then her hand grips the front of my shirt as she kisses me back. She presses up on her toes, chasing my mouth with hers.

I can't get close enough. I can't *hold* enough.

"Nolan," she whispers, in between wet, frantic kisses. "Nolan, *please.*"

Everything below my belt twists, a heavy stone of desire sinking in my gut. I nudge her cheek with my nose and tip her chin up so I can get a better angle. Faster. Deeper. Harder. She whimpers and my magic flares hot, brushing along the back of my neck. Over my arms and somewhere in the middle of my chest.

Fuck.

I don't go slow. I am not gentle. I'm clumsy and overeager. My hunger is a physical thing, a drumbeat of desire telling me to *take, take, take.* She's soft and warm and just as impatient as I am, and I've wanted this for too long.

Her other hand finds my cheek, holding me to her, and I groan, wild, my hand dragging roughly down to grasp the curve of her ass through the material of her smart little skirt. She's always wearing the most ridiculous, impractical things. Colorful sweaters and tiny skirts. Boots that make her legs look like they go on for miles and flimsy, semi-sheer blouses that tease more than they conceal. I press my body into hers, desperate for more, and we go stumbling across the narrow space behind the counter.

Her back hits the wall and something tumbles off, clanging across the floor. But she doesn't stop and neither do I, our mouths still working frantically against each other like this is the only chance we'll get.

"More," I demand against her mouth, my hands tugging at her hips, the curve of her thigh, trying to guide her on the counter so I can have her closer. She complies without hesitation and then I'm licking into her mouth while I spread her legs wide, slotting my hips between her thighs. We're a perfect fit, her soft curves pressed up against all my sharp edges. I haven't felt anything half as good in more than a hundred years. Not in this lifetime or the one before it.

"I need—" she says, all breathy and sweet, and something shatters toward the back of the shop. My magic is singing through my blood, humming in a way I've never felt before. I sink one hand into her thick, incredible hair and *pull*.

I know exactly what she needs. I need it, too.

I pant against her neck, tugging again, my fingers twisting through her heavy curls. How many times have I imagined exactly this? Her hair spilling over my hands, my face against her throat. I scrape my teeth along her pulse and she shivers in my arms. I press my tongue to the same spot and feel the flutter of her heartbeat.

"Please," she whispers. I wrestle enough control of myself to look at her face. She tips her head back, her eyes squeezed shut as she mouths the words. *Please, please, please.*

I don't know what she's begging for, but I'll give it to her. I'll give her anything she wants.

"Harriet," I whisper against her skin, just for the pleasure of feeling her name rattle against my teeth while she wraps herself around me. She tucks both of her hands beneath the hem of my shirt, her palms firm on either side of my spine. Her nails drag up and my hips jump forward. She digs them into my shoulder blades and I almost drop to my knees.

"We should—" She cuts off on a sharp gasp when I nose the collar of her sweater to the side, dragging wet kisses along the line of her shoulder. I grip her thigh and pull it higher against my hip. "We should talk about this. I don't—I don't want—"

Awareness shudders over me. I stop and drop my forehead against her collarbone, lifting my hands from her ass to the counter on either side of her hips. I grip it tight, the weathered wood groaning beneath my hands.

"You don't want?" I ask, winded.

"I don't want this to be a pity kiss," she finishes on a gasp, her voice muffled against the fabric of my shirt.

I lean back. "Pity kiss?"

She nods, keeping her face tucked to my chest. Hidden. "Yeah, you know. Because of the whole stupid teenage boy thing."

I almost laugh. *Pity kiss.* I don't give a flying fuck about that boy and what he did or didn't do—beyond making Harriet cry.

I kissed her because I wanted to. Because I couldn't keep standing in front of her and *not* do it.

I want to see her eyes for this conversation, and selfishly, I want to know what my kisses look like burned against her mouth. I sink both of my hands into her hair and angle her face toward mine, dragging my thumb over her red and swollen lips.

They part and her tongue briefly touches my skin. I exhale a sharp sound.

"What about that kiss felt pitying to you?"

A small smile twists her mouth, then her eyes jump to the mistletoe across the ceiling. I follow her gaze to the trembling, glittering leaves. Hundreds of them, covering every tile.

"Wow," she whispers. "It's beautiful."

I make another vague sound. My magic has never done anything like that before. I have no idea how it happened. All I know is I was thinking about kissing Harriet, and . . . mistletoe.

Harriet presses her face into my hand, still gazing up at the ceiling. "Did you kiss me just because, like, ten million things of mistletoe exploded out of you?" A self-deprecating smile inches across her mouth. "Do Christmas ghosts get penalized for not upholding traditions?"

I move my hand from her jaw to the graceful line of her neck, tracing against the small bruise I worked against her skin, satisfaction burning in my chest. The leaves on the ceiling rustle with another hot flare of magic.

"I kissed you because I wanted to, Harriet," I say. Her eyes find mine. "And I'll kiss you again, if you want that. But know there won't be anything pitying or required about it. I've existed for decades. I don't do things I don't want to do."

She nods. A subtle shift of her chin to her chest. "Okay."

"Okay." I sift my fingers through her hair again. For weeks, I've tried to find reasons to touch it. I want to feel it everywhere. Brushing against my chest. Over my thighs. Tangled across my shoulder while I tuck myself against her in bed.

I clear my throat. "Though I do concede Tommy Hildenbrand is a moron of monumental proportions."

Harriet snorts, her arms looping around my waist in a loose hug. She presses her cheeks over my heart. "He is. Or he was, at least. Who knows what he's up to now."

I rest my head against hers and close my eyes while she traces a gentle circuit across my back with her hands, more of my weight leaning against her the longer she does it. She scratches at the base of my spine and I press my face into her, nuzzling into her neck. She laughs and scratches again, harder this time.

"Feels good," I slur, my mouth against her warm skin.

"Good," she says.

"No one's touched me like this in—in a very long time."

The silence stretches into a yawning, comfortable quiet. Harriet moves her hands against my skin and I relax into the pattern of it, indulging in the rare moment of stillness. I haven't felt this anchored to a place in decades.

"I think I want to kiss you again." I press the words against her skin. "Will you let me?"

Her hands stutter in their rhythm, then resume again, light and teasing.

"Yeah." She releases a deep breath, a decision made in the way her whole body relaxes against mine. She's dropped all that armor she's been holding on to and I've never felt such simultaneous relief and pressure. I want to be worthy of her trust. I want to earn it.

It's just us and the mistletoe in her tiny shop, time slipping slowly around us. If I ever got to choose to come back to a memory, I'd want it to be this one.

"Nolan?" she asks, her voice lazy and slow. "Is this a good idea?"

"This?" I ask.

She traces the line of my spine. "This," she says, her voice hushed.

I tighten my grip around her.

"I don't know," I tell her. The things I want from Harriet don't line up with the things that are inevitable. "I can't—" I swallow around a suddenly dry throat, hating the truth but knowing she deserves it. I can't lie about this.

"I can't stay," I rasp. "I can't give you a future. Even if I don't move on, you won't remember me. Not after Christmas Eve."

"No," she breathes. She tips her chin back to look at me, eyes searching mine. She catches her bottom lip between her teeth. "I'll remember you."

I gently free it with my thumb. "You won't," I correct gently.

She shakes her head. "I'm not going to forget about you. I can't." Her jaw firms. "I won't, Nolan."

"It's not up to you. It's part of our magic. Your memories will blur until they're gone completely."

"Will you remember me?" she whispers.

"Yes," I confess. "I'll remember everything."

Her face crumples. "Nolan."

"Hush." I slip my hand around the back of her neck, thumb rubbing up and down. "This is how it's meant to be."

"I don't believe that. I can't."

"It is," I say gently. "This is not something we can change."

There are forces bigger than the both of us at work. Sand is slipping through our hourglass and it doesn't matter how many handfuls I grab in an attempt to extend our time. Christmas Eve is my deadline.

Her hands press into fists against my back. "What if—"

"What?" I ask.

A sad smile tugs at her mouth. "I know I can't keep you, but—" She saws her teeth against her bottom lip, blinking up at me with her wide, coffee-colored eyes. Her heart on her sleeve and mine in my throat. "What if I hold on to you for a little while? Just until you have to go. What if we . . . pretend?"

Something in my chest fractures. "Harriet," I whisper.

"Can I just—can I have you like this? For as long as I can?"

I make a wounded sound.

"If that's not something you want, that's all right. I promise I won't make things uncomfortable for you. I'll help you get to your afterlife, just as I promised, no matter what." She sucks in a deep breath, collecting her bravery. "But if there's a part of you that wants me the way I want you, then—"

"Yes," I say quickly. "I do. Of course I do." I duck my head down quickly and catch her mouth with mine. I meant for it to be a chaste kiss—quick, reassuring—but I get distracted by the small moan that sticks in the back of her throat. I lick into her hot mouth and suck at her bottom lip, both of my hands anchored in her hair.

When I pull away, we're both breathing heavily, her hands clenched tight in the front of my shirt.

"I do want you," I say, my forehead against hers.

Harriet relaxes. "Then maybe this is what we get to have. Just this. For as long as we can. No expectations, from either of us. We won't worry about the future. We'll have our present."

"Yes," I agree, the weight on my chest doubling, a buzzing in the back of my head and in the palms of my hands. "We can have this."

I almost don't recognize the feeling, but it builds to a dull roar, vibrating everything beneath my feet. *Magic.* We're being pulled away, against my will. Harriet gasps and I reach for her just as my magic does, spinning us away before I can get a good grip on her. Her legs curl around my hips, the counter suddenly gone, and I adjust her in my arms until she's wrapped around me.

My stomach bottoms out as time yanks at us. I wasn't ready for the pull of it and neither was she, her legs scrabbling for purchase against my body.

"I've got you," I yell over the howling, holding her tighter. Flashes of images and sound blur by, her hair whipping around us.

Harriet clings to me. "Don't let go!"

"I won't."

I might as well be yelling into the void. The roar around us masks everything. I've never jumped so soon after another trip before, and I've never done it without tugging on my magic myself. It's violent and unrestrained. Rough. Demanding.

When we finally stumble to a stop, I stagger backward with Harriet in my arms, landing with a rough thud against a cabinet taller than I am.

Nothing around us moves. Nothing around us reacts.

Harriet lifts her face from my neck, blinking blearily at me. "Please tell me you didn't try to avoid a serious conversation by flinging us backward into my past."

I lower her legs from around my waist, smoothing the edges of her skirt down while I take stock of our surroundings. "Why would I want to avoid a conversation I was enjoying?" I nudge her chin with my knuckles and brush a quick kiss to her nose. Reassuring her, I hope, that I won't be in the habit of letting her down. Not if I can help it. "No, this little trip was unintentional."

"Does that happen?"

"It's never happened to me before."

A smile tugs her mouth tight. "Another anomaly."

The room we're in smells like warm brown bread and sea salt, dimly lit by the single window on the far side of the room. Limestone walls and a low, thatched roof. A candle in the middle of a small, wooden table. I can hear waves just outside. A low voice that rumbles the first few bars of a Christmas song, then abandons it.

Harriet's hand reaches for mine. "I know that voice," she says.

A tall figure ducks into the room, shirt untucked and suspender straps around his waist. It's like looking into a slightly warped mirror, my hair longer around my ears and collar than I keep it now. Messy and windswept from being out on the water.

The figure moves closer and I come face-to-face with . . . myself. The winter of 1902, give or take a couple of months. Just before my death.

"Aye," I say faintly, watching myself settle at the table, urging the candle closer. I pull a book out from under my arm and place it flat on the table, leafing through it until I find the right page. "I know it, too."

Chapter Twenty

Harriet

*O*ne Nolan in a room is distracting.

Two feel like a personal attack.

My attention is torn between the Nolan sitting at the kitchen table with a steaming bowl of soup and the Nolan leaning up against a cabinet with his arms crossed over his chest, watching his younger self with a fierce frown on his face. He seems to be handling this trip better than the last, and I wonder how much of that is because we seem to be the only ones here.

Me, Nolan, and past Nolan.

"This is the strangest day of my life," I murmur.

Nolan snorts on the other side of the room. "I know exactly what you mean."

"You doing okay?" I hedge.

He nods, an absent, faraway look on his face as he stares at the single lit candle in the window, the flame dancing in the thick, warped glass.

"Aye, I'm grand." He looks back at the man quietly eating soup at the table, a book open at his elbow. He scratches under his ear. "I'm not . . . panicked . . . like last time."

"Good." I knit my fingers together and try to study the room, but my eyes keep tripping back to the man slouched at the table. Nolan sits exactly the same way, like his body can't help but take up space. Though this version of him certainly has more interesting wardrobe choices.

"Why are you looking at me like that?" Nolan rumbles from across the room.

"I'm not looking at you. I'm looking at him."

Nolan snorts. "Semantics, Harriet." He shifts closer and traces a lazy, meandering path down my spine with his palm. "Why are you staring at *him* like that?"

Because his threadbare white shirt is unbuttoned to the middle of his chest, two thick suspender straps hanging around his waist. He looks like a period drama on steroids. My thoughts are nowhere decent, that's for sure.

"Shirt," I say under my breath. "Suspenders," I add.

A devious smile edges at his mouth, awareness making his eyes bright.

"Ah," he says.

How he manages to imbue a single syllable with so much smug knowing, I'll never understand. I reach under his arm and pinch his side.

"Shut up."

"I don't think I will." He laughs, tugging me close so I can't pinch him again. "You're affected, Harriet."

"Of course, I am." I relax against him, my arm slung low around his waist. Past Nolan flips another page in his book, breaking off a piece of his bread. "It's you."

Outside the small window, waves crash against the rocks. A bird calls from some distance away. A church bell echoes out over the water.

And Nolan sits by himself at a wooden table with just one chair, only a book for company.

My heart aches in recognition. How many mornings have I sat at my kitchen table, staring out at the water outside the window, watching the boats pass by and hoping for something different? Filling the empty space in front of me with a distraction so I don't have to feel the ache of my loneliness?

"My mam used to light a candle in the window every Christmas Eve," Nolan says next to me. He's gazing at the window again. "She said it would help guide lost sailors home for the holiday. That it was good luck." His mouth flattens into a line, his easy strokes against my back stuttering and then smoothing out again. "Sometimes when I was out on my boat, I thought I could see the flicker of it from the harbor. I'd forgotten about that."

"It's a nice tradition."

"There's so much I've forgotten," he says, his voice tight. "That day on the beach. I didn't realize how much until . . . until I felt it again. My father's laugh. The candle. This place. My *home*."

I press my cheek against his arm. "Tell me about them?"

"I'm not sure I remember."

"Try."

He releases a shaky breath and I feel the brush of his chin against the top of my head. Dull pressure, like he's pressed a kiss somewhere in my hair.

"My mother's name . . . her name was Caoimhe," he says, stilted. "She liked to sing while she cooked and she . . . knit. She'd knit misshapen sweaters for my da that he'd wear proudly out on our boat, even though . . . even though the other fishermen would take the piss out of him for it." He pauses, thinking. *Remembering.* "My da used to kiss me on the head when I left the house, even when I was grown. He thought I spent too much time out on the water."

"Did you?"

Nolan shrugs. "Probably. It never felt right to leave. There was the work, yes, but there was something else, too. I always felt a pull. Like there was something I was meant to find."

"What was it?"

"I don't know," he muses, voice light. "I died before I could find it."

"That's a shame."

He snorts a laugh. "For a number of reasons, yes."

I watch the man at the table, so like Nolan but different, too. Younger. Softer. Not yet hardened by time and disappointment.

"It's easier," he says slowly, his voice low and rough. "With you here."

Something soft and warm and glowing lights up inside me. If I had magic, I bet it would feel like this.

"What is?" I ask.

"Remembering," he says. "Everything." He turns to me, eyes crinkling at the corners. One of his dimples appears briefly, and I reach up to trace my finger over it. His face softens, and he turns his head to press a kiss against the palm of my hand.

The man at the table continues with a few shaky bars of another Christmas carol and my heart somersaults in my chest.

You're not alone, I want to tell him. *I'm right here with you.*

"You have a nice voice," I say instead. It's rough and broken-in like that book he has open on the table, the spine worn and the pages faded. It's imperfect in the way real things always are. I love it. "How can I convince you to sing to me?"

"You can't." He peers at me, consideration in the little line that appears between his eyebrows. "You're being very agreeable right now."

"Am I?"

"Mm-hmm." His fingers drift up my back again. "Maybe I should kiss you more often."

"I like to think I'm always agreeable." My cheeks burn hot. "But maybe."

Kiss me as much as you can, I beg in my head. *Kiss me until I can't possibly forget you.*

He says Christmas Eve is his deadline, that I'll forget him as soon as his magic pulls him away. But I can't lock my feelings for him away. Not anymore.

So I'm going to try something new. I'm going to live in the moment without fear of what comes next, enjoy whatever time we have together and appreciate it for what it is. I won't white-knuckle grip my expectations.

Nolan dips his head, expectant.

"You can't kiss me now." I laugh. "You're supposed to be focusing."

His nose drifts along my cheek. "I am focused."

"On the memory, Nolan."

He grunts, then straightens. "Fine. What am I supposed to be looking for?"

"I'm not entirely sure. You said you were looking for something out on the water, didn't you?" I wave my hand at the scene in front of us. "What does unfinished business look like?"

"I haven't the faintest."

My mouth twists. This memory isn't exactly awash with inspiration. He's eating soup by himself at a table while reading a book. The furniture is simple. There are no knickknacks on the counter that I can see. Just a half-eaten apple and a collection of bronze coins. A crumpled-up piece of paper and a pencil. Unless he has unfinished business with a produce stand, I really don't know what we're doing here.

"Maybe it's the book." I shift closer and tilt my head to get a better look at the title.

"Maybe it's the spoon," Nolan grumbles behind me.

I roll my eyes as I bend over past Nolan, my hand planted next to his on the table. His presence is dulled here in the past. I can't smell the salt on his skin. I can't feel the warmth of him. He turns a page and reads the first line under his breath before taking another bite of soup. I smile at the top of his head.

"Stop that," Nolan says at my shoulder.

"Stop what?"

"Making eyes at me."

I snicker. "I'm not *making eyes*." I turn my back to the man at the table and examine the walls instead. They're just as bare as the furniture. A haphazard shelf stacked with books and a windowsill with a single candle. Fishing supplies, discarded on a small table by the front door. A hat. Some sort of biscuit wrapped in a handkerchief. His boots stacked in the corner. His coat on a peg. A dented compass with a broken chain.

"There," I say, pointing at the compass. "What's that?"

Nolan snorts. "The compass?"

I nod.

"That thing never worked right. It couldn't find its way. The arrow always spun around and around, unwilling to land on a single spot, never mind actually find north." He pauses. "My dad must have got it for cheap from one of the lads at the bar. Probably a wager gone wrong."

Damn.

I move toward the crowded bookshelf. Maybe there's something there, wedged between the stacked volumes. There doesn't seem to be any sort of organization as far as I can tell, but—

"Harriet," Nolan snaps, his voice losing its playful lilt.

"I'm not making eyes!" I repeat. For someone who has lived several lifetimes, he sure can be insecure. "And if I was," I add under my breath, trailing my fingers across the spines of the books. "I'm just looking at you."

He ignores me. "Harriet," he says again, voice strained. "Come here."

I turn to look at him. His fists are clenched at his sides, sparks shooting from between his knuckles and dancing over the backs of his hands. They wrap around his strained muscles, coiling up until his arms are wrapped in thin, glittering ropes. His eyes darken, the lines of his body tense. He's vibrating, almost. Barely holding on.

His eyes close for two long seconds, then open again. Something gold blazes inside of them.

"Come to me," he says. "Right now, please."

I cross the small room to his side and he immediately reaches for me, pulling me into his chest. He holds me there, the sparks from his hands sizzling up my spine. It doesn't burn, but it's uncomfortable.

"My magic is pulling. We're going."

"Right now? But we've barely—"

"It's not willingly, Harriet. Hold on to me."

Chapter Twenty-One

Harriet

*H*e barely gets his warning out before we're picked up in a heavy, furious wind. It's rougher than the last time, cutting at my legs until I stumble. He wraps his other arm around my back and tucks his body around mine until my face is buried in his neck and both of my hands are clenched tight in his flannel. I close my eyes and hold on, my brain rattling around in my skull.

It feels like we're being pressed through an impossibly small tube. Pressure, pressure, pressure that doesn't release. It only gets thicker, heavier, until I'm gasping for breath.

And then it stops. It ends as quickly as it began, dropping us in the middle of a crowded street. I blink at the bright light around us, vaguely registering a Christmas market in Baltimore. There are small wooden booths set along a walking path. Lights crisscrossed overhead. A boat docked in the harbor, wrapped in tinsel. Somewhere close by, a group of carolers are singing a jazzed-up version of "Silent Night."

I press my palm to my forehead with a wince.

"Okay?" Nolan asks, pulling back to get a look at my face. His hand squeezes the nape of my neck. The golden ropes are gone now, his eyes back to normal. He ducks down. "Harriet. Are you all right?"

I let my hand drop from my forehead. "Why did that feel like we were being pressed through a meat grinder?"

He makes a face at the metaphor. "We jumped again." His eyes dart around our surroundings, then snap back to me. "I've never—" He winces sharply. "Something isn't right," he finishes, shaking his head once.

"Yeah. That seems to be an ongoing theme with us." I grip his elbows. "Are *you* okay?"

"A bit jumbled up, to be honest." He studies me for another minute, his body seemingly moving slower than the rest of him. He tilts to the side, then catches himself with a sharp shake of his head. I watch him come back to himself like he's breaking above water, blinking the salt out of his eyes.

He turns and looks at the crowd around us. "Do you recognize this place?"

"It's downtown Baltimore." I eye him for another second before gesturing toward a mulled wine stand constructed to look like one of those German clock-tower things. "We're at the annual German Christmas market they set up along the harbor. I haven't been in years."

I catch a flash of cherry red behind him. A familiar head of blond hair, straightened instead of curled. Past Harriet is wandering down a crowded pathway with a ceramic mug in the shape of a boot clutched between leather-clad hands, studying each craft booth with interest. My mother walks slightly behind, her arm looped through the elbow of a young man with a phone to his ear. The look on her face is . . . victorious.

"Ah," I say.

Nolan follows my attention, eyes searching.

"What do you see?"

I point at where the past version of myself has stopped in front of a booth, examining a row of tiny glass ornaments. "There."

"Where?"

I point again. "There. Right there. At the booth with the glass."

He squints to get a better look. "Is that *you*?"

"It is."

"No."

"It is," I tell him, laughing.

"Your hair," he says faintly. "What's been done to it?"

I snort. He sounds winded. *Devastated.* "I straightened it."

"Why?"

Because that's how the man on his phone two steps behind me preferred it. Brent. I met him during my first year of law school and we were dating by fall break. He was charming and electric. Charismatic. Handsome. Everyone wanted to be his friend, and he wanted *me*. Timid Harriet York and her ill-fitting sweaters, sitting in the back of the classroom with her scribbled notes while everyone else tapped away on their computers. When he gave me his attention, it felt like stepping into the sun.

When we started dating, my mother was ecstatic. Finally, I was meeting her expectations, and it was all because of someone else's interest in me. Even so, I loved having her approval. For the first time in my life, I felt seen. Truly seen and adored.

But Brent's preferences were suggestions that slowly turned into demands. He wanted me to change my hair, my clothes . . . the mismatched furniture in my tiny apartment. He wanted me to be more stylish, refined, professional. It was for my own good, he said. How would anyone take me seriously otherwise?

And me? I just wanted to be loved. All those things felt like an easy trade-off for his affection and my mother's approval. My mom adored

Brent and I adored *finally* being worthy of her attention. As one half of a whole, I suddenly found myself the recipient of all the affection she had withheld for decades. Invitations to lunch. Cocktails at the boat house. Spontaneous shopping trips for clothes that *Brent* would like. It seemed the only thing I needed to do to win my mother over was to change everything about myself.

So I did. And I ignored the paper cuts it gave my heart.

"It's easier to manage when it's straight," I deflect, watching the past version of myself try to wave Brent over. He and my mom exchange an amused eye roll. He doesn't join me at the booth.

Look at little Harriet, that look seems to say, *indulging in her whimsical nonsense.*

How long did I ignore those condescending looks? How many times did I make excuses, bending myself into whatever shape they wanted? How much of myself did I lose?

"Actually," I correct, feeling a surge of fierce protectiveness toward this past version of myself. She had no one to look out for her. Not even herself. "I hate it when it's straight. It takes forever and it makes my head look flat."

Nolan makes an offended sound. "Your head doesn't look flat."

"It does. It looks like a pancake."

Nolan is quiet next to me, observant. He watches as I pick up an ornament and hold it up to a strand of Christmas lights, delighting in the rainbows it paints over the sleeve of my sleek jacket. The past version of me laughs and Nolan shakes his head.

"I don't like it."

"I figured as much."

His attention is fixed on the other version of me, his blinks a little too slow and heavy. I frown at him.

"Nolan, are you—"

"It doesn't look like you," he continues. "It's too . . . contained."

"My hair?"

"Yes, your hair. But . . . everything else, too."

"And, what? I can't be contained?"

He shakes his head, eyes narrowed. Past me is halfway down the street now, moving farther and farther away from Brent and my mother. They don't even notice.

"No," Nolan says, matter-of-fact. "You're boundless."

"Boundless," I repeat, unimpressed.

"Aye. Boundless," he says again. "I could spend an eternity studying you and still not know what you might do next. You give so much of yourself, so freely. You're . . . wild with your attentions. Miraculous. I've seen so many lives, Harriet, but I've never seen someone live like you."

My mouth goes dry. "Me?"

His gaze slants down to me. "You," he says.

I blink up at him. No one has ever spoken about me like that before. Like I'm something to be treasured instead of something to be tossed away. *Miraculous.* I roll the word around on my tongue. It's delicious. *Special.* My cheeks burn hot. My hands tingle. It feels like I'm freefalling through the ozone, picking up speed, the edges of me catching fire.

At first I think his words have sent me into some sort of tailspin, but then Nolan's arm snaps out and bands around me. I realize it's his magic. Again. It rushes up around us with a roar, grabs me by the back of my jacket, and whips me backward. I feel like I'm at the end of a very long tether—running, running, running—then yanked to a sharp stop.

We go backward, but this time we don't settle. Our feet barely skim the ground in a new memory—a stone dock, extending out over the water, young Nolan coiling rope on the deck of a small boat—before we twist away again, landing somewhere else. A low-lit tavern, a man playing a fiddle in the corner. Nolan's father, his mouth bracketed in concern. *You're spending too much time out there, Nolan. What are you looking for?*

Away again. A little girl with wild hair, bent in half, digging through the bottom shelves of the antiques shop. Aunt Matilda, laughing. *What are you looking for?*

A lighthouse on the water, a lone figure with his elbows braced on the railing. A long, formal table. Flickering candles. A gravestone with a faded, weathered notebook. Another with a bouquet of wildflowers.

A man sitting alone at a table set for one, eating his dinner.

A woman sitting alone with her arms crossed over the back of the couch, watching the boats in the harbor.

What are you looking for?

Memories twist and braid together. Mine, his, mine again. On and on it goes until I have to squeeze my eyes shut against it, pressing myself into Nolan. He drags me closer, his arms tight around me. I can't hear what he's saying, but I can feel the vibrations of his voice, rattling through his body and into mine. I catch fragments. *Harriet* and *hold on* and *got you* and *won't let you go.*

His hand threads through my hair and he cups my neck, holding on tight.

Won't let you go, I tell myself, trying to quell the fear. *He won't let you go.*

Almost as soon as I think it, we land on solid ground. The sound rushes out in a vacuum until my legs are shaking and my ears are buzzing.

Stained glass lights. A record player in the back. Crowded shelves and a music box tipped on its side.

Time unceremoniously dumps us in the middle of the Crow's Nest, back to where we started. I stumble against the counter at my back, my stomach taking a nosedive.

"What the hell was that?" I breathe, looking over to Nolan.

But Nolan isn't looking at me. He's staring at the mistletoe on the ceiling like he's never seen it before, swaying on his feet. His face is pale, his hands clenched into fists.

"I think," he says slowly, his voice thick. "I think something is wrong."

And then he collapses to the floor.

Chapter Twenty-Two

Nolan

When I was a boy, I got the notion that I could fly.

My mam tried to dissuade me, of course, cuffing me across the back of the head and telling me to sort out the washing instead. That I could *fly* to do that, if I was so bloody eager.

But the idea stuck with me and a week or so later I attempted to jump off one of the small cliff faces in our small fishing village. I didn't fly, but I did manage to twist my knee into a right mess. I couldn't walk straight for close to a month.

I haven't thought of that memory in ages, but I'm thinking of it now, my entire body pulsing like I've hit every sharp edge on that outcrop once again.

I wake with a jolt, my throat tight and my eyes dry. My head is pounding like someone's taken a shovel directly to my temple, but there's a small, warm body nestled against mine.

Awareness drifts over me in lazy waves, ebbing closer and then further away again. Elusive.

Harriet, I think blearily, the body in front of me wiggling. The last I remember, we were spinning through time. Colors and lights and . . . too much sound. Another wave of pain crashes through my skull.

I tug Harriet closer, my hands flexing.

I hold on to her.

She's here, I try to assure myself. *She's safe.*

You didn't let go.

"Whamph—" I mumble, my mouth filled with cotton balls. I lick my lips and try again. "What happened?"

Harriet shifts, the weight of her pressing in the cradle of my hips. She stretches her legs out, then tucks them back against mine.

A gruff sound floats out of my chest. Some of my dreams have started exactly like this.

My head gives another dull throb and I moan. I'd ask if I was dead, but I already know the answer.

I rub my palm over a silk-covered hip. "Harriet?"

"I'm here," she whispers. Her voice is sleepy and slow. Rougher than usual. It eases over my shoulders and settles somewhere low in my belly, right where her body is pressed tight. "Are you back?"

I blink open my eyes and squint. Soft morning light filters in the room through a gap in the curtains. We're wrapped in a cocoon of soft flannel sheets with a thick mint green comforter on top. The sheets are cream colored with tiny bears on sleds all over. I stare at them in confusion.

I'm in Harriet's bedroom. More specifically, I am spooned against Harriet in her bed, clutching her like one of the bears printed on her sheets.

"Back?"

"You've been in and out all night."

I frown. In and out of . . . what? Consciousness? It would certainly explain the headache threatening to split my skull open.

"'M back, I think." I try to move, but I feel like I've been hit by a cargo vessel. I'm weighed down with lead, marbles rolling around in my brain.

"What happened?" I burrow down farther in the blanket nest and realize I'm missing my shirt. I shift my legs. My pants, too. "Where are my clothes?"

"I assume they're wherever mine disappeared to." Harriet eases away from me, sitting up with her shoulders pressed to the plush, green headboard. It's almost a perfect match to the pajama set she's wearing. Silky and slinky, mere scraps of fabric against her creamy skin. She tosses her hair back, watching me carefully. "What do you remember?"

My attention is caught on the delicate strap of her camisole. "What?"

"What do you remember?" she asks again, her mouth moving slowly around the words. "About last night."

Everything is thick and hazy, like trying to look through the bottom of a cloudy glass. I turn on my back in her bed with a grunt, ridiculous sheets tangled around my torso, and dig my fists into my eyes. "My magic was out of control. I tried to stop it, but I couldn't."

I remember the bone-deep panic when I tried wrapping my fist around that golden strand of magic and couldn't grab ahold of it. It grabbed ahold of me instead, curling around my arms in thick, glittering bands.

I remember spinning, flashing images. Memories from Harriet's past and mine, twisting so quickly together that they became indiscernible. Images that mirrored one another so closely that it was almost as if they were merging, occupying the same space.

I remember landing back in the Crow's Nest. A sharp pain at the very base of my skull. Tingling in the palms of my hands, and then—
Nothing.
I don't remember anything.

"Did I pass out?" I ask Harriet.

She nods, her bottom lip caught between her teeth. "You did." She reaches over and brushes her fingers across my forehead. There's a tender spot there, right above my left eyebrow. I tilt my head into her touch and her fingers shift up, dragging through my hair.

Harriet smiles. "You knocked your head pretty good against the counter. I thought I was going to have to summon some sort of spiritual healer."

"There are no spiritual healers," I explain, eyes closed. There are no doctors or nurses that take after ghosts, because ghosts don't get hurt. We're not of this world. We don't bleed. I shouldn't have been able to manage a bruise. "How did you get me back here?"

"I was able to rouse you enough to get you up off the floor, but you were—largely unaware."

Her attention drifts to her bedspread as she plucks at a loose thread. My eyes narrow in suspicion. It's not like Harriet to censor her thoughts. Not with me, anyway.

I root around for my patience, limited though it may be. "What does *largely unaware* mean?"

"You were . . . saying things."

"What sort of things?"

"You talked about my hair a lot," she says. The hair in question spills over her shoulder. "You said I had universes in my hair, whatever that means. That you wished you could wrap yourself in it like a blanket."

Okay, well. At least now I understand her hesitation.

"That's, uh . . ." *Tragic. Embarrassing. Wildly accurate.* I scratch behind my ear. "Did I say anything else?"

"You said some things about your dad. People I didn't know and places I didn't understand. Flying? Cliffs? There was a whole speech about peppermint that somehow morphed into how tired you are." Her mouth twists down in a frown and her hand finds my forearm over the blanket. She traces an absent shape there. "You asked if I had any more lemon drops and you were . . . very affectionate."

"Affectionate," I repeat.

Amber eyes meet mine and then drift away again. Her cheeks flush pink. "Yes."

"I didn't—" I tell myself to settle. "I didn't do anything inappropriate, did I? I didn't . . . make you uncomfortable?"

I am almost painfully aware of my bare skin beneath the blankets. Did I strip down? Did I force myself into her bed? I think of the way I was clinging to her when I woke up. Did I force myself on *her*?

Harriet must recognize my panic because the tension in her face eases, her touch against my forearm becoming more intentional. "No, Nolan. Whatever you're thinking, no." She shimmies down in the bed, her knee knocking against mine beneath the blankets. "You didn't do anything."

A smile brightens her face. "It was nice, actually. You were like— like a big, cuddly bear. You kept saying how much you liked my hugs. And once I got you back here and wrestled you into bed, I was too afraid to let you sleep by yourself. You seemed . . . drunk, almost? Magic drunk. I tried to help you change into something more comfortable, but you—you just sort of *whooshed* all your clothes right off." I groan as she laughs. "Except your briefs. You're still wearing those."

"Small miracles," I manage. My eyes catch on her shiny green pajamas. "And you?"

"Me?"

I nod at her top. "You said your clothes met a similar fate, but you seem to be wearing them."

"Oh." She looks down at herself and laughs. "Barely. You, ah, *whooshed* my clothes away, too, and you gave me these instead?" She plucks at the material of her top. "You said you dreamed about it."

Christ. I press my lips together and look at the ceiling. "Ah."

Harriet huffs a laugh. "I tried to take the floor, but you insisted upon sharing the bed, and well. Here we are." She pokes at my bare shoulder. "You're very clingy in your sleep, you know."

I don't know. I haven't shared my bed with anyone in quite a while besides Builín, and she's not exactly forthcoming with details.

Harriet presses the back of her hand against a yawn, one arm stretched above her head. Her tiny green shirt rises and I get a glimpse of creamy, pale skin. My little episode last night got something right, at least. She looks deliciously sleep rumpled. A pillow line on her cheek and her body loose. Lazy smiles and warm skin.

I watch her face carefully. "If I made you uncomfortable, I—"

"Nolan, stop," she cuts me off. "I already told you that you didn't. You were fine." She tucks her knees to her chest and rolls to her side. "Are you feeling better?"

I mirror her position and shove an arm under a pillow, nudging my leg forward so I'm tucked against her beneath the covers. I'll blame my episode if I have to. I still feel vaguely fuzzy, but my headache is receding to something manageable. "I am."

"Good. I was worried." She pushes her hair away from her face, then tucks her hand beneath her cheek. She looks impossibly soft here in her bed. In her ridiculous sheets and ridiculous pajamas. "Why do you think your magic—" She makes a vague gesture and puffs out her cheeks. Like an explosion.

I huff a laugh.

She smiles. "Why do you think your magic went wild?" she asks.

"I don't know. This is the longest I've ever been on assignment." The word feels clumsy on my tongue. I haven't thought of Harriet as an assignment for a while now. It's an improper label, though I wouldn't know the proper one if it slapped me across the face. She's in a category all her own, and I'm not entirely sure what to do with that.

"Maybe my magic is rebelling. Forcing my hand. It's shoving everything at us at once because of the delay."

"How many memories do you usually visit?"

"Two or three usually does the trick. It's not a particularly complicated process."

Her eyes search mine. "It's different with me."

"Aye."

In so many ways, it's different with Harriet.

I could go back to the department and ask to see Isabella again, but I'm worried it'll raise more questions. I'd like to see this through to the very end, whatever that might look like.

I'd like to have as much time with Harriet as possible.

Harriet walks her fingers up my bare arm, then down again. Greedy for her touch, I tug at the blankets, making it easier for her to touch me.

"Did you see anything helpful?" she asks. "Last night?"

I try to remember what we witnessed in the whirlwind, but all I can remember is Harriet's hair in my face, my palms pressed tight to her rib cage. I had been so afraid she would slip out of my grip. That I'd lose her in the spin of time. Everything happened so fast. "No. I was too busy panicking to be of any investigative help. You?"

She shakes her head. "I didn't see anything that could be a key to moving you forward."

Something pinches in my chest. Moving on to something different has been the driving force behind my existence for several decades, but it's hard to consider it when I'm wrapped up in sheets with tiny bears on them. With a pillow that smells like Harriet's shampoo.

I don't want to be anywhere else. I want to be right here.

She mistakes my hesitation for something else.

"Don't worry," she says quickly, nails dragging up and down my forearm. "We'll keep looking. I was really good at those hidden picture things as a kid."

"What hidden picture things?"

"The ones in the backs of magazines?" I give her a blank look. "Never mind. The point is I'm sure I can figure this out with a little bit more time."

"Aye," I agree, my voice a rough scratch. "More time."

More time.

More time.

More time.

The entirety of my existence, I've been urging time to pass. Now I desperately want it to slow down.

"We'll get back out there," she reassures me, her strokes across my arm getting longer, deeper. I shiver, tilting myself closer. Goose bumps pebble my skin.

I didn't even realize I could get goose bumps.

"Harriet."

"What?" Her touch dances higher, over my biceps, down the slope of my shoulder to the top of my chest. She inches up my neck and I press my head back into her pillow.

"What are you doing?" I ask, my voice a low rumble.

"Oh," she says. Her hand lifts. "I was just— Do you want me to stop?"

I grab her wrist and pull her hand back to my bare chest. "No."

She laughs, resuming her slow, easy pattern. "You said something last night—"

I crack one eye open, watching.

She spreads her fingers wide. My heart pounds beneath her palm. "I was rubbing your back and you were telling me how nice it felt. You said—you said no one has touched you in a hundred years."

I fight off the burn of embarrassment. It's not shameful that I crave touch when I've had so little of it. That after all this time, I enjoy Harriet's attention.

"It's been quite some time," I agree. I pause again, swallowing. "I like how it feels."

I shift on my back and the sheets tug lower against my hips. It feels brazen to do this in the soft light of morning, but my desire to feel Harriet's hands against my skin outweighs any embarrassment. Her palm eases down over my abdomen, mapping new territory.

"Okay?" she asks.

I nod. My body feels like it's coming alive under her touch, my muscles burning with impatience, my skin buzzing everywhere her touch wanders. She's not following any sort of set path. Every time I think I know where she's going next, she deviates.

She traces the stretch of skin along my side. Eases her palms over my chest. Her nails scratch across a patch of freckles and the ends of her hair drift over my neck. I make a bitten-off sound.

She laughs under her breath and taps her fingers across another thin white scar, just beneath my collarbone. "What's this from?"

"Don't remember," I tell her, my eyes still pinched shut. My cock is heavy between my legs, everything leaden and weighted. I'm grateful for the blankets piled over my lap, embarrassed her innocent touch has twisted my arousal so tight.

"And this one?"

She eases her fingers over at a spot near my hip and my back arches. I couldn't summon the memory attached to that particular scar if she put a knife to my throat and demanded it.

"I don't know," I slur, my words lazy and slow. "I don't remember much from when I was alive."

Her hair pools across my stomach. Something warm and wet brushes over my scar.

My hands fist in her comforter.

"That must be difficult for you. Not remembering."

This is difficult for me. Holding myself still for her wandering touch. Trying not to react. Trying not to embarrass myself.

I open my eyes and stare down the length of my body at her. My blood runs hot at the pretty picture she makes. She has one hand propped at my hip, the other flat on my stomach, her body hovering over mine. One of her straps has slipped from her shoulder again, caught in the crook of her elbow. I can see the swell of her breasts. The hard point of her nipples through the thin material. She's looking at me with her bottom lip between her teeth, all that blond hair spilling over her shoulders.

She holds my gaze as her hand dips lower, nails scratching through the dark trail of hair beneath my belly button.

"Can I—"

"Please," I gasp, not letting her finish her question. My hips rise beneath the blankets, chasing her touch. "Please, Harriet, I'll—"

I'd do just about anything to feel her hands on me.

She shushes me with a smile, pushing herself up. She trails a single fingertip from one hip bone to the other and I let out a pitiful, whimpering sound, dropping my head back against her pillows. She grins at me.

"I want you to be sure," she says.

"I'm sure," I mumble back, lust drunk and lost. This feels like traveling through time. Like a rope tied around my chest, pulling tight. "Don't stop."

"I won't," she promises. She finds the blankets trapped around my hips and tugs. "Lift for me," she murmurs.

I do as she asks, tilting my hips up, letting her gather the blankets. My embarrassment has evaporated, traded for anticipation instead. I don't care that I'm painfully aroused from a few innocent touches. I don't care that Harriet will see.

I *want* her to see. She deserves to know how much I crave her.

She yanks the sheets off and tosses them toward the end of the bed without looking, her hands resting against my hips. I tuck my arms beneath the pillow under my head, gripping the feathered material hard. My arms flex. The first time I ever used my magic, I felt like this. Like I was out of control.

Her eyes dart down and widen when she sees me straining at my briefs.

"Oh," she says, her tongue wetting across her bottom lip.

"Yes," I grind out. There's no hiding from it now. I could probably come from just looking at her. "My apologies," I add after another beat of heavy silence, not meaning it at all.

Harriet's eyes snap up to mine. "Your apologies?"

She dips one finger beneath my waistband and traces the delicate skin on the inside of my hip. A spot, apparently, directly connected to my cock.

"Yes."

She slips her whole hand beneath the elastic, the material stretching around her wrist. She keeps her touch deliberately away from where I want it most, her fingers brushing along the inside of my thigh. "Why are you apologizing?"

"I don't know," I moan. "It seems like the proper thing to do."

She smirks. "My hand down the front of your underwear doesn't feel like a time for proper."

Christ. I hope not. She shifts and circles her hand around my cock, her touch far too light.

It's not enough. I need more.

"Harriet. *Please*," I beg.

"Am I hurting you?"

"No." *Yes.* "Tighter. Please. Wrap your hand around me and—*yes*. Like that. I need—"

"Shh." She hushes me again and her weight shifts. She tightens her grip and the gentle amusement leaves her face as she moves her fist up and then down. I make a garbled, gasping sound. "I'm going to take care of you."

"I know you will," I say, nonsensical, too focused on the feel of her small hand drifting up and down my cock. Long, languid strokes. "You always do."

She doesn't even know how well she takes care of me. With her easy smiles and careful touches. Her too-soft heart and that smart mouth. She's made me feel more alive in a handful of weeks than I have in decades. She's lit up all of my darkest corners.

"Harder. Make it—make it rougher for me."

She makes a satisfied sound and tightens her grip. A handful of strokes and I'm already close to the edge, my hips chasing her touch, pushing into her hand. My hands find her headboard behind me, fingers gripping at the edge. The wood creaks.

I clench my eyes shut, trying to hold on to my restraint. I don't want this to end. It's too good.

"Harriet," I breathe, and she makes another low sound in response. I feel it vibrate in my bones, a heavy press of anticipation that starts where she's touching me and spirals outward. It feels like the pull of my magic but warmer. More insistent. It spreads to my chest and pulses out, thrumming in tune with the blood roaring through my body and the motion of Harriet's hand.

"I'm close," I tell her. "I'm—I'm close."

Immediately, her grip lightens. "Not yet," she whispers.

"No. Please." The pleasure recedes, a sharp ache that steals the breath from my lungs. I'm frantic, needy, reduced to a mindless, begging version of myself. I open my eyes and push myself to my elbows, watching as she yanks my briefs down farther, keeping them trapped around my thighs.

"I'm going to take care of you," Harriet says again, and before I can comprehend her intentions, her hands are bracing herself on my hips and her head is sinking over my lap. She takes me in her warm, wet mouth.

"Fuck." I moan. One shaky hand rises to sink into her hair. "I'm going to—I can't—you look—*fuck.*"

She lifts her eyes to mine and I gather up all her hair, using it to guide her tempo. She follows beautifully, moving down and then up and then down again. Her eyes don't leave mine.

"Tell me." I grunt. "Tell me I can."

She gives me permission with a slow blink as she hollows her cheeks and sucks me hard. Her tongue twists around me and—that's it. I'm done. I collapse into the pillows and fist both hands in her hair, giving in and fucking myself into her mouth roughly, pleasure roaring through me like a cyclone. She lets me do as I please, moaning around me as my orgasm grips me by the throat.

I am nothing but sensation. Heat and lust and delirium. Raw power drifts around me, sending out sparks but landing like snowflakes.

I vaguely feel her pull away, her hands still braced against my torso.

"Nolan." Harriet's voice sounds very far away. "Nolan, open your eyes."

"Can't," I pant, chest rising and falling.

Harriet snorts a laugh. She presses against my chest again. *"Look."*

I crack open my eyes with effort. The room is filled with swirling snowflakes, drifting lazily from the ceiling and landing against our bare skin. I must have lost control of my magic when I—when I lost control of myself. Golden sparks dance between the snowflakes, my magic buzzing beneath my skin. Harriet holds out her hand with a laugh, trying to catch some as they dance away. I can feel them melting against my bare chest as I blink dazedly at the ceiling. Kisses of warmth instead of bites of cold.

My magic pulses again, and more snowflakes explode from the ceiling.

"You made a snow globe," Harriet says, delighted.

I reach for her. I need her closer. She lands across my chest with a muffled *oomph*, snowflakes in her hair.

She's the most beautiful thing I've ever seen.

"No," I tell her, my magic racing almost as fast as my heart. The snowflakes pick up speed to match, flecks of gold in between. "You did."

Chapter Twenty-Three
Harriet

I'm quite pleased with myself.

I've never inspired a man to create new weather patterns before, but I suppose I've never been with a man like Nolan. His skin. His taste. The *sounds* he made. The way he moved, desperate and needy. For *me*. My touch.

I felt powerful. Intoxicated. Desired.

Nolan rolls his head against the pillows, looking at me through lazy, half-lidded eyes. Snowflakes are still drifting from the ceiling, catching in his hair before they melt. He lifts his hand and rubs his thumb at the corner of my mouth.

"I like this look on you," he rumbles, voice impossibly deep.

I duck my head against his shoulder. "I like this look on *you*," I tell him. I rest my chin against his arm and peer at his face. "You look—"

He's still wearing the remnants of his arousal—rosy cheeks, messy hair, a satisfied laziness in his intent expression. He's the most relaxed I've ever seen him, and it makes me feel like I should be wearing a medal around my neck.

"Exalted?" He blinks sleepily. His hand sifts through my hair so he can touch my neck. His favorite place. "Incandescent?"

A laugh tumbles out of me. The snowflakes pause midair and tremble, then pick up speed once more, swirling in a new pattern. "Something like that."

He grins at me, wide and beaming, so unrestrained it makes my breath catch. Nolan is so controlled with his reactions—so reserved with his affections—that this sort of smile makes me feel like I've been handed something precious. One of the treasures I keep at my store.

I reach out and gently touch one of the dimples in his cheek.

He turns his head to brush a kiss against my fingers, and something warm and molten twists low in my belly. "You should have orgasms more often if this is your reaction."

He laughs, a rumbling sound that skitters over my skin like the snowflakes that are still falling from the ceiling. "You're incredible."

Heat climbs my cheeks. I just had my mouth wrapped around him in my teddy bear–printed sheets, and his flattery is the thing that makes me blush. Unbelievable. "Again, I think that might be the orgasm talking."

His smile flickers. "Why can't you hear praise without brushing it away?"

"Because," I say, keeping my eyes on his neck instead of his face. "I just ended a century-long dry spell for you. I'm sure those endorphins are having a field day."

"Do you know what I think?"

I give him a look. "You've never once hesitated to tell me."

He gently pinches my chin, holding my attention firmly on him. "I think you don't know how to take a compliment."

"That is . . ." I consider denying it. "Probably true," I answer on a sigh instead.

His forehead creases. I don't think he expected my easy agreement. He watches me for a moment, then dips his face closer to mine, gaze focused on my mouth. "That's something we should work on, Harriet."

"Sure," I tell him, my breath hitching as his hand continues its slow descent. He spreads his fingers wide across my chest and pushes, insistent until I fall back into the pillows next to him. I land with an *oof* and Nolan props himself up on his elbow above me, his hand still lightly collared against the base of my throat, holding me still.

"We're going to start right now," he says. "With compliments."

"What?" I laugh. "We don't—"

"These pajamas," he says over me. "They drive me mental."

"That doesn't sound like a compliment."

He toys with one of the thin straps draped over my shoulder. "They've driven me to distraction since the very first night I saw them."

"Well, you're the one who put them on me last night. So, take that up with yourself, buddy."

"I don't think I will," he rumbles. He twists the strap he's investigating, guiding it over the slope of my shoulder and down to the crease of my elbow. The top of my shirt tugs down slightly, catching on the curve of my breasts. He licks his bottom lip and repeats the process on the other side, until my barely-there top is barely clinging to me.

"Your skin looks like you're glowing when you wear this color." His eyes trail over my newly exposed skin, the straps in my elbows, my hair on the pillow. "You always look like you're glowing," he adds.

I certainly feel like I could be when he looks at me like that. I wiggle in the sheets beneath him, my breath shallow.

His eyes snap to mine and hold. "You're supposed to say thank you."

"What?"

I shift, fighting the urge to cover myself. I've never been particularly comfortable with my body. The men I've been with haven't held effusive praise for my small breasts or the heavy flare of my hips. The awkward length of my long limbs or the unruly nature of my hair. The act of revealing myself has always been practical. The first step in a process that ultimately ended in lukewarm satisfaction.

But Nolan is unwrapping me like one of the colorful treats I keep in a jar on my kitchen table, heat flaring in his eyes with every new inch exposed.

"When someone gives you a compliment," he says slowly. "You're supposed to say thank you."

"Oh." I wet my lips and blink up at him. "Thank you."

He clicks his tongue. "Doesn't sound like you mean it."

"I do. I mean it."

"You'll need to be more convincing." He ducks down and presses a wet, sucking kiss to my neck. His fingers catch in my hair against the pillow. "Let's try another."

I close my eyes as he works his mouth against my skin, impatient scrapes of his teeth and short, rough sounds. It's intoxicating, *feeling* the way he's holding himself back from me. I want to push that meticulous control of his. I want him to forget whatever game he's playing and move his mouth to my breasts instead. But he's a man on a mission, focused entirely on the thrumming press of my pulse and the spot beneath my ear that makes my legs twitch wider in the sheets.

I'm hollow and hot and absolutely aching, but Nolan stays with his mouth against my neck like he's in no particular rush.

How nice for him.

"Your skin is so soft," he says an indeterminate time later, when it feels like I might climb out of my skin. My neck has never been so sensitive in my life.

"Oh," I breathe. "I use, um, lotion."

He presses another slow kiss to the delicate skin just below my pulse. "It's not the lotion that makes you soft, Harriet." His teeth catch my skin and bite. "And remember to say thank you."

"Th-thank you," I stutter, my heart giving one heavy *thump*. I reach for him, my palms sliding over warm skin, his shoulder blades flexing as he moves over me. He rumbles out an appreciative sound, then I dig my nails in the small of his back and some of his endless patience snaps.

His hand finds the front of my camisole, but this time he doesn't bother with the light, teasing touches. He tugs until the silky material pools around my waist, my nipples tightening as snowflakes land against my bare skin. Nolan pushes himself up above me so he can study his handiwork.

"Look at you," he whispers. "Beautiful."

He cups my breasts in his big hands, his thumbs finding my nipples. My back arches and he tugs my body fully beneath his.

"Say thank you, Harriet."

My lips quirk up. "Thank you, Harriet."

His eyes flick up briefly in a half-hearted eye roll, then he bends down to press a kiss right between my breasts, exactly where my heart is trying to pound its way out of my chest. He lets his forehead rest there for a moment, nuzzling, and a warm, hazy feeling cuts through the sharp burn of arousal.

"Your heart," he says against my skin. "This foolish, beautiful thing. It's been bruised, hasn't it?"

My fingers climb the ladder of his rib cage, feeling the way his chest expands and contracts with every breath. Pressure builds behind my eyes. I nod.

"But you still let it tug you forward, yeah?" He settles himself over me, one of his legs between mine. "What a gift that is. To still wish and dream and want. To find the good. To wear it on your sleeve."

"It doesn't feel like a gift." A single tear slips out of the corner of my eye, mixing with the snow that drifts around us. Nolan reaches up and wipes it away. "It feels like a curse. Like I haven't learned my lesson. Like I'm setting myself up for disappointment."

Like I'm being silly and naive, hoping things might be different. That if I'm as shiny and positive as possible, some of that might rub off on the people around me. That I can fix whatever it is inside of me that makes it so easy for me to be tossed aside. Disregarded.

Nolan shakes his head. "I don't think you understand me, Harriet. This isn't a discussion." His voice is gentle, a laugh in there somewhere. "Compliments, remember? I don't want to hear an argument. I want to hear a thank you."

I swallow hard at the lilting command whispering along the edges of his voice and something in me softens and breaks. It's a relief to hand over control. To have my role laid out so easily. To know exactly what to do.

The knot in my middle unravels, liquid heat spilling out.

"Okay," I whisper. "Thank you."

"That's right." His eyes trip a shade darker—so blue they're almost black. Still waters that run deep. "I've lived longer than any man has a right to. I don't dabble in false sincerity. Surely you know that by now."

He plucks at my nipple, twisting lightly. It occurs to me in a startling moment of clarity that if Nolan hasn't been touched in almost a century, then he hasn't done any touching either. What an honor it is to be laid out beneath him like this, bare skin and wild hair.

I relax deeper against the pillows, offering more of myself.

"Shall we try another?"

"Yes," I breathe immediately.

He grins at me, bright and boyish, and so delightfully young that I find myself smiling back. He plants both knees between my thighs and urges them wider, shifting down to tuck his hips to mine. The muscles in his arms bunch and flex, his beard scraping at my skin just before his teeth do.

"You feel——" He inhales deeply, trying to settle himself. "You feel so good. Better than any dream I've ever had." His hand palms my hip, angling it up, our bodies connecting and retreating. "So warm."

I hook my foot behind his knee, trying to pull him closer. "Thank you," I breathe.

"Can I truly have you like this?" He settles more of his weight against me. "Is this not another dream?"

"It's not a dream. I'm here, and you're here, too, and I need—I need you to—"

He hushes me, digging his hips into mine, pressing me deeper into the bed. "I won't be rushed, Harriet."

I groan.

"I thought about doing this when you wore those red pajamas," he tells me. "I thought about pulling those shorts to your ankles, going to my knees, and putting my mouth on you."

My stomach twists. "I thought you hated those pajamas."

"I do hate those pajamas," he says. "Those pajamas make me stupid. Those pajamas make me wonder what other sorts of things you have in that wardrobe of yours. And that dress." He makes a deep, rumbling sound. Something tortured with his teeth bared against me. "*Fuck*, that dress."

"What dress?"

"You know the one." He yanks my top down farther, a useless loop of silky fabric around my middle. "The dress I picked out for you. You were so lovely."

I close my eyes with a sigh. *Lovely.* He's called me that before. In a tiny dressing room with his warm breath against the back of my neck. It's just as thrilling now as it was then.

Has anyone ever looked at me and seen anything other than someone falling woefully short of expectations? *Lovely* is meant for other people. Those who are soft and glowing, held between careful hands.

"What are you supposed to say?" he rasps against my skin and the tension in my belly pulls tight, a pulse that echoes in time with my heartbeat, settling right between my spread thighs.

"Thank you," I breathe, the words bursting out of me without hesitation.

"Good, Harriet," he says and it's almost better than his mouth against me, the electric feeling those words ignite. "See? It's not so difficult, is it?"

I shake my head and he chuckles knowingly, one hand pressing between my thighs. He grinds there roughly, following the desperate motion of my hips. The sound that falls out of my mouth would be embarrassing if I wasn't so relieved at the friction.

"Lovely," he says again and I bite my lip against a whimper. "Is this what you need?"

I nod and try to spread my legs wider despite the tangle of blankets holding me immobile. My fingers release his body and tangle in my hair instead, pulling it off my sticky neck. I need something to hold on to. Something to keep from floating to the ceiling with the snowflakes.

More and more land against my skin, picking up speed as Nolan's hand keeps the heavy rhythm, tiny white crystals that tickle at my bare breasts and the heaving hollow of my stomach. The flare of my hips and my open, panting mouth. Each one feels like a kiss. Like Nolan's hands and lips are everywhere.

He tilts his head down, watching the way his hand works between us.

"More?" he asks.

"Please."

He drags his hand up my thigh, slipping it beneath the loose hem of my shorts.

"You did need this." He grunts. "*Fuck*. You're wet."

I should be embarrassed, but I'm not. Not with Nolan. He thinks I'm *lovely*.

"Yes," I tell him.

"I made you this way, didn't I? With these little touches." He fixes me with a heavy, hot look. "With my cock in your mouth."

"Yes." I hiccup a moan as he presses one finger, then two, inside me. It's like he's too impatient to wait, all his restraint snapped like a string being pulled from both ends.

"Tell me." He circles my clit with the pad of his thumb, leans down, and presses his mouth to mine in a hot, licking kiss. "Tell me how much you needed it," he says, each word accompanied with another rough thrust of his fingers.

"I did. I needed it," I babble immediately. He deserves to know. He's exactly right. He did make me this way. "I've been thinking about this, about you. I needed you to touch me. I needed you to want me."

The words spill out of my mouth, careless, twisted up in desire. I flinch as they echo around the room, dancing between the snowflakes. It's too much. Too much of the secret I've been tucking close to my heart, only peeling back to examine in the stillness between sleep and awake when consequences feel far away and dreams are within reach. My affection for Nolan has steadily been growing into something unmanageable. A balloon in the middle of my chest that I'm afraid is going to pop and leave me scattered in pieces on the floor.

I close my eyes and hold my breath, my body stiffening beneath his. Nolan slows his touch and I tuck my arm across my naked chest, feeling exposed.

I always do this. I say too much. I make it into something it's not supposed to be. I've mistaken Nolan's affection for something more, when he's made it perfectly clear from the very start that I'm an assignment. A means to an end. An end he's been waiting a very, very long time for.

It's not fair of me to lay the weight of my growing feelings across his shoulders.

"Harriet," Nolan whispers, and I twist my face to the side, hiding in my pillow. I try to close my legs but his other hand settles over my knee, pressing it back to the bed, keeping me open for him. He moves over me, his nose pressed to my temple. "Harriet," he says again, sharper this time.

"I'm sorry," I say quickly, my voice higher than usual as I try desperately not to cry. I ruined it. We were having fun and I ruined it. "I didn't mean—I'm just—"

I'm overwhelmed, I think. It's never been like this for me. Magic and heat and desire so sharp I feel like I'm slicing myself against the edge of it.

"You didn't mean it?" he asks. I shake my head, not trusting myself to speak. Maybe if we just get back to the pleasure, I'll forget the way my admission burns at the inside of my chest. I try to rock my hips against his, but Nolan holds me still, a hiss tucked against my ear. "Look at me."

I ignore him, biting my lip. Fingertips touch my chin, guiding my face to his. "Look at me," he says again, softer this time. "You needed me to want you?"

I search his face, waiting for the rug to be pulled out from under me. But there's nowhere to hide when I'm caged beneath him like this, and I nod before I can convince myself not to. Nolan might not have seen the worst of me yet, but he has seen more than most. The broken parts that I've done my best to patch up on my own.

"You needed me to *want* you," he repeats, not a question this time, his voice cracking around that word.

I shrink beneath him, tucking my chin to my chest. Tears burn behind my eyes. I'm so embarrassed.

"It's okay." I press my palms to his shoulders. "We don't have to—"

"Harriet." He bites down around the edge of my name, his voice crisp. "You misunderstand me."

"I don't—"

"We bypassed *wanting* long ago." He shakes his head. "Your pajamas and your candy canes. Your smart mouth and your big heart. All of this *hair*." He digs his fingers into it with his free hand, dull nails scratching against my scalp. "How could you possibly think—even for a second—that I wouldn't *want* you?"

"I don't know," I say, sounding winded. I'm still trying so hard not to cry. "You yell at me a lot."

He arches an eyebrow. "You tried to assault me the very first time you saw me."

"You broke into my house."

"I didn't break—" The corners of his mouth twitch in amusement. "Is this really what you want to discuss right now?"

He traces a slow path against my skin, right below my belly button. His fingers are still wet from me, my desire banked but not forgotten.

"I don't even really know what we're talking about," I breathe.

He dips his head closer to mine, his hand sliding back up my thigh. "Do I need to convince you?"

I squeeze my eyes shut tight. "No."

Two fingers find the soft heat between my legs in a rough press before he lightens his touch again. Teasing. I make a choked sound in the back of my throat.

"Okay, maybe."

I feel his grin against my jaw. "That's good, Harriet, because I intend to." He cups me fully and rolls his wrist, grinding right where I need him, the pressure delicious. I spread my legs wider and shift down in the bed, chasing his touch. "We'll start like this."

He finds the same pace without hesitation, working me right back up to the edge he had me balanced on. Except this time he doesn't stop, two fingers pressing back inside me with rough, heavy insistence. I grip the arm bracketed by my head, then dig my nails into the muscles of his biceps when it all becomes too much.

"Nolan," I whine, and a wild sound tears out of his chest. He grips my chin with his free hand and drags my lips to his, licking into my mouth.

"Next time I'll be patient," he says against my mouth when he pulls away, both of our chests heaving, his fingers still pinching my chin, making sure I can't look anywhere else except right at him while he works me toward a frenzy. His fingers move faster between my legs, like he needs it as much as I do. "I'll take my time, and I'll prove my point, and I'll hear you say my name like that over and over again. Next time, I'll take off these damned shorts and watch how well you take me." His teeth flash white as he clenches them, barely holding on to his own composure. His hips bump up against the back of his hand as he moves against me. Like he's fucking me with more than his fingers.

"I'll sink into you inch by inch and you'll be so good for me," he grinds out. "You'll say thank you. Won't you, Harriet?"

"Oh *god*," I grit out, everything within me pulling tight as I tumble over the edge, the rest of the fantasy he's weaving lost to the white noise in my head. To the messy, unpracticed way he touches me. It's not the promise of *more* but the promise of *again* that has me trembling beneath him, grabbing on to whatever I can reach.

I haven't ruined it. Not at all.

I've made it *better*.

Nolan works me through my orgasm with a low rumble of encouragement, his forehead pressed to my temple as I shiver and shake beneath him, his chest brushing against mine with every panted exhale. I keep my eyes closed and let myself feel it. How he mumbles things like *good* and *beautiful* and other words I've never, ever associated with myself.

But Nolan makes me think that maybe I could.

I smooth my palms over his shoulders, down to his wrists, and back up again as the pleasure ebbs out of me like a wave retreating from the shore. I'm suddenly exhausted, my body loose and warm.

Nolan huffs a laugh, collapsing at my side, his hand at my hip. He squeezes once. I let my hands drift over his warm skin as I wait for the next part. The part where he tells me he's only here for a little bit. That he can't make any promises. That what we just did was a mistake, and we can't do it again.

But all he does is drift his mouth along the shell of my ear, the snowflakes slowing until none remain.

"Do you believe me now?" he asks against my skin, not moving an inch. My hopeful heart leaps in my chest, even as I try to stomp down hard on it.

There's still an hourglass hanging over our heads. There are still things Nolan doesn't know. We can't ever have anything beyond this, these fleeting moments we steal for ourselves.

But it's hard to worry when Nolan rolls out of my bed, half-moons from my nails decorating the skin of his lower back, his hair standing on end. He peers at me over his shoulder and smiles at whatever look is on my face, his hand reaching out to cuff my ankle and squeeze.

"Yes," I tell him. "I believe you."

Chapter Twenty-Four
Nolan

*I*n the back corner of Harriet's antiques shop, I hold a silver platter in front of my face and study my reflection. I trace the edge of the purple bruise on my forehead I got when I smacked my head against the counter, then tilt the platter down, angling up my chin to get a look at the mark on my neck. A different sort of bruise.

I grin.

I didn't expect this morning with Harriet. I had hoped for it—in some distant part of myself that's still capable of such a thing. Waking next to her, though. Feeling the warmth of her body. Her mouth around me. The warm, wet heat between her thighs—

I drop the platter, a loud clang of metal against the hardwood floors.

"What was that?" calls Harriet from somewhere in the front of the shop.

"Nothing," I yell back with a wince, reaching for the platter and placing it back on the shelf I retrieved it from.

I've been sitting in a cozy armchair by the windows for the last hour and a half, flipping through books I've found tucked into various nooks and crannies, listening to Harriet as she shuffles around, humming to herself. Every now and again I can hear the jingle of bells from the man dressed as Santa on the corner. The laughter of children as they streak past the windows.

It's nice. Comforting. I'm supposed to be looking through inventory for anything related to my past, but the truth is, I haven't bothered to look at all. I have no desire to.

Harriet appears in the doorway. She poured herself into a pair of skintight jeans and a creamy white sweater with a big red bow before we left her house this morning. She looks like a present I want to unwrap.

"Did you find something?"

"No."

She raises an eyebrow. "Have you even been looking?"

"I have," I say, gesturing to the stack of books at my side. "During our last trip to the past, I was intent upon my book. I thought I'd start there."

"Doesn't look like you've done much starting," Harriet quips, giving me an amused look as she leans up against a shelf full of teapots shaped like various produce products. She picks up a tiny one in the shape of a cabbage and smiles at it, wiping some of the dust from the top with the edge of her sweater. I get a glimpse of the pale skin of her belly and my mouth goes dry.

I know what that skin tastes like now. I know the exact sound she makes when I drag my scruff against it.

I've been riding a high of endorphins since I left her bed. We had coffee in her small kitchen until I got distracted by the stretch of her bare thigh beneath her green shorts. Then I coaxed her onto my lap and proceeded to kiss her until she was making tiny, bitten-off sounds in my mouth, both of my hands fisted in her hair, her legs spread wide over mine.

"Anything of use?" Harriet asks, setting the cabbage pot back on the shelf. At my blank look, she laughs. "With the books, Nolan."

"Oh," I say, distracted. "No. Not quite yet."

Her head tips to the side. "Are you sure you're all right?"

"'M fine," I say. I lean forward so I can hook my finger in one of her belt loops. She so rarely wears jeans, and these look like they've been painted on. I love them.

I tug at her until she's standing between my legs. "Did you find anything?"

She cups my jaw with her hands, her thumbs easing over my cheeks. I make an embarrassing noise. Something between a rattle and a growl. Her smile pulls wider.

My magic strains and buckles in my chest.

"I haven't been looking," she murmurs.

I drop my forehead against her stomach with a sigh of relief, encouraging her to scratch her nails through my hair. My fingers flex on her hips. "That makes two of us."

"Do you want—"

"Yes," I cut her off immediately.

Her smile tips wider, her eyes crinkling at the corners. "I didn't finish my sentence."

"I don't care."

"I could say I want to go ice skating again." Her eyes shine in amusement. "I could say I want to go cut down a Christmas tree."

"Whatever you want."

I want to do whatever Harriet wants to do. Sit in silence or arrange hardware by size. Go to the little bakery down the street she seems to like so much or add more baubles to the Christmas tree. I want to keep her company, be with her with whatever time we have left.

I swallow hard. "Maybe we could—"

A startled screech echoes from the front of the store, closely followed by a crash that's much louder than my rogue silver tray. There's some vague yelling, a gasp that sounds a lot like *holy shit*. And then *what in the frankincense fuck.*

Harriet flinches, turning halfway toward the register.

"I think Sasha is here."

I grunt, tightening my hands against her.

Harriet laughs. "I should probably go see what the problem is." I don't let her go. "Since I own this place." I still don't let her go. "And she's my employee." I press my face harder against her belly. "Nolan." She laughs.

"Or," I offer, "you could stay back here with me." I nuzzle into her stomach, gratified when her breath hitches. My palms inch down over the curve of her ass and squeeze. "We could see how quiet you can be."

She hums. I let my hands play over her curves. I can feel her resistance deteriorating, the same way I could taste coffee on her tongue this morning while she sat in my lap. She sways closer.

Then something else crashes in the front of the store, accompanied by a shriek.

"Harriet! I think the mistletoe is moving!" A pause. "Related question. Where the hell did all this mistletoe come from?"

"I'll be right there!" Harriet shouts over her shoulder, untangling herself from my grip. "Be right back," she tells me. "I'm just going to—" She points over her shoulder, wincing. "I'm going to try and explain why we suddenly have about seventeen thousand boughs of mistletoe across the ceiling."

I slouch down farther in the chair, satisfied at the reminder of our kiss and the things it made my magic do. "I'm not sorry about it."

"Me either."

"Good."

Her face eases and an answering softness blooms in my chest, dancing happily with my magic. Harriet is so *good*, and it has nothing to do with the things we did to each other in her bed this morning. She makes me feel all sorts of things I have no business feeling.

"Harriet," I begin, a confession on the tip of my tongue. "I—"

Another loud noise echoes from the front of the store. "Harriet!" Sasha shouts.

"I'm coming!" she yells, whipping her way to the front with a roll of her eyes. I watch the sway of her ass in her tight jeans as she goes, all that blond hair hanging loose down her back. I drop my head against the chair, annoyed at the interruption but grateful for it, too. If I have no business feeling the things I'm feeling, then I certainly have no right to share them with Harriet. It feels selfish. She deserves better than that.

I bend and retrieve one of the books from my stack, flipping it to read the back cover. Something about a duke and an island princess. I'm intrigued. I flip through the first couple of pages in interest.

"Didn't mark you as a historical romance kind of guy," says a smooth voice from the corner by the window. I jolt in my chair and almost send the book across the room.

Isabella pushes off the shelf at her back, a sharp smile curving her mouth. Her reindeer headband has been abandoned for a single gold clip, just above her left ear. She plucks at a piece of lint at the bottom of her sweater. "You've been avoiding me."

"I'm not avoiding you." My magic sparks along my arms in warning. Isabella makes me nervous on a good day. A sudden appearance in the mortal world is not like her and I'm on high alert. "I was under the impression you were handling Reaper business."

She crosses her arms over her chest and looks up at the ceiling. Her dark eyes turn assessing, cataloging the mistletoe spread across the tiles. It somehow managed to wander all the way back here, to the farthest corner of the shop. It's probably a bad time to take pride in that.

"I did have Reaper business to attend to," she agrees slowly. Her eyes slide back to mine. "But Gideon has decided to get involved and he is more than capable of handling the situation. All office heads are to resume business as usual."

My back goes straight. "Gideon?"

While Reapers are fearsome in general, Gideon is . . . formidable. As the oldest Reaper in existence, some say he's Death himself. Cold. Malicious. Calculated. If he's in the mortal world, the situation is more fraught than Isabella is letting on.

"He *is* in charge of the Grim Reapers," Isabella says. She picks up the same teapot Harriet was studying, her lips twisted in a frown. "And while his sudden appearance after three hundred years is unprecedented, it is no longer my issue." She sets the pot back on the shelf and folds her hands together. "I'm here to talk about you."

"What about me?"

Her eyes flick up to the ceiling. The magical mistletoe shivers under her perusal. "Are you having trouble controlling your magic, Nolan?"

"Not that I'm aware of."

"Hmm." She trails one finger across the edge of an oak nightstand with a peacock painted on it, then wipes the dust away on her tailored black pants with a faint look of disgust. "Let me tell you my observations, and then you can tell me yours."

"All right," I agree reluctantly. I'd rather fling myself from the window and walk through the inlet, but I don't think that was a suggestion so much as an order.

"My receptionist tells me that you appeared in a frenzy, rambling about trips to your past and wayward dreams. Then when she appropriately suggested a different course of action, you abruptly changed your story." She takes another step closer. I press back in my chair, shoulder blades tucked tight against the plush material. "I figured I'd stop in and check on you personally, given how long it's taken you to close this case, and what greets me? Clear evidence of magical extravagance." She frowns up at the mistletoe again. "This is against the rules, Nolan."

I slide my palm against the back of my neck, squeezing. "It was involuntary."

"Involuntary," she repeats. "Is your magic rebelling, Nolan?"

"I have everything under control." At her arch look, I elaborate. "Now. I have everything under control *now*."

"You have a bruise on your forehead," she points out.

"I know. I'm—I'm handling it."

"You are not," she snaps. "You are toying with forces you do not comprehend, Nolan. Do I need to remind you about your deadline? Christmas Eve is quickly approaching. You *must* pass Harriet on to her next ghost before then."

I keep quiet.

"Let me remind you what happens if you miss it, since I can see you're not concerned. The bruise is just the start. Things will continue to change. You won't be the only one who will bear the consequences."

Dread settles like ice in my gut. My magic plucks sharply at the back of my neck. "What's that supposed to mean?"

Isabella releases a short breath, frustrated. "I've told you. Harriet was assigned to you for a reason. The decisions you make will impact the both of you."

"And what does *that* mean?"

"It means as I said."

"You haven't said anything!" I manage through clenched teeth, careful to keep my voice low so we don't attract the attention of Harriet. If Isabella is trying to coerce me into doing my job, she's found a very effective way of doing it. "Are you threatening Harriet?"

"I'm explaining what happens if you fail," Isabella replies calmly. "It's very simple. This is your job. If you don't complete your *job*, you don't move on." She tilts her head to the side, her hair a dark curtain around her face. "Though I find it very interesting that the perception of a threat against Harriet is what finally garnered such a reaction out of you. You're more attached than you should be, Nolan. Do you deny it?"

I drag both hands through my hair. "I—" The words stick and hold. I want to deny it. I feel like I probably should, given how this conversation is going. But I can't. I've been orbiting around Harriet since that very first night. Since she threw a television remote at my head and accused me of an entire suite of misdemeanors. Amusement and intrigue have slowly melted into affection, and after this morning, I'm afraid it's only the tip of the iceberg.

"No," I finally say. "I don't deny it."

Isabella's face turns thoughtful, lips twisted down in a frown. "I appreciate that you're not lying about it."

"Perhaps I should," I grumble back, studying the floor instead of bearing the full weight of her judgment. I can hear low voices at the front of the store, Harriet and Sasha as they move things around. My stomach sinks. "If you intend to reassign me, at least let me say goodbye first."

I don't want to be another person who disappoints Harriet. Who leaves her behind. If I'm being forced out, I'd like the opportunity to explain things. To tell her—

Well. I'm not sure what I would tell her.

"She won't remember you when you go," Isabella says.

I stare hard at my hands. "For me, then."

I would like to have the opportunity to say goodbye.

Isabella rolls her eyes. "You can stop with the sad boy martyr act, Nolan. I won't be replacing you." My head snaps up. "You have your orders. You've received your warning. I expect you to adjust course accordingly. Channel your inner captain, or whatever it is you used to be."

"That's it?"

"Were you expecting something more dramatic?" She inspects her nails. "Shall I conjure some hellfire, just for shits and giggles?"

"*Shits and giggles*," I repeat slowly. "I didn't know you knew that expression."

She grins at me. A shiver works its way down my spine. She really is terrifying. "I do enjoy these little phrases the mortals use." She gestures at me, a dismissive flick of her wrist. "Now, come. Show me the girl."

My relief trades places with trepidation. I'm going to have an ulcer by the end of this conversation. "Pardon?"

"Surely you didn't think I'd come for a visit and not want to see her?" She tucks her hair neatly behind her ears and starts moving toward the front of the store without me. "I'd like to meet the woman you're so hell-bent on breaking all our rules for."

Chapter Twenty-Five
Harriet

ou're telling me you got all of this"—Sasha gestures to the mistletoe on the ceiling—"on discount from some Podunk tree farm down on the coast."

"It's not a Podunk tree farm. They actually run a pretty robust operation," I explain. "They have an ice-skating rink. And a bakery."

Sasha looks at me over her glasses. "Okay. You're telling me you got ten thousand pounds of mistletoe from a *robust operation*. And you installed all of it yourself. On the one day I wasn't working this week."

I scoop up another handful of rogue buttons and deposit them in a vase in the shape of a hedgehog. The original glass jar met its demise on the hardwood floor of the shop courtesy of Sasha's oversize handbag. She had been too busy staring open-mouthed at the ceiling to realize she was destroying half of our seasonal inventory.

"Yes," I say. "That's what I'm telling you. Three times now."

"Don't cop a tone." Her eyes narrow. "What did you use?"

"For what?"

"For the mistletoe." Sasha points aggressively at the ceiling. "What did you use to install the mistletoe?"

"Oh. Um." I study it, squinting. "String? And some . . . double-sided tape?"

Sasha makes a disbelieving sound. "There must be a whole lot of holiday magic up there with it, if double-sided tape is doing the job."

Yes, I want to tell her. *There is a lot of holiday magic up there. I kissed a Ghost of Christmas Past and it made his magic spin out of control. I'm supposed to be helping him move on, but instead I'm getting attached. These choices are going to hurt me when he eventually disappears, but I don't know how to stop. I don't want to.*

I collect another handful of buttons, dropping them in the back of a prickly little hedgehog. Leave it to me to develop feelings for the most unavailable man in the room.

I've been floating on a cloud since we left my house this morning, but now my feet are slowly returning to the ground. Nolan is a *ghost*. He's going to *disappear*. And I'm indulging in these feelings like I've got nothing to lose.

But I can't turn off the hopeful piece of my heart. It's as much a part of me as breathing.

The string of unanswered text messages on my phone is proof enough of that.

I texted my sister this morning while Nolan was in my shower, wanting to talk to *someone* about everything bumbling around in my chest. But all I got in response was a quick: in a meeting, will text you later.

She never texted me later.

I'm not sure why I keep bothering.

Because you hate feeling like you did something wrong, the little voice at the back of my head whispers. *Because you miss your sister.*

I used to think the only place I fit was with Samantha. That if we could make it through our turbulent childhood—if we could with-stand my mother constantly pitting us against each other—then we'd always have a place to land. But I think that's gone now, destroyed with a handful of caustic words tossed out in the heat of the moment.

Maybe I don't fit anywhere. Maybe I'm not supposed to.

Maybe my best bet is a ghost with a guilt complex.

I laugh, slightly hysterical, and reach for some of the buttons that skittered under a coffee table. Sasha gives me a concerned look.

"Are you all right?"

"I'm fine," I tell her. Out of my depth and almost out of time, but I'm fine.

She gives me another critical look, but she doesn't push. It's one of my favorite things about Sasha. She can hold me accountable when I need it, but she gives me the space to live in my own delusional little bubble when I need that, too.

Her attention flits back to the ceiling. "Do we need to, like, water them?" She stands so she can touch a bundle, mesmerized. "They're so pretty."

They are pretty. Pretty and achingly romantic. Every inch of my store is covered. Even the storage closet has mistletoe clustered around the busted bulb I haven't bothered to replace.

"Holy *shit*," Sasha whispers, backing up a step and almost sending another glass object crashing to the floor. I grip her by her sweater and pull her away from the crystal, but she's pressing up on her toes, peering over my shoulder. "They're pretty, too." She starts slapping at the top of my head, trying to get me to turn. "Have they been here the entire time?"

I swat her hand away and stand, brushing at the backs of my jeans, my hedgehog vase of buttons clutched protectively in one arm. "What are you talking about? Stop hitting me."

"Them," she explains with a whisper, shaking me back and forth. "Look at *them*."

I finally look. Nolan is walking up one of the aisles, a heavy frown fixed on his handsome face. It's a sharp departure from the cuddly, affectionate man I left at the back of the shop, but no less striking. He's rolling his thermal up over his forearms with sharp, practiced movements, but his frustration only makes him look more windswept, in a sexy pirate sort of way.

The source of his discontent appears behind him in the form of the most beautiful woman I've ever seen.

"Whoa," I whisper and Sasha makes a sound in agreement. Nolan looks like he's trying to communicate something with his face, but I'm too focused on the stunning brunette slightly behind him to do much decoding.

"Harriet," Nolan says. "I'd like to introduce you to Isabella."

Isabella. Isabella. *Isabella*. A tiny bell of recognition rings somewhere in the back of my mind. She extends a graceful hand in my direction while my brain tries to work it out, her sharp eyes flicking down my body and up again. I struggle not to fidget with the edge of my sweater. She has shiny, dark hair. Elegant brows. Cheekbones for days. She looks like she could kill a man with the heel of her shoe and then slurp up their soul with a silly straw.

I'm unironically wearing a giant red bow and I'm pretty sure I have a dust bunny clinging to my ass.

I grab her hand with mine, feeling stupid and small and more than a little intimidated.

"Nice to meet you," I squeak out, the second half of the statement twisting up like a question.

"It's really not," Nolan mutters under his breath.

A catlike grin flirts with the edges of Isabella's mouth. "I'd like to say Nolan has told me all about you, but he's been . . . tight-lipped."

Like Nolan, her voice is tinged with a light accent. Her eyes cut in his direction. "I can see now he has his reasons."

I drop her hand and cling to my vase. I look to Nolan for reassurance, but he's got his nose pinched between thumb and forefinger. I blink back to Isabella. "What do you mean?"

A throaty laugh tumbles out of her. "You have a bruise on your neck."

I remember Nolan's rough growl this morning, his mouth working against my skin while his fingers twisted between my legs. I saw the purple half-moon below my ear in the hallway mirror when we were leaving and did my best to hastily hide it with drugstore concealer.

Not well enough, apparently.

I clap my hand over the mark, my face flushing hot. "Curling iron," I explain.

Sasha, Isabella, and Nolan all give me varying looks of disbelief. Isabella's is tinged with amusement, Nolan's with faint satisfaction.

Sasha looks like she's about to pull a bag of popcorn out of her purse and use one of the sideboard tables as her bench seat.

"You don't curl your hair," Sasha whispers out of the side of her mouth.

My blush deepens. "Thanks for that, Sash."

"Is it a hickey?" she continues.

"Sasha."

"He has one, too. Did you make out with this hot man?" She pauses, shifting incrementally closer. "He has a mustache," she says, scandalized. Maybe a little enamored.

I know the feeling.

My lips twitch. "Sasha. Please."

"Who are these people? Where did they come from? Have they been here the whole time? Are they customers? Did they bring the mistletoe? They don't look like they work at a farm."

Isabella's smile grows into something predatory.

"I didn't see them come in," Sasha adds. "How did they get in?"

She shouldn't have seen them at all. Or, if she did, she shouldn't have *noticed* them.

More things are changing, then. Isabella and Nolan exchange a knowing look.

"I see what you mean," Isabella says to Nolan. Her gaze flicks between Sasha and me. "This is an unusual situation."

Nolan releases a long-suffering sigh. "I told you," he says to her under his breath. He looks at me and his lips quirk in reassurance. "Everything is fine," he says. "Isabella is just checking in on our mutual ... project."

The pieces slowly slot themselves into place. Isabella, Nolan's boss from the afterlife. The one he needed to check in with when everything started going off the rails.

She settles her attention on me with a sly smile. I shiver.

Sasha nudges me with her elbow.

"Oh. This is Sasha. She helps me run the store." The four of us stand there, awkward and silent. "Maybe she could show you around a little bit? Are you interested in anything?"

"I saw what I came for," Isabella says, her gaze unwavering. She shifts her attention to the counter behind me, cluttered with various items. "Though I wouldn't mind looking around a little bit. I'm intrigued by your collection."

"Is that necessary?" Nolan asks, sounding like he's standing at the very edge of his patience. He gives me a weary look. I shrug.

"I don't mind," I offer. No way she's worse than New Balance guy. I give Isabella a shy smile. "Let me know if you see anything you'd like to know more about."

She moves toward a shelf full of snow globes I set out for the holiday season. As she crosses the room, I'm seized by the sudden, irrational urge to defend Nolan. I don't know why she's here, but I have my guesses. Nolan doesn't deserve to suffer for my own indecision.

"Nolan's been great," I blurt out, my pulse fluttering like butterfly wings. "He's been very . . . helpful during this process. So if he's—if he's in trouble or something, he—um. He shouldn't be."

Sasha frowns at me. "What in the hell are you talking about? Who is Nolan?"

Nolan lifts his hand. "I am."

"What process?" Sasha hisses, ignoring him. She looks at the ceiling again, suspicious. "Is this about the mistletoe? Are you dealing illegal Christmas greenery now?"

I hush her, holding eye contact with Isabella even though it makes me feel like there's a tuning fork vibrating up the length of my spine. "So if he violated some sort of rule with the—with the *greenery*, I just want to assure you that he's, um, doing everything he can to deliver the final, uh, product on time."

The final product being my reckoning, I guess.

Isabella's face softens, her eyes losing some of their fire and brimstone. "All is well, Ms. York," she reassures me. "I'm assured Nolan will deliver the project on time." Her eyes narrow as she shoots him a look. A warning. "He always does."

Nolan shoves his hands in his pockets, rocking back on his heels. "Always a pleasure to see you, Isabella."

"And you have always been a terrible liar." She laughs. She looks at me. "Harriet. This has been very illuminating. Thank you."

"You're welcome," I respond. "I think."

She wanders back to the snow globe shelf as I exchange another heavy look with Nolan. I'm not exactly sure what's happened in this conversation. He takes a half-step closer, hand reaching for my elbow.

"Harriet," he says. "Can we—"

"Where did you find this?" Isabella snaps. She's crouched in front of the lowest shelf, cradling the dainty birdcage music box I never bothered to return to its proper place. Instead I put it with the snow globes, hoping someone might stop by the festive display and pick it up.

"The music box?"

She nods wordlessly, standing slowly. She reaches for the knob underneath without looking, twisting it easily three times to the right. The light, tinkling melody winds its way around the room, and her eyes flutter shut, body swaying.

"I think my aunt got it at a flea market in Baltimore," I offer, though Isabella doesn't seem to be listening. "It's usually mostly nonsense and garbage, but sometimes you can find good stuff if you spend the proper time looking."

"A flea market," she whispers, her hard edges melting away and revealing something soft beneath. She traces the bird. "My father gave me one just like this when I was a girl. Voliere de la Cour," she whispers. She lifts her head and presses it to her chest. "How much do you want for it?"

"You can have it," I offer, hoping it might earn me a little goodwill with the tiny, terrifying boss of the spirits. Maybe some for Nolan, too.

Her dark eyes turn assessing. "Are you sure?"

"Of course. It's no problem." Nolan makes a low sound of protest. I ignore it. "We have some gold paper I really like. I could wrap it up for you, if you wanted?"

"Harriet," Nolan interrupts. "You don't have to."

"Why not? She obviously likes it."

"So do you."

"Not like that," I say.

Isabella stands at the register with the music box cradled in her hands, oblivious to the conversation happening around her. She only has eyes for the small metal bird and the precious box beneath. It's the same way my aunt Matilda used to look at boxes that arrived at the doorstep of the Crow's Nest. That very first look, when she cracked open the cardboard, dust motes spiraling out and old, faded things settling in. She knew the value of the trinkets inside exceeded anything anyone could pay with money. She knew there were memories attached.

She honored that.

The melody stops and Isabella immediately winds it again, the first note slightly out of tune.

Nolan drags a hand through his hair, jaw clenched tight. "You don't need to do things to make other people happy." He moves closer, ducking his head. "Don't be a steamroll, Harriet."

I laugh. "A steamroll?"

"You are almost stubbornly self-sacrificing." He huffs. My smile fades. "I wish you'd assert yourself more."

The hit lands somewhere in my softest spot.

I wish you'd assert yourself. Toughen up, Harriet, it's not a big deal. Why are you crying? Come on, Harriet. You're acting like a child.

It's the same sentiment I've heard more or less for the past two decades, and heat climbs my cheeks. Nolan pales, his face immediately falling into something apologetic. "I just meant you don't have to give up the things you enjoy for the contentment of others."

"I know what you meant," I whisper. It's the best I can manage. "If you haven't noticed, this is an antiques shop. We sell antiques." And the first time I sold that specific music box, it was to an ungrateful woman in matching athleisure who thought the dove was a sparrow. In my mind, it's going to an infinitely more appreciative audience.

His lips flatten in a line. I flit my gaze to Isabella, who is watching our exchange with interest. "Sasha can wrap that up for you," I offer. "I'm going to grab a broom from the back for the rest of this—" I gesture at the odds and ends decorating the floor from Sasha's earlier mishap. I can relate deeply to the shattered crystal serving bowl, tipped on its side. "For the rest of this stuff," I finish.

Nolan tries to reach for my wrist as I move past him, but I evade his touch, wanting the sanctuary of the dark closet. It doesn't take a lot of introspection to realize why Nolan's words feel like a balloon slowly losing air, wedged beneath my rib cage.

This morning, Nolan made me feel like my softness was the most beautiful thing about me. Now he's using it as a weapon to lash out. I understand he might be tense with the sudden appearance of his boss, but I don't deserve to be on the receiving end of his frustration.

Nolan allows me exactly thirty-two seconds of reprieve in the dark before he shoulders his way in. I lean against a shelf.

"We've gotta stop meeting like this."

"I'm sorry," he says immediately. "I didn't mean for that to sound as it did."

"I know you didn't," I tell him, staring dutifully at one of my storage shelves in the dark. I rearrange a wayward can of silver polish and try to move past the boulder in my chest. "Doesn't mean it's not true, though."

Doesn't mean it didn't hurt to hear him say it.

"Harriet," he says again, and I feel the brush of his hand between my shoulder blades. He toys with one of my curls. "I let my temper get the best of me. Isabella's appearance was . . . unexpected." He pauses. "And I don't like her touching your things," he adds with a grumble.

"None of these things are mine," I say quietly. "They're things I've found. Things I've taken care of. But they don't belong to me." I can see him only in lines and shadows, his features obscured by the dark. It reminds me so much of our first meeting that my heart turns over in my chest. "Are you worried?" I ask. "About Isabella."

"I'm not entirely sure," he says. "It was a warning, I think. Or as close to a warning as Isabella gets." He makes another low, frustrated sound. "I can't see you back here."

I gesture up at the ceiling. "I still haven't replaced the light bulb."

He reaches above us without looking and twists the busted bulb. Soft, golden light immediately fills the room.

A laugh tumbles out of me. I can't help but be charmed every time he uses his magic.

"Show off."

A dimple flashes in his cheek as he drops his hand, cradling my jaw instead. He holds my face the same way Isabella was holding the music box.

"This is better," he says. "I like it better when you smile."

"Then don't make me frown." I circle my fingers around his wrist and hold on, all of my frustration unspooling at the look on his face. "Talk to me," I whisper. "Tell me what's going on."

"Isabella said—" He swallows heavily, his throat working with the motion. "Isabella said the consequences of my actions will affect the both of us."

I frown. "Okay?"

He drops his hand from my face, settling it on my hip instead. His fingers search beneath the thick material of my sweater until he reaches skin, and a relieved sigh rattles out of him. "I don't know what happens if I miss my deadline. I thought I would bear the weight of that decision alone, but now—"

Ah, I see. "You're worried it will affect me as well."

Nolan nods, hesitant.

"What are the consequences?"

"I'm not sure."

I picture rusted chains. A lone prison cell. Fire pokers. *Keeping Up with the Kardashians* on loop. "Should I . . . ask her?"

"No point to it. She's already left," he responds, tugging at my hips until he can rest his chin on the top of my head. His exhale ruffles my hair. "I didn't like her being here."

"Your worlds are crashing together." I give in to the urge to touch him the way I want. I slip my palms up the back of his shirt, scratching lightly between his shoulders. He slumps against me.

This morning seems so very far away now, a touch of the reality we've been avoiding casting storm clouds over whatever it is we're doing.

How many more times will I get to touch him like this? How many seconds can I stretch into hours before he's gone?

I tuck my forehead against his collarbone and close my eyes. I know what my consequences are. I'll forget all of *this*. Mistletoe ceilings and fathomless blue eyes that crinkle at the corners. His hands in my hair and this soft, tender feeling in my chest. I'll forget that for one perfect holiday season, I was important to someone. That someone thought I was *lovely*.

Nolan's hands tighten against the small of my back. Something like determination settles across his harsh features.

"I'm going to keep you safe," he promises me.

I nod. My mouth quirks up at the corners and I scratch lightly at the back of his neck. Right where his hair starts to curl up.

I smile at him. "I know you will."

His eyes flash as his magic pours out of him, white-capped seas and night-flecked skies instead of shimmering gold. It twists around my legs and slips over my shoulders, hugging around my middle. My hair rises around us like a curtain and his magic hops playfully through the strands, twisting the same way his fingers do. I laugh at the ticklish, bare-feet-in-the-grass feeling and Nolan's expression tumbles from something serious to hopeful. Yearning.

It's the last thing I see before it's nothing but color and sound, the tug-tug-tug of time yanking us back once more.

Chapter Twenty-Six
Nolan

We land without fanfare on the brick walkway outside of a pristine colonial home. White lights twinkle from the landscaped gardens that sit perfectly symmetrical on either side of the entryway. A brass knocker on the door in the shape of a Venetian mask watches us impassively.

Harriet snickers. "The irony of this moment is not lost on me."

"Irony?"

She gestures at the knocker. "You know. The movie? The book? The thing with the face on the door." She twists her features into something solemn and I rub my knuckles over my grin, trying to hide my amusement. Her face wasn't meant for frowning.

"I have no idea what you're talking about," I tell her.

She blinks, surprised. "You've never read Dickens?"

"*A Christmas Carol*? Aye, I've read it."

"And?"

"And I thought it was boring when I was alive. My opinion hasn't changed in death."

Harriet scoffs. "Even though it turns out everything he wrote about is true? That didn't impress you? Even a little?"

I roll my eyes. "The things he wrote in that book are hardly true, Harriet. Do I look like a flickering candle to you?"

Her lips twitch as she stares up at me. Her eyes look like they're glowing in the reflection of the lantern hanging above us, her chocolate brown a bright and brilliant gold.

Maybe she's the candle, and I'm the idiot drawn to her flame.

She's so damn beautiful.

"No," she says. "You look like a surly sailor."

"I believe the term you previously used was *rugged*."

"A rugged, surly sailor, then."

"Better."

Harriet turns to the door, studying the knocker. "I would have thought someone cracking open your entire secret universe would be more impressive," she muses.

"Secret universe?"

"The whole traveling through the past thing. Ghosts. Spirits. Whatnot. Dickens knew *something*."

"Ah. Yes. Well." I clasp my hands together. "I always preferred *The Muppet Christmas Carol* version. There's something oddly captivating about Miss Piggy."

A laugh sputters out of her. "What a surprising man you are, Nolan Callahan."

"I am a man with layers."

"Apparently."

Her amusement slowly evaporates as we linger on the front porch. I've noticed that the past gives her more time to come to terms with her memories than most. We never drop into the middle of one. We're always given enough time for Harriet to ease her way into it.

"I suppose we should go in, then," she says.

I shrug. "Or we could wait. I'm in no rush."

Her shoulders fall. "No, we should. Best to get it over with, and all that."

This memory is different. Harriet isn't curious, or delighted. She's bracing herself for something.

She knows where we are.

She knows *when* we are.

Footsteps sound behind us on the walkway and we turn to look. Past Harriet stands at the end of the walkway, her hair twisted into some sort of sleek bun. She doesn't look much younger than she is now, maybe a handful of years. But she does look more strained, stretched far too thin. Lines that bracket either side of her mouth and an uncharacteristic dullness to her amber eyes. The idiot with the phone trails two feet behind her, still preoccupied, still not paying her an ounce of an attention. Harriet turns to look at him, frowns, then lifts her hand to the brass knocker. She's wearing fitted leather gloves. A jacket that's tailored within an inch of its life. There is no pink coat. No candy canes. No color.

She knocks twice and waits, firming her shoulders. She looks like she's preparing for battle.

"Shall we keep an eye out for clues?" I suggest, watching with interest as the past version of Harriet bites at the tips of her gloves, whipping them off and cramming them in her pockets. Her nails are bare, free of the polish she favors now, and it's almost as jarring as whatever it is she's done to her hair.

"This isn't a trip for clues," Harriet says. "I know why we're here."

The door swings inward, her mother appearing in the entrance. She's older than the train memory. Older, but no less dignified. She greets her daughter with two air kisses against her cheeks, but saves her true enthusiasm for the man behind her. A wide grin splits her face as she greets him.

Next to me, Harriet sighs. "This is the night I broke my mother's heart."

Harriet slowly grows more rigid as we follow her memory through the house. By the time the past version of herself is sitting down for dinner at a table overflowing with shiny silver dishes, she looks one touch away from shattering across the floor.

Whatever it is that happened in this memory for Harriet, it isn't good. I reach for her, relieved when she doesn't pull out of my grip.

"I'm here," I tell her. "I'm right here with you."

She threads our fingers together, gripping tight. "I know," she says. She exhales a shuddering breath. "I know that," she says again, quieter, and I think, maybe, that might be the problem.

That I'm here. That I'm going to experience whatever this memory is with her.

My magic bounds another restless loop on the inside of my chest. I'm unnerved by this silent and cold version of Harriet and my magic is reacting accordingly. It settles like pins and needles against the palms of my hands. An itchy restlessness at the base of my spine.

In the formal dining room, the five people staring dutifully at their plates have barely exchanged more than pleasantries since they sat down. Cardboard cutouts of people playacting at love and family. Her mother and father sit on both ends of the table. Harriet and her sister anchor the other two sides. The . . . fopdoodle with the phone seemingly surgically attached to his hand sits to Harriet's left.

My forehead creases. "Well, this is certainly lively."

Harriet shifts on her feet but doesn't say anything. I busy myself by studying the room. Despite Harriet's insistence that this isn't a reconnaissance mission, I treat it like one all the same.

Fine china. Artfully arranged flowers. Woefully depressing and

probably heinously expensive artwork. This place looks like a mauso-
leum pretending to be a dining room.

"I think I lied to you," Harriet whispers as I'm studying some of
the carvings on the oversize chandelier hanging low over the middle
of the table. I can't figure out if it's a fox in distress, or a particularly
ugly man.

The whims of the wealthy. I'll never understand.

"How so?" I ask, distracted.

"I think I might be a bad person," she whispers.

I stare down at the top of her head with a frown. She's curled in on
herself, holding my hand with both of hers in front of her body. "Ah,
yes. A tiny woman who favors colorful sweaters and thinks candy is
one of the primary food groups. You're a proper villain, indeed."

"I'm serious, Nolan."

"As am I."

She falls silent. In front of us, the conversation moves around Harriet as she pokes at her potatoes. It's like she's another vase on the
table. No one asks her how she is. No one asks her opinion.

How sad it must have been, to be so lonely in a room full of family.

"What if your opinion of me is wrong?" Harriet asks as her mother
prattles on about something involving monograms. "What if *my*
opinion of me is wrong?"

"I don't think so."

"But what if—"

"No," I cut her off easily.

I don't know how or why she's gone from confident to discrediting
herself at every turn, but I don't like it. I don't like how she's done her
hair or the idiot at her side or the way no one seems to realize she's
sitting at the table. I do not like this memory. "Are you about to leap
across the table and stab your father with the serving fork?"

"No, but—"

"Perhaps set fire to the curtains?"

"No, but what—"

"They'd certainly deserve it. That pattern is atrocious."

A small smile cracks through her turbulent expression. Then she releases my hand. "There are things you don't know about me."

"And there are things you don't know about me." I nudge her shoulder with mine. "One overly formal dinner won't change my opinion."

Glass rattles on the table. Silence descends. I didn't realize how much the limited conversation was filling the room until it's gone entirely. My attention snaps from the Harriet next to me to the one at the table, gripping her fork with a white-knuckled grip.

She places it beside her plate, then folds her hands in her lap.

"It's the right choice for me," she says, her voice trembling at the edges. I watch as she physically gathers her courage, eyes flicking up to her mother and away again. She blows out a breath. "I know it might be a disappointment, but—"

At the head of the table, her mother laughs, caustic and sharp. "It's not a disappointment, Harriet. It is a betrayal."

Both Harriets flinch. Clearly, I missed a part of the conversation.

"What's happening right now?" I ask.

"I just told my mother I don't want to be a lawyer."

Shock grabs me by the back of my neck. I'd be less surprised if she told me she trained lions for the circus. Or competed at one of those competitive-eating competitions the town of Annapolis seems so fond of during the summer picnic months. If she told me she was crowned Queen of the Blueberry Pies, it would make more sense than this. "You were a lawyer?"

"I don't like to talk about it." She meets my eyes briefly. "I know it's hard to believe. It sounds ridiculous when I say it."

"*Ridiculous* isn't the word I'd use," I reply. Incompatible, maybe. Out of character. Harriet fits at the Crow's Nest in a way that's intrinsic. I cannot imagine her in a courtroom.

It's too small for her. Too . . . gray.

"I only worked in law for a couple years." She wraps her arms around herself, palms cupping her elbows. "This is the night I told my mother I intended to leave the role she secured for me at a prestigious firm. She, uh—she took it personally."

Personally seems a bit of an understatement as Donna York visibly seethes at the head of the table.

"Mother," her sister interjects. "Maybe we should let Harriet finish."

Her mother's face pinches, her posture rigid. "Yes, Harriet. Please continue explaining how you intend to destroy our family's reputation."

Harriet's date snorts a laugh into his closed fist. "Told you," he tells her, loud enough for the rest of the table to hear. Harriet's cheeks burn scarlet, and I want to slam his face into his dinner plate. Maybe shove the device he seems so fond of down his throat.

"Maybe you should sleep on it," Harriet's father offers, an apathetic look on his face. He doesn't look up from his green beans, continuing his dinner like this is a typical Sunday evening conversation. "This is a big decision. You haven't thought it through."

How many times has Harriet gathered the courage to speak, only to be dismissed like she never opened her mouth at all?

"Well, I'm—" Harriet pauses and swallows heavily, shifting in her seat. "As you are aware, I've been—"

"For god's sake," her mother snaps at the head of the table. "All this dithering. Spit it out."

"I don't like being a lawyer" bursts out of her. She presses her palm to her mouth like she wants nothing more than to shove the words back in. "I don't—it doesn't make me happy. I want to be happy."

"*Happy.*" Her mother sneers. "Your career isn't supposed to make you *happy*. It's supposed to build your *legacy*. The legacy of your family. Or have you forgotten?"

"I disagree," Harriet says. She fights to hold eye contact with her mother. "There are other ways to honor our family's legacy. Law hasn't been a good fit for me. You know it hasn't. Aunt Matilda says—"

Donna York goes still. Harriet's just poured kerosene over an open flame. "You've talked to Matilda about this?"

"I have." Harriet hesitates. "But it's not what you think."

"And what do I think?"

A hush descends over the table. Even her father looks invested now, his eyes darting between mother and daughter.

"She had to dig it out of me. I didn't go to her with the intention to complain. But she can tell, Mom. She can tell when I'm unhappy."

Her mother arches one elegant eyebrow. "And I can't?"

Harriet doesn't respond, but her silence is loud enough.

You can't. You haven't.

"I see." Her mother places her fork to the side and folds her hands beneath her chin. "And what did my sister have to say on this family matter?"

"I don't think—"

"No, no. I'd love to hear what Matilda has to say about this. *Matilda*," her mother says, her voice twisted with sarcasm, "who is so very adept at disregarding familial responsibilities. Did she have some tips and tricks for you? Best practices?"

Harriet looks to her sister for support, but Samantha stares down at her plate, pushing her vegetables back and forth. Harriet's boyfriend is just as useless, reclined in his seat, arms crossed over his chest with both of his eyebrows raised while he watches the conversation like a tennis match.

"We had coffee after the Jacobs case last week," Harriet begins.

"Oh, wonderful," her mother interrupts. "You've been weighing this decision for a *week*."

"Longer than a week," Harriet says, her voice wobbling. I remember an argument in a closet where I accused her of being just as rash.

How long have you been thinking about this? I squeeze her hand in mine.

"The Jacobs case was quite the fumble," her dad guffaws while he cuts a piece of his steak. Harriet's face turns crimson. "The clerks were talking about it all week."

"What happened?" I whisper to Harriet.

She shakes her head, running a trembling hand along her forehead as she watches her memory unfold. "I was nervous to present in court. I . . . threw up in a trash can midway through my opening argument. Then I kicked over the trash can."

"Oh, love." I know how much Harriet cares what others think. She must have been mortified. "That's awful."

"It was," she agrees.

At the table, Donna continues to stare down her daughter. "So? What did my sister have to say?"

Harriet looks like she wants to sink through the floor. "She told me I should think about what I really want. That I've been blindly pursuing this path for years. That maybe . . . a little time wouldn't hurt."

Donna laughs, mirthless. "Of course. Matilda has spent her entire life floating on a breeze, chasing her little whims. She's been everyone's favorite shop girl while I've had to maintain *everything*. She lives in a fairy tale, Harriet. This is real life." Her mouth pinches and she resumes eating her dinner. "This will pass. One stumble won't set you back. You just need to work harder. Apply yourself."

Harriet's eyelashes flutter against her cheeks. "I have been," she says quietly. I can tell she's trying not to cry.

"I heard she *applied herself* all over the courtroom floor," her dad snickers. Brent joins in with a loud bark of a laugh.

"I've said the same thing, Donna," he says as soon as he's done laughing at Harriet's expense. He dabs at the corner of his mouth with his napkin, shooting what I'm sure he thinks is a charming grin down the length of the table. I have no idea what Harriet is doing with a man like this.

"Brent," she whispers, shooting him a betrayed look he doesn't even notice. "You told me you understood. You said—you said you'd help me figure it out."

"I didn't say I'd help you quit." He nudges her cheek with his knuckle and she flinches. It's dismissive and juvenile, and my blood hums angrily in response. "I get it. You were embarrassed. I bet you'll feel differently in a week or two. I'll talk to Jim. See if he can put you on a new case." He pats her shoulder and my hands clench into fists at my side.

"Finally, a productive solution." Harriet's mother beams at him. "That's an excellent idea, Brent, thank you." Case closed, as far as she's concerned. She gestures with her knife. "Samantha. Tell us about the arbitration you're working on. You're the lead, yes?"

"Hank is happy with your work," Harriet's father says around a mouthful of green beans. He points his fork at her with a wink. "Good work, hotshot."

Samantha spares a fleeting glance toward Harriet. Harriet, who is staring at her plate with her bottom lip caught between her teeth, her eyes far too shiny for the dim lighting. Harriet, who has once again been treated like an inconvenient object, and not another person with thoughts and feelings and dreams.

She truly thought *this* was her great atrocity? Choosing herself?

"Thank you," Samantha says slowly, flicking her gaze away from her sister. She forces a smile. "I feel good about the opportunity."

Just like the others.

My magic pulses and golden sparks dance between my knuckles.

"Time to go," I tell Harriet.

"Not yet," she says. "There's more."

"I don't need to see more."

"I do," she says, completely defeated. She cuts a look in my direction. "And I think it's good for you, too. So you understand."

"I've already told you. I know the truth of your character."

"We'll see."

I keep my eyes on her past, watching the way she wilts at the table. So much of her is unfamiliar in this moment. Her hair, her quiet. Her overly formal clothes and the string of pearls around her neck. But I recognize the look in her eyes. The hurt she's trying desperately to hide.

But then something changes. The table explodes in laughter and Harriet's eyes flick up. She considers each person, her gaze lingering the longest on her sister. She seems to find a well of defiance.

A little girl with a boat in her hand.

"I wasn't done," she says. The table quiets. "I've made my decision, and it had nothing to do with Aunt Matilda." She swallows. Braces herself. "I won't be continuing my role at the firm. I've given them my notice."

Her mother's face pales. "You've what?"

"I've put in my notice," Harriet repeats. "I plan to conclude my role during the last week of January. This wasn't meant to be a discussion. It was a courtesy. It's done."

Donna sets down her silverware so hard, the crystal glasses rattle. "And what will you be doing instead? A retreat to the wilderness, perhaps? A séance to discover your true calling?"

Harriet firms her jaw. "I haven't decided yet."

Donna laughs. "Oh, excellent. You don't have a plan."

"I'm going to take some time to figure out what I actually want." She pauses. "I'll be spending time at the Crow's Nest, helping out Aunt Matilda in the interim."

Donna shakes her head. "Of course you are."

"I have a few calls set up with various opportunities, but I think time is the thing I need most," Harriet continues, voice clear. Confident. "I'm—I'm happy there. It's a good place for me while I figure things out."

Donna holds her daughter's gaze across the length of the table, expressionless. "What a fine punishment you've crafted for me, Harriet. Well done."

"Punishment?"

"Is that not what this is? You've chosen the cruelest blow possible to follow your so-called dreams."

Harriet blanches. "I'm not— I don't want to be cruel. This decision is about me. It has nothing to do with you."

"It has everything to do with me," she seethes. "You went to my *sister*. The one person who has always made her disappointment in me crystal clear. She hasn't deigned to speak to me in years, yet she has no trouble speaking to you. You eat up her placations, content to be perfectly ordinary when I have always pushed you for more. So, yes. This is about me. This *decision* is about me. It *is* cruel. And selfish. I didn't think you capable of either of those things, but you have, at long last, finally figured out how to exceed my expectations. Congratulations."

"I didn't—"

"I'd like for you to leave."

Harriet's face fractures. "What?"

Donna picks up her fork and resumes eating her dinner. "You've picked your side. I would like for you to get out of my house."

"I didn't pick a side. I'm doing this for me, because I—"

"I don't care who or what you're doing this for. You've made your decision and now I've made mine. Get out of my house. This is a family dinner."

Not a single person at the table says a word. Harriet is motionless, and then she's not.

She pushes back from the table, folds her napkin neatly, and drops it next to her plate. "If that's what you want."

She hesitates—hoping, I'm sure, for someone to come to her defense. But no one does, and I have to watch as Harriet moves carefully around the chairs her family occupies, seeing herself out of the room. She keeps her face angled down, but that neat bun of hers makes it easy to see her face. The way her eyes shine in the candlelight. The way she's pinching her lips together.

Harriet and her hopeful heart.

"If you cared about what I wanted, you would have talked to me instead of my *sister*," her mother says tartly, just as Harriet is about to leave the room. She tilts her head toward the hallway. "Fetch your coat on the way out."

I can't bear to watch Harriet walk out alone. I reach for her hand and tug her into me as my magic explodes in a rush, relieved for the outlet, spinning around us both and wrenching us forward through time. Harriet is wooden against me, one hand fisted in my shirt and her forehead pressed to my collarbone. I sift one hand through her hair to cup the base of her neck, the other holding tight to her hip.

But it still feels like I can't grip her close enough. I want to stop the roaring around us and find a time and place where no one knows us. Where there aren't expectations or consequences. Where there isn't a clock counting down above our heads or memories of a darker, lonelier time.

A teasing glimpse of the dark, lonely future that awaits.

I want to stop. I want to breathe. I want to hold Harriet.

We land back in the storage closet of the Crow's Nest with a dull thump. It feels like I've taken a barrel to the head. Flipped down a flight of stairs and rolled the entire way down. Time reminds me in no uncertain terms that I don't get to *want* things. I'm a slave to the role I've been assigned. There is nothing but this.

Harriet steps back, her hair curtained around her face. She won't look at me, and that's another sort of disappointment entirely.

"Harriet."

"I need to get back to the front," she says, her voice subdued. "We've been gone awhile. I'm sure Sasha is wondering where I am."

Never mind that we both know that only a handful of seconds have passed for Sasha. Harriet wipes quickly under her left eye with the back of her hand. Something in me splinters.

"Harriet," I try again, reaching for her.

"'M fine," she mumbles with a sniffle.

"Please don't cry." I grip her elbow gently, trying to tug her back into me. "I can't stand it when you cry," I confess to the top of her head.

"I'm just—I can't talk about this right now, okay? I need—I need to get back to work." She presses up on her tiptoes and brushes a quick kiss to my cheek, avoiding my eyes the entire time. "I'll see you up there."

She's gone before I can convince her to stay. I wait before I follow her, caught between coming and going. Something is holding me here in this tiny room and the light bulb above me flickers, a manifestation of my indecision. Off and then on and then off again.

I reach to fix it just as light bounces off of dented metal, pushed back on the top shelf. I step closer to inspect it. A coiled chain. A cracked face. Flecked green paint and an arrow that never points where it's supposed to.

Ice settles in my gut.

There, on the top shelf of the tiny supply closet in the very back corner of Harriet's antiques shop, is a compass with a broken chain.

A compass I've held in the palm of my hand. A compass that *should* be at the bottom of the Atlantic.

Harriet was right. She does have something that belongs to me.

Because that compass is mine.

My stomach dips the same way it used to when my boat was cresting waves I couldn't see the top of. Up and then down, down, down— tumbling over itself. I can't—I can't get a deep enough breath. I should feel elation. Relief. The key to moving forward is right in front of me, gathering dust on the back shelf of a supply closet.

But all I feel is panic. This isn't how it's supposed to be.

Hide it, my brain whispers. *Hide the compass. Harriet doesn't need to know.*

I hesitate for only a moment before I find an old crate and toss it underneath. I push it to the very back of the shelf, then step away.

I'll deal with it later. When Harriet isn't so sad and when I don't feel so out of control.

It can wait.

Tomorrow, maybe. Or the next day.

But I can't be here any longer, my control hanging on by a golden thread looped tight around my rib cage. I close my eyes, tug on that quickly fraying strand of magic, and disappear.

Chapter Twenty-Seven

Harriet

I smooth another strand of hair into place and trap it with a bobby pin, flinching when it pulls at my scalp. I hate my hair like this. I hate the bobby pins and I hate the hairspray, but I need to keep my curls restrained.

I let my hands drop by my sides, staring at my reflection in the mirror. My makeup is perfect. My hair is straightened into submission. I'm wearing the pearls I dug out of my nightstand drawer and my shawl is waiting, draped over the edge of the bed. I look exactly as I should, ready to settle into my appointed role as the accommodating daughter.

The one that defied all expectations and became an even bigger disappointment than anyone could have anticipated.

After that dinner confrontation, my mother didn't speak to me for months. Then the holiday season rolled around, and my formal invitation to the York Family Christmas Gala arrived in my mailbox. I still remember the icy feeling that settled in my gut when I opened that letter. I knew it wasn't an olive branch. It was a smoke screen.

My mother has always valued her image above all else. Of course she'd want me to continue to play my part.

And I wanted the connection, even if it is a hollow one. I've been just as guilty of enjoying the show. I've taken her scraps and thanked her for them.

My hot flush of embarrassment is familiar, but this time it's chased with a new and foreign feeling. Anger. I've turned that memory over a thousand times. It's been reserved for dead-of-night ruminations. Early-morning examination. Every unanswered text message from my sister or unacknowledged milestone from my parents, I've stared down at the blank screen of my phone and thought about that night.

Get out of my house. This is a family dinner.

I did that. I made my mother react that way. I shoved my fist through the delicate web of cracks littered across the foundation of our relationship. I knew what it would do to her when I decided I no longer wanted to work in law, and I knew how she'd feel about my aunt Matilda's role in the decision. I knew she'd see it as a betrayal, but I did it anyway.

I've shouldered the consequences without complaint because I felt like I deserved them.

But now my perspective is shifting.

What did I do that was so horrible? I changed my career path, I didn't . . . set an azalea bush on fire. I didn't fling a fork across the room and accidentally take out someone's eye.

I made an informed decision about my own future. I stood up for myself.

I know who you are, Harriet.

I pass my hands over the silky plum material of my skirt and turn halfway in the mirror, looking at the bare expanse of my back. It's the only thing about me tonight that doesn't cater to my mother's expectations. It felt like a sign last night when I saw it waiting in the window of the shop on my walk home from the Crow's Nest.

Now I'm not so sure I'm ready to boldly defy the dress code.

I could still change. I have time. I could put this dress in the back of my closet for another day and pull on the navy dress that's waiting for me on the bathroom door. I could wear this one another time. Maybe when I'm feeling a little braver.

I reach for the hanger. My fingers brush against the material just as a knock sounds at my door. I freeze.

"Harriet." Nolan's voice drifts through my glass windowpane and up the staircase. "I know you're in there. You can't keep avoiding me."

I abandon the blue dress and fist my hand in my silky skirt, turning and stepping carefully down the wooden steps.

"You've been avoiding *me*," I mutter to myself, wood creaking under my bare feet. "Mr. Disappear-from-the-Supply-Closet-Without-a-Word."

Despite the hasty departure I made from the closet, I thought Nolan would eventually join me at the front. I thought, maybe, he'd go back to his cozy armchair in the corner and I could sneak back for a glimpse of him whenever I needed it. Like a hit of dopamine, or one of my blueberry Danishes. We could look through inventory together or we could just sit in the quiet. I wanted to chase more of that light, buzzy feeling that Nolan gives me until my past was exactly that—my past.

But he left. He left without saying goodbye and I shouldn't be upset about that. I asked him for space, and he gave it to me.

I don't know why I'm holding on to my disappointment.

Because you wanted him, and he left. Because you waited behind that desk, hoping, and he never showed.

Maybe his opinion of me did change after seeing that memory, just as I feared. Maybe now that he's seen the broken-up parts of me I've been doing my best to hide, he doesn't want to keep doing . . . whatever it is we've been doing.

I'm an odd combination of overwhelmed, heartbroken, and . . .

tired, I think. I'm so tired of trying so hard to make everyone around me happy, only to fall miserably short. Time and time again.

Nolan bangs his fist against the door again, impatient as always.

"I'm coming!" I shout, sharper than I mean to. I swing the door open mid-knock and he pauses with his fist still raised, eyes widening slightly. They flick down quickly then back up, taking in the dress.

I cross my arms over my chest.

I wish I had changed. I feel stupid. Like I'm pretending to be someone I'm not. Like I'm a kid in a costume that's one size too small.

"Fucking *hell*." He shakes his head slightly, eyes fixed somewhere around my middle, his hand scrubbing roughly against the back of his head. "You went back for the dress."

I fidget. "Yeah. Last night."

"You look—" He pauses. "You look nice," he finally says, the barest hint of his accent sneaking through.

"Nice," I repeat. Disappointment curls its fingers in the middle of my chest and squeezes. It's worse than the feeling I had when I was waiting for him yesterday.

He used to think I'm *boundless* and now he thinks I'm *nice*.

"Aye. Very nice." He shoves his hands into his pockets. I look down at my feet.

"Thank you," I whisper. There's a crack at the bottom of my door, right at the hinge. Did it strain under all the pressure? Did it buckle from the weight? "If you're here to travel," I say slowly. "I'm going to need a rain check."

"What do you mean?"

I rearrange my skirt, easing out wrinkles that aren't there with my fingers. "I have somewhere to be tonight. I'm not available." I spare his face only a brief look. His jaw is clenched tight. "Maybe you could come back tomorrow? Or we could set up a time—"

His eyes snap to mine. That stubborn little line appears between his brows. "Set up a time," he says.

I nod. "Yeah. If you wanted."

One of his hands finds the door frame, curled around the wood. I let my attention settle there.

"You think I'm here out of duty?"

"Why else would you be here?"

"Why else." A short huff of a laugh puffs out of him. "Are we back to this, then?"

"This?"

"*This*," he says, closing the space between us so quickly I stumble back. He doesn't relent, towering over me. The door slams shut behind him, and his chest rises and falls with a frustrated breath. "This, Harriet. This dance where you and I pretend we're not what we are."

"And what are we?" I manage in a voice that feels too tight.

"Is there a word for what this is?" he says. His eyes hold mine. "Because if there is, I'm not familiar with it. I think about you all day long. I fall into a sleep I don't need and I dream of you. Of your smile, and your laugh, and the way your mouth tastes. The sounds you make. I wake up wondering where you are, how you're feeling, and I hope—" His eyes search mine. "I hope you're thinking of me. You make me hope, Harriet. You make me want. I am haunted by you." He slips his hand around my neck, his palm squeezing at my nape. "Do not mistake me for a good man. I am not here out of some misplaced sense of honor or duty. I demand your attention and I desire your affection."

A breath rattles out of me. "Last night, you left without a word."

"I did." He holds my gaze with his, unwavering. "I was too angry to stay."

My stomach twists. "With me?"

"No, not with you," he says simply. "With the universe, perhaps, and its dreadful sense of timing."

"What does that mean?"

"It's not important." A shadow flickers behind his eyes, but it's gone just as fast as it appeared. "I'm sorry for leaving the way I did," he rasps.

I tip my chin up. "Don't do it again."

His thumb inches up the side of my neck, tracing over my pulse point. "I won't."

I trace my palms over his shoulders. That's a fine promise to make, but we both know it's a hollow one. He could very well leave tomorrow, without a goodbye or an explanation. Our time together does not belong to us.

"I'm always apologizing to you," he says softly.

"I don't mind apologies."

"No?"

I shake my head. "Apologies mean you want to try again." I relax in his grip, staring up at him. "I do, however, have a suggestion. A way you can really put a stamp on this apology, if you're interested."

His gaze trails down to my mouth and holds. "I'm interested."

"You could kiss me," I tell him, trying to stay stern but failing miserably.

Nolan sways closer, one dark eyebrow arching high. "I certainly could."

I tip my head back, letting go of all the complications that twist knots between us. I chase the good feelings, instead. My favorite silver lining.

"Make it a good one," I whisper. "And you're forgiven."

He laughs. "I'll do my best."

Nolan certainly kisses me like he's apologizing for something. He's slow and steady and deliciously thorough, his mouth working over mine while his hand squeezes at the back of my neck. But then I make a small, bitten-off sound, whisper his name, and he loses his grip on the tether of his control.

He stops kissing me like an apology and kisses me like a demand instead. Like the exclamation point at the end of a sentence. He marches me across the foyer until my back hits the wall at the bottom of the stairs, a sharp exhale that he immediately licks from my mouth. The hand on my neck holds me still, his other hand finding the slit in my dress, rucking up the skirt, his palm against the bare expanse of my thigh.

I shiver and let my knee fall open for him.

"You went back for the dress," he says against my mouth.

"Yes."

"Good." He grunts, and his teeth find my collarbone just as his fingers brush the line of my thin, delicate underwear.

I let my head drop against the wall, giving him more room, staring at the golden paper stars strewn across my ceiling. Wallpaper scratches across my bare back and Nolan's scruff brushes against my neck. I'm nothing but sensation, pressed between him and the wall, my knee at his hip, his fingers teasing between my legs. He brushes his knuckles against the front of my underwear and I sift my fingers through his hair.

"You look like a dream," he murmurs.

"You don't dream." I laugh.

"I do. I dream of you." His voice is low. "Every time I close my eyes, it's you I see. You I want."

I want to pause time right here. No past or future or foreboding consequences hanging over our heads. Just now. Just this.

Just us.

"I want you, too," I whisper.

Nolan makes a shaky, pleased sound and presses his thumb to my chin, guiding my mouth back to his.

"I want to make a mess out of you." His teeth catch and pull at my bottom lip. "Want to twist this dress up around your hips and get on my knees."

I laugh breathlessly, my belly clenching tight. "And undo all my hard work?"

He nods. He gives me one more gentle press of his fingers between my legs and then withdraws his hand to safer territory at my hip. The heat and frenzy of the moment passes us by, my nose buried in his neck, smelling the salt that's somehow always on his skin. I close my eyes and try to memorize everything about this moment. The way I fit against him. The way his fingers tap-tap-tap across the curve of my hip, palm squeezing. The way he holds me like he doesn't want to let go.

I want to remember this. All of it.

I hope I remember.

"You make me want impossible things, Harriet."

I know the feeling. "Yeah." I sigh. "You, too."

I scratch my nails against his neck and he shivers. Somewhere on the other side of the room, the ornaments on my tree rattle. I peek over his shoulder and watch the lights twisted across the mantel of my fireplace. They glow intermittently, gaining strength before dimming again. I shift my hand against Nolan's neck so I can feel the heavy pound of his pulse. I realize with a small burst of pride that the lights dim and fade in time with his heartbeat.

I grin.

I wish I had magic, too. I bet the whole room would be dancing in the glow of my refurbished C9 bulbs.

Nolan leans back, brushing a quick kiss to the bridge of my nose. "You have your gala tonight."

I sway in place. "I do. I should have let you know yesterday, but I was—" *Frustrated. Irritated. Confused about my irritation and why some of the guilt I've carried for the better part of a decade has started melting into anger instead.* "I was distracted."

"It's your mother's gala, yes?"

"My family's, technically, but it's always been the crown jewel in her social calendar. She likes to make a big deal of it."

"I'm sure she does," he says. He studies my face. I let him, telling myself not to hide. His eyes crinkle at the corners, but the smile never reaches his mouth. "Let's talk about last night."

"What about it?"

He pulls his hand from beneath my skirt and presses his palm flat to the wall at my side instead, leaning heavily into my space. It's like I have a Nolan-shaped clove-and-flannel-scented blanket.

"Your past," he says. "That memory and your subsequent belief that you've somehow orchestrated a great betrayal worthy of the behavior you've received."

"I don't know what you want me to say."

Nolan's stern expression eases into something fond. He fingers a lock of hair that must have slipped free during our furious make-out and tucks it behind my ear. I close my eyes and drop my forehead against his chin, letting myself have this single moment, wishing I could stretch it out like taffy.

"I don't want you to say anything," he tells me, his voice rough. Like pebbles on a beach. "Not if you don't want to. I, however, have a few things I'd like to say."

I snort. "Of course you do."

He taps me lightly on the curve of my ass in admonishment and my breath leaves me in a soft *whoosh*.

"The first time I met you," he says slowly, his mouth moving against my forehead, "I thought you were insufferable."

A surprised laugh tumbles out of me. "Is this a motivational speech or—"

"Hush. I'm not done."

"Oh, good. Can't wait to hear the rest."

"I thought you were naive, petulant, and far too cheery."

I drop my face against his shoulder and rock my forehead back and forth with a laugh. Only Nolan could deliver that sentence with enough fond exasperation to light a firecracker in the middle of my chest. His big palm settles at the base of my spine.

"Then I started spending more time with you—

"Haunting me," I correct.

"—and I realized that you choose to be those things."

I push myself away from him so I can see his face. I grin. "This might be the worst pep talk I've ever had."

His eyes soften, twinkle lights reflected in the deep blue. Stars in the ocean. It's the most ethereal he's ever looked.

"You make the choice, Harriet. Every morning. You wake up and you pull on one of your colorful sweaters and you wander down a crooked street, smiling at everyone you see. You choose to be in a place where you can honor your aunt's memory. Where you're doing work that feels important and good. You made that choice. And despite the disappointments life has handed you—" The back of his hand brushes over the thin strap at my shoulder. Down over the dip of my collarbones. Across the slight valley between my breasts. He knocks lightly against the center of my chest. "Despite the disappointment and the hurt and the heartbreak, you choose to be these whimsical, colorful things."

I release a slow, shuddering breath. I want to believe him so badly, but a lifetime of shaving myself down to fit in the boxes people create for me has me wobbling on the edge of indecision. It's easier for me to think I've done something to deserve my mother's hostility because the alternative is devastating.

To be such a disappointment for no reason at all? Because my mother is intent on holding on to an old feud that started before I was born?

It's easier to withstand her venom if I've done something to earn it.

Nolan can see it. I know he can. The corners of his mouth quirk up in a sad, understanding smile.

"You're not the villain of your story." He pushes off the wall and fiddles with the sleeve of his cuff. "And you're also not going to this gala alone."

"No?"

"Frankly, I'm insulted I didn't receive an invite."

"You don't seem like a black-tie sort of guy."

"Now I'm even more insulted. I look very good in a suit, thank you very much."

"The dress code states tuxedos."

"Lord Jesus and all the saints," he mutters. "Fine."

"There will be Christmas carols. Socialization. I wanted to spare you."

He rolls his eyes. "I'm already dead, Harriet. One night of socialization is hardly an inconvenience."

"You love the dead jokes."

"Not a joke." A smile lifts one corner of his mouth. "I'm dead serious."

I groan and lean my head against his chest as he laughs, a rough rumble that I press my ear to. His arms wrap around me and squeeze, his laugh trailing off to a happy sound as my hands brush across the strong planes of his back.

"Ask me."

I dig my nose into his shirt. Asking for the things I want is still so difficult for me. Like using a torn muscle or putting weight on a bad knee.

"Want to come to my mother's gala with me? There will be fancy champagne and too-small appetizers and awkward dancing. It's going to be a miserable time."

"Yes, Harriet," he says with a hint of mischief, his mouth moving against my temple. His body tenses and relaxes, the hot flare of his magic lifting the edge of my skirt. His shirt is suddenly starchy and stiff, a bow tie nudging at my nose. I lean back so I can fully take him in, draped in formal wear.

"Of course I'll go." His eyes crinkle in amusement as he adjusts his cuff links. Two small, round pieces of sea glass that match his eyes. My mouth goes dry. "How nice of you to invite me."

Chapter Twenty-Eight

Nolan

I haven't told Harriet about the compass.

I intended to tell her tonight, but then she opened her door wrapped in that deep purple dress, looking a devastating combination of hopeful and wounded, and I couldn't.

You won't be the only one who will bear the consequences.

Consequences. Timelines. Memories and mysteries and magic gone rogue. Things are changing. I should be seizing this opportunity with both hands, hell-bent on being somewhere—*anywhere*—other than here.

But instead, I'm wandering down a neatly curved brick path toward a faintly glowing colonial estate, Christmas music drifting from the open doorway. I've decided to be selfish tonight. I'm giving myself this night with Harriet. I won't worry about the implications hanging heavy over my head. Tonight, I want to pretend. I want to be *with* her.

Car tires crunch across the gravel drive and Harriet's heels click against the walkway.

"You could walk next to me, you know," she says over her shoulder, shooting me a knowing look. It's a marked change from the frown she wore for the duration of the drive over here, her shoulders steadily winding tighter and tighter until she resembled something carved out of stone.

I let my gaze trail appreciatively down the curve of her ass. "I like the view from back here."

She laughs and then reaches behind her, looping her fingers around my wrist and tugging. We're close enough to the water for a light breeze to lift the edge of her coat, wrapped around her like cotton-candy-colored armor. She insisted on parking at the small church down the street, joking about a quick getaway, instead of waiting for the valet. But then her jaw had gone tight and she got that glassy, faraway look in her eyes and I don't think it was a joke. The rest of the drive was spent in silence.

I fall into step next to her, settling my hand at the base of her spine. "All right?" I ask.

She nods silently, watching her feet as she ascends the wide porch steps. She offers a strained smile to one of the attendants standing by the door, then steps to the side. She crosses her arms over her chest and stares out at the dark estate grounds.

A pier extends out over the water, twinkle lights wrapped around the docking posts that bob up and down with the tide. Weeping willows drift lazily around a glowing white tent, the catering staff coming and going with trays balanced on their upturned palms. A man dressed like a high-end Santa smokes a cigarette behind a short fence, and two Rockette-clad reindeer adjust their stockings.

Ridiculous. All of it.

"I just need a minute," Harriet tells me, shifting on her deadly looking shoes. Her breath explodes out of her in a cloud of white. "One more second, and I'll be ready."

I want to gather her in my arms and disappear down a garden path with just the stars and a bottle of champagne for company. If she wants a quick getaway, I have more than a few ideas.

"I'm in no rush," I tell her easily, shoving my hands in my pockets. I'm not used to wearing formal wear. I don't think I've put on anything more complicated than a raincoat in close to three decades. "Take as much time as you need."

An older woman in a white fur wrap gives us an inquisitive look as she passes. I summon all my ghostly energy and glare at her until she pales, rushing forward into the manor.

Harriet shakes out her hands, mumbling something under her breath. I catch a few words: *you'll be fine* and *just one night* and *not alone this time.*

My stomach hollows. She's not alone this time, but it's likely she will be the next. And the time after that, and the time after that until—until there's another man standing in my place. Someone else who will hold her hand and kiss her up against the wall of her tiny, cluttered house. Someone who will keep his pockets full of candy canes, just in case.

The thought fills me with barely banked panic, imagining someone else in all the places Harriet has allowed me to be.

The only thing I've ever wanted is to move forward, and now I'm hesitating. I'm unsure, wavering. I hate the idea of leaving Harriet here alone almost as much as I hate the idea of spending any more time in this place. Maybe more.

Another couple enters behind us and Harriet fixes a plastic-looking smile on her face. I hate that most of all.

"Harriet." I duck closer so most of her body is blocked by mine, her big brown eyes blinking up at me like I'm her lifeline. "Listen to me."

I tangle our fingers together and give her hand a reassuring squeeze.

"We're going to go inside," I tell her, keeping my voice low, mindful of the attendants behind us and the steady stream of guests flitting in and out of the manor. "We're going to drink the fancy champagne. We'll eat some of the tiny appetizers. And then we're going to dance."

Her eyes spark in interest. "You'll dance with me?"

I get that balloon-in-my-chest feeling again and I squeeze her fingers harder. "Aye. I'll dance with you. And I'll whisper inappropriate things in your ear and make sweeping judgments about the people around us."

She smiles. "And you won't leave me alone? Not even for a second?"

I shake my head. My heart *aches*. "I won't. I promise. Not unless you wish it. We'll do this together, yeah?"

"Together," she repeats. The barest hint of a smile appears. "Okay." She nods. "Okay, I think I'm ready."

"Not quite yet." There's been something bothering me since I showed up at her home a couple of hours ago, fire in my veins and desperation in my belly.

I settle my hand around the back of her neck, fingers tangling in the hair at her nape. It disrupts the smooth, tidy bun she's pulled it into.

"What are you doing?" She tugs at my hand. "You're going to mess up my hair."

"I know."

My magic flares to life in my palms and she stills against me. Golden sparks slowly weave their way through her hair, uncoiling it from the harsh bun she's forced it into. She lets out a small sound of relief as it drapes across her shoulders, the straight strands twisting back into the curls I have an unhealthy fascination with. I drag my thumb over the curve of her ear and holly berries appear, nestled in a comb of gold.

"There." I study my handiwork, pleased. "That's better."

Harriet's cherry-red lips curve in amusement. "Was that necessary?"

"Very much so." I reach for her hand and start tugging her toward the entrance. The sooner we get inside, the sooner we can leave. "Now you look like you."

"As opposed to—"

I pull off my wool coat as soon as we're through the doors, handing it off to an attendant standing to our left. I intercept him before he can help Harriet with hers, unwrapping the heavy sash from around her middle. I tug her coat from her shoulders and she shivers lightly as I drag my thumb down the length of her exposed spine. I brush a quick kiss to the back of her head, then duck down to whisper in her ear.

"As opposed to the woman who lets others twist her into something smaller. Remember who you are, Harriet. And remember you're not alone." I hand over her coat, then guide her forward. "Let's find some drinks."

Harriet exhales a sharp breath. "Let's do that."

Her mother finds us before the champagne does.

She greets Harriet with two air kisses on either side of her cheeks, her mouth etched in a polite-looking smile. She looks like she's barely aged since that first memory. There's not a single strand of gray in her dark blond hair, nor a wrinkle to be found across her forehead.

Her eyes are the only thing that give her away. Her eyes look tired.

"Harriet," she says, her smile polite and distant. Her gaze flicks down and then up. "You're wearing purple."

Not *hello*. Not *happy holidays*. A criticism, handed over like one of the paper Christmas crowns my mother used to make out of old fishing ledgers.

A surge of fierce protectiveness rushes through me, twisting with my magic. But Harriet doesn't wilt or fold. She smiles. "I am." Her eyes find mine. "It's lovely, isn't it?"

I'm so damned proud of her. I give her a quick wink.

"I believe I specified navy," her mother says.

"You did," Harriet replies, turning back, her voice calm. The only concession to her nerves is the slight tremble in her hand. "You look beautiful, Mom. Everything looks beautiful. You've done a wonderful job with the venue."

Her mother ignores the compliment. "And your hair."

Harriet's smile falters. "Yes?"

"It's . . . different."

"This is how I normally wear it," Harriet says. She touches the bunch of mistletoe nestled behind her ear. "Well. A little fancier than usual."

Her mother's mouth twists. "A little fancier," she repeats, her voice dry.

I step closer and press my palm to the small of Harriet's back. "I think she looks beautiful."

I say it like a threat. In the same tone of voice I'd probably say *I hope you choke on your cranberry martini*, or *You should be deeply ashamed of yourself*, or *The napkins you selected hardly match the silverware for this ostentatious show of wealth.*

The full force of Donna York's attention is oddly intimidating. She'd do well in the office of Poltergeists, should she find herself in need of an occupation in the afterlife.

"And who is this?" she asks.

Harriet leans into my touch. "This is Nolan. He's a friend."

"A friend who didn't RSVP." Her face pinches, souring in increments. "You failed to mention him when we discussed optics on the phone the other day."

"It was a last-minute decision. I wasn't sure if he was going to be able to make it."

"It seems you made a few of those."" Her top lip curls into a faint sneer before her etiquette lessons kick in and she smooths her features. I've seen statues with more warmth in their expression.

This woman. Harriet's memories of her have been far too kind—lit with the glow of Harriet's ingrained optimism. The reality of Donna York is like wiping a layer of dust off an old mirror and finally getting a good look. I see all of her imperfections.

I drum my fingers against Harriet's back as the three of us stand in an awkward silence. In absolutely no hurry to fill it, I scan the room for the server with the champagne. Harriet taps along to the beat of "Little Drummer Boy" played by the string quartet in the corner. Donna studies me out of the corner of her eye and I keep my features impassive. I have no desire to win her approval or acceptance, and she seems to know it.

"What is it you do, Nolan?"

"I work in auditing," I answer with a shit-eating grin.

Harriet snorts.

"Oh? Is the shop in some sort of trouble?" Donna sounds far too gleeful at the prospect.

Harriet's amusement vanishes and my hand creeps up higher, my thumb easing over the bare skin just above the smooth cut of her dress.

"Not in the least," I say smoothly. "What Harriet has done with the shop is remarkable. You should be proud of her achievements."

I deliver that last bit with a little too much venom.

Harriet holds her breath next to me, bracing for whatever vitriol is about to spill from her mother's mouth. But either Donna York didn't hear me, or she's decided to take a vow of silence in the past three minutes, because she drifts off without another word, a polite smile fixed on her face as she greets a bleached-blond couple draped in silk and pearls.

It's the best response she could have had, I suppose.

"You didn't have to do that," Harriet says, flagging down a waiter for a glass of champagne. "I could win the Nobel Peace Prize and the Daytona 500 in the same year, and my mother would still find something to be disappointed in."

"What's the Daytona 500?"

"It's a car race," she explains. "You really haven't heard of it?"

I shrug. I could not care any less. "Can't say I'm invested enough."

"Well." Her gaze trips around the room, taking in the finery. The oversize oil paintings on the walls and the gold, glimmering plates. The pretty people in their pretty clothes, rotten to the core. "Are you invested enough to dance with me?"

"Now that is something I can muster some enthusiasm for." I thread my fingers through hers. "Off we go."

Chapter Twenty-Nine

Harriet

$\mathcal{N}$olan—to my complete and utter surprise—is a good dancer.

"What?" he asks on our third turn around the dance floor, his footsteps smooth, his thigh briefly pressing between my own before he gracefully turns me again. I feel like we're floating, drifting on a cloud above the rest of this party. His palm eases half an inch lower over the curve of my ass and his mouth hovers over mine as we spin around and around. It's probably too much for a dance at my parents' holiday gala, but I don't care.

This is what I thought his magic would feel like. This spark in my chest that flares brighter every time his eyes crinkle at the corners. This tingling in my hands when his nose drifts across my cheek. I close my eyes and exhale a breath, letting him lead.

This weightlessness in my head and in my heart. This complete and total trust that he has me. No matter what.

Nolan does a neat two-step and extends his arm, whipping me out and spinning me back like a top on a string. I land against his chest with a quiet *oof* and he spins us away again, my hair flying around my shoulders.

"You're looking at me like I've just pulled a fully decorated tree out of my arse," he says with a wicked smile.

"Is that . . . something you can do?"

"You may find this shocking, but I've never attempted that particular parlor trick."

I consider that. "I can't stop thinking about it now."

"Maybe later." He laughs and glances his fingers along my cheek. "What's got this look on your face?"

"You're a good dancer," I explain. "And I'm having fun. Both of those things are unexpected."

His smile turns crooked. "There's an insult in there somewhere."

"Please." I give him a look. "You forget I've seen you on ice skates."

"Fair point." We take another spin around the dance floor and I let myself relax in his hold. He watches me with soft eyes. "What do you normally do?" he asks. "At these events?"

"Usually, I stand by the kitchen and wait for the appetizers to come out." I frown over his shoulder at my mother, standing in the center of a cluster of tables. She hasn't looked at me since that disaster of a welcome, though I'm sure she'll seek me out later in some dark corner to let me know my failings. I brought an unsanctioned date, wore purple, *and* left my hair natural? I might as well have set the drapes on fire and stolen a golf cart.

Maybe I *should* set the drapes on fire and steal a golf cart. Maybe we *can still* set the drapes on fire and steal a golf cart.

"I don't know," I continue. "I usually try to hide."

I've never felt particularly welcome, so I usually find somewhere to make myself small. I don't attract attention. I put in my yearly allotted three hours of family face time, then I go home and eat a takeout pizza on my couch in my matching pajamas.

I feel that same foreign burst of anger from this morning. *Why* do I do that? What did I do to deserve that sort of treatment from my *family*? The people who are supposed to love me no matter what.

Nolan's right. I'm not the villain in my story. Not even close.

"I don't know why I do that," I whisper, something hot pressing behind my eyes. "I think it's easier for me when I do what's expected. It's my way of making up for all my other disappointments. It gives me hope they might change their minds, I guess. But maybe I should let that go. I'm not happy, and neither is anyone else. I think I'm tired of hiding in the corner, eating the canapés."

Nolan's eyes flash in the twinkling lights, then settle into something dark and intent. "We're not hiding tonight."

My lips lift up at the corners. "No," I say. "No, we're not."

"Good," he murmurs. That word settles low in my belly, pulling tight. I might be edging away from seeking the approval of others, but I still like to know when I've pleased Nolan.

I like it very much.

Nolan watches me with his dark eyes, his thumb doing another deliberate sweep across the bare skin of my back. I imagine that thumb working at my body with the same deliberate touch. Slipping into my mouth and pressing against my tongue. Dragging slow and rough between my thighs, my pretty purple dress hiked up around my hips, my delicate underwear hanging from one ankle.

"What are you thinking about now?" Nolan rumbles.

You, on your knees in a hidden alcove. Your hand fisted in the material of my skirt, mine in your hair.

"Nothing," I breathe, trying to blink away the image. "Why do you ask?"

"Your cheeks are pink."

"You said my cheeks are always pink."

"Not like this," he says. "This is what you look like when my mouth is on you."

"Nolan," I whisper, not sure if I want him to stop or keep going.

The string quartet finishes the final lingering notes and we slow to a stop at the edge of the dance floor. He lifts my hand to his mouth and brushes a kiss against my knuckles. "Let's get a drink. Then maybe I can convince you to tell me about those dirty little thoughts you're having."

"I'm not having dirty thoughts," I lie.

His grin is something two shades shy of smug. "Sure."

I'm about to lob another denial in his direction when a familiar head of blond hair over his shoulder catches my attention. My smile freezes on my face before cracking right down the middle.

On the other edge of the dance floor, Samantha is standing at a table with an ice sculpture, talking to a man in a blue velvet smoking jacket. She gestures gracefully with her hands and he laughs. I'm struck by how comfortable she looks. How relaxed. This whole time, I've been hiding in corners and Samantha paraded down the middle of the room.

Where did I make the wrong turn? When did I become someone that was easy to discard?

"I see my sister," I tell Nolan quietly, my pulse hammering in anticipation. I told Nolan we're not hiding tonight, and I meant it. "I'm going to go talk with her."

"Do you need me?"

He asks it quietly, earnestly, and my heart stumbles over itself. I could tell Nolan I needed a plate full of fancy Brie for this conversation, and he'd disappear to the cheese board without another word. No one has ever taken care of me the way Nolan has. I'm not sure anyone ever will again.

I shake my head, then lean up on my toes and press my mouth to his. It's brief, and chaste, but he chases my lips with his, one of his hands gently cupping the back of my head to keep me close. He tucks our foreheads together, bumping my nose with his.

It's impossibly sweet, and my heart does another barrel roll in my chest.

"I'll be by the bar. Signal if you need me."

"What sort of signal?"

He thinks on it. "Do you know how to do a bird call?"

I grin. "I'd ask you to demonstrate, but I'm a little bit afraid of what might happen."

Amusement shines behind his eyes. "It'll be a surprise then." He pats my side, steering me in the direction of my sister. "I'll keep an eye on you."

"Thanks." I take two steps forward, feeling brave, then turn back, feeling honest. "And thank you for being here. I'm really glad you knocked on my door tonight."

Nolan's face softens. "I'm glad to be here." He gives me a nudge. "Go on. Don't leave me with the wolves for too long."

I skitter away before I can second-guess myself, approaching Samantha just as the man she's talking to departs. She's wearing a floor length A-line dress—navy, of course—her hair pulled back in a sleek-looking ponytail. Her attention catches on me and holds, awareness taking a moment or two to sink in.

Her eyes widen.

"It hasn't been that long since you've seen me," I tell her as I approach, fighting the urge to readjust my skirt. Two weeks ago, I would have felt like the *before* to her *after* photo, an inadequacy I've spent most of my life battling against.

But not tonight.

Maybe it's the dress, or maybe it's the high of being spun around the dance floor by a man who cares about me, or maybe it's the heavy, protective feel of Nolan's gaze on my bare shoulders . . . but the only thing I feel is a low rumble of frustration. I'm so damn tired of begging for scraps of affection. Not when I now know that it can be given so freely.

"It's been almost a year," Samantha says, her voice smooth and rich. She studies my hair while she thinks, her perfectly shaped, caramel-colored brows crashing together. "Spring, I think?"

"That sounds right."

"Well, you look great." Samantha's smile is strained. "That's quite the dress."

"Yeah, it's nice." I huff a laugh. "Are we really going to do this, Sam?"

She sets down her empty champagne glass. "What?"

"Are we really going to make small talk? Us?" I step closer, careful to keep my voice low. Old habits die hard, and confrontation is enough of a challenge for me. I don't want to cause a scene while I do it. "You've barely talked to me for months. You haven't been responding to my text messages or answering my calls. What's going on?"

"I've been busy at work," she answers, not quite making eye contact. "They've increased my caseload and I'm in charge of a new special-interest cohort with the corporate law group. It's a ton of work, Harriet. It's not personal."

Ice lodges at the base of my throat. *Not personal.* It should be personal. I *want* it to be personal.

"That sounds really great, Sam, but—" I drag my teeth over my bottom lip, debating whether or not I want to push. "Is that the thing that's made you distant? Work?"

Her stern expression falters, exposing something soft and tender beneath. But then she wipes it away, settling back into cool and indifferent. She looks so much like our mother I want to cry.

"I'm not distant, Harriet. I'm just busy."

"Don't do that," I say. "Don't make it seem like I'm making it all up. You've been avoiding me."

"I just told you, the—"

"Corporate law group, I know." I swallow hard and tell myself to be brave. "But I want to hear about you, Sam. Not work. I know we had that argument, but I never meant for you to pull away."

I showed her a sliver of the pieces I keep tucked away from everyone else and she punished me for it. She's still punishing me for it.

296 B. K. Borison

"That's the problem, Harriet."

"What is?"

"When I tell you about work, I *am* telling you about me." Her eyes dart away again, and I don't have to turn to look over my shoulder to follow her gaze. My mother and father are holding court in the middle of the room, guests flocking to them like moths to a flame. "I'm doing really well right now and things feel good. I don't want to mess it up."

"Mess it up," I repeat numbly.

Samantha takes a fresh glass of champagne from a passing waiter. "I'm in a good place. I don't need the family drama to distract me from my goals."

A laugh catches in my throat. "Oh, okay. You don't want *me* to mess it up."

She shakes her head, frustrated. "That's not what I meant."

"Yes, it is," I reply, fighting hard to keep control of my voice. "It's exactly what you meant. All I've ever done is try to be exactly what everyone needs. Instead, this family treats me like I'm a disaster. I don't understand what I've done."

Color blooms in her cheeks. "You really think you tried, Harriet? You hit one roadblock and you threw everything away. You have no idea what I've gone through trying to smooth over the damage you've done."

I angle my face away, feeling like I've been slapped. It wasn't one roadblock. It was a perpetual bad fit. I chose my own happiness, not the destruction of some false legacy. If she knew me the way I thought she did, she'd see that.

I swallow, meeting Samantha's gaze with difficulty. "And then you threw *me* away when I couldn't play pretend anymore. Wouldn't want anything to rock your boat with Mom and Dad, am I right?"

I've been trying to cross the chasm between us for months, but I'm the only one reaching across. Sometimes bridges aren't meant to be rebuilt. The idea that I was making things difficult for *her* while trying to mend our relationship is unbearable. My mother believed me to be selfish and cruel for years. I suppose she's not the only one.

It's just like I said to my aunt Matilda. I don't fit. I've never fit.

Maybe I need to stop trying.

"It doesn't matter," I say quietly, already scanning the crowd for Nolan. The quartet has just started up what sounds like Ariana Grande's "Santa Tell Me" and there is an alarming amount of retirement-aged law people grinding on the dance floor. "We don't have to talk about it," I say. "We don't—we don't have to talk at all." I spot him on the opposite side of the bar from where he said he'd be, a thunderous expression on his face.

I meet Samantha's eyes again, my anger leaving me in a rush. Instead, there's just exhaustion. I force a smile. "I really am happy for you, Sam. And I wish you the best."

I turn to leave, but Samantha grabs my hand.

"Harriet, wait." My heart gives a hopeful flutter in my chest. "The family picture is in a few minutes. Mom will want you to stay."

I blink at her, my hope turning to ash.

"Right," I say. How could I forget? My mother's favorite performance of the night. When she artfully arranges us in front of the Christmas tree and links her arm through mine, pretending like she's never been happier. "I'll meet you over there."

Samantha's mask slips. "Harriet," she says again, only for it to be repeated louder and with far more venom six feet behind me.

"Harriet," my mother whisper-seethes, marching across the dance floor in her stilettos. She smiles politely at every person she passes, but spares no kindness for me. She curls her fingers around my arm and tugs me close. "Where on earth did you find that man and why is he *here*?"

My attention darts over her shoulder to Nolan, bewildered. We make eye contact and his eyebrows fall in a heavy line. He takes a sip of his drink, then sets it to the side. He slowly starts making his way to me.

"I told you. He's my friend."

I thought Nolan would be able to evade questions with whatever ghostly smoke cloud he carries with him. But my mother is laser focused on his presence. I guess that's another thing that's changing for him.

My mother's face pinches. "He's rude, is what he is. Do you know what he said to me?"

A hot flare of protective irritation swells within me. Whatever Nolan said, I have no doubt she deserved or instigated it in some way. I yank my arm out of her grip.

"I don't care what he said."

She gapes at me. I've never talked back to my mother in my life. It's oddly . . . freeing.

"What on earth is this attitude?"

"My attitude. My hair. My dress. My date. Are there any other transgressions you'd like to add to the list tonight?"

She rears back, offended. "What's gotten into you?"

I think about that little girl with a wooden boat clenched tight in her first. For the first time in my life, I think *I've* gotten into me.

"Everything all right?" Nolan asks, coming to my side, his hand finding it's usual spot against the small of my back. I try to ground myself. I didn't come here to argue. I didn't come here to make a scene.

I came because I thought I was holding a door open, but the hinges broke off long ago. There's no point in forcing a relationship with people who don't want it.

"Everything is fine," I say, tired down to my very bones. "You okay?"

Some of the tension melts from his face. "All is well, love. You ready to go home?"

Love. Home. The words sound like a wish I made upon a star. I want to curl my fingers around them and press them into my skin so that when he's gone and I'm alone I can remember what it felt like to be adored. If only for a little bit.

"Yeah." I give him a small smile. "Let's go home."

"Absolutely not," my mother interjects, grabbing for my wrist again. I don't know if she intends to hold me against my will, or if she just wants my attention. Either way, it's wildly out of character for my composed mother. Her nails bite into my skin. "We haven't taken the family picture."

Nolan's face darkens.

"I suggest you take your hands off her."

"And I suggest you keep your opinions to yourself about *my daughter*." My mom's eyes flash, more uncharacteristic emotion breaking through. "I believe you've said quite enough for one evening."

I tug myself out of my mother's grip, tucking my palm protectively over the half-moon marks. I had low expectations, but this evening has been a disaster. None of it has gone the way I thought.

And yet, it's hard to be concerned about what my family will think of me when I already know they think the worst. Why not try something new? Why not try . . . not trying?

"What did you say to her?" I ask Nolan.

"He called me a fool," my mother rushes to answer. "Never in my life have I been treated—"

"I said she was *foolish*," Nolan corrects, his attention unwavering on me. "I said she was foolish to have the incredible privilege of being loved by you, only to ignore it in favor of criticism." His eyes snap up to my mother and hold. "That is what I said. Exactly."

My mother halves the space between them, getting in his face as much as is polite in Annapolis high society. "And what gives you the right to say such things? You don't know anything about our relationship."

"I know enough," he says simply. He's *seen* enough.

I place my palm against his chest. I'm afraid if I examine what he just said too closely, I'll split at the seams right here at the edge of the dance floor.

No one's ever defended me before.

"I'd like to go home now," I tell him, my voice tight.

He nods, splitting his attention between me and my mother. "If you're sure."

"I am." I swallow heavily and touch a trembling hand to my cheek. My face is numb. My fingers are cold. There's a buzzing in my ears that's growing louder as the pressure in my chest builds and builds. I'm standing at the edge of something. I'm about to clip my own wings and see how far I fall.

"Could you grab my coat?" I ask. "I'll meet you by the door."

He looks like he wants to protest. I squeeze his hand. "Please," I add.

"Aye, all right," he says. He lingers for another moment, then leans forward and brushes his mouth right above my ear. His magic skims my neck in reassurance, lighter than his touch and twice as warm. "I'll be waiting."

"We still haven't taken the picture," my mother says, keeping her face carefully neutral as Nolan makes his way around the dance floor. The "Waltz of the Flowers" from *The Nutcracker* drifts lazily around us and I almost laugh. I feel like a flower. Something delicate, bending toward the light on my trembling stem. Always trying so damn hard to be seen. To grow. To build a bouquet and flourish within the group.

I'm so damn tired.

"I think I'm going to pass this year," I tell her, working hard to stand my ground. Even though I know it's the right thing, it's still a difficult thing, and my heart and my head are screaming at me to smooth the edges. Fix it. Make everyone else comfortable. I push down against that feeling and ball my hands into fists. "I know I've made some choices in my life that you've disagreed with, but I like what I've built for myself. It's okay if you don't want to be a part of it, but don't—don't make me out to be a horrible person just because I chose something different than what you wanted. I'm tired of being diminished for some imaginary sin. I'm tired of having to beg for your attention. I try so hard and for what? You don't even notice. I wish you would be honest with me instead of"—I gesture around us at the ornate dining room—"whatever this is."

This entire song and dance. This senseless hope that I can somehow turn myself into someone my family *likes*. That with enough pressure and positive thinking, I can subdue all of my quirks and idiosyncrasies and be someone they're proud of. That I'm one conversation starter away from fitting in.

"I suppose I'm to blame, yes?" A bored expression settles across her face. "I'm a horrible mother? I've done this to you? Your aunt Matilda would never. Is that right?"

My heart turns over in my chest, disappointment a fist around that vital organ. I'm being the most honest I've ever been, and she's still not listening.

I cast a quick look at Samantha, but she's staring holes into her perfectly sensible stilettos. I'm alone in this conversation, just as I've always been.

"I'm not placing blame," I say as patiently as I can manage. "I'm sharing how I feel."

"You're being sensitive," my mother snaps.

"Then I guess I'm sensitive," I reply. "I'm sensitive, and I'm softhearted, and I'm emotional, and I'm probably delicate, too. I cry during sad commercials and I say sorry all the time—most of the time for reasons I can't articulate. I never wanted to be a lawyer. I hate arguing. This conversation right now is killing me because I just want to give you what you want from me until this feeling in the middle of my chest goes away."

My hands clench into fists, the words coming faster. "So, yes. I care too much. I've always cared too much. I'm irresponsible. I eat cake for breakfast. I feed my neighbor's cat and my Band-Aids usually have some sort of Disney princess on them. I'm colorful and sentimental, and I—I like these things about myself. I like my cluttered shop and I like my tiny house filled with things that make me happy. I like my hair when it's curly. I like this dress. And I like that man waiting patiently at the door for me, despite what I'm sure was an overt attempt to chase him off." I take a deep breath and roll my shoulders back. "This is who I am. I'm proud of it. You can choose to know me, or not. But it's up to you now. I won't be trying any longer."

My mother firms her jaw. "If you walk out that door now, you won't have another chance."

I smile tightly. Once upon a time, that statement probably would have devastated me. But now?

I lean forward and brush a quick kiss to my mother's cheek. I don't need another chance to force someone to love me.

"I think I'm okay with that."

Chapter Thirty

Harriet

The drive home from the gala is quiet, both Nolan and I lost to our thoughts. He lays his hand on my knee as we pull out of the small church parking lot, but otherwise gives me space, staring out the window as we wind our way back to my house.

I thought I'd be immediately ravaged by guilt. Second-guessing myself. But instead I just feel an odd sense of weightlessness. Like I could float right into the night sky if I wanted to.

Nolan clears his throat from the passenger seat.

"You've been sitting here with your chin on your steering wheel for seven minutes," he says calmly.

"Oh." I lean back and turn off the ignition, releasing my death grip on the wheel. I didn't realize we were parked on the small parking pad behind my house. Muscle memory guided me home while my brain conducted an overthinking Olympics.

The low rumble of the engine cuts out. Silence descends. I pocket my keys in my jacket and collapse against the seat. "Sorry about that."

"Don't apologize to me." He frowns. "Are you all right?"

"I'm fine." I poke at the feeling, examining it for cracks, and realize it's true. I do feel fine. I feel better than fine. I feel *good*. Euphoric, almost. Drunk off the power of finally speaking my mind. "Actually, I think I'm good."

I said what I wanted to say and the world didn't end. I'm still here. I've opened a door, or . . . kicked a pebble down the side of a mountain. I chose myself, and I didn't worry about how my relationships would suffer for it. I didn't contort myself into some absurd shape for the comfort of someone else. I was strong, and brave, and a little bit of a badass.

It's a relief, honestly.

"Good?" Nolan asks, sounding dubious.

I nod. "Really good, yeah."

I look over at him, cramped in the passenger side of my car, his knees almost to his chest, and my palms itch. I want to chase this feeling. I want to hold on to it with both hands.

"Would you like to come inside?" I ask.

His eyebrows jump in surprise. "Do you want me to come inside?"

"Why wouldn't I?"

"You haven't said a word to me since you told me to fetch your coat."

"Oh," I say again. "I'm sor—"

Nolan's long fingers squeeze my thigh. He hasn't moved his hand since we got in the car. "If you say you're sorry one more time," he says slowly, "I might lose my mind."

I button my lips shut. *Sorry* is right there on the tip of my tongue, but I swallow it. He lets out a breath through his nose, the smallest of smiles shadowing his cheeks. "Good," he rumbles.

That word again. It glides over my shoulders and settles in the middle of my belly, warm and liquid. I shiver.

Nolan watches me, solemn.

"I'm the one who should be apologizing to you," he says, his voice a low scratch. "I overstepped tonight. I'm sorry for that."

"How?"

"Your mother came over to me while I was waiting for you at the bar." He squeezes and releases my leg like he's trying to convince himself to let go, but can't quite manage it. "She wanted to know the nature of our relationship. She was—well. She's a bit of a hag, really."

I snort a laugh. "She really is, huh?"

My mother isn't ever going to change. Oddly enough, it's a relief to know it. I've tried to change so many things about myself to get her to like me, but it's never been about me. I know that now. She's holding on to old hurts, unwilling to forgive or forget.

Now that I've said my peace, I can let that wound start to heal.

Nolan drops his head back against the headrest. "I lost my temper. It wasn't my place to correct her behavior."

I give a noncommittal hum and inch closer. I don't want to have this conversation in the car with a console between us. I want to be somewhere I can see his face. Where I can smooth my hands against his warm skin and raised scars and reassure myself that he's still here, sitting in the space next to me.

I settle for tangling our fingers together on my thigh. "What else did you say to her?"

Nolan swallows hard, still nervous. "I might have told her that her head resembled a potato."

A laugh bursts out of me. "You what?"

"You have to admit she does vaguely resemble a root vegetable." A flash of a dimple appears in his cheek. "I didn't like the way she was talking about you," he says softly. His touch brushes along the inside of my knee. "My frustration got the best of me."

I snicker again, leaning forward to press my mouth to his. My bright, bubbly feeling expands. Nolan was there for me tonight. He

showed up, he stayed, and he defended my honor. He made me feel
good.

I catch his bottom lip between my teeth and suck at it, an indulgent kiss that makes him shift in his seat. He melts against me.

"You're not mad," he breathes when I let my mouth drift down the
line of his neck.

"Of course I'm not mad." I fumble with his bow tie, frustrated with
how many buttons and clasps and closures are between me and his
skin. He grunts when I tuck my finger in between his neck and the
material, my nails scratching. "Why would I be mad?"

"Because I compared your mother to a yam."

"I thought you said it was a potato."

"There's a saying about potatoes, but I don't want to give in to Irish
stereotypes."

I laugh against his neck, letting my forehead rest against his jaw.
Tonight could have easily been another bad memory of Christmas
Past to add to my already extensive collection, but it wasn't. I danced,
and I laughed, and I said the words that have been hammering holes
in my heart for years. I was brave, and it was because of Nolan.

"I don't want to talk about this anymore," I murmur.

"What do you want to talk about?"

"I don't want to talk."

"Noted," he says.

His fingers inch up my thigh, disappearing beneath the high cut of
my dress. When I don't protest, the rest of his hand follows. I spread
my knees wider in the limited space of the driver's seat, encouraging
him to explore. He takes the direction beautifully, his rough palm
scraping at my hip, gripping it as his mouth dips back to mine. I sink
into him, mindless and warm.

"Let's go inside," I breathe, draping my arms over his shoulders.

"Aye," he grunts. "Hold on to me."

"I am holding on to—" I shriek with a laugh as his magic explodes out of him in a rush. It coils around my ankles before brushing up the backs of my legs, over the curve of my waist, up along my spine. It sends my pulse skyrocketing, that happy-spinny feeling twisting low in my belly. I close my eyes and hold on, laughing again when we land with a bounce in the middle of my bed.

I blink up at Nolan perched above me on his hands and knees. His bow tie is crooked and his hair is a mess, but he's wearing a soft, somewhat bewildered smile. Like he can't quite believe his luck.

I know the feeling.

"I love when you laugh like that," he says.

I grin. "Like a hyena?"

"Like you're happy." He pushes some of my hair away from my face. "Like you can't contain it."

That tender, soft place beneath my ribs glows. "You make me happy," I confess quietly. A second ago we were wedged in the front seat of my car. Now we're splayed across my bed. Nolan's holding himself above me on his elbows, my arms still wrapped around his shoulders. "That was very efficient," I tell him.

"Best use of my magic in decades."

I drop one hand and trace a finger down the line of my dress strap. "I have some other ideas on how you can use it."

His smile sharpens into something hungry. "Not quite yet." He settles his hand at the base of my throat, urging my chin up with his thumb. He holds me steady, looking me over. "My control is tenuous at best, Harriet. I need to go slow."

I don't want him in control. If I get to keep him for only a little bit, I want proof that I had him while he was here. I want snowflakes from my ceiling. I want bite marks on my belly. I want magic pulsing from his palms and rattling my windows in their frames.

"You don't have to be careful with me," I say, voice hushed, my hands tugging at him. I finally get a good grip on his bow tie and untangle it from around his neck. I toss it blindly off the side of the bed. "I can take it."

His breath stutters out of him in a rough laugh. "I know you can." That laugh tumbles into a darker sound when I unbutton his top two buttons, exposing the hollow of his throat. I scratch there lightly.

"And you will," he rumbles. "I promise you that. You'll take everything I give you, won't you?"

My skin flushes hot. I nod.

"But maybe I need you to be careful with me, hmm?" He props himself up on his palms, staring down at me. "There's so much I want with you."

"I'll be gentle with you," I whisper.

His eyes soften. "I know that, too."

I've never cared very much about what's fair and what's not. It hasn't mattered. I've taken what the universe has handed me and made the best of it. But I'm not sure how I'm going to smile through the heartbreak that's coming.

Nolan belongs to another time. Another place. He's meant for a well-deserved afterlife, and I have no desire to keep him from the things he wants.

So I pack away the bruises I can already feel forming and do my best to exist in the moment.

"Your face got sad," he whispers. "Where did you go?"

"Nowhere," I answer. "I'm right here."

I'm not going to spend tonight worrying about what's next. I'm going to be here. With Nolan.

I tiptoe my fingers down his chest, undoing more of his buttons. I pat at his chest. "Up."

He leverages himself to his knees without hesitation and I'd laugh if I wasn't just as eager. Our easy affection melts into frantic desperation, his fingers working at his buttons from the bottom while mine work from the top. He rolls his shoulders back and tears the material from his body, exposing smooth skin and a smattering of dark chest hair. Lean muscle and a heavy cut at his hips. A body honed by work, honored by time.

I press up on my elbows and brush my mouth against the middle of his chest, right where his heart is thundering out a furious rhythm. Both of his hands tangle in my hair, holding me against him.

Like this, he doesn't feel like a spirit at all. He feels like a man. Warm skin and rough sounds. Scars littered across his chest and arms.

Like this, he feels like *mine*.

"Harriet," he bites out from between clenched teeth when I sink my nails against his hips. He's kneeling above me, straddling my left thigh, and I can't get close enough.

"What?" I whisper, drifting my mouth lower, licking at a scar just above his hip. I undo the buckle of his belt and his whole body jolts.

He sucks in a sharp breath when my knuckles drift over his cock.

"I can't—" he says. "I won't be able to—"

I stop and rest my chin against him, staring up along the length of his body. My arms wrap around his torso, holding him close. "What is it?"

His eyes grow heavy and his hands sink into my hair. He looks decidedly—*deliciously*—disheveled.

"I want to be inside you when I come."

Everything beneath my belly button tightens.

I blink. "Oh."

"And if you keep doing what you're doing, it's likely we won't get that far."

He lifts his hand and cups my face, his thumb tracing over my mouth.

"Oh," I say again.

I part my lips and let his thumb slip inside. His face collapses into stern lines, attention focused entirely on my mouth. He dips his thumb farther inside and I curl my tongue around it. He grunts.

"*Fuck*," he whispers. He pulls his hand away from my mouth, his eyes wild. "I need more."

"I want more," I say quickly. I want it so bad it feels like I'll crawl out of my skin waiting for it. I lay back against the pillows. "Come here."

Nolan lowers himself on top of me, his arms straining on either side of my head. He dips his mouth to mine, kissing me like *I'm* the one who is meant to disappear. Both of my hands anchor in his hair, our mouths working hot and wet and slow. I try to stretch out every moment until I'm warm and pliant beneath him. Aching, in all my hollow places.

My back arches. I fumble with the zipper at the base of my spine.

"No." He roughly pins my hips back down. "Keep the dress on."

"Why?" I whine.

He tugs at my skirt until it's folded up over my hips in a puddle of silk. I'm wearing pale pink underwear, cut high around my hips, and he whispers another low *fuck* under his breath. His tongue drags along the inside of his cheek.

"Because," he says, "I want to have you exactly like this."

Then he pushes himself off my bed, drops to his knees, and drags me down the length of my bed by my thighs. I shriek at my ceiling as he settles my hips at the very edge, my legs dangling uselessly over the side. He arranges me exactly the way he wants, roughly tipping my knees wide before slotting himself between them. I can only see the top of his messy hair, bowed over me.

"I need this," he whispers, and any thoughts of self-conscious hesitation drift away with the raw desperation in his voice. He presses a soft kiss just below my belly button. "Can I have this, Harriet?"

I open my legs wider.

"Yes," I whisper. "Please."

He doesn't hesitate. He hooks two fingers in the front of my pretty, lacy underwear and tugs the material to the side, pinning it against my thigh with his thumb. Then he drops his mouth against me and lightning rockets up my spine.

It's messy and honest in the way Nolan always seems to be and I can't breathe through the intensity of it. The way he opens his mouth wide against me, tongue licking, mouth sucking. It's like he's trying to taste as much of me as possible, as quickly as he can.

My hands hover over his head. I want to thread my fingers through his hair, but I don't—I've never—

He takes in my hovering hands from between the cradle of my thighs and my favorite crinkles appear. He grins and guides one of my hands to the back of his head.

"Go on," he says. "Show me where you want me."

I thread my fingers through his hair and his eyes slip shut. I pull and he moans, face crumpling in agonized pleasure. Overcome and out of control, I press my hips down against his mouth and rock. I expect him to hold me still, make me take what he gives me, but he surprises me again. He blinks open heavy eyes and stares at me lazily, letting me grind against his mouth. Letting me take what I need.

He's always letting me take what I need.

I press myself up on one hand so I can see him, the angle better like this, the other still in his hair so I can hold his mouth tight between my legs. I roll my hips again. Again and again and again.

It's the most selfish I've ever been.

It's *fantastic*.

Heat pulls tighter in my belly and my head drops, the ends of my hair tickling the bare skin of my lower back as I work myself against him.

"Nolan," I whine. "Yes."

He pulls away with a gasping breath and his fingers take the place of his mouth, swirling wide, wet circles against my clit. He sucks a mark in the crease of my hip and I hear the clink of metal, his belt buckle dropping against hardwood.

"'S good," I breathe, scratching my nails against his scalp, trying to guide his mouth back to where I want him. I'm so close I'm vibrating with it. "Please. I need you."

His face darkens and he drops another kiss, right above where his fingers work at me. "Pull your top down," he grinds out.

I yank my arms free of the straps and the dress pools around my middle, a thick, tangled band of silk. Nolan grips it and he uses it to tug me flat to the mattress. He yanks again until I'm positioned exactly the way he wants me.

Which is hanging half off the bed, my thighs propped on his wide shoulders, hugging his ears. If he was using any restraint before, it's gone now, his attention focused on sending me over the edge as fast as possible. One of his biceps nudges against the inside of my thigh in a quick, tight rhythm and I roll my hips to match. It's so good. So, so, so good.

I close my eyes and give in to it, whimpering and moaning and whispering his name, tracing my fingers through his hair, over the tops of his ears, across the back of his neck, and down his jaw to where his mouth is warm and wet against me. I choke on nothing when I feel the wet slide of his tongue across my fingers, my orgasm tightening in my belly.

"Nolan," I breathe. *"Nolan."*

"Don't be polite, Harriet." Dark blue eyes meet mine. *"Take it."*

Then he ducks his head down and makes me.

It's slow and thick. Indulgent. It dances up my spine before easing low in my belly, snaking down my legs, and making my thighs tremble. I break apart while Nolan watches, leaning back to rock the palm of his hand firmly where his mouth just was, letting me grind my way through the rest of it. He knows exactly what I need without my even having to ask, amplifying the pleasure until it feels like my orgasm has been going on for hours. I'm sweating, incoherent. I whimper nonsense as my hips work, my body unspooling like thread beneath him.

Nolan arches over me when I finally quiet, one hand pressed next to my hip, the other with a firm grip around his cock. His teeth clamp down on his bottom lip as he strokes up and then down, the tendons in his neck standing out in sharp relief.

"This is enough," he pants. He edges forward and his knuckles bump where I'm wet and sensitive, the blunt tip of his cock pressing down against me. He grinds there, his hand still working. "This is more than enough."

I urge my knees wider and shake my head. "Not for me," I say. "Want you inside."

He makes a wounded sound and falls on top of me, catching my mouth with his in a messy, furious kiss. I can taste myself on his tongue and it makes me burn hotter, my desire reigniting, my body demanding more.

"Harriet." He moans. "I don't think I can—I won't last."

"That's okay." I push my hands into his hair, trying to soothe him. "It's good. It's so good."

He nudges against me again, mumbling under his breath. I catch words like *beautiful* and *incredible*, his accent a rough scratch somewhere under my ear. Then he tilts my hips up and presses his way inside, a thick slide of heavy heat.

He goes slow. So slow I'm wiggling and pushing for more by the time his hips are flush with mine. Both of our bodies are sticky with sweat, my dress still caught between us. Nolan props himself above me and hooks one finger beneath the tangled, ruined material, a sly smile curving at the edge of his mouth. With a flash of heat, the dress is ribbons against my skin, his magic a tingling aftershock. A single strand loops around my torso, a pretty bow knotted between my bare breasts.

"A gift," Nolan pants. "Just for me."

I laugh and Nolan brushes my hair away from my face with trembling hands, smiling with a barely there quirk of his lips. He keeps watching me as he moves his hips, his jaw going slack. His rhythm is slightly sloppy, unpracticed, but everything feels better because of it. The friction. The press of my thighs at his hips. The way his fingers catch and tug at my hair. I'm reduced to feeling everything in pieces because I'm not sure I can handle the whole of it. How thick and hot and syrupy sweet it is to be pinned beneath him like this. To lie here and take it. To give him what *he* needs.

Nolan's forehead creases, his hips moving faster, and I know he's close.

"Show me," I whisper, and he shakes his head, clenching his teeth. "Let me see," I beg.

He wedges his hand between us, fingers searching.

"Not yet," he orders. "Need to feel you again. Need to feel you on my cock."

He already knows how to touch me, I think somewhat deliriously as his thumb rubs. *He knows exactly what to do.* "You don't have to—"

"It's not for you," he bites out. "I need it."

He flips his hand and drags two knuckles on either side of where he's still moving inside me, trapping my clit and forcing friction, and that's—that's it. The pleasure chokes me, sweeping me under. A sharp, furious orgasm burns through me like a storm, stealing my breath.

Somewhere through the haze, I hear him groan, his hips punching against mine as he chases his own release. I drag my nails lazily up and down his bare back as he tenses, his muscles rigid as he works his way through his pleasure.

He looks beautiful. Furrowed brow. Open mouth. Hair damp at his temples and his bottom lip swollen from my kisses. I cup his face in my hands, watching the way his face collapses in relief.

When his eyes blink open again, they're a startling shade of blue. One I haven't seen before. His magic lurks at the corners with flecks of gold and I beam at him. He grins back, chest still heaving, and then the both of us are laughing like love-drunk idiots, our mouths bumping together as we try to kiss our way through it.

When he finally collapses at my side, I'm kiss-bitten and beaming. Nolan looks equally stupefied, his hair practically standing on end.

Remember this, I tell myself as he laces our fingers together, his eyes closed as he tucks my hand against his mouth. He drags a kiss across my knuckles and I slot it in the secret place right next to my heart.

Please, please, please.

Remember him.

Chapter Thirty-One

Nolan

There's a cat sitting in the middle of Harriet's kitchen.

Specifically, *my* cat is sitting in the middle of Harriet's kitchen, offering me the feline equivalent of a smug and knowing look.

"Builín," I greet her over my mug of coffee, blinking hard in the morning light and trying to figure out if I'm having an orgasm-induced bit of hysteria. The window over the sink is open, presumably from where Builín let herself in, and her orange paw is raised against her mouth. I haven't seen her in a couple of days. I suppose now I know where she's been disappearing to. "Did you . . . need something?"

The cat blinks at me. I blink back. Two arms twine around my bare waist and I feel a kiss pressed between my shoulder blades.

"Why are you talking to a cat?" Harriet mutters, sleepy and lazy, her lips pressed against my skin.

"Good to know you can also see the cat."

"Of course I can."

Harriet tilts her face toward my neck and sucks a quick, wet kiss to the side of my throat. We've just barely managed to untangle ourselves from her sheets, but I'm eager to go back. Given all the things we did to each other last night, I should be nothing more than an empty shell. A husk, gasping for breath and sustenance.

Yet I feel Harriet's lips against my skin and my cock gives an eager twitch beneath the red plaid pajama pants I stole from her dresser. They're far too short, cut just above my ankles, but they're soft. I don't even care how ridiculous I must look. The comfort is . . . unmatched. I can see why Harriet enjoys them so much.

"Oliver likes to let herself in for treats," Harriet says, shuffling her way over to a tiny tin canister. She opens the lid and pulls out a treat, then holds her palm out to Builín. Builín gobbles it up, then butts her head against Harriet's thigh in gratitude.

"She's harmless, and I like the visits." Harriet's attention snaps over to me. "Oh! I suppose she can see you, huh? You said cats can always tell when there's a ghost around."

"She can," I say slowly. "She does. For a multitude of reasons. One of which is that she's actually my cat."

Harriet's brow furrows in confusion. "What?"

I gesture at the cat with my empty mug. "Builín belongs to me."

"But this is Oliver."

"No. That's Builín."

"Uh, actually—"

"Builín," I croon. "C'mere."

She nudges Harriet once more, then prances her way over, leaping off the edge of the dining table before perching on my shoulder. Her purr rumbles in my ear as she drags her soft nose against my jaw in affection.

Harriet stares at me, one hand on her hip. "Huh."

"Aye," I agree. "It appears we've both been duped."

"Apparently." Harriet brings the coffeepot over to fill my mug, pecking me on the underside of my jaw once she's done. It cracks open some needy, neglected part of me and I tilt my head, catching her mouth with mine. Builín launches herself from my shoulder, soft feet padding across the kitchen floor. But I don't care, because Harriet tastes like mint and coffee and the fig jam that's open on the counter. It's the start of every good dream I've ever had, and that's exactly what it feels like, too.

A dream I'm about to wake up from. A dream I was never supposed to have in the first place.

Harriet pulls away with a laugh, shaking her head. "Keep kissing me like that and we'll never get anything done."

I loop my arm around her waist and blindly place my coffee mug on an overcrowded counter filled with gingerbread houses of various shapes and sizes. I take the coffee pot out of her hand and set that aside, too. I nose my way under all her hair and press kisses down the line of her throat.

"What do we need to get done today?"

"Oh, I don't know," Harriet breathes. I walk her two steps backward so I can press her to the refrigerator. The contents rattle. A magnet falls on the floor. "Little things. The farmers' market, if you want. Solving the mystery of your afterlife, after that." She combs her fingers through my hair. "Maybe dissuading your boss from sending me to burn in eternal hellfire."

I pull away from her neck. "Eternal hellfire?"

Harriet shrugs. "We still don't know what these very mysterious consequences are all about. Maybe your spirit friends will damn me to burn for eternity."

I shake my head, amused. "That's not what hell is like."

"Oh?"

"I've been told it resembles a corporate waiting room, complete with fluorescent lighting."

Harriet's face pinches. "Gross."

"There's a water cooler that never stops dripping and the air-conditioning is perpetually set to seventy-eight."

She gasps. "Why even have air-conditioning?"

"Precisely." I lean back, propping myself against the fridge. "What's the likelihood you let this go for the afternoon?"

"What? The mysteries of the universe? Not likely, buddy." She reaches for my abandoned coffee. "We have an afterlife to get you to."

It hits me like a slap. My afterlife. It's not something I want to think about when I can still see the marks I worked into her skin.

I still haven't told her about the compass. I left it beneath a crate on the top shelf of her supply closet because I don't want to know what happens if it comes back into my possession. What happens if I touch it? I'd like my unfinished business to remain exactly that . . . unfinished.

I want to stay where I am. Here, in Harriet's kitchen, in a pair of borrowed pajama pants with sunlight streaming in through the windows. Paper stars hanging from the ceiling and Harriet, in a pale pink robe with her eyes shining bright.

I don't want to move on. I don't want to be taken away from Harriet. It's the cruelest twist of fate that the thing I've wanted most is finally within reach and I don't—I don't *want* it anymore.

I'm coming *alive* again, and for what? To leave it all behind when I finally claim my compass? To get one last tease of what it felt like to be human?

It's not right.

"We could stay here today," I offer, staring hard at the kitchen floor. At our legs, tangled together against the fridge. Harriet's slipper-covered feet and my ridiculous pants. "We could—" The rest of my sentence drifts as I struggle to figure out where we go from here.

She cups her hand around my chin and guides my face up until I have no choice but to look right at her.

"Pretend," she says. "We could pretend. That's what you want to say. Isn't it?"

I exhale and nod. That's exactly what I want. I want to pretend I get to have this for longer than a handful of stolen moments.

"And you want to go to the past," I point out, my voice barely more than a rasp. "You want to keep looking."

She presses her lips together and I want to kiss her so badly it hurts. But kissing her during this conversation feels like stealing something back that never belonged to me in the first place.

"What I want," she says slowly, "is to keep you. But we both know that has never been in the cards for us. We knew that from the very start, Nolan."

"We could spend our days like this." I drag my knuckles over the front of her robe. "We could—"

She shakes her head, cutting me off with her fingers against my lips. I quiet, and her palm soothes along my jaw.

"If I don't get to keep you, I want to at least make sure you're happy. Wherever you are. And that means resolving your unfinished business and sending you on your way." She wipes the sleeve of her robe under her nose, then under her eyes. "So, yes. I want to keep looking. Because you deserve to be happy, Nolan. And it's important to me that I get to be a part of that."

I am happy, I almost say. *I'm happy with you. I'm happy like this.*

But I don't. Because she's right. I don't get to stay and I won't hurt her by saying something different, just to spare her feelings. There are rules and I've broken every single one.

I can't break this one.

I don't even know how I would.

"I want to keep you, too," I murmur, hoping she can hear the things I'm not saying. I brush some of her hair away from her face, then cup my hand around the base of her neck. I close my eyes and feel the flutter of her pulse, butterfly wings in the palm of my hand.

"We'll go later today," I say, reluctant.

She nods. "We'll have breakfast first."

"And lunch," I add. "Then a nap."

She leans back to look up at me. "A nap?"

Her eyes are red-rimmed but bright, the very tip of her nose pink. But she smiles through it, just like she always does.

My hands tighten against her.

"An excuse to get you back in bed," I explain. She laughs and I lean forward to lick the sound off her tongue. She melts against me. I tangle my fingers in the sash of her robe.

I pull, and the material slips free.

I won't get to keep Harriet, but I will get to remember.

I intend to make the most of it.

Chapter Thirty-Two
Harriet

"You're stalling."

"I'm not."

"You are."

"I'm *not*."

I laugh. "Nolan. I've watched you debate putting your arm in that sleeve for the past four minutes. You've rearranged all my gingerbread men twice. You're looking at my garland like you want to redo it."

"It's hanging slightly crooked."

"No, it's really not." Maybe a little. In the middle. But we don't need to redecorate right now. We need to visit my past. Or his. Wherever his magic takes us.

Nolan lets his head drop back, his eyes pinched closed and his navy peacoat hanging off one arm. He rumbles something under his breath about *stubborn* and *more time* and *should have gotten another blueberry Danish.*

I soften.

"I know you don't want to go." I loop my arms around his waist and rest my chin on his chest. He peers down at me. "I don't want to go either, but it's the right thing to do."

It's the only thing we can do. Last time we ignored his magic, it spun out of control. I'd rather not have a repeat performance.

I also need to keep a firm grasp on myself. I can't lose sight of how this ends. It'll hurt bad enough when I have to say goodbye. I don't want to pretend it's not coming.

His jaw tightens and then relaxes, the sleeve of his jacket still hanging limply at his side. His eyes search mine, his hand finally raising to tuck some wayward curls behind my ear. He sighs heavily. From the very depths of his soul.

"You're right. We need to do it." He swallows, eyes searching, a flash of guilt tightening his eyes. He tries for a smile and falls woefully short. "You sure I can't convince you to spend the afternoon at the shop with me instead?"

"We can go to the shop after." I pause, dancing my fingers across his neck, right beneath his hairline. He closes his eyes and his shoulders slump. "I don't want to spend the rest of our time together waiting for the end of it. Okay?"

His eyes stay closed and his mouth flattens into a line, but he nods. "All right."

"Good. Now kiss me and let's go."

One eye peeks open. "Look at you. *Demanding* little thing."

"I learned from the best." I pucker my lips. Nolan laughs. "I'm waiting," I singsong.

There's a rustle of fabric as Nolan pulls his coat on the rest of the way, then his palms trace up my arms, over my shoulders. Slow. Firm. Steady. A reassurance that he's here. That he's *with* me. His nose nudges mine and I'm not sure I've ever had a more perfect moment in my life.

"Kiss me," I demand again, and I taste the edge of his rough laugh the moment before his mouth catches mine.

He's slow, and careful, and deliciously thorough. He holds my face and his mouth stays patient. Slow, slow, slow. I feel lit up inside. Glowing.

I don't realize we've gone back to the past until Nolan pulls away and we're somewhere else, the remnants of his magic sparking in his palms. Stone-gray skies and open water greet us. Seagulls hovering above the horizon and choppy, uneven seas.

Nolan frowns as he looks around. "My past," he says.

"Definitely," I agree, peering around the deck of the small ship. "Is this your boat?"

Nolan's gaze is still fixed somewhere in the distance, his eyebrows tugged down low. Thinking. "Aye," he says, distracted. "She's mine."

A laugh bubbles up my throat. "It's a she, huh?"

"All good vessels are." He shakes his head, then looks down at me. A wind off the water ruffles his hair. He winces. "That sounded horrible, didn't it?"

"I wouldn't say *horrible*."

"By vessel, I meant ship—"

"Uh-huh."

"Strictly in the sense of a nautical nature, not—"

"Right. I understand."

Nolan narrows his eyes. He's so damn easy to tease.

"Are you done?" he asks.

I grin at him. "For now."

He shoves his hands in the pockets of his coat, then gives me a pointed look when I try to do the same. I pulled on my pink, ankle-length jacket with the too-tiny pockets before we left the house.

I hold up my mittened hands and wave them at Nolan.

"Thank you. I have no desire for you to lose access to your hands while on the deck of a ship."

I look around the boat. If I spread my arms wide, I could touch my fingers to either end of it. There's a white cabin at the back. A collection of nets and rope littered in neat piles.

I don't see Nolan, though. Nothing but a discarded woolen cap, tossed over the edge of an old crate.

Another gust of wind lifts my hair.

"Do you know what memory we're in?" I ask. There's a *thunk* every now and again from beneath us. I suppose he's belowdecks, doing . . . whatever it is fishermen do when they're down there.

Battening down the hatches? Shivering his . . . timbers?

"Most of my time was spent on this boat. I don't know what specific day this is or why we're—"

The rest of his sentence cuts off abruptly as the ship rocks beneath our feet. Thick, black clouds gather in the distance, moving quickly in our direction.

Nolan reaches out to steady me, his grip firm.

"What is it?" I ask. He looks spooked.

"Do you see the lighthouse?"

I turn and stare in the direction of the shoreline. I catch the barest hint of a light, flashing and dimming. Flashing and dimming. But there's a thick fog creeping around the edges of the boat, and I lose sight of it easily enough. It's like it was never there to begin with.

"No," I say faintly. "I thought I could, but now I can't."

"Church bells," he says to himself.

A low, eerie sound echoes out over the water. Far in the distance. The slow chime of heavy church bells splits the air before the wind carries it away.

The hair on the back of my neck rises.

"*Hell,*" Nolan curses. "I know this day."

He swallows hard. "This is the day I died."

Chapter Thirty-Three

Harriet

The day you died?" I repeat.

Nolan nods, his gaze fixed somewhere far off. He's still holding on to my arm.

"Well." I lean and peer over the side of the boat. The swell is slowly growing more violent, raising the boat and then dropping it again. Like Poseidon himself has lifted a hand from the water and is toying with the small ship. "That doesn't seem like a good thing."

Nolan frowns, eyes searching the boat for . . . something. An escape hatch, perhaps. "No, it's really not."

Rain begins to drum heavily from the sky in thick, heavy sheets. It weighs down my hair, but I can't feel the temperature or the moisture of it. It's an odd sensation. Like being pelted with cotton balls. Or walking through a spiderweb.

The boat rocks again, and past Nolan appears from belowdecks. He's wearing a thick white sweater and a frantic look on his face, rushing to the wheel. He spins it, attempting to turn the boat around and head toward shore, but even I know it's useless. The storm is moving too fast. The fog is too thick. There's no way he knows where he's going.

"Why are you out here alone?" I yell over the sound of wind and rain and foaming, trembling ocean. We might not be able to feel the effects of the storm, but the sound is horrible. A runaway train. An echoing roar. "You should have someone with you!"

Nolan grips me tighter on a particularly vicious lurch, one arm coiled around my waist. He's soaking wet, from his dark hair to his black boots, water trailing down his cheeks like tears. I can't see a damned thing, the storm a curtain pulled tight around us.

"It's a small boat!" he yells back.

The boat jerks, and we go skidding two feet to the left. Our feet scramble across the wet deck while behind us, past Nolan is trying to secure the ropes.

My Nolan watches him with an impossibly sad face, his jaw clenched tight. "We need to go," he says.

For once, I don't want to argue.

"Yes," I agree. "Let's go."

Except as Nolan tries to drag me toward him, the boat lurches again, a rogue wave crashing over the side. Water cascades over the deck and I lose my grip, my hip hitting the deck hard. I start to slide as the creaking ship lists to the right and my hands reach for anything I can grab. A rope. A mast. Something.

But I'm clumsy with adrenaline and fear, the fog and the wind and the rain and the ocean swirling together until everything is painted gray. Nolan yells for me, but I can't see him. I can only see the past version of him, clinging to the wheel of the ship with one hand. His sweater is stuck to his skin like plaster, the angle of his arm all wrong.

"Nolan!" I shout, not knowing if I'm calling out to the past or the present. Both, maybe.

He must have been so afraid out here alone. Did he know he

wouldn't make it back? Or did he still hope? Up until his very last moment?

Another wave hits the boat with an ear-splitting roar. There's a ferocious crack, like the earth is splitting open, and past Nolan loses his grip on the wheel. I reach out to him, but it's too late. The boat is almost perpendicular with the water and he rolls across the deck, his head hitting the mast of the ship before he topples over the edge.

He goes into the water without a sound.

"Harriet!" I hear from somewhere behind me, frantic and afraid. "Harriet!"

"I'm here," I try to yell. But I can't move. The deck of the ship is too steep, the wood too slippery. The waves are relentless now, one on top of another, battering the wood and breaking it apart beneath their monstrous grip. There is only the roar of the ocean and my heartbeat in my ears. My quick, panicked breathing and Nolan's voice, yelling in the storm.

I need to get to him.

I push up on my knees and try to turn, blindly feeling my way in his direction. Wood groans beneath my palms and the world spins, water crashing down on me like a hammer. I lose my slippery grip with a scream and I go over the edge.

Beneath the water, it's silent.

I'm aware in a way I probably shouldn't be as I slowly sink beneath the surface. I can feel the water but not *feel* it, my body adapting to the new environment seamlessly because I'm not *here*. Not really.

I don't need to breathe.

I don't need to see.

I just *am*.

A wisp. A memory.

I belong to another time. Another place.

Hazy and dreamy and draped in blue, I float down, down, down.

Some distant part of my brain sounds the alarm, but it's far away, and I'm so very, very tired. I'm tired of thinking and fighting and wanting and yearning. I'd like to rest now. Just for a moment.

I know I need to claw my way back to the surface, find Nolan and let him take me back to the place I belong, but I can't muster the energy. Instead, I let myself sink, blinking against the weight of the water.

It doesn't sting at my eyes, or burn at my nose, or choke at my lungs. There's a vague sensation of pressure, but it's easy enough to ignore. Debris from the ship float lazily around me and I drift my fingers along a piece of wood. Maybe I could use this to get back to the surface?

I don't know. It's too much to think about. A worry that's easy enough to let go of. My thoughts grow sluggish and I'm reduced to color and sensation. Cold water and numb fingers.

Blue. Purple. The faded white of a sweater.

The water shifts, and I see him.

Nolan is there, in the water across from me. His arms are limp at his sides and his hair is a halo around his head, lightened to a dark bronze beneath the surface. There's a cut across his forehead that bisects his eyebrow, but it's not bleeding anymore. He looks frozen in time. Peaceful.

His eyes blink open, sluggish and slow.

Yes, I think blearily. *Here I am. You don't have to be alone anymore.*

I'm glad I can be here with him at the end, even if he won't know it.

No one should be alone when they die. Not Nolan. He's been alone enough.

I reach for him across the expanse of open water and he blinks lazily, his features softened. He lifts his hand as if to reach back and we drift closer. Together we twist farther and farther down, the ocean growing darker around us. We've come so far from the surface, but it's—it's nice down here.

Quiet.

Warm.

I don't need to be afraid.

This isn't where you belong, a voice whispers. *Come back to me. Swim, Harriet. Fight.*

In a second. I'll start swimming again in a second. Right now, I just want to be with Nolan.

With Nolan.

With—with Nolan.

Nolan.

Shockwaves ripple in the water around us. Golden sparks light up the dark.

Pretty, I think with a giggle, bubbles slipping from my mouth. Nolan drifts away, farther out of reach.

No, I think. *No, stay with me.*

I don't want him to go. I don't want to watch him disappear.

He sinks farther. His eyes are closed now.

A hand grips the collar of my coat. There's a yank, a pulse of magic around my middle—

And then there's nothing at all.

Chapter Thirty-Four
Nolan

We land in the middle of her living room, soaked to the bone.

I grip her pink coat and try to tear it from her shoulders, but it's too heavy and her arms are trapped. Her body is limp and uncooperative underneath mine, her eyes closed, her lips tinged the faintest shade of blue.

"Fuck." I yank at her jacket again, her head lolling to the side. "Fuck. Harriet. *Please*." Magic bursts out of me and the jacket disappears, the thin blue oxford she has on underneath clinging to her chest.

She's too still.

She's too cold.

"Harriet," I snap, shaking her once. I pinch her mouth open and lean down, pushing air into her lungs. But I don't know if it'll work. I'm a—I'm a ghost. I don't *breathe*. I lean back and settle my hands over the middle of her chest, pressing with a firm rhythm.

She doesn't stir.

"Harriet," I say again. How long was she under water? One minute? Two? Time is fleeting, especially in a memory. I never should have let go of her.

Christ, I'll never forget the sight of her tumbling over the edge, terror blowing her eyes wide, her hands reaching for me. I scrambled to follow, but she disappeared too quickly. I couldn't see her beneath the surface. I couldn't see anything.

"Harriet," I whisper again, begging now, my hands still pressing over her chest. I count to thirty, lift my hands, and wait to see her lungs fill.

They don't.

I press my mouth to hers again.

"Harriet, please. Please, love." I cup her chin with a trembling hand. I stop trying to breathe air into her lungs and soften my mouth against hers in a kiss. I'm desperate. She's so fucking *cold*. "Come on, now. Wake up. Wake up for me."

Is this the consequence Isabella warned me of? Is this the price I need to pay?

If so, the cost is too steep.

I stare down at her pale face. "Harriet." My voice cracks. "Come back to me."

I trace her cheek with my thumb. Water drips from the ends of my hair to the floor. I'm aware of the silence, the quiet pressing down on me as it wraps us in a cocoon on Harriet's floor. It squeezes at my lungs and at the back of my neck, my breaths overly loud in the absence of Harriet's.

"Please," I whisper.

Harriet lurches beneath me with a sputtering gasp, choking on water. I quickly turn her on her side as she empties it from her body against the hardwood, coughing and sputtering, my hand firm against her back as I help her through it. Relief is a razor blade slicing me open. I'm so grateful it hurts.

"It's all right," I soothe as she curls onto her side, her knees tucked to her chest. Her body trembles violently, her wet hair a tangled clump against her neck. "We're back. I got you."

I found her beneath the water. I got her back and I didn't let go. She's safe now and she's—she's going to be fine.

Her gaze is bleary, her teeth chattering. "Co-co-cold," she stammers.

I spit out an ugly word. Of course she's cold. I chuff my hands over her shoulders and let my magic flow through me, shivery and bright. My control is tremulous at best and it explodes out of me in a frantic wave, rattling the ornaments on the tree as it covers Harriet like a blanket. She whimpers as she's wrapped in gold. My hands grip her tighter.

"You're all right," I repeat. I can't stop shaking. "We're back."

We never should have returned to the past. Not when I know the key to moving me forward is hidden on the top shelf of her supply closet. These trips are nothing but a distraction, and now a threat to her safety. I should have grabbed her hand and pulled her back to this time as soon as we landed on that boat. I knew where we were.

It was selfish, not to tell her.

My magic pulls back, caressing her gently as it returns to me. Pink cheeks. Messy hair. Tired eyes. She's exhausted but *alive*, lying curled in a half-moon on her living room floor.

She glances at her chest with a surprised sound.

"You ch-chose the nutcracker ones."

She plucks at the top of her matching flannel pajamas, smiling faintly at the dancing nutcrackers. I can't say it was a deliberate choice. I chose whatever would get her the warmest the fastest. She shivers and I frown, waving my hand again. A sweatshirt appears on top of the nutcrackers.

It's far too big. She's dwarfed in the soft material, the sleeves extending over her hands. She tucks her fingers in the cuffs, curling herself into a ball. "Is this y-yours?"

"Yes," I reply immediately, my heart still hammering in my chest.

I can't stop touching her. I trace my palms over her arms, her shoulders, the line of her neck. I press my hands against her warm skin and finally release a breath when I feel her pulse fluttering, steady and sure.

Another shiver twists its way over her shoulders and my magic explodes out, adding mittens on her hands and a hat over her hair. I blink and she's wearing snow pants, cinched tight around her waist.

An amused smile quirks the corner of her lips.

"While all of this is very helpful, I think it would be best if you dried yourself off." Her eyes soften, her hand raising to brush some of my wet hair away from my face. "Your hands are cold. You must be freezing, Nolan."

I pull away from her. I've been dripping on her warm, dry clothes. Touching her with my frigid hands.

"'M sorry." I reach for my magic again. My wet clothes disappear in favor of jeans and a gray T-shirt. "I don't—you were—and then—" I clench my jaw, my molars snapping together. "I'm so sorry," I finally grit out.

"Oh, Nolan," Harriet whispers. She extends her arms, shifting closer on the floor. "Come here. Don't apologize. I'm okay."

But she almost wasn't, and it's because I couldn't keep her safe. Because I'm too cowardly to tell her the truth. Because I can't stay away.

I haul her into my lap and bury my face in her hair, exhaling a heavy breath. She clings to me just as fiercely.

"No more trips," I say into her neck. "No more, Harriet. We're not going back."

She combs her fingers through my hair. "But we haven't—"

"No more," I say again, my voice hard. I press my hand to the middle of her back, trying to tuck her closer. "I won't take you. I won't do it, Harriet."

"Okay," she agrees. She scratches her nails against my scalp. "That's okay. We'll stay here."

I nod, my nose against her neck. I should have told her about the compass. We never should have gone to the past. "I won't—we're not going back again."

"Okay," she says once more, reassuring me. "We won't go, Nolan. It's okay. I'm all right."

"Okay." I squeeze my eyes shut, wrapping my arms around her. I can't stop seeing her beneath the water, her golden hair drifting around her. Her amber eyes bright, even through the dark. Her pink coat and her hand, reaching for mine.

My brow furrows and I twitch my head to the side, *remembering*. Not when I yanked her from the ocean, but before.

Cold water. A splitting pain across my forehead. Pressure against my chest and burning across my nose.

Everything blurry and dark, and then light.

Her hand. Reaching for mine.

I thought she was an angel.

My eyes snap open.

"I saw you," I murmur.

Harriet rearranges herself in my lap until her arms are draped over my shoulders, her cheek resting against my shoulder. "Hmm?"

"Beneath the water," I say, my voice shaking. "I saw you."

"Oh. Yeah, you did. I didn't see you, but I could feel your magic." She presses a kiss to the tip of my ear. "Thank you for coming to get me."

I shake my head. "No, Harriet. I *saw* you. I remember you. I—I remember when I was drowning," I stutter, not knowing how it's possible, but feeling the truth of it in my bones. I *remember*. "I saw you beneath the water. You reached for me. You tried to grab my hand."

A line appears across her forehead. Her eyes search mine. "You mean you saw me when you pulled me out," she says slowly. "Right?"

I shake my head. "No. It's my memory. From before. It's hazy, but I remember you. *You*, Harriet. I remember your coat." Church bells.

Robin's-egg blue. Sea glass green. Pale, pale pink. *Pink.* The pink of her coat. "Harriet. It was you. I was dying and I saw *you.*"

"How?" she breathes.

I shake my head. "I don't know."

I remember that itch that first night we met. When she was sitting on her couch with her hair pulled into a messy ponytail. I looked at her and something felt familiar. A wisp of a memory, floating at the edge of my consciousness.

She's always been there. This entire time, Harriet has been there.

"What does it mean?" she whispers.

"I don't know," I whisper back.

I press my forehead to hers and breathe in her peppermint sugar smell. I feel the softness of her hair. I close my eyes and try to connect the dots.

"Maybe I was always supposed to find you," I rasp.

Maybe, my heart adds, *you were always supposed to be mine.*

Harriet takes the news—and her recovery from almost drowning off the coast of 1902 Ireland—in stride.

She makes pancakes with her puffball hat still pulled low over her ears, her mittens discarded on the kitchen counter as she wields the spatula. The realization that I somehow saw her present self in my dying moments more than a hundred years ago has validated her every theory regarding my presence in her life.

"I knew it," she says for the fiftieth time since we entered her kitchen, her eyes bright with enthusiasm. A wet clump of batter goes flying off the end of her spatula. "I knew I was supposed to help you move on. And now, look! We have proof!"

I think of the compass sitting on the top shelf of her storage closet and shift uncomfortably. "It's not exactly proof," I counter, still trying to stall. Still trying to drag out our time together.

Apparently, I haven't fucking learned my lesson.

She sets both hands on her hips, glaring at me from the stove. She looks adorable in her oversize sweatshirt and flannel pajamas. Wild hair and rosy cheeks.

"I thought you'd be happy about this," she says. "It's a guarantee that you're going to move on."

"It's no such thing," I say wearily. "We have no idea what it means. Not really."

Half of me is still hoping it's a string of coincidences, meaningless in their frequency. Two ships passing in the night, nothing more and nothing less.

Harriet turns off the stovetop. "It means something, Nolan. You know it does."

That's what I'm afraid of. How can I move on if it means I must leave this behind? Afternoon pancakes and a cluttered kitchen with mismatched tea mugs. Harriet and her pajama sets.

The irony is breathtaking. Harriet is the key to my salvation, when salvation means I'll be somewhere without her.

I pick at the edge of my pancake. The chair across from me screeches against the floor. Harriet's hand reaches for mine. "Hey. Talk to me. What's going on?"

Our fingers knit together. I don't know how to articulate the guilt and the trepidation and the hesitation, so I say, "I'm having trouble figuring out how to say goodbye to you."

She makes a small sound under her breath, her hand tensing and then relaxing in mine.

"We knew this was going to happen," she whispers.

"Aye. I know."

I didn't realize how hard I'd fall. I had no idea how important she'd become in such a short amount of time.

I think of her beneath the water. The look on her face. Her hand, reaching for mine.

I didn't realize I'd already been missing her for more than a hundred years. Now I'm going to miss her for an afterlife more.

"I don't want to leave you alone," I say, my throat tight.

"I won't be alone. I have Sasha. And Oliver." She tries for a small smile, mouth trembling. "You don't have to worry about me. I'm going to be okay."

I know she will be. She's resilient, and intelligent, and so damned lovely it makes my chest ache. She's a force to be reckoned with and I've seen her steadily rebuild her confidence over the past few weeks. She has a solid belief in herself now—that she can stand her ground and be okay. That she's worth the effort it takes to demand more for herself.

I know she's going to be fine without me. She'll be better than fine. She'll shine so fucking bright. Just like she's been shining.

I know it.

It's *me* I'm worried about.

Chapter Thirty-Five
Harriet

Three days until Christmas and I am faking it until I make it.

I told Nolan I'll be fine because I don't want him to worry. I want him to go into his afterlife without any hesitations. He deserves that.

But the truth is, saying goodbye is going to devastate me. It doesn't matter that he says I won't remember him when he's gone. My heart will. I know it.

Nolan doesn't say anything about my forced cheerfulness, choosing instead to kiss me wildly every time I suggest another festive activity. I ask him if he wants to make gingerbread houses and he pins my hips to the kitchen table. I ask him if he wants to go ice skating, and we make out in my car for fifteen minutes. I catch him humming along to a Christmas song and I grin so hard my cheeks hurt.

"What?" he asks.

"You're singing."

"I'm not."

"You're singing a *Christmas* song."

"I'm not."

"So you *do* like Christmas. Even after all that rumbling and grumbling."

"Or perhaps"—he snaps his fingers and a sprig of mistletoe slowly grows from the lamp above my head—"you're rubbing off on me."

We don't act like there's a deadline barreling down on us. We're just two people enjoying the holiday season, doing our best to be ignorant of the last remaining grains of sand in our hourglass. I don't want my final moments with Nolan to be spent waiting. I don't want to anticipate the goodbye.

Which is exactly how we find ourselves celebrating Christmas early, spread out on my living room floor with a pile of blankets in front of my fireplace and enough Chinese food to feed a small army. I know I'm not supposed to remember anything, but I study him beneath my tree like if I try hard enough, I will. How he looks like *this*, sitting with his legs crossed at the ankle under the glow of the lights, a box of lo mein open on his lap and a paper crown crooked atop his head.

"You have such interesting traditions," he tells me with a sideways grin, piercing a piece of broccoli on his fork. He pops it into his mouth.

"Were you expecting fine silverware? Maybe a candlestick or two?"

He shakes his head. "I was expecting plates in the shape of sugar-plum fairies, at the very least."

I sit up in eager interest. "Have you seen those somewhere?" He rolls his eyes. I point my fork at him. "There's that infamous Holiday Spirit enthusiasm again."

"There's only so many times one can hear 'Crabs for Christmas' before the holiday season begins to lose some of its sparkle."

I gasp. "You take that back. It's a Maryland tradition."

"It's a Maryland travesty."

I clap a hand over my mouth and laugh so hard I topple backward.

Nolan sets his plate to the side and crawls over me with a grin, settling in the cradle of my hips, one edge of his paper crown drooping over his forehead. My heart turns painfully in my chest, a key twisting in a rusty lock.

"You're so beautiful," he says. "I haven't told you that enough."

It's the closest we've come to acknowledging the inevitable in days and pressure burns behind my eyes.

"You have," I assure him, my voice thick.

Of course I had to fall in love with a ghost. I've always loved the broken and forgotten things best.

"I got you a present," he tells me, his voice low. "Do you want to see it?"

I snicker. "Why does it sound like you're about to open your pants?"

"That's not what I'm talking about." He pauses. "Though, good to know. For later."

Heat simmers low in my belly. "Later," I repeat.

I keep experiencing bittersweet fragments of what could be. Maybe somewhere in an alternate universe, a different Harriet and Nolan are sitting in front of the fireplace without any ultimatums hanging over their heads. Maybe they're happy.

Nolan pushes off of me, settling on the blankets, his eyes growing serious. There's a lick of warmth, a brief shower of sparks, and a box appears in my lap. It's imperfectly wrapped—kraft paper with duct tape holding uneven edges together—and my heart gives another painful *thud* in my chest. I imagine Nolan wrapping it himself. No magic. Just him.

I pick at the tape carefully and peel the paper back.

"It's not that great," he says as a precursor. "I don't want you to get excited."

"Too late," I singsong. "My expectations have spun wildly out of control."

"No pressure," he murmurs, his hand rising to scratch roughly at the back of his head. I laugh when I finally peel away the paper.

It's an old tackle box. Navy blue and faded. Marks at the place where his hand has picked it up and put it down, likely hundreds of times. I fit my fingers to his and smile at the match.

"I think I've had quite enough of the open water," I say, tapping my fingers over the handle. "But it's lovely. Thank you."

I'll use it for spices in the kitchen, maybe. Or maybe my jewelry upstairs.

He rolls his eyes to the ceiling and reaches for the small latch at the front of the metal box. "It's holding the present, you beast. Didn't have any proper boxes. It's been a while since I've given anyone a gift." He flicks open the front and lifts the lid.

Inside is a neatly folded square of fabric, the same material as his mittens that are still shoved in the pockets of my pink coat by the door. I pass my hand over the butter-soft material.

"It's a scarf," he explains. "That store I told you about? In 1978? They were selling scarves, too. I, ah, I found this at my flat. Thought you'd like to have the matching set."

I pull it out of the box. The material is thick and cozy, not worn down with age like the mittens. The color is also slightly brighter, like the yarn was purchased recently. I run my hands over the uneven rows. "I thought you said it was 1976."

"What?"

"You told me you got the mittens in 1976 at a mercantile store."

"Oh. Well . . ." He swallows heavily. "Must have gotten the scarf at the same time and misplaced it."

I twist the scarf neatly around my neck. There are initials stitched at the very bottom. *NC.* I love that even though he's insisting on lying to me about where he got the scarf, he's selfish enough to want me to walk around with a piece of him.

"Thank you," I whisper. "I love it."

"You don't have to love it."

"I do. I love it," I say again. "It's mine now. Stop hating on my scarf."

He ducks his chin to hide his smile and I lean sideways, grabbing a wrapped package from beneath my tree. I hand it to him, immediately clasping my hands together beneath my chin. I've been buzzing about my gift since I found it two mornings ago at the shop, anxiously awaiting his reaction.

He stares down at the parcel in his hands, brow furrowed. "You got me a gift?"

"Of course I got you a gift. It's Christmas." I run my hand over my scarf. "You got me a gift."

His long fingers trail over the pretty gold paper. "No one's gotten me a gift in"—he tilts his head to the side—"in a very long time."

I pause, then say, "Is that why you hate Christmas radio so much?"

He snorts a laugh. "No. I hate Christmas radio because I can't stand the song about the Christmas shoes." He shudders, then murmurs to himself. "Who makes such a depressing song? I'll never understand."

"Get over the damn song." I laugh. "And open your present."

Nolan grins at me and tears into his gift like a madman, gold paper falling to my hardwood like tiny, fallen stars. It reminds me of his magic. The way it sparks and glows and burns brighter whenever I laugh.

I chew on my bottom lip and stare hard at the box in his hands. There's a part of me that wants to toss it out the window and keep living in this quilt of denial we've wrapped ourselves in. But I know what's coming. I knew it as soon as I saw his gift at the shop.

Our ending is inevitable.

I can't keep playing pretend.

Much as I'd like to.

Nolan opens the small white box and goes absolutely still.

344 🐦 B. K. Borison

"Harriet," he breathes.

I lean forward so I can see the compass nestled in the middle of the box. "I found it in the storage closet at the shop. Can you believe it? It was under an old jam crate. This whole time and it was there." I laugh, but it sounds wooden. Hollow. "I can't be sure, but I think it might be yours. And if it's not, it's a pretty good replica. It doesn't even work. Just like you said. Remember?"

He doesn't look up from the compass. "Aye. I remember."

He recognizes it. I know he does. Awareness sends goose bumps scattering up my arms, my throat thick. My pulse skitters into double-time and that clock that hangs heavy over my head begins to chime.

Our time is up, I think sadly. *I can't hold on to him any longer.*

"It only ever points in one direction. Isn't that—" I saw my teeth over my bottom lip, trying so damn hard not to cry. This is what I wanted. This is what I hoped for. So why is it so damned hard? "Isn't that funny?" I ask, my voice wobbling.

Nolan twists the compass back and forth lightly, watching the arrow at the top of it. When I was holding it, it only ever pointed at my chest. It didn't matter which way I stood, it always pointed in one direction. Now that Nolan is holding it, though, it points—

"It points to you," he says, his voice low. Blue eyes flick up and hold mine. A sad, knowing smile edges at one side of his mouth. "It points right at you."

"Oh. That can't be—"

"This compass is mine," Nolan cuts me off gently. "You were right. About everything, you were right. You are the key to moving me forward, just as you thought. You and your little shop."

My face crumples. "I'm so glad," I say, my voice breaking.

Nolan curses, closing the space between us, his forehead finding my shoulder. "Don't cry."

"I'm not," I say, absolutely crying. Silent tears spill down my cheeks.

I sniff and drag the back of my hand under my nose. "I'm so happy I could give this to you. Best Christmas present ever, am I right?"

Nolan snorts. But there's no humor there. Only frustration. Resignation. "Aye. It would have been, if I hadn't found it first."

I shake my head. "I don't understand."

He rocks his head back and forth against my shoulder. "I'm the one who put the jam crate on top of the compass. I didn't want to see it. I didn't want to touch it. I knew if I did, that perhaps it would take me away. I thought if I ignored it, we could go on as we were. I didn't realize you'd find it, too." His eyes close on an exhale, his jaw tightening. "Should have thrown the bloody thing into the harbor."

"I think I still would have found it," I whisper.

"Aye, me, too." He twitches his head minutely to the side. Like he's saying *no* to some voice I can't hear. "I don't want to go."

"Nolan."

His hand reaches for mine. He threads our fingers together as gold sparks begin to dance from his knuckles, landing like kisses over the back of my hand.

"I don't want to go," he says again.

"Your magic," I whisper.

He nods. "Aye. It's calling me back."

"Back to where?"

"I don't know."

I stare hard at the compass discarded on the floor, more tears filling my eyes. I've spent so long *not* thinking about Nolan leaving that I have no idea what to do with myself now that it's happening.

"How much time do we have left?"

Bright blue eyes blink open, his gaze faintly beseeching. "I don't know." He swallows, strain in the lines of his face. "Not long."

I nod and tell myself to be brave. I knew this was going to happen. It was *always* going to happen.

But that doesn't make it easier. If anything, I've only made it worse. I've stretched out my heartbreak like a rubber band and now the center of it is vibrating with tension. When it snaps, I'm going to be left in pieces. Just like the gold paper on the floor.

"It's okay," I whisper, a single tear slipping down my cheek. I wipe it away quickly and try to smile. "It'll be okay."

"I don't want to go," he says again, and *my* chest cracks open, a strange combination of guilt and sadness and affection pouring out. I feel like I'm beneath the waves again, scrambling for the light at the surface.

"No, Nolan. This is good. This is what you've been waiting for." I sniffle. Another tear falls and he shakes his head, reaching out to brush it away. I press my face into his palm. "I'm so happy I get to be with you at the—at the end." I suck in a sharp breath. "This is how it's supposed to be."

"It doesn't feel like it." His eyes flare, another ferocious tug around his body. His magic is a rope, pulling him in the opposite direction of me. "I don't know how to say goodbye to you. I need more time."

I shake my head, smiling sadly. "This is all we have."

"No. No, I need more."

"We can't."

"Harriet," he begs. He guides me to him with the hand on my cheek, pulling me into his body, coiling his arms around me. He holds me to him fiercely. Like he can ground himself here with me by sheer force of will. "Harriet, I've never—" He swallows, his entire body rattling under the force of his magic. "I'll think of you every day. Every moment. It'll be only you."

I close my eyes.

"Please don't say goodbye to me," I whisper, my lips against his cheek, my voice crumbling to pieces. Another tear chases the first. Then another and another until I'm quietly weeping against his skin.

Nolan's arms squeeze me tighter. His big body shudders against mine. He's resisting the pull of his magic so hard he's trembling with it, just to stay for another moment.

It makes me love him more. This stubborn, impossible man.

"What would you have me do?" he rasps.

I lean back until I can hold his face. I trail my touch over his eyebrows. That thin white scar. The slopes of his cheeks and the strong line of his jaw. I try to get one last good look at him.

I'm going to remember him. I *will*.

"I want you to kiss me," I manage through my tears. "And tell me you'll see me tomorrow. Just like that first night."

His nose nudges mine. His lips brush the corner of my mouth. One side and then the other. So, so tender.

"Harriet," he says, his lips moving against mine. "I'll see you tomorrow."

His voice breaks on the last word and I nod, sniffling, pinching my eyes shut. I don't want to watch him when he goes. The only things I want are his mouth on mine and my body pressed tight to his. I tip my mouth up and he kisses me, slow and sweet and so damn earnest another sob rattles out of me. I grip his hair in my fists and hold on until I can't anymore.

Until there's a shower of gold sparks and a pained whisper of my name.

Until I'm sitting on the floor in front of my fireplace by myself.

I keep my eyes closed and bring my knees to my chest.

"Don't forget," I say to the empty room, burying my forehead against my knees. I trace his name against the fabric of my pajamas. I chant it, over and over.

Nolan.

Nolan.

You love him. And I think he could have loved you, too.

With a little more time, I think he could have loved you forever.

"Don't forget," I say again. "Please, please. Don't forget."

Chapter Thirty-Six

Harriet

I wake up in the middle of my bed with swollen eyes and a scratchy throat and I stare at my ceiling.

Nolan, I think, and my eyes shut in relief. *His name is Nolan.*

I didn't forget.

I think of the way his hair curls at his collar. The way his laugh feels pressed against my back, his arm slung heavy over my hip.

A tear escapes the corner of my eye.

Remember, a coaxing voice in the back of my mind whispers. *Remember and wait.*

I pull myself out of bed and shuffle down the stairs. I pick up the discarded compass from the floor and set it on the mantel. Then I make a cup of coffee, and I wait.

I sit by the window, I watch the water, and I wait.

I watch the sun move through the sky, and I wait.

I watch the stars wink to life, and I wait.

I fall into an uneasy sleep on my couch. In my dreams, I wait.
Nolan doesn't come, but I wait.
Tomorrow comes and goes. So does the next day.
I place a candle in the window and I remember.
I remember and I wait.

Chapter Thirty-Seven

Harriet

Are we going to leave the trees up through the end of January like usual?"

Sasha has been approaching me with kid gloves since the holiday, no doubt reading the melancholy I keep draped around me like the scarf I haven't bothered to take off. Christmas has come and gone, and Nolan hasn't come back.

I'm being a sad sack. I know that.

It's hard not to be.

So I'm letting myself feel my feelings as I shuffle around the Crow's Nest, thinking about Nolan. I take inventory of my memories, checking off each box to make sure nothing has wavered. The ice-skating rink. The tree field. The back corner of the shop where his favorite arm chair is, and my bedroom. My kitchen. His tea mug.

Everything is still there. Every crack and crevice Nolan filled up.

Maybe it was his last gift to me. A little magic to hold him in place.

Whatever it is, I'm grateful I don't have to forget the rasp of his laugh or the reluctant way his mouth always pulled into a smile. Like even after a hundred years, he wasn't quite sure how to do it.

"Harriet," Sasha says carefully. "Are you all right?"

The million-dollar question.

"Yes and yes," I say, chewing on the inside of my cheek. "The decorations will stay up until the end of the month, and I'm—I'm okay."

Okay feels like a fine enough word for what I am.

Sasha frowns at me from around the side of an antique mirror. I get a good look at myself in the gilded frame and wince. My hair is in a messy bun on the very top of my head. My eyes are shadowed and tired. And my shoulders are hunched to my ears, the scarf Nolan made me looped three times around my neck.

"Maybe I'm slightly less than okay."

She nods, solemn. "I used the mirror on purpose. You needed to take a good hard look at yourself."

I give her an unamused look. "I figured as much. Thank you for that."

Sasha scurries around the edge of the mirror and rounds the counter, joining me where I'm trying to scrub off sales stickers from the bottom of dusty glasses. We absorbed some stock from a neighboring antiques shop that had to close its doors, and they inexplicably put stickers on everything.

"Does your sad potato act have anything to do with the scarf you refuse to take off?"

I nuzzle my chin down into the material. It still sort of smells like Nolan. Cloves and sea salt.

I *miss* him.

"Maybe."

Sasha pauses, waiting for me to elaborate. I don't.

"Does it have anything to do with that hot guy who was in here with that hot girl?"

I stop trying to take out my heartache on the bottom of a wineglass. "You remember that?"

Sasha's face pinches. "It was last month. Of course I remember."

Yes, but . . . I sort of assumed she wouldn't. Nolan said that ghosts aren't remembered. That once a mortal sees him, he abruptly disappears from their consciousness. I wonder what else—

I abruptly stomp down on the thought. No. *No.* It doesn't mean anything. Nolan is gone and I am here.

There's no use in debating the intricacies of a world I'll never know more about.

"That guy sort of looked at you like you hung the moon," Sasha continues. "And I haven't seen him around since."

I nod, picking at the edge of a sticker. "Yeah. There was . . . we had a thing." A thing that felt like *everything.* A thing that has potentially ruined me for any other *things* for the rest of my life. "But it was temporary and we both knew it. He's . . . moved on."

I snicker to myself. It sounds suspiciously like a sob.

Sasha gives me a look. "Is he coming back?"

I shake my head.

"Oh. Bummer." Sasha leans her hip against the counter at my side. "Do we need to get drunk about it?"

"No." I smile and rest my head against her shoulder. "I'm dealing with it. I'm just—giving myself the space to mourn what could have been, I guess."

"That's fair," Sasha says. "Hey, if you want to talk about it, I'm here, okay?" She pats lightly at my back. "I promise not to pull any more shenanigans with the mirror."

"Appreciated." I laugh.

"But you do look a little like Miss Havisham, walking around in the scarf."

I roll my eyes. "Noted."

Sasha hitches her thumb over her shoulder. "I'm going to go catch up on my reading while pretending I'm counting inventory. Yell if you need me."

"At least you're honest," I call after her.

She waves over her head. "You are always welcome to join me!"

"Some of us still have work to do!"

I let my mind drift as I work my way through the rest of the glasses. I keep the scarf around my neck and press my face into it every now and again. I might be Miss Havisham, but it's nice to feel like I have a piece of Nolan here with me still.

I don't have any other tangible reminders. The compass disappeared from the mantel the morning after Nolan left. All that remained was the little white box I wrapped it in and the flecks of gold paper in between my floorboards.

I like to think it's with Nolan now. Wherever he is.

The bell above the door jingles with a new visitor.

"I'll be right with you," I shout. "Feel free to look around and let me know if you have any questions."

The door closes and stilettos click across the uneven floors. A shadow falls over my mismatched glasses.

"I was actually hoping to talk to the owner." I look up and my sister offers me a hesitant smile from the other side of the counter. "If that's all right."

I make us tea and find two dining room chairs in one of the back corners, arranging them so that we can talk by one of the windows. It's snowing today, a light flurry on the other side of the glass that makes me think of lazy mornings in bed. Nolan's hands in my hair and his bare skin beneath my mouth.

I blink and focus on my sister, stirring my spoon a little too aggressively. It *clink-clink-clinks* against the edges of my mug.

"I'm surprised to see you," I offer. She hasn't said anything besides a half-hearted *thank you* since I handed her the mug, and while I'm content to let her work up whatever nerve she needs, I have no idea what she's doing here. It's possible she's doing reconnaissance for my mother, but that seems a little too desperate for Donna York. "I wasn't expecting you," I add, forcing myself to hold still. To *wait*.

Samantha nods, peering into her tea mug like it holds the secrets to the universe. "That makes sense, given how our last interaction went."

I smile tightly. "Also seeing how you haven't responded to a single one of my text messages in months."

She flinches. "That's fair."

I stay quiet. If she's waiting for an apology, she's not going to get one. I don't regret anything I said the night of the gala. For the first time in a long time, I was honest. I was brave. Nolan showed me I could be both of those things without apology. I don't intend to undo all of that hard work by making it easier for Samantha. And while it *is* difficult for me not to fill the space between us with assurances, I hold my ground. I blow the steam off the top of my mug and I wait.

"I always envied you, you know," Samantha finally says.

I almost spit out my tea.

"What?"

A dry smile pulls at her cheeks. "Is that really so hard to believe?"

"Yes," I say immediately, emphatically. "You—you—" I set down my tea on the window ledge. My hands are shaking too badly for me to maintain my grip. "You envied *me*? Why?"

How? I want to ask. *When?* Samantha was always the put-together one. The one my mother measured me against only to find me woefully wanting.

Her smile turns sad. "You always got to be exactly who you wanted, while I had no choice but to fit the mold that was made for me."

I blink at her, shocked. "Samantha." I have to steady myself. I don't know if I'm furious or amazed that we've both managed to be hurt so profoundly by the exact same thing. Maybe a combination of both. "I've spent my entire life trying to *fit into* that mold. It felt like—it felt like no one wanted me to fit."

She nods. "I realize that now. Or, I guess, I realized that after what you said at the gala. I thought you had some well of confidence I never figured out how to access and you were just—doing what you wanted, damn the consequences." She sets her mug down next to mine, the ceramic handles kissing. They're mismatched, but they pair beautifully. I stare at them for a long time.

"When you made the decision to leave law and run this place instead," Samantha continues, "I was furious. It felt like you got to do whatever you wanted while I was trapped. While I had to clean up after your messes. It isn't a fair response and it's something I'm working through with my therapist, but—I don't think I ever considered that you weren't given the same choices."

"They liked you more," I tell her. "They *always* liked you more."

"I think Mom was afraid of how quickly you got on with Aunt Matilda," Samantha says. "I think Mom struggled to understand you, and it was hard for her when Matilda got it right on the first try. I'm not making excuses for her, but I think she felt she lost you before she ever had you."

"I was just a child."

Samantha nods. "I know. It's not fair how she treated you. Our parents are people, too. They make mistakes and poor choices. But you—"

She trails off. My heart stomps a furious beat in the middle of my chest. "But me?"

"You were so brave," Samantha continues in a whisper, eyes flicking up and then down again. "So much braver than me. Everything Mom threw at you, you seemed to handle it. You didn't crack. You didn't wilt."

"I did," I interrupt. "It hurt me. Every time."

Samantha nods. "I can see that now. But you were also very good at making other people believe you were okay. I thought you had something I lacked."

"Yeah." I laugh. "A people-pleasing complex."

"And apparently I've been nursing an inferiority complex," Samantha replies. A rueful smile tilts her lips. "As I grew older, I think my admiration twisted into irritation. I've spent so long being envious of you, I think I forgot that we're supposed to be on the same team. We used to be partners, remember?"

Tears burn behind my eyes. "Yeah. We used to be partners."

We used to tell each other everything. We used to lie beneath her blankets at night, our faces inches away from each other on her pillow and whisper about all the things we wished we could be. We used to be best friends.

Samantha's face softens. "I'd like to get back to that, if we can. I think—I think it'll take some time, for both of us. And I know I owe you an apology. But I'd like to try."

I sniffle, discreetly trying to wipe under my eye with the edge of the scarf. But it's game over when I feel the tiny *NC* embroidered at the bottom.

I might have been the key to moving Nolan forward in his afterlife, but I think he was the push I needed in *this* life. He forced me to see myself in a different light. He made me brave enough to stand up for myself, and because of it, Samantha got to see me in a different light, too.

It's like Nolan's reached above my head and fixed that busted light bulb in the supply closet. I'm seeing everything from an angle I haven't before. Light in all my dark corners, discovering the forgotten things.

"I'd like to try, too," I tell Samantha. I take a chance. I reach out my hand toward her. When she tucks her palm against mine, something in my chest realigns, shifts, and settles. I let out a breath and smile my first real smile in weeks. "I'd like that a lot."

Chapter Thirty-Eight
Nolan

*I*f I knew the afterlife was merely another waiting room with white walls and a bland landscape painting, I wouldn't have fought so damned hard to get here.

"Am I in hell?" I ask.

Isabella inspects her nails, completely uninterested in my tantrum. "For the fifteenth time, may I reiterate: No. You are not in hell, Nolan."

"Do you intend to hold me against my will for all of eternity, or only a short period of time?"

"My, you are dramatic lately."

I cross my arms over my chest, leaning back in the plastic chair I've been assigned. It creaks ominously. "You've kept me here for weeks without explanation. I believe I'm entitled to my fair share of dramatics."

She clicks her tongue and a nail file appears out of nowhere. She starts to shape her nails. "There is no such thing as *weeks* in this place, Nolan. Please do try and control yourself."

I *can't*. I've been a mess since I landed in this room—however long ago that was. It certainly feels like weeks.

Weeks of not knowing if Harriet is okay. Weeks of thinking about the look on her face when she told me not to say goodbye. Weeks of feeling the absence of her like a knife in my side.

I was sent to haunt Harriet, but she ended up haunting *me*.

"I would like to leave," I say, for perhaps the eighty-sixth time.

"No," Isabella says, moving from one nail to the next. "As I've already stressed, we are waiting for an associate to arrive." Dark eyes flash up at me from beneath thick lashes. "Be patient."

"My patience is gone."

She rolls her eyes. "No kidding."

"I want—"

A knock sounds at the door, light and upbeat. Three quick raps in a row.

Isabella keeps her eyes on me. She snaps her fingers and the nail file disappears. "Can you behave yourself?" she asks.

"Depends."

Her mouth settles into a line. "I suppose that's the best I can hope for. Come in," she calls.

The door squeaks open and a small orange blur darts through. Builín scampers over and sits at my feet patiently, her orange and white tail swishing merrily through the air. I blink at her.

She meows a greeting and hops into my lap, nudging my chest with her cheek and then draping herself dramatically over me. I scratch lightly under her chin, as confused as I've ever been.

"Why is my cat here?"

"She's not your cat," a familiar voice says, laughing. My attention snaps to the woman standing next to Isabella, a soft smile on her face and her arms crossed over her chest. Her eyebrows fly up when our eyes meet and hold, a slow smile curving across her familiar mouth.

"You recognize me?" she asks.

I nod. Harriet's aunt Matilda is standing in front of me in a colorful sweater with wide sleeves, her hair the same curly disarray as Harriet's. It sends a pang of longing so ferocious through the middle of my chest, it's a wonder I don't fall out of the chair.

"Good." She claps her hands together. "I've been wanting to talk to you."

"Gathering recently departed spirits from their respective resting places takes time," Isabella explains. "That's what the wait was for. There was quite a bit of"—she and Matilda exchange a loaded look—"red tape."

Matilda snaps her fingers, and an armchair appears. It's the same armchair as the one I favored at the antiques shop. The one right by the window, where I'd read my books while Harriet bustled around the front. She collapses into it, a steaming mug of tea at her elbow.

It's in a Christmas tree mug, because of course it is.

I smile.

"I am of the understanding that we have a mutual acquaintance," Matilda says. Her face softens. "How's my girl?"

I lean forward in my seat, my elbows resting on my knees. "She's a mess," I answer, voice breaking. "Color everywhere. A laugh that's just a shade too loud. Painfully addicted to candy canes." I pause. "As lovely on the inside as she is on the outside."

I miss her so much.

Matilda laughs and it fills the room, bouncing off the plain white walls. A laugh that's just a shade too loud.

"Sounds like my Harriet." Her eyes close and a wistful smile tugs at her cheeks. "I miss her," Matilda says quietly.

"She misses you," I reply. "You haven't . . . checked in?"

She shakes her head. "Can't. There are restrictions on timing. If ghosts were able to check in on their loved ones as soon as they departed, I'm not sure anyone would move on." She smiles sadly, her eyes turning sharp. She nods at Builín, still in my lap. "Though I've found my ways to keep tabs."

"Builín is yours?"

"I prefer Oliver, but yes. She's mine. She kept Harriet company when I couldn't." That sad smile again. "I didn't want my girl to be alone."

I drag my hand over Builín's arched back. Her tail swishes at my chest.

I didn't want to leave Harriet alone either. I'm sick to my stomach just thinking of it.

"Are you—are you here to guide me to the next place?" I ask. "Because Harriet was the one to move me forward?"

Matilda blinks at me, tea mug frozen halfway to her mouth. "You don't know?" Her attention snaps to Isabella. "He doesn't know?"

Isabella shakes her head. "He hasn't put it together yet."

My face tightens. "What don't I know?"

They ignore me.

Matilda sets her Christmas tree mug to the side on an end table that appears out of thin air. Another knickknack I've seen around the antiques shop.

"Surely he doesn't think it was all a coincidence."

Isabella shrugs. "For such an intelligent man, it appears he is remarkably stupid."

Matilda makes a thoughtful sound. "I suppose he did die by sailing directly into a storm. Not the brightest bulb in the bunch."

"You make a fair point."

"Excuse me. Would someone mind explaining?" I look between them. "Is it Harriet? Has something happened?"

Matilda's face softens. "Harriet is fine. Or rather, as fine as she can be." She pauses, tracing her thumb across her bottom lip. I've seen Harriet do the same thing a million times, and my heart gives another painful thump in my chest. "What do you think you're doing here, Nolan?"

"Being tortured."

Isabella snorts.

"Not that. Why do you think you've moved on to this place, Nolan?" asks Matilda. "This"—she gestures at the open space around us—"waiting room."

"Because—" I glance at Isabella, but she keeps her expression carefully blank. "Because Harriet figured out what my unfinished business was. She found the compass, and it satisfied some decades-long conundrum. I was able to move forward when she set me to rights."

Isabella pinches her nose with a sigh. Matilda stares at me.

"My," Matilda says. "You are stupid."

I grind my teeth together. "I'd appreciate an explanation."

I can't take another second of this vague discussion. My patience is at its very limit. Every time I close my eyes, I feel Harriet shuddering in my arms. I see her big brown eyes, filled with tears. My goodwill has run dry.

"The compass was never your unfinished business." Matilda plucks her mug back up from the table. Builín hops from my lap and returns to her, winding between her legs. "Harriet was," she says.

Everything goes still and tight. Like one of those toys I had as a child, where the string was pulled from the back. My string has been pulled, yet nothing comes out. White noise fills the space between my ears, my throat bone dry.

"What?" I breathe out.

Isabella smooths her hands over her skirt. "Have you ever wondered why you remain a ghost, despite fulfilling every request I've ever asked of you?"

I remain quiet.

"You've been waiting, Nolan." Something uncharacteristically tender and soft transforms Isabella's harsh features. "You've been waiting for Harriet. To exist in the same time as her. Your souls were together in the beginning, and so they shall be in the end."

My hands brace against the edges of my seat, knuckles white. I hardly dare to hope. To breathe.

"How do you—" I exhale. "Are you sure?"

Isabella raises an insolent eyebrow. "Aren't you?"

The compass. That day in the ocean. The way it always felt like I was being pulled incessantly into her orbit. How I spent my lifetime *looking*. The vibration beneath my skin every time she so much as glanced in my direction. The way I thought I recognized her, that very first night. How much I *miss* her.

Aye, I'm sure.

"It doesn't happen for all spirits," she explains calmly, an old sadness flashing behind her dark eyes. "And sometimes there are . . . complications . . . that prevent two souls from finding each other again. You are extraordinarily lucky, Nolan."

"Lucky," I repeat, voice dry.

Isabella nods.

"*Lucky*," I say again. I let go of the edge of the chair and press my palms to my knees instead. My hands are trembling, my entire body shaking with the force of this . . . feeling. "You're telling me I was forced to exist in another time without the woman I—" I swallow down the word, not willing to say it to anyone who isn't Harriet first. My hands clench into fists and I try again. "I've lived lifetimes, waiting, without reason or warning. I've been *miserable*. And you call me *lucky*?"

Isabella fixes me with an impenetrable look. "And now that you know, how many lifetimes more would you wait? For your Harriet?"

My frustration leaves me in a rush. I'm suddenly exhausted. Tired to my very bones.

"As many as it took," I answer. "However long."

"Good answer," Matilda says from her cozy armchair.

"But you couldn't have mentioned it?" I ask Isabella, dragging a frustrated hand through my hair. "All this talk about consequences, and you couldn't have just *told* me that she was meant to be *mine*?"

Her face remains impassive. "I couldn't have."

"Why?"

"Would you have believed me? *Nolan, this isn't a training exercise. This is your Harriet. Yours. She is made for you, as you are made for her.*" She smirks. "You would have laughed in my face."

I consider that, then begrudgingly accept she has a point. "Perhaps."

Isabella huffs, crossing her arms over her chest. "I told you as much as I could. Anything more, and I would have faced consequences of my own. Your trips to the past were meant to speed the process along. Don't you see? The boat, when she was a child. How you kept singing the Christmas songs she loves best, before you knew her. She even made the same jam that your mother used to serve you as a boy. She's been waiting for you her entire life, and you've been searching for her just as long."

I think of the memory where Harriet was on her couch, her chin resting on her crossed arms, staring out over the water. Another where I was sitting at the table in my home, doing the same.

Both of us alone.

I drag my hand across my mouth, my throat tight. There's a pressure behind my eyes I can't blink away. "Is that it, then? Is that why I'm here? I am to wait more?"

Matilda leans forward. "You're here because now you need to make a choice." She snaps her fingers and a candy cane appears in her hand. A grin tugs at her mouth as she unwraps it. "And it better be the right one."

Chapter Thirty-Nine

Harriet

I stare at the candle in my window, the flickering flame reflected in the glass. A deep goldenrod yellow that burns orange, the dancing flame steady and sure.

This candle has been burning since I first lit it weeks ago—day and night—the last remaining bit of magic Nolan left behind. The wick hasn't worn down. The wax hasn't melted. I've come and gone and still, the candle burns. It shines bright in my window, calling lost sailors home, just as Nolan's mom used to do.

Except my sailor isn't coming home.

That's the problem, I think. I need to stop thinking of Nolan's home as somewhere with me. This was never his home to begin with. He was never mine. This was just a stop before something better.

A lesson, maybe, for the both of us.

"It's just a candle," I tell myself. I fist my hands in the sleeves of my sweatshirt. "You won't forget him if it's out."

I can't keep going like this. Every time I look at the candle, it feels like a sucker punch through the middle of my heart. I miss him. I want him. The candle just reminds me of everything I lost. Everything I no longer get to have.

I'll make a wish. I'll close my eyes, blow out the candle, and make a wish. Just as I used to do when I was a girl.

I bend forward, take a deep breath, and—

A knock pounds at my door, rattling at the hinges. I freeze, half an inch away from the flame. Hope is a wild, fickle thing. It bands tight around my middle, stealing my breath.

It couldn't be.

It's not possible.

I abandon the candle and trip my way over to the door, stumbling over the Christmas decorations I still refuse to pack away. My hand trembles. I yank at the knob and—

And I find myself nose to nose with Darryl, my wayward mailman.

He grins, stepping backward on my porch. "Whoa there, Harriet. Quite the welcome."

I slouch against the frame and run a trembling hand across my forehead. I've told myself to stop wishing on stars for impossible things, but the second I'm given a chance, off I go again.

"Hi, Darryl."

"Evening, Harry." He adjusts his bag over his shoulder. "You don't look so good."

I nod. This is the problem with hope. It only ever leads to heartbreak.

And as it turns out, I am especially good at stretching out my heartache.

"I'm fine." I drop my hand and try to fix a smile on my face. "What can I do for you?"

He reaches into his bag and pulls out a small cardboard box. "Got a package for ya."

I frown. "You have a package for me at nine thirty-two at night?"

He nods. "Sure do!" He wiggles the cardboard box in front of me, something rattling around inside. It's probably the little cup and saucer I pity-ordered for myself. The one with a tiny cupid shooting an arrow instead of a handle. I grab the box out of his hands before he can shake the damned thing into pieces. "I got turned around earlier today, but have no fear. I always deliver packages where they're supposed to go."

That is factually untrue, but I'm too tired to argue with him.

"Well, thanks for bringing it by, Darryl. I appreciate it."

"No problem." He rocks back on his heels, turns to leave, then pauses. I cross my arms over my chest and linger in the doorway, watching him on my little stone walkway. Behind him, the street is lit in softly glowing lamps. The stars, a bright blanket in the sky. "You sure you're all right, Harry? You seem down in the dumps."

"I am down in the dumps," I answer with a laugh. "But it's getting better. I think I've been holding on to things too tight. What's that saying about *if you love something, let it go*?"

Darryl frowns at me. "I always thought that was a dumb saying."

I laugh. "Yeah, me, too." We both smile. "I'm going to be okay."

"Of course you are." He nods once. "I'll be seeing you."

I give him a little wave. "See you."

I shut the door behind him and go back to my candle. I stare at the orange and gold flame. How the reflection makes it look like there are fifty candles, all in a row.

I am going to be okay. It might take some time, but maybe someday soon I'll be able to think about Nolan without wishing we had a different ending. I don't need to keep a candle in the window to hold on to all the good things he brought to my life.

So I close my eyes, think about the way his hand cupped the back of my neck, and I blow out the candle.

A knock sounds at my door.

I roll my eyes to the ceiling.

"Darryl, I swear to god." I didn't check the label before I discarded the package on my small entryway table. He probably delivered the wrong thing to the wrong house and wants to continue his late-night delivery special. I snatch the box and wedge it under my arm, swinging the door open.

Except it's not Darryl.

Strong jaw. Broad body. His hands held loose at his sides. He steps closer and the light from the tree I still haven't taken down hits his face.

His hair is dark. Lightly curled. Windswept and messy.

Nolan smiles at me from my front porch, a little unsure.

"Hello, Harriet."

I drop the box.

He swallows, looking nervous. His hand pushes through his hair in a move so achingly familiar I could cry. "You might not remember, but we've met before. I—"

I don't wait for him to finish the rest of his sentence. I launch myself at him, my arms around his neck and my knees hugging at his hips. His arms snap around me immediately, tugging me higher against his chest, one hand fisting in my hair.

"I remember," I say, my voice too high, my mouth busy pressing frantic kisses to his chin, his jaw, the little hollow beneath his ear. "Of course, I remember."

"*Fuck*," he whispers, emphatic, his face somewhere in my hair. "Harriet. *God*, Harriet. I've missed you."

I laugh and sob at the same time, then squeeze at his forearms, his biceps, his shoulders. I twist the fabric of his flannel in my fist and hold on tight.

He's *here*.

"What's happening? Are you really here?" I blink furiously, trying to get rid of the tears. I want to see him clearly. I want to be sure. "Why didn't you move on? Did something go wrong? Do I need to fix it?"

Nolan shakes his head and marches us forward into the house. He kicks the door shut behind us and tucks his body more firmly around mine, his chin on top of my head.

"I'm here," he says against me and a shiver twists down my spine. How many nights did I fall asleep to the fantasy of exactly those words, whispered exactly like that? "I'm here, Harriet. This is real."

"Are you sure?" I ask, my words thick as I sob my way through them.

"Aye, I'm sure." He pulls away from me, wiping my tears away with his thumbs. His smile is tender. His eyes are warm. He looks different, somehow. Like he finally got a good rest. Like he found exactly what he was looking for. "There's nothing for you to fix. I moved on, just like I wanted."

I shake my head. "I don't understand."

"I was given a choice. Two doors to walk through. One would move me forward to a place of rest and peace. And the other—"

He pauses. I study his face, my eyes searching. "The other?" I ask.

A smile starts at one side of his mouth and slowly unfurls until his dimples wink to life beneath his scruff. The lines by his eyes deepen.

"And the other would return me to the woman I love," he rasps.

A broken sound cracks out of me. I drop my forehead to his chest and start to cry in earnest. "I don't understand."

He sifts his hands through my hair, a laugh rumbling in his chest as he rubs at my back. "I don't think we need to understand." He rocks us back and forth. "It was you, Harriet. You are the one I've been waiting for. You were never supposed to move me forward, you were supposed to hold me here. Keep me tethered." He presses his forehead to mine. "It was always supposed to be you."

I feel like I'm caught in a dream. Like I'm going to wake up suddenly in my bed, all alone. I want to believe him *so badly*, but I'm afraid.

"Could you kiss me?" I ask, my cheeks still wet with my tears. I don't know how to stop crying. "Can you kiss me so I know this isn't—"

Nolan cups my jaw and drags my mouth to his, kissing me like his life depends on it. And in a way, I suppose it does. He came from another time to love me, and I've been waiting to love him in return. That's what this hollow ache in my chest has been about.

We just had to find each other.

His calloused hands catch in my hair and tug roughly as he gets carried away, kissing me harder. Licking into my mouth, pushing me forward, knocking me into the wall with a dull thud.

"Sorry," he mumbles against my mouth when my head bumps up against a light fixture. He runs his palm over my hair. Gets distracted and wraps it around his fist.

"Don't be sorry," I breathe. "Kiss me again."

I'm not dreaming.

This is real.

He came back to me.

He's *mine*. Someone I can have. Someone I get to keep.

We kiss until I'm dizzy with it. Until I don't know what time it is or where we are.

When he finally pulls away, his lips are swollen and his eyes are bright.

"What happens now?" I ask, tracing the rare proof of his happiness. I lean up and drop a kiss against his jaw. Because I can. Because I never thought I'd be able to again.

Nolan grins, so breathtaking I almost start crying again. Or maybe I'm still crying. I don't know.

He leans forward so the words are whispered against my mouth. "I'll see you tomorrow, Harriet." He brushes a kiss to my bottom lip, the dip in my chin, the hollow of my throat. His hand finds my jaw and he holds me steady. "I'll see you the tomorrow after that, and the one after that, and the one after that."

He punctuates each statement with a kiss, his scruff tickling at my skin. When he pulls back, he holds my face between his hands, gazing at me with tender, aching longing. Deep, sure possession.

"I'll be with you for every tomorrow you allow, and I suspect a time after that, too."

I curl my hands around his wrists, holding on. "Are you sure?"

He nods. "The unfinished business I have is with you, Harriet York. You better get used to having me around."

I sniffle. "Haunting me?"

"No." He smiles. "Loving you."

Acknowledgments

Thank you for reading Harriet and Nolan's story. I know it's a little bit different from what you're used to from me, but it's a story that's been bursting in me for a while now. The idea of a wayward Ghost of Christmas Past sent to haunt the wrong woman came to me right after I wrote *Lovelight Farms*, but I placed it on a shelf for when it felt like the right time. And apparently the right time was eight months pregnant with an unavoidable deadline of my own barreling down on me.

I had a friend tell me once that writing a book is like slotting a bookmark into a chapter of our life. So much of what we're going through as people is reflected in our work as authors. I like to think this book is a reflection of how hopeful I felt while carrying my son. The big, soul-filling love I already had for this tiny person I hadn't yet met. The waiting and the watching and the knowing that everything was about to change for the better.

So, thank you for picking up this book. I hope it brought you something you needed. I hope that if you feel like a lost and forgotten thing, that you realize how beautiful and special you truly are. And I hope that if you feel like you've been left waiting, that there's beauty in that, too. That maybe, the thing you've been searching for is right around the corner.

In the business of books, I'd like to thank my agent, Kim Lionetti, who listened to me ramble about ghosts in an empty restaurant in

New York and nodded her head and told me to write it. It's an incredible thing to have someone believe in your ideas before you can articulate them, and I feel so incredibly lucky to have Kim on my side.

Thank you to the team at Avon, who welcomed this project with such incredible enthusiasm. If it's a wonderful thing to have someone believe in your ideas before you can articulate them, then it's downright magical to have a team react so emphatically when they're on paper. Shannon, you shaped this so beautifully into the book of my heart. I can't wait to see what else we do together. And DJ, who has believed in me from what feels like the very start, what an absolute joy it is to (finally) work with you.

Thank you to everyone who has ushered this book to its final form: the copy editors, the marketing team, the formatters, all foreign publication teams, and the absolutely incomparable Brittany Keller, who made the cover of my dreams. It truly does take a (very talented and specialized) village.

And to my village. Thank you to Adri, for always giving me the pep talk I need. Thank you to Annie, for knowing and loving my brain so well. Thank you to my writer friends, who make this weird, wonderful job so much less lonely. And thank you to every person who has ever read, sold, loaned out, shared, yelled about, or made something for my books. This community of love is what makes this the very best job in the world. I am so, so grateful.

My biggest and most heartfelt thank-you to my husband, for loving me even when I turn into a deadline troll, hunched over my desk and snapping at you whenever you enter the room. My compass always points right at you.

And to my children, who still think Mommy works at a bookstore. I've been waiting my whole life for you.

I hope you'll come back for another visit to the Department of Hauntings and Spirits. I heard a rumor there's a Reaper on the loose.

ONE PLACE. MANY STORIES

Bold, innovative and
empowering publishing.

FOLLOW US ON:

@HQStories